BEYOND THE AETHERIAL VEIL

BEYOND THE AETHERIAL VEIL

ODYSSEY OF THE ETHEREAL BOOK 2

Jamie Kojola

Podium

BEYOND THE AETHERIAL VEIL

CHAPTER 1

The Story Thus Far

Massive sheets of ice covered the entire shattered peak of a volcano on the fiftieth floor of the Tower of Aetherius. The ice held an otherworldly sheen of red to it—one did not find Ethereal ice naturally. An abandoned altar of ice lay dormant now. No other sign remained that a mere hour ago it had been the site of powerful summoning and resurrection magic. A dozen meters away stood a large, elaborate tent, and within sat three individuals at a gorgeous wooden table, although one sat on top of the table itself instead of on a chair.

The individual sitting on the table was a black house cat with yellow eyes. Arkaziel, the black cat, was a race called a StarMane. The shapeshifting feline was a draconic cat whose true form exceeded fifty meters. Additionally, the cat was an Ethereal light and shadow Cultivator (one well into the third tier), who possessed the genetic memories of his predecessors and an appetite for nearly everything. The combined arrogance of a cat and a dragon instilled a natural belief in him that he was the main character of the universe.

Arkaziel lapped at a bowl of milky alcohol they had gained in the tower city of Nivathar between bites of ambrosial fruit salad.

"So, are you ready to start now, Blue?" Arkaziel impatiently asked.

"No, yeah, I can talk while you two eat, I guess," Aetheria answered. The aqua-haired woman sat next to the feline. Occasionally, she petted him.

The woman's hair glowed with an internal luminance that defied the natural order. Her eyes also glowed, a red, eerie light that left those who witnessed it to question the meaning of existence within the universe. Although she was the only woman in the room, she was the tallest. Her full height measured 188 centimeters, although she could change that at her whim. Like the cat, she was also a shapeshifter. Aetheria wore a long, red trench coat, an aqua-blue scarf, a black tank top, black canvas pants, fingerless black gloves, and dark reddish-black boots made of dragon scale.

Like the cat, she was a third tier Cultivator of the Ethereal, but her specialty lay with ice and freezing.

"Unless you want me to wait?" Aetheria asked the man who sat across from her.

Werylin Amaryllis, once Imperator of a kingdom, former ghost, nodded eagerly.

"Please, I'd like to hear what has happened since you stumbled into my tomb." Werylin, an elf, had long purple hair, lavender eyes, pale skin, and the awkwardness of someone freshly resurrected after thousands of years spent as a specter.

"So polite. You could learn a thing or two, Ark." Aetheria chided her companion, who hissed at her in annoyance.

"Alright, so I guess my story starts on planet Earth. I grew up in a wonderful place called Minnesota. It's not entirely relevant, beyond saying my gaming hobby brought me into the spotlight of some gods. When I died there, two Primordials offered me the chance of skipping the cycle of reincarnation and remaining myself if I toppled a goddess for them. Seemed like a great deal to me. Live the life of adventure I'd spent my entire life on Earth reading, playing, and dreaming about? Who wouldn't say yes to that?

"So, I got reincarnated into a new body in the world of Grief, an ancient world ruled by Oizys, Goddess of Misery. I reincarnated in the lost city of Nova Azura, original galactic home of the Aetherial race. I technically qualified to be born there, as an adopted child of Nyx and Aetherius, although I'm still human."

"Are you still human?" Werylin inquired softly.

"Evolved human? I think of myself as human, and that's the important part, maybe? Anyway. A god called the Trickster apparently talked Oizys into terms that the Primordials used to make me, and once she realized she got swindled, she got pissed. After millennia of trying to destroy Nova Azura, she succeeded, but only after I escaped. I found myself on the island with the Tower of Aetherius, learned I could regenerate from almost anything, found your lodge, met you, then entered the tower."

"Wait, you aren't going to tell him about getting eaten by a lizard?" Arkaziel asked sweetly.

"It isn't important. The tower is . . . well, the tower. On the fourth floor, I found a training city. I learned a lot during the years I stayed there. Basic cultivation techniques, a few arts, alchemy, blacksmithing, dancing, and a whole slew of languages. It was my first time meeting an Ethereal Cultivator too, when the Soul Witch took me under her wing."

"Yeah, she did." Arkaziel snickered.

"Shut it. Ignore the cat. Although yes, I bound my soul to Aoibhe's, and we're committed to one another. She'll be joining us when I become at least an Ethereal Scion, but I want to be her equal when I summon her, so maybe when I'm an Ethereal Lady."

Werylin coughed, looking slightly nervous. "Just what tier is she?"

"Oh, Aoibhe is on the fifth tier. She's an Ethereal Lord, well, Lady."

Werylin sputtered a little. "She could destroy a planet on her own!"

"Well, yeah. I probably could myself, even at the third tier. I am the Etherfrost Asura, after all."

Arkaziel snorted. "No destroying worlds until I'm big enough to eat them. That's my food!"

Aetheria bopped the kitty on the nose. "No eating worlds."

"Anyway, oh yeah, I ran into your great grandkids on the second floor. They were doing well, although your great-grandson, Tasmin, had some Nether curse, but I was able to remove it. Also, I maybe slept with your great-granddaughter, Ithyrra. Don't look at me like that. I had just started cultivating Aether, and you know how new power feels. I was high on power, super horny, and things just happened. Anyway, moving on. Oh, it turns out Tasmin's curse went back to your daughter, Alora. She turned to necromancy inside the tower, turned herself into a lich."

Werylin sighed. "She was a wonderful little girl but always had a dark twist to her thoughts. She had the most amazing skill with pastels."

Elven lifespans being what they were, Werylin's response to the death of his daughter struck Aetheria oddly. *Maybe his time as an undead left him with no sympathy for someone who turned to it willingly?*

"Sorry. I destroyed Alora on the fourth floor, along with a lot of Death Knights and other powerful undead." Aetheria said the destroyed part a little reluctantly.

"The only outcome for a lich." Werylin's sadness shone through clearly there. She gave him a few moments of silence to come to terms with things before she continued. After a few minutes, and the positive energy infusion of the ambrosial fruit, Werylin nodded for Aetheria to continue.

"After that, it was a lot of loneliness and violence until I came across Ark here. I helped fight off some nasty insects, we forged a bond, and we climbed the tower as partners. We kept running into encounters Aetherius had set up in the tower. A goddess once called Thalassa, or Aetheria, ended up being my first mercy kill, but she gave me her Flame. We met Ymir, the Ice Giant, and he gave me his Flame, too."

Arkaziel laughed at the simple glossing over of their adventures.

"After that, it's a lot of violence. I bridged into Tier Two and then Three. I got the Flame of Khaos and made a few mistakes. The Origin, the source of Ethereal energy, is now accessible to me through a conduit within my soul. Turns out people don't do that for a reason. I keep getting bombarded with emotions and desires from the Origin that are really a pain in my ass. Beyond the whole "climb the tower" thing, my priorities right now are to figure out how to make a working core, and to fix the emotional bleedthrough."

"You connected your soul to *the source of Ethereal power?*" Werylin's lavender eyes expressed grave incredulity every bit as thoroughly as his voice did.

"Humans, right?" Arkaziel laughed, to the discomfort of the human and elf. A cat laughing felt unnatural. The judging look Arkaziel gave both of them, however, was perfectly in line for a cat.

"Cripes, can't a girl make a minor mistake here and there? I acted rashly and made a mistake, *maybe*. If this works, though, I get to say I told you so. Now, how to move forward . . . Themis said it was possible. I just need to figure out how to make a new type of core. Since I can pretty much draw unlimited power from the Origin, a regular core won't help me. I need to find a way to create a specialty core that could be useful while still covering the requirements to hit Tier Four."

"Wait a moment," Werylin said. "I've joined the most ridiculously over-powered climbing party Grief has ever fielded, because I helped you? You didn't even think, hey, I bet he's great in a fight if he fought off an Orc Tide?" Werylin's offended pride seemed liable to break if someone didn't answer right. Arkaziel, shockingly, stayed quiet.

"I've met a lot of your clan; they were all competent and mostly awesome. Karieth, however, sold me on your capabilities. I might have unlimited power from the Origin, but I'm still a third tier and can't manifest nearly as much as I can draw. I'm a brawler, a tank, a defender, whatever term you want to use. Arkaziel is a ranged skirmisher with close-quarter capabilities because of being a StarMane. Another close-quarter fighter with magical support is a perfect complement to our party, especially since Aoibhe is a witch."

That Aetheria had put at least some thought into things seemed to mollify the elf.

"How did you get my sword, by the way?" Werylin hefted the sheathed blade.

"I don't know how it got there, but a collector in Dragon's Roar, the Arena City, had your sword. I had to trade some Nidhogg scales, some rare alchemical ingredients, and a whole pile of demonic cores for it. Did I overpay?" Aetheria honestly did not know, but once she heard the merchant had Harmonious Tempest, she had moved quickly to gain it.

"It is hard to say. On Grief, Harmonious Tempest is an unparalleled blade forged in the earliest days of the world. It is a legend not just in Clan Amaryllis, but across all of Grief. They forged the blade from a fallen star and quenched it in the donated blood of an ancient silver dragon. They made the hilt from a branch gifted to our clan by the Lord of the Forests, and they crafted the guard from fragments of armor from the first Imperator. On top of all the unique components, every wielder of Luminous Aria adds an ability to the blade. Every generation to wield it makes the sword more powerful."

Aetheria whistled appreciatively.

"Money well spent then." She smiled.

"More than you know. I entwine part of my soul to the blade. Your summoning may not have worked without it." Werylin laughed.

"So, can you tell us a bit more about your exact abilities?" Arkaziel inquired.

"Well, as I informed Aetheria in the tomb, I started my path as a minstrel and spellsinger. Familial responsibilities forced me to abandon that direction and walk the path of a warrior-mage. Cultivation-wise, I am a third tier Cultivator."

"Which path?" Arkaziel pushed.

"It is a bit of a mess, but I walk a path called the Aria of the Ever-Changing Tapestry."

"Never heard of it." The StarMane sounded unimpressed.

Not offended in the slightest, Werylin nodded.

"I named it myself. In short, I practice the sword style of Clan Amaryllis, and mix in the power of the Words of Creation. The Words of Creation are a creation myth among my people, that the gods brought the universe into being by Speaking it. Think of spellsong, but with less emphasis on music. Much of my magic still resonates with the harmony of the universe, but I do not use spellsong the way I did as a minstrel."

"That sounds sweet. So you're muddling through on your own path? That's awesome. Welcome to the club." Aetheria gave Werylin a big, encouraging smile.

CHAPTER 2

Showing Off

After the darkness of teleportation faded, the trio found themselves in a dimly lit arena. Aetheria, Arkaziel, and Werylin stood in a sandy pit with high walls on all sides. Aetheria sighed softly, rolled her shoulders, and let Ethereal power flow from her soul aperture into her body to increase her physical abilities even more. Arkaziel, annoyed by her shoulder roll, hopped onto the ground, where he took a panther-sized form. Werylin, newest to the party, took stock of the arena, and his hand settled over the hilt of Harmonious Tempest.

The arena had three doors. While they readied themselves, the first door opened, and a swarm of golden retriever-sized beetles rushed toward them while the sand churned beneath the door. With Aetheria's Ethereal Sight, she could see the life energies of tunneling insects that used the surface group as a distraction.

"Want to take the first wave, Werylin? There's a group of submerged diggers using these beetles as cover."

The warrior nodded, and in a flash, he appeared among the swarm of dog-sized beetles. A quick draw attack severed five of the beetles in half. Werylin's katana left stray magic behind his swing, the motes of which slowly formed clefts and musical symbols before fading. Not that the swordsman stayed stationary. His blade flowed from the broad sweep attack into a few quick slices that volleyed slashes of power projected from his sword to bisect multiple beetles in a row.

"Damn." Aetheria whistled. Werylin, perhaps unsurprisingly, moved with a speed that made her feel slow. The swordsman had no competition for the claim of fastest in the party, his elven dexterity putting both shapeshifters to shame. *I thought he'd be more like a strength/magic fighter, but he's definitely dexterity/magic. I should have realized that as soon as I saw the katana.*

Werylin dispatched the initial wave with no issues. The sand he had kicked up while slaying the beetles fell around him, but he held Harmonious Tempest lazily until the surrounding sand churned. The sand broke. Werylin leaped into the air and said a single word. Although he whispered it, it carried across the arena with no dampening from the loud clatter of hundreds of teeth snapping and missing the mark of where he had stood.

"Hemorrhage."

Five sand sharks attacked empty air, but with that word, they all flopped onto the sand and flailed as cuts wracked their bodies. *Internal bleeding, too. I just barely caught the flares of magic inside the sharks' brains.*

Werylin landed gently on the sand before casually thrusting his blade through each flailing animal's brains, putting them out of their misery. He then flicked the blood off his katana and sheathed it.

"What, no cleaning cloth?" Aetheria quipped lightly. Arkaziel and Werylin looked at her like she was an idiot. *What? That's what an anime character would do.*

"It's a legendary magic artifact, Aetheria. It cleans and sharpens itself." Werylin then shrugged. "I dislike blood getting in the scabbard, though. It is uncivilized to walk around smelling like blood and death. I'm not an orc."

Note to self: Werylin will have issues with orcs, won't he?

"Nicely done, elf. Now you can handle the next batch, too. Just call if you need help." Arkaziel licked the back of his front right paw with a feigned indifference that didn't fool Aetheria. He was as interested in watching their new party member as she was.

"Not a problem." Werylin smiled with confidence. "It seems fighting with a flesh and blood body is easy to fall back into." The spellsword rolled his shoulders and took a step forward. Within the same doorway that had opened previously, a gate held bestial shadows behind its closed bars. Then it opened.

The gate contained five enemies, a race of lizard-men that Aetheria had never seen yet, equipped with five distinct sets of equipment. One wielded two daggers, one a white crystal wand, one a red staff, one a bow, and the final lizard-man had an axe and shield. Werylin looked undaunted. Well, he did fight hordes of orcs for a hundred years and was ahead of Aetheria on the Winding Way. It'd be kind of weird if he wasn't confident in his abilities.

The lizards split into a unit formation, with the fighter in the front, the ranger and rogue in the middle, and the two mages in the rear. A spell that read as water-aligned to Aetheria's Ethereal Sight formed from the chants of the wand-wielder. The staff wielder chanted a lightning spell, no doubt meant to be a combo attack. While the ranger filled the air with arrows, the fighter held his ground and the rogue prepared to back him up. Their unspoken tactics obviously meant to drive the elf to them on their terms.

Werylin did not hesitate. The elf appeared to dance lazily through the oncoming arrows, and the warrior's axe slammed against his own shield in a terribly discordant screech. The sound sent a light tingle through Aetheria's nerves, but Werylin did not seem affected by it. Instead, he blurred forward to match weapons with the first lizard-man. Delicate-looking blade or not, Harmonious Tempest easily parried the harsh axe blows, and it was the blade of the axe, not the katana, that got chipped.

The rogue could not find an opening to support the fighter with, and on the third parried axe-blow the warrior overextended. One fast slash and the warrior's head tumbled across the ground.

It had not been a total failure on the warrior's part, though; he had bought time. A large sphere of water formed around Werylin when the first mage's spell finished. Within a breath, the second finished and a bolt of lightning flared from the sky.

In the terrible sounds of magic unleashed, Werylin's voice spoke over everything once more.

"Reflect!"

As commanded, the water-sphere vanished and reappeared on the mage who cast it. Unfortunately for the red staff, he was in range and also trapped within the water ball. The lightning arced wildly to strike the original caster, the sphere of water took the lightning, and both lizards died, painfully. Ranger-lizard took two hops backward and shouted some language Aetheria did not understand. Its arrow suddenly glowed and gave off the impression of a shooting star.

Werylin casually cut the arrow in half, but when the sliced arrow hit the ground past him, each half exploded with tremendous force. Aetheria contained it with a quick ice wall, which nearly made her miss the rogue's attempt to assault Werylin.

The lizard was quick and charged forward fractions of a second behind the explosive arrow. Double daggers ripped the elf's throat apart in a spray of blood. The rogue unleashed a flurry of blows. Aetheria counted at least fifteen, but she may well have missed a couple. It moved that fast. When the form of Werylin hit the ground, it vanished into motes of magic. Panic filled the lizard's eyes for a brief second.

"Retaliation."

Every strike the lizard-man just made appeared on its own body, while Werylin reappeared, completely unscathed behind it and to the right, which was where the ranger lizard stood. Harmonious Tempest contemptuously finished the last of the lizard-men off, splitting the creature from head to toe. Its bisected body fell to the sand precisely at the same moment Werylin's sword clinked into its sheath.

~I'm feeling more like a big dumb brute than ever, watching him fight.~ Aetheria commented to Arkaziel.

+You are a big dumb brute, Aetheria. You are a brawler. He's a spellsword. You take damage; he deals it. Don't forget that our new companion is just shy of Tier Four himself, while you just hit Three. You'll get there. I'll show you how to step up your game.+

While the two talked, the third gate of the first entrance opened. A single creature emerged. The monster looked like someone had mashed together a tiger and a bear, then gave it a big horn in the center of its forehead. When the thing moved, its fur rippled, and it seemed to vanish from view. Like the infamous Predator's cloaking system, it had a chameleon effect.

"Harmonious Cascade!"

Harmonious Tempest flew from its sheath. The magical edge cut the air in a wide sweep that sent a storm of golden lightning through the air to strike the cloaked cat-bear-unicorn-horror. Within Aetheria, the Flame of Khaos hungered in response to the display, but she resisted. Instead, she watched the golden lightning destroy the monster, until it dropped to the sands and Werylin mercifully ended its suffering.

"What the heck was that?" Aetheria asked, unable to contain her hunger or curiosity. A small manifestation of the Flame of Khaos appeared and began to eat the residual energies.

"An ability added to Harmonious Tempest by its first wielder, the Imperator of Order."

An indiscreet cough pulled Werylin's and Aetheria's attention to Arkaziel. The still panther-sized StarMane stood before a newly opened door. Before him, the ground writhed in shadows. Aetheria barely glimpsed the vanishing forms of murdered chickens before the all-consuming Devouring Darkness ate them.

Werylin arched a brow at the spectacle. Aetheria failed to contain her laughter.

"A light appetizer for your first round, Ark?"

"I love to eat chicken." A multitude of fangs showed in a hungry smile that Aetheria had become accustomed to. Werylin looked somewhat off-put by the cat's antics.

With no time to prepare, the second gate behind the second door opened. A swarm of fifty flying puffer fish darted through the gates toward Arkaziel. Each of the fish puffed up as they swam through the air and unleashed volleys of quills at the panther. Aetheria's Ethereal Sight told her that the quills had a spiritual component and were not just a physical attack.

Arkaziel's fur shimmered, black draconic scales formed underneath, and he inhaled. The quills pelted against his scales ineffectively. Arkaziel exhaled. A beam of light and darkness filled the intervening distance and disintegrated the entire swarm in one go. Any remaining quills exploded in a vortex of spiritual energy, which the cat opened his maw and ate, as if he'd been waiting for it the whole time.

"Quillshots were a staple of the planet Acarda," Arkaziel said. "Their flesh is absolutely putrid and toxic to even a StarMane. Their quills, however, are rife with spiritual energy. Gather enough together and they hit a critical mass and produce the tastiest spiritual explosion."

"Were a staple?"

"Grandpa ate all the fish, then the planet. What a jerk. They were so good!"

Aetheria sighed wearily, and Werylin stared at the cat, open-mouthed.

The third gate opened to reveal a murderous cockatrice who raised its head and unleashed a terrifying caw from its rooster head, catching Aetheria off guard and instantly paralyzing all three of them. It had been a while since an enemy had stunned one of them, let alone both her and Arkaziel. Her body refused to react to her commands, and Werylin seemed to be in the same boat.

With the arrogance of an apex predator, the cockatrice approached the stunned panther. Its massive beak opened to take a bite out of Arkaziel. Centimeters from its beak hitting the cat, hundreds of tendrils of shadow emerged from the dark fur, and a different squawk escaped the beak as blood and feathers filled the air.

It did not give up, even while pierced by spears of shadow. The cockatrice ripped at the panther with its beak, but Arkaziel suddenly appeared underneath its legs, still paralyzed, based on his identical posture. The cockatrice got a mouthful of sand, its target long gone.

Arkaziel's tail swished, and then a halo of light formed around the cat. The StarMane rippled, its form becoming the true draconic glory of a sixty-meter-long cat-dragon. He contemptuously ate the cockatrice.

"Exponential growth on the enemy's attacks, Aetheria. If you're going to show off like both of us, you'd better bring it."

"I don't feel the need to show off. I need to practice holding aggro. You two murder everything while I keep it pissed off at me."

With no time for planning a strategy, the third door opened to reveal three Tyrannosaurus Rexes. *How do you taunt dinosaurs?*

CHAPTER 3

Murder in the Arena

Arkaziel reduced his size down to a mere three-meter dragon, instead of the hockey-rink-sized behemoth he truthfully was. Aetheria internally heaved a sigh of relief. *How would I pull the attention of things off something that huge?*

Aetheria darted ahead and left a trail of snowflakes in her wake. Then the Ethereal snowflakes that swirled around her shot ahead, peppering the three T-Rexes with dozens of minor wounds, and drawing the ire of the monsters toward the Etherfrost Asura.

"Haste." Werylin's soft voice filled Aetheria's ears. Surges of power rose in her, her reflexes and mental acuity jumped to levels higher than she was used to, and she experienced support magic for the first time. *I could really get used to this. I'm still slower than Werylin, but it's a lot closer now than it was before.*

Aetheria's snowflake flurry enraged the mighty dinosaurs, who stomped and lunged forward to bite her. With the alacrity upgrade, though, the monsters couldn't even get close to biting her while she danced past the first, and then into the middle of them.

"Etherfrost Nova!" Aetheria shouted out the warning to her companions, before blue flames swallowed her body then exploded outward in a fifteen-meter radius. Frostfire raged for a brief second before the nova dissipated. Patches of hoarfrost covered the T-Rexes and continued to freeze and burn the creatures. Her freezing domain expanded outward, and thicker frost appeared on the monster hides, while patches of ice flickered in and out of existence under their feet.

Pillars of ice rose and sank around Aetheria. She used the pillars to practice her parkour on, obviously. To an ordinary human's perceptions, she was little more than a red-and-blue blur between three incredibly fast dinosaurs that each tried to bite at the blur. To Aetheria, Arkaziel, Werylin, and the dinosaurs themselves, she stayed just ahead of the oncoming attacks. The T-Rexes were excellent practice for her, as they only employed three attacks so far: bite, stomp, and tail smash.

Arkaziel let her play for a few seconds. "Try not to ruin the corpses. They look tasty."

The cat lifted a paw, and a glowing claw unleashed a blast of darkness at one target. The black, inky *something* seemed to tighten and constrain the poor creature. Its efforts to break free became frantic, but it was to no avail. Its death came after ten seconds, when the darkness seeped inside of it, and then the hide fell to the ground. The flesh, blood, and all other organic material that made up the monster were gone.

Arkaziel burped.

"Mm. Yeah. Those are tasty." He purred happily.

Werylin did not sit idle while the cat played with its food. He blurred behind a T-Rex, ran up its tail, then removed its rather enormous head from its shoulders before it could even recognize there was a threat beyond the blue-and-red blur it kept trying to eat. A second slash sent a wave from his blade, which beheaded the last of the survivors.

"Well, I guess I don't need to play up the tank role if you guys are just going to one-shot them." Aetheria endeavored to keep the annoyance from her tone. She failed miserably. Werylin landed next to her, just as the gate to the next batch of creatures opened.

"I could hold back?" Werylin suggested. "I am the furthest along their path in our party."

Aetheria gestured, and a turret rose from the sand before her, followed by two more. Spears of ice shot through the air without warning, piercing the scaled hides of camouflaged reptiles on the walls.

"That's unnecessary. Holding back now that we're past the Aetherial Veil is counterintuitive. The faster things die, the better." Aetheria said the last without a second thought. She had a minor flashback to EFWO—one mage in the raid party who worried about their absolutely bonkers damage made the rest of the group feel underperforming, but the goal wasn't for everyone to have a long line on a graph or chart; the goal was to kill a raid boss. In this scenario, the goal was to reach the next floor, so whatever got them there faster and didn't compromise moral or ethical lines was on the table.

Aetheria felt confident the Administrators would increase their challenges to match the growth in power that the duo-turned-trio had undergone. *Way to jinx your own party.*

The ice turrets fell silent when Aetheria could no longer see any more blurred monsters on the walls. Ethereal Sight proved its value yet again. The third gate opened. Not a single reptile had launched even a single attack. Perhaps because she jinxed them, or perhaps because it was the last fight of the floor (if she guessed its layout properly), a dragon roared. The creature had electric-blue scales streaked with red, its full length easily forty meters long.

The draconic enemy's forces charged forward, a proverbial horde of little half-lizard half-dog men, armed with deceptively powerful weaponry. How was the weaponry deceptive? While they appeared to be standard spears and pitchforks, they glowed powerfully to her Ethereal Sight. So did the kobolds. *Oh, come on, a dragon with an army of Tier Three kobolds?*

Aetheria darted forward, still under the effects of Haste, and then leaped through the air to deliver a jump kick to the face of the kobold who led the charge. Her foot exploded his face like a melon, even while the three kobolds behind the first jabbed spears and pitchforks at her. Blades and tines pierced her body, but she smiled grimly through the pain.

"Etherfrost Nova."

The Frostfire flames surrounded her for a moment before exploding outward toward the kobolds. She didn't bother with an omnidirectional blast. The forward-directed nova crashed in waves against the kobolds. Hoarfrost glistened on their red hides, and behind her she heard Arkaziel make a self-satisfied grunt. Three wells of darkness appeared, spread out amongst the kobolds. From within each of the wells dozens of long black tentacles of darkness attacked kobolds. Darkness entwined the unlucky kobolds that veered close enough, pulling them into the fount of shadows.

Werylin hummed three notes, then blurred through the kobold minions to their back lines, where a sweeping attack demolished the enemy casters before they could even get a spell off. The kobolds had no defense against the raw speed of the elf, but the dragon seemed to have no such limitations. Lightning shot from its maw in quick breaths. One lightning bolt Werylin could dodge. In fact, he evaded the first three before the fourth and fifth struck him. The dragon's eyes flashed red, and beams of energy flared toward Werylin's convulsing form.

When Aetheria raised an ice wall, expecting the smooth surface to reflect the energy beams, she discovered the beams weren't a strange form of red lightning like she assumed, but rather heat. The beams bored through the quickly raised wall, but it did buy Werylin enough time to shake off his convulsions and retreat. As he did, another beam of energy came from behind her to strike the electric dragon. The enemy dragon endured the scorching of its scales inflicted by Arkaziel's twilight breath, with only a few of them being dislodged or shattered.

Aetheria lifted a hand and tossed an orb of ice into a group of kobolds. The orb exploded into concentric rings of jagged, red Ethereal ice shards. *Oh, that's disgusting.* The test run of ice fragmentation grenades landed them on the list of *only in dire situations.*

Aetheria launched a few lances of ice at the dragon while she slipped across the packs of kobolds. Werylin had switched targets and blurred between groups to finish them. He used the ice turrets on their own back line and Arkaziel's founts of darkness, kicking a kobold into one of them for every two or three he dispatched with swift swings of his katana.

Arkaziel remained on the back line. The cat launched precision light strikes from his eyes. Soundlessly, laser beams killed kobold after kobold. Aetheria reckoned the duo would have the kobolds defeated by the time she reached the dragon.

The dragon opened its mouth and drew in a heavy breath. As she ran toward it, Aetheria filled her aura with the Primordial Flame of Aetherius, which consumed the massive amounts of lightning it sent at her. When the brilliance of the lightning ended, the dragon was a scant five meters away from her. Large draconic eyes looked shocked to see a human survive such a blast, but it quickly reacted and leaned forward to bite her. With Werylin's Haste effect still active, Aetheria sped through the space between the dragon's teeth and, once in its mouth, shot pillars of ice up to force its jaws wide apart.

The dragon flailed in rage at the increasing number of icy pillars preventing it from snapping its jaws shut. It tried in vain to overpower the ice, and its full body thrashed with the effort. Even the undulating tongue beneath her couldn't break free of the pillars of ice that pinned it to the bottom of the dragon's jaw.

The red pillars of ice darkened when Aetheria applied the Flame of Nyx to them, which caused the ice to leach the life force of the dragon with each second they were in contact. The change in danger represented by the pillars pushed the dragon's attacks against the ice toward frantic desperation as it couldn't resist the drain on its life. Fear gave way to panic, as it failed to destroy the ice.

The entire dragon shook as loud magical explosions rocked the electric dragon's thick hide. Aetheria maintained the ice pillars, even as she heard it swallow more air and magical energies spiked at the back of its throat. She let them build until she lifted a hand and invoked the Flame of Khaos. The gathering electrical energies, once exposed to the Flame, shifted from a blue hue to a red one, and then shot outward into the flesh of the dragon's throat.

Again, the enormous beast thrashed. The internal attack had rent fissures in its throat, and her energy senses let her know it had expanded into the head and upper chest of the dragon.

Suddenly, light filled the dark maw of the dragon, and the dragon's head and neck separated. The faint clicks of Werylin sheathing his sword drew her eyes to him. The elf had a large frown on his face as he looked at Aetheria through rows of sharp teeth.

"Just what the hell was that? I heard the most discordant note I have ever heard in my life, and then red lightning began to hew the dragon apart from the inside."

"Flame of Khaos," Aetheria answered honestly, despite the disapproval from the elf.

"Mm." Werylin's tone conveyed inner conflict.

"Something wrong with using the Flame of Khaos?" Aetheria's question was earnest, which seemed to mollify Werylin some.

"No, I just did not expect it. Among my people we are taught to seek balance with the universe in our paths. Spellsong, the Words of Creation, even our sword styles, all involve joining in this balance and using it as a form of limited precognition to enhance all we do through a unifying force. Harmony, or as some call it, *Order*."

"Oof." Aetheria let out a sigh. "Actually, that is fantastic. Hang on one second, though."

Aetheria stepped out of the jaw to see Arkaziel in his full form. The StarMane had already begun to clean the dragon corpse, and was in the process of collecting scales, skinning, and filleting it.

"What? We can divvy up the loot however you want, I want to get at its organs while they are still warm and juicy." Arkaziel licked his lips, which only put on display the fact he was salivating quite a bit.

"Okay, you eat up." Aetheria couldn't contain the laughter at Arkaziel's antics.

CHAPTER 4

More Jigsaw Puzzles

The fifty-second floor ended up being a noncombat floor. The trio found themselves inside of a large room with three tables, each with one of their names assigned to it. A ticker floated above each table, and each currently read 1,000.

"I hate puzzles." Arkaziel groaned.

"They look easy?" Aetheria noted, pointing out the lack of many pieces.

"That's almost worse. If we have to do a thousand puzzles each, and they're mind numbingly boring, it's just torture," Arkaziel whined.

"First and second place get prizes; third place gets a punishment." The sports-announcer Administrator had returned briefly to give them the only incentive they needed: loot.

Arkaziel took on his human form. "Stupid thumbs."

Aetheria patted him on the shoulder before she moved to her table. The two men did the same.

The Administrator kicked off their competition. "Ready, set, puzzle!"

A quick count showed that Aetheria had fifty-one puzzle pieces on her desk. She processed the number of pieces while organizing them by edge or middle ones, and then she started from a corner and worked her way around quickly. It was not a complicated puzzle; it was the sort she would have pulled out for a six- or seven-year-old back at the library. When she finished, there was an extra piece.

"Not this again." Aetheria growled, the other two looking up from their almost finished first puzzles.

"Extra piece." Aetheria waved it at the men, before her finished puzzle vanished, and a new set appeared on her table. The extra piece in her hand remained, and all three swore softly. Her ticker dropped to 999.

Moments later, Werylin and Arkaziel followed suit.

The puzzles proceeded like that: each complete puzzle left them with between one to three extra pieces that kept accumulating. The simplicity of each puzzle quickly became complicated by the growing number of extras their desks held. Werylin seemed to be the least put upon by the extra pieces. The elf hummed a beautiful tune to himself and seemed to never pause or doubt where the next piece of the puzzle went. His long, delicate fingers maintained a smooth, if slightly slow, pace while continuously putting together the puzzles.

Arkaziel, on the other hand, was a creature of chaos. He moved in bursts of speed and then would have a few seconds of slowdown, followed by more bursts of speed. There was no harmonious connection to the universe for the StarMane. It reminded Aetheria of children trying to run down the big hills of Duluth before they were ready. Aetheria would never forget the mixed looks of victory at success followed by the horrific realization that once you started down a hill it was a challenge not just to stop, but to keep going as well.

Aetheria fell between the two. She'd had enough puzzles thrown at her inside the tower already that she easily fell into a rhythm, but she lacked that connection to order that Werylin possessed. If her supposition that chaos and order were opposite ends of the same sliding scale were true, couldn't she employ her Flame of Khaos to assist her in some way? She called upon the Flame of Khaos, and Aetheria's vision swam. For some reason, the Primordial Flame of Nyx seemed to call to her, so Aetheria drew upon it as well. Between the two Flames, she found she could sense something like a natural order. Aetheria threw herself into the sensation. Her hands worked almost of their own volition.

Puzzles came and went. Aetheria lost track of time until Arkaziel's telepathic calls pulled her out of her meditative trance.

"What, Ark? I was trying stuff!" She was annoyed.

"You started bleeding from your eyes a few minutes ago. Figured you'd want to know." Arkaziel shrugged and went back to his puzzle. Werylin frowned at the two of them.

"Whatever you were doing, you may have overdone it. Not all aspects of the gods are meant for us mortals, even if they give us their power." Werylin pointed up at the tickers. The elf had 231 left, while Arkaziel had 260 left. Aetheria had 1 left, but her entire table was covered in what looked like thousands of pieces.

"I tried to enter a state similar to what you were employing, I think. I didn't feel a oneness or any harmony, though, just a compulsive sense of where things should be and what I needed to change to make it right." Aetheria bit at her lower lip, but she no longer bled from her eyes. The pain had already receded, but clearly employing the power for so long had taken a powerful toll upon her. She wanted a nap.

"That sounds closer to fate or destiny than harmony?"

"Maybe. It involved the Flame of Nyx, so I definitely went off the rails with what I intended and what I accomplished." Aetheria rubbed at her face in an attempt to fully rouse herself. When that failed, she pulled one of the Ethereal apples from her repository and had a restorative snack.

"Perhaps you turned your senses toward fate instead of order?" Werylin's tone made it sound more impressive than if she had sidled up to order.

"Maybe. Nyx is associated with fate, and the Fates are her daughters." Aetheria shrugged. Once more, she encountered a scenario where if things were neatly labeled, or she had an action log, or even a list or description of abilities, she might know. Even now, she could only tell you that the pale blue-white Flame of Ymir was the Flame of Ymir because it appeared when Ymir gave her the Flame. How many facets of abilities were going unused because she simply didn't know enough?

"Exploration of possibilities is a good thing, Aetheria. You've got a lot to explore, but you also have the means to do that exploration."

Aetheria's arched aqua brow prompted Werylin to continue.

"You are the only Immortal I've ever met. We elves can enjoy exceptionally long lives, but eventually we die. The same is true for all the races or beings I've ever heard of. You have the capacity to survive the results of your experimentation, and the time to do it in." Werylin laughed. "Many will envy you your capabilities."

"You don't?"

"What is the point of envy when it comes to things you cannot yourself attain? I have my own strengths to focus on and grow, and it would be a terrible soul who covets the power of one who resurrected them." Werylin winked at the words. Aetheria laughed a little, surprised at her lack of reaction or internal flailing at Werylin. *He's gorgeous, a swordsman, an elf, intelligent and learned . . . I must have really given myself totally over to Aoibhe if our minstrel can't even make me squirm.*

Arkaziel's irritation hit Aetheria like a Mack truck, and it made her laugh because she could even feel his conflicted emotions about it. Aetheria could put together the StarMane wanted them to shut up, but he also wanted them to keep distracting each other so he could catch up or at least get ahead of Werylin.

"That's a healthy mindset, Werylin. Are you trying to distract me from winning?" Aetheria's inquiry carried a heavy dose of sarcasm. She didn't actually think that, but Werylin's cheeks reddened. Only after that blush did Aetheria notice that Werylin's hands never stopped sorting and placing pieces. *That cheeky minstrel.*

How did my table get so full of pieces? Downside to totally spacing out there, I guess. If there were one to three extra pieces per puzzle, and I'm down to the last puzzle, that means I have somewhere between a thousand to three thousand pieces on the table. Are they all going to be part of the puzzle?

The obnoxious task before her daunted Aetheria for once. There were so many pieces that the puzzle couldn't possibly use all of them. The mere idea of sorting all of them manually left Aetheria with a sour stomach.

"Guess I'll try this again," Aetheria muttered under her breath, but this time she focused on the Flame of Nyx only. She sought the foresight of Night, a path through the pieces before her. Aetheria silenced her thoughts and stilled her mind. She focused on the vast darkness in her mind's eye while she aligned herself with the Primordial Flame of Nyx. Aetheria could feel shadows seep out of her pores and cover the table, as hundreds of shadowy pencil-thin appendages formed to prod at the puzzle pieces on the table. A dull sensation filled her mind, and imagery slowly formed out of the darkness.

The first image was that of a figure fighting on the front lines of a battle, one holding off many. A word flowed into her mind, accompanying the image. *Vanguard.*

The second possibility revealed by the Flame of Nyx was of a figure raining destruction on enemies in the form of icy whirlwinds and tornadoes. *Tempest.* Less clear than the first two, the third option showed itself as someone constructing weapons, creatures, and everything else out of ice. *Shaper.* The last option she saw was even vaguer than the last, and she could see why right away. It had no synergy with her. The *Frostforged Warrior* relied on icy armor and weapons, and Aetheria wasn't about either armor or weapons.

While the idea of a Tempest seemed entertaining, that wasn't Aetheria's nature. She'd never done well as a damage class in any game. The idea of a Vanguard appealed to her. *Are these stupid puzzles self-actualization tricks pushing us subconsciously toward realizations about our own paths? Did I do myself a disservice by touching fate to find paths? Well, I've already made my choice. Let's bring it forward.*

Aetheria embraced the Vanguard. Once she focused on the creation of the Vanguard puzzle, she fell into a half-trance state where over three-fourths of the puzzle pieces were discarded from her table. She tossed them carelessly onto the floor behind her with two hands, and whenever she found a desired piece, Aetheria put it together with her other two hands.

+*Shapeshifters.*+ Arkaziel sent the single word to her, laced with both mockery and teasing. Aetheria perked up out of her trance just enough to notice that Ark had also forsworn a mere two hands and had adopted the four-armed form that she employed.

Eventually, Aetheria slid the last piece of the puzzle into place and beheld the image she had wrought. It looked nothing like the mental image she had seen of the Vanguard. Mostly because the puzzle showed a depiction of Aetheria herself, surrounded by an icy aura and a swarm of icicles. The artistry of the image made her smile. Aetheria didn't know if she looked like that much of a badass in a fight, but now hoped she did.

A holographic prompt appeared before her, the first words congratulating her on beating her companions. It offered her four choices of rewards, which were:

1. *Strategy and Treatises on Ice Cultivation*
2. Single-Use Enchantment: Of the Glacial Sovereign
3. Frostshaper's Glacial Eye
4. *An Idiot's Guide to Core Creation*

While the first three were all solid, the fourth didn't hold any interest for Aetheria. Themis had told her straight up that she would have to build a unique construct for her core. No prize for a random tower level would hold the answers she needed to construct such a core. Similarly, she already had several tomes on Ice Cultivation, most of which, while interesting, held basic knowledge she had already gone beyond. The Glacial Eye sounded interesting, but with no further information, she wasn't inclined to pick it. It could easily be a cursed item, and she had no issue shaping ice anyway.

She tapped the second option, and a glowing sphere of energy appeared in Aetheria's hand. Knowledge of which items she could apply it to, but not what it exactly did, flowed into her mind. Aetheria laughed like a madwoman as she slammed the orb into the scrunchy in her hair.

"Behold, I have gained the Scrunchy of the Glacial Sovereign!"

Aetheria's form glowed brightly as the red scrunchy absorbed a colossal amount of magical energy.

CHAPTER 5

Seabreeze

I can't believe I lost. StarMane tradition dictates I now eat one of you," Arkaziel muttered unhappily. His dissatisfaction at losing to Werylin was eclipsed only by his disbelief at the curse the Administrators had placed on him for the next seven days: everything smelled like wet dog to him.

"It's okay, Ark, you were really close." The appearance of the door to the next floor had never been such a relief, although when they appeared on a small tropical island with the sea spread out in every direction, Aetheria had a sinking feeling in her stomach.

"Even the salt smells like wet dog!" Arkaziel complained.

"Water level," Werylin said somberly.

"Yep," Aetheria agreed. The small island, barely three hundred square meters by Aetheria's estimation, held no room or indication that it was to be part of this trial.

"Yay, wet dog and getting wet. My two favorite things." Arkaziel scowled even more before his form rippled into that of a dark blue-black water dragon. He snapped his jaws at the air a few times, practicing for the inevitable fish genocide to come.

"I haven't seen you take on other draconic forms before, Ark," Aetheria noted with curiosity.

"I've realized more of my gains. Took some time to digest the parts of the phoenix." Glee and malice alike filled the StarMane's eyes.

I kind of feel sorry for whoever we run into on this floor.

"What's the plan?" Werylin inquired while going over his equipment.

"Can you breathe underwater? I guess that's the first thing."

"If you give me an hour I could cast a ritual." Werylin sighed, uneager to go about the elaborate process.

"Just take one of these." A flask appeared in her hand, followed by two more. "It should last a full day. Here's a couple extra in case we get separated."

"Thank you, Aetheria. Do you carry many alchemical supplies?" Werylin seemed surprised that she had potions which were of dubious benefit to the party of two. "Why do you even have these?"

"Yeah, a lot. Some bought, some I made. Never know what you're going to find in the tower, and we've run into floors with denial of magic or certain energies before. Got to be prepared in case others need help, or we ourselves need help." Aetheria offered a little shrug, wondering if she needed to explain the Girl Scouts to Werylin.

Arkaziel chimed in. "Why not carry everything? Aetheria's repository is infinite. Even if we never need it, she can employ its mass to destroy people."

"Alright, enough dillydallying. Let's figure out what we're supposed to . . ." Aetheria trailed off, as half a kilometer offshore the water foamed, and an interesting submersible broke the surface. While only parts of the craft had emerged above the waves, it was enough to clearly see the design similarities to that of a large blue whale.

"Oh man, they are so lucky they surfaced. I would've eaten them," Arkaziel said.

"I told you to stop eating metal. I can use it in my repository, and it barely helps your cultivation."

Werylin pointed back at the craft. "We've been spotted."

In minutes, a smaller craft departed the whale submersible and landed on the beach. Three people hopped out of the scout craft, and one remained on the boat. Two were humans with blue hair, while the other two were merfolk, with blue skin, scales, and gills at their necks that seemed displeased with the ocean air.

"Hail and well met." Aetheria tried in the most common of the human tongues she'd learned.

"Greetings. Our prayers to mighty Pontus and his illustrious father, Aetherius, have been answered at last! For weeks, our priests have performed the sacred rights to call for divine aid, and now our prayers have been answered!"

Arkaziel snorted, which seemed to make the three nervous.

"That's right, we've been sent by Aetherius. What problem plagues your people so that you must turn to the gods for aid, instead of solving them yourselves?" Aetheria inquired, while internally she wondered if their problems were naturally occurring or if an Administrator had just rewoven the fabric of reality on this floor to present a challenging scenario. *Thinking about how the tower works is too headache inducing. They're sentient, at the least, so they get helped.*

"I am Captain Coral." The seaman spoke before the human. "The Free City of Seabreeze is under assault by nefarious forces. If you can free us of them, we shall reward you greatly, and Pontus has offered one of Thalassa's creations, Ocean's Serenity, to the one who frees us."

~Oh, that sounds promising!~ Arkaziel kept his greed confined to telepathy.

"We shall assist you. That's quite the vessel you have. I don't suppose I could get a tour after you explain the situation to us?"

Which is how the trio ended up aboard the *Narwhal's Shadow*. Coral gave them a brief tour of the ship. Arkaziel had returned to cat form, while Aetheria and Werylin, each almost a head taller than the fish people and the other humans, struggled to be graceful in the cramped, confined quarters of the submarine. Luckily, the tour was brief, and they were served refreshments in the galley while the ship set course for

Seabreeze. The journey to Seabreeze took just under four hours, and it left Aetheria wondering how long the ship had been waiting for them.

The situation that lay before Seabreeze was multifaceted. A creature they called Tiamat's Daughter had taken up residence in one of the vast aquatic crevasses near Seabreeze. Since its arrival, the people had suffered increasingly dark dreams, and already three citizens had attempted to harm themselves or others because of the terrible dreams. Many fish and other aquatic life had fled the area, which pushed the Sharktooth Clan to increase their raids upon Seabreeze. Finally, something had destroyed the city's linkage to a nearby volcano that powered most of the city's infrastructure via what sounded like a complicated magitech reactor.

Seabreeze proper surprised Aetheria. She had expected a domed or bubbled city under the ocean, but instead the city was actually open to the ocean. A magical field clearly marked the boundaries of the city. According to Captain Coral, a sacred relic called the Breath of Pontus let all who dwelt in its range breathe. While curious about such a relic, its effects were strange to experience. Breathing water felt awkward, but after a few minutes, each of the party became accustomed to the oddity. The ability to breath water didn't confer the experience to quickly adapt to it. Everything underwater became more difficult. Eating, talking, bodily functions; anything and everything was worse underwater, and Aetheria pointedly didn't think about where everyone peed whenever she felt warm water.

Without concern for the necessity of oxygen, the trio were capable of soaking in the grandeur of Seabreeze without the nagging problem of drowning, and there was a lot to enjoy about such a beautiful city. The architectural style looked like coral reefs Aetheria had seen on so many documentaries, with rounded and curved shapes native to such reefs blown up to a much larger scale. *How many of these fish are carnivores? Don't let them swim free if you don't post* DANGER, CARNIVOROUS FISH *signs everywhere.* They had worked out a plan of action during the four-hour journey aboard the *Narwhal's Shadow*. The city would supply the group a few enchanted items for breathing underwater, as well as local maps. While they could have just used Aetheria's alchemical potions for Werylin and shapeshifting for Arkaziel and Aetheria, it just wasn't in Aetheria's nature to turn down loot. Their first order of business was to investigate Tiamat's Daughter, as they all felt the Sharktooth Clan's aggression tied directly to that, and they might avoid slaughtering the warlike sharkmen by dealing with the underlying cause first. The volcano would come second, and the sharkmen and other problems after.

Werylin chose an amulet for his enchanted breathing item. Arkaziel went with a gaudy collar, while Aetheria opted to pay an enchanter to add the effect to her own belt. A few thousand gold coins, monster cores, and a couple of reagents later, and her black belt held two new effects: water breathing and increased swim speed. The enchanter couldn't tell her how much of a speed increase it would be, just that she'd be "faster." Once more, Aetheria longed for a properties screen for her items and abilities, but it wasn't to be.

Which brought the trio to a large sentry outpost on the north side of Seabreeze. Captain Coral had accompanied them to the edge of the city.

"Good luck out there. The ocean has been changing lately, so who knows what you'll find. This is a whirlpool grenade. It can buy time to escape almost any normal threat that should be near Seabreeze." The shrug of his shoulders conveyed the uncertainty of its effectiveness against larger threats.

"I think we'll be okay, Captain. We'll be back when we've got things sorted." Aetheria gestured and the water churned and froze into the form of a teardrop-shaped hull pulled by ice dolphins. Aetheria flicked her wrist, and the Reins of the Ice Queen appeared in her hands, connecting to the creations and bolstering their speed and control. They left Coral sputtering something about the beauty of the vessel as it shot off into the ocean proper.

"So what do you think this Tiamat's Daughter will be? Think it will have any actual relevance to Tiamat, or are we heading into a fight where it's deliberately misleading?" Aetheria inquired.

"Well, we've got different Admins now. Presumably they know a thing or two about subterfuge, misdirection, and not just basic-bitch floor ideas, unlike the one I ate—whatever their name was."

"Superbia, I believe."

"Wait, you ate a Tower Administrator? You skipped over that one in the recap. Might have been good to know." Werylin sounded annoyed, and Aetheria didn't blame him. Something that could bring blowback probably shouldn't have been so casually forgotten.

"It was all fair. Aetheria challenged him, he lost, I ate him. Aetherius didn't care, so it's all good. He loves StarManes." Arkaziel beamed. "He's one of the few gods that shares a fondness for us. It's mostly just him and Chronos, among the big names."

"Might have something to do with you constantly trying to take a bite out of the others. Presumably, like people, gods don't like to be eaten." Aetheria smirked as she teased Ark.

"If they don't want to get eaten, they should stop being so delicious."

The scenery they passed amazed Aetheria. Massive reefs, giant fields of seaweed, the occasional fissure that created warmer water. She noted, however, a distinct lack of aquatic life that left the beauty of the ocean marred. The farther the trio traveled in their ice-craft, the more haunting the absence of life became. Every kilometer closer they came to the crevasse on the map, the more desolate the oceans became. Even plant life thinned out. When the crevasse became visible at a half kilometer, no life remained. Not even microscopic life, as best Aetheria could tell with her Ethereal Sight.

The closer they came to the trench, the more the Aether diminished and Nether dominated. The Flames of Nyx and Khaos both feasted on the ambient energies without being directed to. Aetheria perked up when she noticed the strength of the Flame of Khaos, actually intensified from its feeding.

"Disorder," Werylin murmured, fingers caressing the hilt of his katana.

"My Flame of Khaos is eating most of it. Stay in my vicinity if you're worried about being affected by it at all. Whatever we're about to find, it's increased the Nether presence so much that the Aether has thinned out, and it's producing some strange fluctuations in the Nether to boot. Any ideas, Ark?"

The house cat-sized water dragon gave her a baleful look.

"All I can smell and taste is wet dog. I hate wet dog." If anger alone could make the water boil, the ocean would have cooked around Arkaziel. Instead, he just looked miserable.

The vehicle's occupants went silent. All three felt the predatory gaze of another being fall upon them. No visible signs showed they were being watched, but each of them could feel the remote viewing of a powerful, and uncaring, creature focus upon them.

Aetheria flicked a hand out, unleashing a pulse of Ethereal power that shattered the remote viewing spell.

"How'd you do that?" Werylin asked with confusion.

"I can see spellforms. What I can see, I can destroy."

"Haste." Werylin hummed three bars before he said the word. As usual with his Words of Creation powers, the syllables seeped into Aetheria's mind and immediately improved her alacrity. Aetheria nearly asked what he was doing, when the form of a colossal monster rose from the crevasse. Hundreds of eyes lit with madness glared at them, and a massive wave of chaotic energy hurtled toward the trio.

"Take the reins," Aetheria muttered. She let the translucent reins go free, while her hands both moved before her to invoke a powerful replica of the Flame of Khaos that formed five meters ahead of their vessel. The colors of the flames did not shift like typical fire, but varied by the second, shifting through the whole RGB spectrum in a way that hurt to look at. Nor did the flame dance in a way normal fire, or even other Flames Aetheria possessed, did. The Flame of Khaos followed its own rules, ignoring gravity, conventional spatial movement, and even cohesion.

The giant wall of gray energy struck her manifestation of Khaos and vanished completely. The multicolored Flames vanished as well, while Aetheria struggled with the amount of chaotic power she had just absorbed. The Flame of Khaos helped there, eager to digest the power. Each second pushed the intensity of Khaos in her mind higher, closer to reaching equilibrium with her other Flames at Tier Three.

Hundreds of eyes focused on them, and the ocean lit up with the aura of the monster that swam above the crevasse.

"That's terrifying," Werylin said.

Arkaziel, however, disagreed.

"It looks like it'll taste worse than Nidhogg's asshole. Good thing I can only taste wet dog right now."

"Let's kill the terrible Elder Abomination Thingie before patting ourselves on the back." Aetheria sighed and conjured another Flame of Khaos to stop an even greater wave of power.

CHAPTER 6

Spawn of Tiamat

The so-called daughter of Tiamat looked nothing like a dragon. The beast that swam above the crevasse looked more like a hydra with three eel heads, and inexplicably, its lower half had hundreds of tentacles covered with eyes—eyes that seemed to break causality, as wherever their gaze fell, the flow of water became chaotic. With her Ethereal Sight, Aetheria watched mana flows become unpredictable. The effect on Aether and Nether was subdued, for now.

"It's screwing with mana. No idea how that'll affect your powers, Werylin. Ark, stick to Ethereal power." She gestured, and a few Ethereal apples appeared for him. "If you need one of the big fruits from Cryostrialis, let me know."

The ice vehicle dissipated at about fifty yards from the creature. The Reins of the Ice Queen swelled with magical power, and Aetheria stowed the reins before they could succumb to a chaos surge. The water itself churned and heaved Aetheria and Werylin closer to the massive abomination. The Flame of Thalassa allowed Aetheria incredible control over water, and she made use of it to propel herself like a missile toward the monster.

Dozens of tentacles shot forward, but all failed their attempts to knock the Etherfrost Asura off course. One of the eel heads almost caught her, but she forced the water to slow the movements of the hydra. With the help of the water, Aetheria deftly evaded being bitten, and then her fist contacted the torso of the creature. She landed the first blow a dozen yards from where the necks joined the body. The body of the creature rippled as force transferred from Aetheria's arm into its torso; its scales shattered, and blood filled the water. Blood partially obscured her sight, but Aetheria's Ethereal Sight revealed the delivery of Ethereal power into the hydra's body.

Power that turned into needles of ice inside the monster. Two of the eel heads roared in pain, while the third moved to bite at Aetheria. Werylin sliced the attacking head cleanly down the middle, his katana completely unhindered by the scales and blubber. The eyes along all the tentacles focused on Werylin and Aetheria. Each of the optical organs glowed with a baleful red miasma, and then beams of power shot forth in a massive volley of chaotic power.

Complicating matters, Arkaziel unleashed his own attack at the same time. Hundreds of bolts of radiant energy struck at the eyes of the tentacles, even as their own beams fired at Aetheria and Werylin. A third of the blasts counteracted one another. Another third, Aetheria devoured with the Flame of Khaos. Unfortunately, the Tier Two Flame could not cope with any more, and the vast surge of chaotic power rippled through her even as the rest of the beams struck her. Werylin, at least, had gotten out of the way.

It had been a bit since Aetheria had truly appreciated the extent of pain and damage her Tier Three body could soak up. The discordant energy ripped at her body and tried to break it apart. Sensations of being ripped apart like this were usually reserved for tiering up, but unlike with that process, the bolts of chaotic power didn't have enough oomph to shatter her cells. Instead, Aetheria was struck with pain, then another bolt would hit her, more pain, more tearing, more healing. The cycle was brutal, and although it was over in three seconds, it felt like an eternity.

Shivers wracked her body for a moment as she healed. At that point, the tentacles had opted to entangle her and hold her for one of the eel heads to come down to eat as a snack. Even if she were not mildly stunned, she wouldn't have fought it. Killing gigantic creatures from the inside had proven effective in the past.

Werylin, not comfortable in water, tried to provide aid, unleashing an attack he called Moonlit Aria. The surrounding water filled with glimmering moonlight and pale white flowers, but nothing else happened.

"Misfire!" The elf snarled, as Aetheria got swallowed by one of the hydra's eel heads.

~I'll do some damage from inside. My Flame of Khaos is almost Tier Three. That should even things up.~

Arkaziel did not respond to her. She assumed he heard her, but even his emotions in the empathic bond seemed dampened as she entered a world of darkness inside the monster. After the memorable experience of being swallowed, Aetheria did not end up in a stomach. Instead, she stood on a floating island in a sea of floating islands. The void expanded in all directions. This was not what she had expected when being swallowed by a stupid hydra.

"Hopefully, I didn't just screw up."

The Flame of Khaos crystalized in intensity, finished with its absorption of the last attacks. New strength and power flooded through Aetheria's being. Nothing attacked her while multicolored flames licked at her skin. The flames left no damage and faded once the Flame of Khaos finished its transition to Tier Three. A cursory glance at the mirror of ice showed her hair had become two-tone: streaks of red shot through her usual aqua hair. With a touch of concentration, it went back to normal. *Better than black. I'd look evil if I added any more black to my appearance, or at least emo.*

There did not seem to be a single other living thing in this place, just floating islands. Nothing gave off any signs of energy to her Ethereal Sight. Did her sight cease to work in this place, or was this some kind of illusion? Aetheria attempted to draw ambient energies, but no Aether or Nether answered her. It was like she was a normal human again and breathing in didn't carry tides of power.

Of course, her inner sun, Frostfire, still churned out constant Ethereal power feeding into her soul, so this was not really a problem.

"How am I supposed to get out of here?" No gates were visible. Neither her internal sense of energy nor Ethereal Sight provided any help. With a disgruntled hiss, Aetheria closed her eyes and thought about her options. Nothing came to mind. Aetheria was uncertain of her location, making this difficult.

If only I could teleport . . .

That was the only method she could think of to get back to where she should have been.

"Trial and error time, I guess."

Previous attempts to use teleportation had all failed her, but she had one Flame she had not tried to attempt it with. A rainbow of fire licked her skin once more when she drew deeply on the Flame of Khaos. A doorway of ice appeared before Aetheria, and she focused on the idea of the doorway activating with the power of Khaos, to take her back to the fight. Energy flickered and sputtered, but nothing happened.

"Wrong mental imagery, maybe? Maybe that's not the way. What other types of teleportation are there besides doorways?"

The doorframe of ice crumbled to pieces, and chaotic energy formed an oval window that looked elsewhere. Aetheria glimpsed Arkaziel and Werylin fighting the hydra before the window fell apart. It seemed like she was on to something, but she couldn't get another window to form even partially after twenty more tries.

"Okay. So . . . maybe I can just . . . bamf?" Aetheria didn't have any more ideas. All the times she'd seen teleportation depicted, it really came down to either doors, portals, or just a thing that happened. Aetheria focused on the multihued Flames of Khaos and imagined them engulfing her, swallowing her, and spitting her out back in the fight. A disorienting sensation struck her, followed by the reawakening of her bond with Arkaziel, and the sensation of being once more in the ocean.

It worked!

The feel of the teleport differed from the smooth transitions between floors of the tower. There was no intervening time. Aetheria reappeared next to Arkaziel instantly. The aquatic dragon form of the StarMane was still intact. Werylin, likewise, showed no injuries, but if that was from raw skill or Arkaziel healing him, Aetheria wouldn't find out until later.

The gigantic form of the abomination now had about a third fewer tentacles. The boys had destroyed the eyes on half the remaining tentacles while she was gone, but already the damaged ones had begun regenerating.

"Don't get eaten by it. I ended up in some kind of strange dimensional space," Aetheria noted lightly. Immediately, the ocean reminded her how uncomfortable it was to talk underwater.It didn't hurt, but the distortion, the pressure, the subconscious fear of getting fish piss in your mouth made the experience borderline unpleasant.

"Take the thing's attention. If I can get a minute to build an attack up, we should be able to overcome its defenses," Arkaziel commanded his minion. His tone left no doubt he expected Aetheria to fall in and fight the monster immediately.

"If you could distract it, it has generated enough disorder that I can unleash Harmony's Vortex. I believe between our attacks, the hydra will die." Werylin, Aetheria noticed, at least actually asked.

While the three casually chatted, the hydra opened all three mouths and unleashed a gray-and-red-flecked cloud of energy at them. Aetheria flashed forward a few yards and deployed the Flame of Khaos to consume the energy. Now that it had reached Tier Three, the Flame ate the entire attack. Only minimal amounts of power escaped from the ravenous Flame to cause minor damage within her body. Minimal to the point that Aetheria merely grimaced through the internal damage and its subsequent healing.

With a heavy pull of Ethereal power from Frostfire, Aetheria employed the Flame of Thalassa to take control of the surrounding ocean. Immediately, her awareness of the ocean expanded in a very distracting way, but she focused on the task at hand. Aetheria generated about twenty geysers of water that launched horizontally at the hydra. The Primordial Flame of Ymir provided the freezing, creation, and devilish intent to do harm.

Twenty batches of frozen ice ripped the hydra's hide to pieces. To say that she had its undivided attention was a minor understatement. All of its remaining eyes locked upon her, and rather than make one giant attack, the hydra fired forty-nine separate energy beams at her. All of those beams seemed to have a massive debuff on their aim, though, as the hydra grappled with the existential crisis of meeting eyes with Aetheria.

The ocean lit up as Werylin appeared behind the hydra. Harmonious Tempest embedded into the blubbery flesh. A shockwave flowed into the creature, and then Werylin and his katana retreated into the darkness.

Aetheria absorbed many of the attacking beams with judicious use of the Flame of Khaos, but even so, she was still struck by at least a dozen. The effect of the attack was not what she expected. Her reflexes slowed down, her strength ebbed, and even her regeneration seemed to suffer under the exhaustive power of the strange attack.

~Enervation. Purge it with a purification power, quickly.~

Arkaziel's input pushed her to do what he said. Through her sluggish reactions, she activated the Flame of Aetherius and purified her body with the sacred power of the divine.

Arkaziel's jaws opened, and beams of pure shadow immediately darkened the ocean, but not for long, as thousands of spears of light shot out of the orb in his mouth. Both the light spears and darkness beams concentrated on the torso of the behemoth hydra.

The hydra's back suddenly ruptured as a whirlwind of golden energy ripped free of its body but did not go far. In fact, Harmony's Vortex couldn't be shaken off. The hydra flailed tentacles at it, tried to swim away from it, but second by second, the creature lost more of its body to the devouring light of order. Things went poorly for the creature once Arkaziel's assault landed. The destruction wrought by the light and shadows and the order vortex ripped the monster apart; the ocean filled with body parts and viscera.

"You two overdid it!" Aetheria hissed, while Werylin lifted his sword and the golden vortex vanished back into the curved blade. Previously unseen, a glyph glowed on the blade for a few seconds before it vanished from Aetheria's ability to perceive.

With the vortex gone, Arkaziel moved faster than Aetheria had ever seen. It looked like he was imitating a Hungry Hungry Hippo, darting through the water to try and eat as much of the hydra as he could.

"Wet dog must taste *really* good."

"Maybe he just likes the scent?" Werylin countered.

CHAPTER 7

The Volcano

With the defeat of the Spawn of Tiamat, the trio had two other problems to tackle. First, they needed to check on the volcano's power relays. Depending on how that went, they would need to deal with the increased aggression from the Sharktooth Clan afterward. Aetheria had hoped that dealing with the monster at the heart of the nightmares and changes to the ecosystem would solve the problem. Internally, Aetheria had her doubts. Sometimes the tower allowed for simplistic video game-like solutions to scenarios; other times, it followed the more complicated situations of real life. *Is there a standard, or does this all just come down to the whims of the Administrators? How much free will actually exists inside this place?*

Aetheria crushed those thoughts. Pondering the meaning of life, existence, and free will was a fast track to depression town, and Aetheria could not afford to stay there. Even though the mysterious entity in the Origin had toned down their longing and loneliness, it still proved to be a constant companion to Aetheria. If she was not on guard with her own emotions, it would be effortless to fall into another depressive episode. Aetheria wanted to be stronger than that. *This is another trial, and I will come out on top.*

The trio rode on top of a giant manta ray made of ice. With the Reins of the Ice Queen in her half-gloved hands again, Aetheria controlled the ice mount effortlessly. Werylin settled back, his lavender eyes constantly scanning the ocean around them. His paranoia seemed justified once they had left the domain of the Spawn of Tiamat. Aquatic predators had started to appear once more. So far, they had four different ambush predators attempt to make a snack of one of them. None of the attacks had resulted in more than a scratch, but the annoyance of small-fry ambushers attacking the trio of Tier Three Cultivators seemed to personally slight Werylin. Arkaziel, in a rare show of empathy, commented that they must be starving.

The volcano lay nearly on the opposite side of Seabreeze. They did not stop in the city; instead, Aetheria made a straight path for the dominant source of thermal energy she could sense in the distance. Eventually, Arkaziel pointed out the line of beacons they had been told to look for. Since the beacons were inactive, they were not yet to the problem. Several minutes later, they encountered a broken beacon. Magical sparks shot forth from the destroyed magitech transformer, and the three moved in to get a closer look.

"Looks like fiber optics, almost," Aetheria murmured to herself.

"Like what?" Werylin inquired.

"A glass cable that transmits light. Technology from my old world."

"Why would you transmit light through glass cables? How would you even make a glass cable?" Arkaziel actually looked curious, but Aetheria suspected it had more to do with his searching out a new use for one of his affinities, and less to do with technical inclination or interest.

"It was a whole thing. You'd flash the lights like a code, and the receiver would translate that to data. So you could, say, translate your voice into information sent over the line, and have a conversation with someone far away." Her summary was overly simplistic, but neither of the two had a technical background so the general idea seemed better than finely nuanced and technically correct answers.

"I thought you said your old world didn't have magic?" Werylin gave her a "you lied to me" look.

"We had technology, and we used that to make vehicles to fly, go to the moon, make weapons of mass destruction, and other fun stuff. A lot of things magic can do, you can do with technology, too."

"Technology isn't that great," Arkaziel said. "Sure, it lets the Tier Ones feel empowered, but to make correspondingly dangerous technology to matching higher tiers requires components of that tier. It doesn't elevate the average being from the unwashed masses to a Cultivator's power. There's plenty of technocracies out there in the universe. My great-great-grandfather ate a few of them."

"Getting eaten by a StarMane is hardly a damnation of their path. A world-eating StarMane is what tier?" Aetheria asked a question she'd never bothered with before.

"Tier Seven."

"Seven, right. Most Tier Seven Cultivators can destroy planets, too, no?" Aetheria's red eyes narrowed at the cat.

"Sure, but they don't *eat* planets. They just blow them up."

Werylin started to open his mouth, but Aetheria shook her head slightly at the elf. Arkaziel's defensiveness and superiority were in danger of spiraling.

"Does anyone else feel like we're being watched?" she said suddenly. A nagging sensation would not leave Aetheria alone, as if someone was talking about her just out of her audible range. When she examined their surroundings with Ethereal Sight, she noticed distortions in the flows of mana—moments before invisibility fields dropped, revealing a squad of approximately thirty shark people that had them surrounded.

The Sharktooth Clan were humanoid sharks, yes, but very little of them was human beyond their slightly short arms and opposable thumbs. At the end of thick, strong legs were powerful flippers. The weapons of choice amongst the squad seemed to be spears and harpoons, and aside from three of the back-row combatants, they all possessed Tier Three auras.

"Surrender, and your deaths will be merciful. Fight, and we will eat you alive." The squad leader had gray skin covered with dark black natural markings. The multiple rows of teeth inside the shark men's mighty jaws were disconcerting when combined with the raw hunger in their beady fish eyes.

"I'm going to have to pass on that. You could just fix the damage you've done here, and our StarMane companion won't turn you into fodder for his cultivation." Aetheria counteroffered with a smile she didn't feel.

While she spoke, Werylin hummed a few notes that the water distorted. *That might make it difficult to follow music- or harmony-based paths in aquatic cultures,* Aetheria reasoned.

Arkaziel simply hissed in his water-dragon form, and tentacles of shadow rose up from the sea floor and pulled the three Tier Two Cultivators down to their deaths, dropping the numbers to three versus twenty-seven. Although with three more aquatic versions of Arkaziel summoned by his Twilight Duplication power, it went up to six versus twenty-seven.

"You will suffer!" the commando shark shouted, his weapon glowing with a baleful cursed light.

Aetheria summoned five orbs of red Ethereal ice. The orbs encircled Aetheria, and then immediately started to fire ice spikes at the sharks. The attack was less effective than on the surface, sadly. Between water slowing the spikes' velocity and the raw aquatic speed of the sharkmen, most of the spikes missed their targets.

Werylin's answer involved a move straight out of an anime. The elf had assumed a battōjutsu stance, and the moment he saw a cluster of four sharkmen dodge ice spikes and shadow tentacles, he unleashed a sword-draw attack that bisected three of the four. The attack did not end there, intentionally or not. Werylin's sword-draw had created so much pressure that it produced a vortex that sucked in anything in front of him within eight meters. Six of the enemy squad were caught in the current and dragged toward the swordsman, who dispatched the first two sharks with ease before the vortex ran out of power and the other four broke free.

Arkaziel did not waste any time. His doppelgangers ran rampant, flashing into the melee to engage the physically weakest-looking sharkmen. The StarMane himself remained next to Aetheria. Arkaziel gestured with his claws and unleashed tendrils of shadows that seemed to waver in and out of reality while they traveled. The first sharkman to fail to dodge the tendrils was ripped apart, as if it had been caught in razorwire. Its struggles to escape only sealed its death.

Inspired, Aetheria finessed the Primordial Flame of Thalassa to create invisible but exceptionally strong spider-wire nets of water, then willed them to shoot toward a few clusters of sharkmen. The results were every bit as gory and bloody as the tendrils that Arkaziel used, or the cutting vortex Werylin created with Harmonious Tempest.

In seconds, only two members of the Sharktooth Clan remained: the leader who had threatened Aetheria to begin with, and another warrior with an aura nearly as strong. Aetheria guessed they were on Werylin's advancement and were getting close to Tier Four.

"Not too late to surrender," Aetheria shouted to the two.

The ocean had turned red with the blood of their brethren, and Aetheria had a sinking feeling as the two suddenly inhaled. All the blood, gore, and corpses of their companions that Arkaziel had not used Devouring Darkness on were sucked into the sharks' mouths. If it were not so immensely disgusting to watch, it would be almost comical.

Unlike Aetheria, Arkaziel did the practical thing. While the two cannibalized their squad mates, Arkaziel flung a mass of shadows at them, creating a ten-meter area of wobbling, flailing tentacles that attacked everything. His quick thinking denied the sharkmen a small amount of sustenance, but they still ate enough to make the cat's jealousy surge through the empathic bond he shared with Aetheria.

Unexpectedly, the two remaining sharkmen chomped down with their large shark jaws and consumed the Devouring Darkness, before their two now-larger forms shot out of the gloom in a headlong rush toward the trio. Aetheria flung one of her Thalassa-powered razorwire nets at the oncoming rush, but somehow the water shattered against the leader's snout, became fodder with a chomp, and with barely any slowdown the leader almost bit Arkaziel's head off. Instead, Aetheria pushed Arkaziel away by controlling the water, and delivered a powerful punch to the side of the jerk's head.

Usually when Aetheria punched things, there was some reaction. This time, there was none. Cannibalizing the remains of its companions had pushed the leader firmly, if temporarily, into the fourth tier, and its defenses were stronger than Aetheria's normal attack. She was about to try again when the shark turned and bit at her face. Instinctively, a flare of rainbow energies surrounded Aetheria, and she appeared on the other side of the shark. Aetheria was so shocked by the sudden teleportation that she missed the opportunity to get a sneak attack in.

The second-in-command had gone for Werylin. The elf seemed to be the least suited to water. He had to use water-breathing items, and he had no flippers, nor any other adaptation for the aquatic combat. Sure, Arkaziel and Aetheria had opted to employ the magic items, but in a pinch both could just grow gills. Even Aetheria was slightly shocked when the elf casually waited for the shark to be mere centimeters from biting him when the elf said a single word.

"Revenge."

Then the shark's teeth bit into Werylin, mawed his pale elven flesh, filled the water with his blood, snapped his bones, and gulped his meatbag body. A massive discordant note rang out, and Werylin reappeared next to Aetheria. The second-in-command suffered all of the damage it had just inflicted upon Werylin without any of the degradation of attack due to tier disparity. Tentacles of shadow rose from the darkness to consume the second-in-command. Arkaziel had no intention of allowing it to regenerate or recuperate.

"You don't eat us, we eat you!" the sole survivor, the Sharktooth Clan war leader, shouted at them.

Aetheria conjured the Primordial Flame of Nyx and attacked the leader's life force directly with the limitless hunger of the night. Strength, power, vitality, all leached from the leader into Aetheria. With each flicker of the Flame in her mind, she stole just a little bit more from the war leader. Yet it was a slow attack, and the death of its companions and second-in-command had sent the leader into a frenzy. It launched itself at the human woman.

Arkaziel's eyes flared, and six arcing bolts of radiance shot toward the shark. None managed to pierce all the way through its thick Tier Four hide. Werylin, similarly, tried to strike the leader from the side. The furious war leader deftly dodged the golden katana, then was past the elf. Aetheria, slower than Werylin, had no chance to dodge the ridiculously fast enemy, and row upon row of horribly sharp teeth pierced her flesh.

CHAPTER 8

Sharp Shark Teeth:
Slicing Surfers Silently

The sheer number of teeth in the Sharktooth Clan war leader's mouth caused a lot of damage. The temporary Tier Four teeth pierced her clothing and flesh like they were no defense at all, despite last moment density shifts pushing Aetheria to the equivalent of a full plate armor wearer. The nonlinear increase in power between tiers had never felt quite so vast before, but Aetheria did not have time to worry about that.

Aetheria flared the Primordial Flame of Thalassa with all of her might. The ocean itself counteracted the jaws of the war leader, buying her just enough time to teleport into a flare of chaos. When she reappeared twenty meters away, there were still some shark teeth in her body, which she dumped into her repository. Even with the last-minute save, she had practically been bitten in half.

Empowered with Ethereal energy, Aetheria's regeneration kicked into overdrive. In seconds, grave wounds turned to flesh wounds, which also vanished. Yet Aetheria was in anguish. Almost instantaneous healing meant suffering the pain of regeneration that hurt almost as much as the attacks themselves.

For the first time, Aetheria learned her teleportation could also function as an attack. Discordant rainbow energy clung to the war leader's maw, where it acted like a strangely sticky corrosive power. Unlike a normal acid, it became quickly clear the Ethereal power acted with a quintessential property of Nether: wither. Why her teleport should do that, Aetheria had no idea, but it seemed to cause the war leader so much pain he was driven to mindless rage. *I'd be pretty mad if my jaw and upper mouth just kept deteriorating into nothing.*

The ocean became dark above them. All light sources other than Aetheria's glowing hair and Arkaziel's maw vanished. With Ethereal Sight, Aetheria could tell that Arkaziel's eclipse covered a few kilometers of area, nearly including the city of Seabreeze. In a second, all that swallowed light reappeared as a glowing sphere inside the dragon's mouth, before it fired at the war leader. Yet Aetheria was shocked to see an attack that finished bosses off previously, only took the sharkman down to maybe half. *Maybe.*

The war leader's dense hide had been damaged by the intense twilight attack, and in some places the light had even managed to penetrate to the point of damaging organs. Unfortunately, the shark's regeneration kicked in immediately. While nowhere as fast as Aetheria's regeneration, the trio could not afford to slack off.

Werylin followed up Arkaziel's attack with a few hummed bars and a solitary command word.

"Wither!" commanded the elf, and the rainbow flames around the shark's jaw spread across the war leader's body. It was a slow spread, but with the thick armor and hide of the war leader already pierced, the withering chaos disintegrated more and more of the shark by the second. Aetheria's imaginary health bar for the war leader went down slowly, and she estimated it wouldn't be enough to finish the sharkman.

Aetheria darted forward to draw the shark's attention, even as her hands each glowed with different colors. Her right hand took on the holy, cold skies of Aetherius. Aetheria's left hand flared with the frigid black and purple Primordial Flame of Nyx. Her right eye shifted from red to a pale blue-white as the Flame of Ymir activated, while her left eye became the blue of oceans with the Flame of Thalassa. Activating four Flames at once took an immense amount of energy, but the Ethereal sun (Frostfire) in her soul dumped near infinite amounts of power into her soul faster than she could draw it.

The war leader charged at Aetheria as she charged at him. The disintegrating maw came for her once more, and at the last second Aetheria altered herself to the size of a minnow and continued her charge down the creature's throat. All four Primordial Flames hit critical mass at the same time she entered the creature's stomach.

"Etherfrost Nova." Tiny Aetheria piped the words out before her energy shot outward in a massive full area nova attack. Only, unlike normal, this frigid attack had been infused with four Primordial Flames. The rigid power differentials of Tier Three versus Tier Four shattered before the Etherfrost Asura's power mixed with that of multiple primordial gods. Shards of aspected ice ripped the war leader apart. A whirlwind of icicles acted like a blender, and the ocean filled with blood and gore, as the Sharktooth Clan war leader was blended from the inside out, all as a miniature Aetheria stood in a small cocoon of safety surrounded by a disgusting slurry of fish.

A slurry that Arkaziel somehow sucked into his mouth like a vacuum.

"That was gloriously spicy, and also bitter, but really sweet, and kind of gross while also superb. Your Flames make great cultivation seasonings, Aetheria!" Arkaziel swooned over the complicated taste of his shark slurry, while Aetheria returned to normal size.

"Wait, how are you tasting anything!?" Aetheria exclaimed in confusion.

"I am so amazing I broke the curse!" Arkaziel crowed triumphantly, then shifted his eyes to see if the Administrator had heard or a new punishment might be on its way.

Werylin watched the StarMane with a mixture of disbelief and humor.

"Glad you approve of my attack. Now then, that's the Sharktooth Clan taken care of . . . maybe. Let's see if we can fix the magitech relays, and keep an eye out for any more signs of raiders."

None of the three possessed any training or knowledge enough to repair the strange cables that ran between relays, but Werylin proved another use of his strange path. The elf hummed almost a full song before he waved his fingers at the broken relay and said, "Mend!"

Magic is so cool. I need to work on my own magic more between fights.

Over the course of sixty seconds the cables reattached themselves, and delicate components melded back together.

"Seems kind of like cheating, to just use magic to fix things, doesn't it?" Aetheria laughed, while the other two gave her flat looks.

"Cheating? You're the definition of a cheater, Ms. I Have Multiple Primordial Flames." Arkaziel laughed at her while rolling his eyes. "It's only to be expected, though. Aetherius obviously arranged our partnership, and without the Flames you couldn't keep up with me."

"It seems as fair as your automatic regeneration," Werylin commented lightly.

"Don't be a green-eyed monster, Arkaziel." Aetheria waggled her finger at the dragon before she summoned an icy megalodon with the Reins of the Ice Queen for the three to ride back to Seabreeze.

Twenty minutes later, they sat at a large table in the government center of Seabreeze. Opposite them were three of the important people of the community. The trio were offered a vast assortment of snacks, but none of that really mattered to Aetheria. When things wound down, Captain Coral presented Aetheria with a set of earrings.

"As promised, Ocean's Serenity, created by Thalassa herself and given as a reward from Pontus for protecting our community."

The earrings were composed out of a heavy, white metal similar in appearance to platinum. The power Aetheria felt from the set exceeded the enchantment on her Scrunchy of the Glacial Sovereign and the Punch Drunk enchantment on her gloves. What was the comparable tier of a Primordial to mortals? Aetheria didn't know, but she slipped the earrings into her repository and bound them to herself, and they appeared on her ears.

The white metal earrings were a gorgeous, almost fractal, representation of waves. As usual, the acquisition of new magical gear made Aetheria disgruntled. She had no clue what her gear actually did. Aoibhe had mentioned rituals that could allow you to understand the capabilities of magical items, but Aetheria hadn't tried that yet. It was now on the list, because despite the serene feeling that swept over her when she put the earrings on, there was no other immediately discernable change in how she felt.

Maybe it'll help me resist the melancholy of the Origin?

There were other minor rewards. Money, a few basic magic items, new alcohols, and after bartering, a lot of rare aquatic food ended up in Aetheria's repository. When the door to Floor 54 opened, the trio didn't hesitate to leave the aquatic city behind. If there had been any crafters in their cultivation tier, maybe they would have lingered, but there was little else on offer in Seabreeze.

The trio appeared on another island. This one held small mountains, tropical jungles, and the chatter of great and varied wildlife. A ghostly blue projection of an Administrator appeared before them. This Admin had a human appearance, but all of their features constantly swam and morphed into different ones. Even their voice constantly shifted tone.

"There is a treasure on this island. Find it before your enemies do or take it from them if they acquire it before you."

The projection vanished.

"I like treasure." Arkaziel laughed while his body flowed into a five-meter-long dragon-cat.

"Who doesn't like treasure? How do you guys want to do this, spread out or stick together? Anyone have a sense treasure ability?" Aetheria looked back and forth between her companions.

Werylin shook his head. "My spells all require I know more about something to find it than just 'treasure.' It is too vague for me to do anything with."

"I can smell treasure a mile away," Arkaziel bragged.

Aetheria was on the fence on whether Ark could actually do that or if he was just being his usual narcissistic cat self.

"Alright. You are up; don't disappoint me." Aetheria generated a wyvern of ice with the Reins of the Ice Queen and hopped onto its back. She knew better than to suggest Arkaziel just let them ride him, even if he was the one taking the lead on this particular quest. He would just retort with why they don't ride her, since she was the best mount the tower had ever seen, and that just felt like a conversation that Aetheria never wanted to have. Ever.

"This island is called the Emerald Enigma." Arkaziel informed the other two while they all got comfortable on the ice wyvern. "According to my memories, it's almost always a mystery or competition-based floor. It's also a total pain. A lot of the normal wildlife can mimic sounds, so that babbling brook or bird caw could be a thunder lizard, or who knows what. Lots of fae touches on the island, too. Glimmerflies, shimmer lizards, and of course the always fun leaf leviathans. Why they aren't called treeants I don't know, since they're just living trees."

"Any idea where the treasure is going to be?" Aetheria inquired.

Arkaziel sniffed the air. "Take us toward the center of the island."

Four minutes later, the wyvern hovered in the air before a giant waterfall.

"There's definitely structures back there." Aetheria nodded.

"Told you so." Arkaziel's pride threatened to burst out and eat them all.

Werylin wordlessly leaped from the back of the wyvern, through the waterfall, and landed in a cave on the other side. Shortly after, he called out to the two.

"Looks like a temple or labyrinth. Others have come through here recently; they didn't hide their tracks."

Arkaziel and Aetheria joined him and found themselves in an ancient tunnel. The walls, floor, and ceiling had all been carved with magic at some point long ago.

The once-smooth stone had been weathered by constant exposure to moisture in the first area. No art or plaques of any kind were in the first chamber, but if they had opponents it was possible that everything had just been looted already.

"How many came through here, Ark?"

More sniffing and the dragon suddenly had a happy look on his face. Which never boded well for *somebody*.

"Four. A human, a half demon, a dragonoid, and a squirrelfolk. Coincidentally, squirrelfolk are delicious, so please don't ruin their corpse before I eat them."

"Fine, fine. Let's get some treasure. Keep your eyes open for traps; I'll take the lead." The air around them chilled as her domain expanded outward five meters. Snowflakes occasionally flickered in and out of existence in the air of her domain, while little patches of hoarfrost appeared on any surface but the floor.

"Does your domain freeze traps?" Werylin looked quite curious.

"It might, but I've pushed my domain's primary function into slowing things down. Hopefully by enough to let me react to traps before they spring. After that shark, it is always possible we'll run into Tier Four traps."

Click. Aetheria's latest step made a small sound.

"Way to jinx us." Ark snorted.

CHAPTER 9

Race for the Treasure

oes your domain freeze traps?" Werylin had asked her. The question received an answer a fraction of a second after Aetheria's booted foot set off a pressure plate. The telltale *click* had stopped all three in their tracks.

A hail of projectiles fired from the walls and ceilings. Given the faint glow and sickly green coloration to the tips of the attack, Aetheria didn't want to get hit by them. Her domain did not stop the projectiles, but the freezing domain did slow them down enough that she plucked them all into her repository once they got within two meters of her.

"That hardly seems fair." Werylin laughed.

"You'll get used to it," Arkaziel smarmily replied before Aetheria could respond.

"Is the protagonist getting jealous of his sidekick? Wow, Ark, way to undermine yourself." Aetheria mimed wiping away tears at her bonded companion then flashed him a smile with pearly whites. Then she tapped the tip of her boot against the floor, and a sheet of ice two centimeters thick covered the floor, ceiling, and walls.

The corridor came to an intersection where the forward path split into three different paths. Markings on the walls gave a brief idea of what lay before them, and Aetheria felt a little better once they deciphered the pictures.

"The safe path, the path of alacrity, and the path of combat," Werylin said. "It's like the story of Sir Reymon, honestly. In that tale the safe path led to an exit. Safe, yes, but without risk there could be no reward. The path of alacrity and combat both led to the treasure. Alacrity contained traps, puzzles, and mazes." Werylin stopped his explanation to wait for Arkaziel and Aetheria to stop groaning.

"Combat it is, then?" The elf seemed amused at the aversion of the other two to puzzles and traps.

"Definitely combat. I'm hungry." Arkaziel showed more teeth than was necessary with the words.

"Which way did the other group go?" Aetheria couldn't see any footprints on the rocky floor.

"They took the safe path." Arkaziel snorted in rebuke of their cowardice.

"So we'll need to keep an eye on our rear. Let's steamroll the combat side and get the loot." Aetheria stretched her arms a little before she took point.

The path continued straight for some time, until it opened into a large chamber. Three basilisks lazed in the middle of the room gnawing upon the corpses of a strange goatlike creature. Like most lizards, the basilisks did not like ice magic, and Aetheria's opening combo of a dash and Etherfrost Nova caused all three lizards significant damage, to the point Werylin's blade and a couple of spears of shadow finished off the basilisks in the first volley.

The route to the next room followed the same pattern of a long hall, then a chamber with monsters. The second chamber contained no enemies, at least so it seemed, until Ark pointed at the ceiling. "Bat swarm."

Once again, the trio employed the same tactics, and they wiped the entire swarm out in just a few attacks.

"It's been a while since we've fought things that die this easily." Aetheria didn't trust it.

"I'm just that awesome, Aetheria. This is how fights usually go when you're me, and you're an Asura, so of course things are easy. Since this is a floor I know about, and Werylin knows a story based on it, it probably hasn't been altered to challenge us that much." Arkaziel didn't come out and say the Administrators were lazy, but Aetheria felt that was his real point.

The third chamber, however, held a nest of large, almost transparent spiders, four of which were the size of a van. Each of the big spiders gave off the aura of a Tier Four monster, while the smaller person-sized spiders exuded the aura of a high Tier Three Cultivator. Werylin offered to start this particular fight and hummed a few quiet notes before he quick-drew Harmonious Tempest and said another of the blade's keywords, "Wave of Final Order!"

The sweep of the katana through the air generated massive waves of energy. Like ocean waves, they rose and fell as they swept across the web-filled room. The energy shifted its coloration as it rose and fell along the waves, alternating from gold at the lowest to pitch-black at the top. The attack hit every creature in the room, and the far walls shuddered under the impact of the waves on that side. The spiders underwent a number of effects.

From what Aetheria could tell, the attack slowed enemies. She wasn't sure whether it was an exhaustion-based slow, or some kind of other ordeal. Every spider became very stiff and slow-moving, even while crackling gold energy attacked them with a damage-over-time effect.

"Oh, it causes exhaustion. That's a nice attack. Good one, elf." Arkaziel complimented Werylin. Aetheria wasn't at all jealous of his genetic memories that allowed the StarMane to identify things he had no other way to know.

Aetheria darted into the center of the room and launched another Etherfrost Nova. The explosion of cold killed off the Tier Three spiders before the shards of ice that followed even hit. The Tier Four spiders, on the other hand, were barely wounded. Three of the large spiders shuffled toward Aetheria, though slowed by Werylin's and Aetheria's attacks.

Arkaziel generated twenty spears of light that arced around and over Aetheria to strike the large spiders—five each into the slow-moving targets. For the first time on the floor, their enemies did not go down to the trio's opening salvo. The ice that slowed the spiders down inexplicably shattered, and the golden energy that had been attacking them vanished, too.

"They overcame those effects quickly. Fighting above your tier is always like that." Werylin grumbled. The elf hummed a few bars and cast Aetheria's favorite support spell. "Haste!"

The spell glowed around all three and bolstered their speed and alacrity.

Aetheria, still in the center of the room, tapped her foot against the hoarfrost already formed on the floor by her domain. Spears of ice formed on the floor and shot up to pierce the two spiders to her left. The closer of the two managed to dodge the sudden attack. Ice impaled the farthest spider, and almost instantly a coruscating beam of light and darkness struck the sitting target . . . and kept hitting it. The spider managed to endure five seconds of the breath attack before the spreading internal ice and the twilight breath finally killed it.

The spider to Aetheria's right leaped straight for the blue-haired woman. Its speed through the air diminished with every centimeter of progress it made through Aetheria's domain, and then it started to take small wounds as well. Aetheria could see a second domain had been erected in the room. Werylin's Domain overlapped her own without incident, and it cut opponents.

Either way, between Haste and the slow effect on the spider, Aetheria's right arm went back and then shot forward toward the midair spider. Her arm elongated into a two-meter limb made of the red crystal of the Luxentian people; her hand at the end of it had become a single spike that pierced through the spider's mouth and head entirely. As quick as it happened, Aetheria's arm was normal length, the excess mass returned to energy.

Then the last spider was upon Aetheria. It moved at full speed, seeming to resist her domain as well as the shallow cuts of Werylin's domain, which were unable to pierce its hide. Not for the first time, Aetheria wondered how much variance there could be between the same monsters. Did each monster have its own capabilities, like Arkaziel and his siblings had, despite all coming from the same clutch?

Aetheria dodged the first of the eight limbs with its nasty-looking claws. The second nicked her, despite Haste, and pain immediately flared throughout her whole body. *Must be magic. The toxin couldn't hit my brain instantly.* The pain fell between burning alive and being covered in acid, and Aetheria pulsed Aetherflame through her body to purge the ill effects. It slowed her reaction time down enough that the spider closed in, and its mandibles pierced both of her sides.

Accompanying her scream were surges of Ethereal power that coated the spider in ice.

Twenty shining spears of light arced around Aetheria to strike the spider, and before the afterimage had cleared of the shining attack, Werylin appeared behind the spider. The elf flowed like a dancer, and Harmonious Tempest flashed and flicked with each step of his beautiful dance. Werylin attacked each place the radiant spears had struck, which allowed his blade to cause significant damage. He dismembered the spider while Aetheria recovered from her wounds.

"I really hate spiders," Aetheria muttered as her shirt restored itself.

"Have you considered wearing armor?" Werylin seemed confused by the way her clothing regenerated.

"It seems unnecessary. I think it'd slow me down, and I haven't encountered any armor more durable than forms I can shapeshift into."

"Mm. Well, I suppose you'll figure something out. Just because you can take a hit, doesn't mean you should." Werylin shrugged lightly. "Not that it seems to slow you down that much."

Aetheria laughed at how diplomatically the elf tried to approach the gap in her fighting style.

"You aren't wrong. Maybe when we get to the next city you can help me shore up my defenses a little more. In fact, you probably could use the same, huh? We didn't have all your old gear. A shopping spree is in order."

"I hope the next town has jumbo shrimp, ideally as big as a house. It's so much more satisfying to eat things in my real form," Arkaziel interrupted.

"Focus, guys. We've got to finish this floor, and then five more to hit our next city."

Two daggers appeared out of nowhere; one slit Aetheria's throat and the other pierced through her back into a kidney. The daggers were held by a purple-haired woman with black eyes, small horns, and a small tail who wore leather armor.

"No need to worry about what you'll never see, cutie." The half-demon laughed before she pulled the blade free, then stabbed both daggers back into Aetheria's other organs.

When the half demon attacked Aetheria, three other forms shimmered into existence, their invisibility field broken. A brunet human man looked displeased the rogue had broken his field, and he began chanting and gesturing again.

Next to the caster, a dragonoid in full armor charged Werylin, who blocked the enemy's sword-swing easily, but a volley of rocks from the squirrelfolk woman's sling distracted Werylin, and he got bashed in the face by the dragon-man warrior's shield. The blow sent the slender elf through the air, and he crashed painfully into the stone wall before falling to the floor.

Darkness swallowed the room.

"Lisa, you were supposed to stun the feline, not the elf! Zar, get some light cast."

The sound of a large being sucking in air caused silence to fall over the group, before the squirrelfolk and dragonoid man spoke simultaneously.

"Dragon!"

Three figures attacked the four. Each of the twilight duplicates currently mimicked Arkaziel's draconic form at four meters long. They darted in with speed bolstered by Haste, a flurry of claws and bites forcing the party to fall back-to-back.

A flicker of light appeared underneath the feet of the half demon a fraction of a second before a pillar of light appeared. The half demon's arm fell to the ground—the rest of her body had been vaporized by Arkaziel's holy light attack.

"No one gets to hurt my sidekicks." Arkaziel's voice boomed across the room, and the other three climbers got a full view of their opponent. A ten-meter-long black dragon with a feline face, ephemeral glowing purple fur, yellow eyes, and a look that left no doubt they were no more than food in its eyes.

CHAPTER 10

Snacks

The opposing party barely had time to react to the angry boom of Arkaziel's voice and the death of the half demon in a pillar of light. Then the twilight duplicates were upon them in a flurry of claws and snapping teeth. Evasion went out the window when the three survivors allowed themselves to be pressed together; they were forced to rely on blocking and parrying. The human male attempted to block the swipes of claws with a staff in one hand and mystical shields generated by the other, but the sharp, knife-sized claws ripped through the barriers with nearly no resistance. By the third assault, the man bled from multiple wounds.

The dragonoid withstood the onslaught the best. His heavy armor, large shield, and impressive strength allowed the warrior to defend against the attacks of the twilight duplicate. In his element, the warrior called upon arts to unleash a high-powered shield bash against the copy of Arkaziel. Fire licked the shield and burned at the copy, but a moment's distraction in destroying one duplicate did not go unpunished. Tentacles of darkness grasped his extremities and pulled the dragonoid down, armor and all, into the Devouring Darkness. And then there were two.

The squirrelfolk woman had taken on a gray appearance. Her skin had become as hard as stone. Her agility did not seem to be hindered by the change, as she still dodged the attacks of the twilight duplicate. A pulse of golden light illuminated the fallen form of an elf against the wall, and also showed the druidic Cultivator another glimpse of the draconic feline that stalked toward her and the remaining mage.

Terror filled the woman's eyes. Unknown to her, Arkaziel had activated one of his rarely used abilities all StarManes possess. All she knew was that an impossibly powerful beast king stalked the darkness and kept killing her companions in one hit. Sure, there were a lot of powerful monsters and beasts in the towers. Worlds rife with gods, demons, and monsters left denizens with no shortage of harrowing experience, but the squirrel girl had likely never encountered a true beast king yet. This one, with its horrible yellow feline eyes, promised only death.

Tremors overtook her body. She opened her mouth to scream, only to be devoured in one bite.

The last survivor of the party, the brown-haired human mage, sobbed at the quick defeat of his companions. Two twilight duplicates remained, and they flanked the mage to toy with him for a few moments while the dragon watched him. A plea for mercy almost escaped his lips, before a strike of Arkaziel's tail shot the mage across the room into the wall, where shadows then pulled the broken body into the darkness.

They died before Aetheria had even finished pushing extra Ethereal power into her regenerative capabilities. Yet in the precious seconds it took her throat and internal organs to heal, the darkness had abated, and the only piece of the opposition party that remained was the severed arm of the half demon.

"No one hurts my sidekicks." Arkaziel hissed before he licked his paw.

"Jeez, Ark, you didn't have to go full murder cat on them. Why don't you heal Werylin? He looks a bit out of it yet." The purple-haired elf had a slightly vacant look in his eyes that made Aetheria think of head trauma or a concussion. Still, Aetheria smiled a little. Arkaziel rarely got emotional. It was nice to be loved.

"I already gave him a light heal, but yes, he may need more attention."

Aetheria bit her lower lip, while Arkaziel went to heal Werylin.

Had the opposing party deserved to die like that? Given the sneak attack and slit throat and organ attacks the assassin had used on her, Aetheria had a hard time with feeling guilty about the result, but she didn't feel good about it either. Murder and consumption seemed like an especially bad way to die, but perhaps it was karma? *Were they climbers, too? Or natives? Is there even a tangible difference? Rest in peace; better luck next incarnation.*

Aetheria shied her thoughts away from the idea of the wheel of life, reincarnation, and the Samsara. There were so many questions that filled her mind about those things, but none of them applied to her anymore, although they did still pertain to her friends and companions.

After a couple of different healing techniques, Werylin's concussion and its accompanying mental fog lifted. The swordsman seemed exceptionally embarrassed by the fact he'd been taken out by a counterattack like that. Aetheria understood the embarrassment. The half demon's attack would have killed her if she weren't immortal.

The path onward ended in a room with a pillar of light shining upon a large chest. The scene reminded Aetheria of a video game. All that was missing was a triumphant soundtrack surging in the background. Instead, Arkaziel burped. "Sorry. The warrior's armor isn't digesting very well."

"You shouldn't eat your prey, armor and all. No wonder your stomach is upset."

"Aren't green dragonoids usually toxic?" Werylin arched a fine lavender brow.

"I ate an incarnation of Nidhogg. What's a little humanoid dragon Cultivator compared to the apocalypse dragon?" Arkaziel puffed up his chest, then groaned and transformed into a house cat. In his cat form he climbed into Aetheria's arms.

"Poor kitty. Let's see what loot we get. That'll make you feel better." Aetheria gave Ark a good chin scratching while she and Werylin looked over the chest.

"I don't see any traps." The elf's hand hovered over the lid.

"Me neither. Nothing with Ethereal Sight. Pop it open."

"Oh my," Werylin murmured when the lid opened, revealing the contents of the chest. Atop its other contents lay a small blade in the same style as Harmonious Tempest.

"Is that a wakizashi?" Aetheria asked quietly, but Werylin just looked at her strangely.

"It's a shorter blade, yes." The weapon emitted a powerful aura to Aetheria's Ethereal Sight, but compared to the power of Harmonious Tempest, it was a pale shadow.

"Congratulations on getting a new sword. It looks sweet," Aetheria said, but Werylin just grunted while he handled his new blade and affixed it to his belt.

"Let's see what else we've got here. Aunt Belinda's Stomach Drops, 'for when you eat things you shouldn't.'" Aetheria laughed, and let a few drops hit Arkaziel's tongue.

"Ooh. Sweet relief. You know alchemy—learn to make those. It'll solve so many problems when I eat worlds."

"We can look for recipes. I can't just learn to make something by looking at it, you know." Aetheria again lamented her lack of a gamelike analysis or investigation ability. She would have to check her recipe books or find some alchemists on the next city floor.

Three more things remained in the chest. The first was a thick book titled *What are Cores, Anyway?* A quick skim through the first few pages showed it to be a philosophical treatise in the first half, and a detailed compendium of odd, special, or interesting cores the author had encountered in their travels. The only name attributed to the work was a signature on the last page that Aetheria thought said Jaim Lightbringer.

Werylin, upon hearing her mutter the name, looked shocked.

"Jaim Lightbringer? How would something of his end up in the tower?"

"You know the name?" Aetheria inquired while she rubbed Arkaziel's stomach.

"That is the name of the Sun-paladin who aided my clan against the orc horde."

"What happened to him, anyway?"

"After the Orc Tide was defeated, he excused himself to go fight a dragon. I heard no more of his activities before they put me to judgment. If he is still alive, somehow, I should like to meet him again." Werylin rubbed at his chin in thought.

"We'll keep an eye out for him, then. If he is still alive, maybe we'll encounter him while we travel between towers?" Aetheria offered encouragingly.

"Can't we just fly between towers?" Arkaziel whined, although the drops seemed to improve his mood slowly.

"May I read the book first, Aetheria?" Werylin asked. "I intend to form my core when we find suitable reagents."

"Of course! Let me know if there's any really great insights you find in there. You've got a lot more experience with this stuff than I do. What do you need to make your core, anyway? Do you have to make a core, Ark?"

Werylin answered first.

"Predominantly, I just need energy, but some order-attuned items would make it easier."

"StarManes don't make cores. That's for you humanoids. We just eat, process the power, consolidate our gains, and repeat. No cores needed. Ooh, yeah, keep rubbing right there, Aetheria." It was hard to take Ark seriously when he was being held on his back and Aetheria kept rubbing his tummy.

"What's that orange thing?" Werylin frowned into the chest.

A small pillar of ice lifted an orange ball out of the chest and slowly turned it.

"It smells fantastic," Aetheria murmured.

"That's an ambrosial orange, called a Daybreaker. It will bolster affinity with light," Arkaziel recited encyclopedically.

The three looked at one another. Objects that were useful to all three hadn't shown up much yet.

"You want it, Ark? You use light magic."

"I want it. That might push me into the next breakpoint of light affinity." Aetheria gave it to the cat.

"What do you mean *breakpoint*, by the way?" A fine aqua brow arched with the words.

"Points at which you gain a noticeable benefit from an increase. Every bit helps in some fashion, yes, but at certain affinities your spells, arts, and abilities gain a quantifiable improvement. With my Radiant Burst Art, for example, when I cross a breakpoint, the technique gains an extra projectile."

The other two nodded at the explanation.

"Can my affinities still improve even though I have a bunch of Flames?" Aetheria wondered.

"Sure. Your Aether, Nether, and ice affinities should have room for growth, since you've tiered up a few times now." Arkaziel tried to keep the "duh" from his tone, just this once.

"We're having a fruit party when we hit Tier Four, then. We've got a lot of ambrosial fruit left."

"Most of those were lesser ambrosial fruit. They'll still help, but we should eat them sooner than later. They'll have the most pronounced effect on Tier Three and below," Arkaziel said.

"Okay, fruit party after the last thing in this chest."

The last thing Aetheria lifted was a metal sphere the size of a beach ball. Its contours and lines looked like what Aetheria recalled of the ancient map of Grief. While she handled it, she noticed it was actually a puzzle that could be shifted around.

"Magic puzzle." Werylin grunted.

"Not mechanical, but that's just weird as hell." Aetheria's finger tapped the island that represented where she had appeared on Grief, and she could just drag it around the map. The metal flowed and reshaped to her input.

"It looks like Grief." Werylin agreed with Aetheria's assessment.

Arkaziel, however, shook his head.

"It looks like Arcadia. I bet that if you unlock the puzzle, it will have some kind of heavenly treasure inside of it. Why would they give you a puzzle that could be easily solved? You're from Grief, right?"

"Good point." Werylin nodded.

"What's Arcadia?" Aetheria had no clue.

"It's a pocket dimension. The gods use it as a trading post for who's who of the universe. Apparently way back when they pretended to live there, but they don't bother with that kind of posturing anymore. We should totally go there after a few towers. We'll probably have so much stuff to trade for objects more beneficial to us. Aetherius has been good to us so far, but now that we're across the Veil, we'll get more stuff that isn't tailor-made to us. Sure, everything here seems good, but not all the stuff we find will be useful to us."

Aetheria could practically see the dollar signs in Arkaziel's eyes.

"Why are you so interested in money, anyway?"

"It is what you use to buy food, Aetheria." Arkaziel did not hold back any of the scoffing in his voice this time. "Bring on the fruit buffet, my minion." The belly rubs had made Arkaziel complacent in his phrasing, which earned him an orb of water falling on his exposed belly.

CHAPTER 11

The Azure Expanse

Before entering the door to Floor 55, the trio devoured a host of ambrosial fruit and rested up. Arkaziel claimed to have hit the next breakpoint in his shadow affinity, while Werylin raised his Aether affinity dramatically. The progress of nearly nothing, to above normal levels of Tier Two Cultivators, was a massive increase for one meal. Werylin offhandedly remarked he could feel a small spark of lit, blue-flamed kindling burning in the back of his mind now.

Aetheria's ice affinity had marginally improved, but more importantly, she'd somehow gained some new senses. Ethereal Sight could now identify a golden haze around Werylin's katana that represented order. Unlike with normal energy signatures, the golden haze had a density and patterns far different from ice, fire, or lightning. Aetheria took this as further proof that order and chaos were a state, and she didn't think it related to matter state, but the overall system that composed reality.

If that were true, then Aetheria wasn't sure how useful the power of Khaos on its own was. She really needed to do more research, ideally in a place with learned scholars, to more fully understand what she was dealing with. Her gut, however, suggested that the Flame of Khaos would work best when combined with other forces. A small, overly cautious voice in the back of her mind suggested she think things out fully before messing with fundamental aspects of the universe. *After all, you're just a human.*

If she didn't experiment and pull out every tool in her arsenal, though, how was she going to make it through ten of these damned towers without losing herself or a companion along the way? The devil's advocate in her mind whispered lazy, seductive whispers. *The Administrators just match the challenges to your progress. Growing stronger will make it harder for you and your companions.*

Get bent.

The doubt of exploration did not last long, but it would need to be done while on the move. Arkaziel and Werylin were eager to test out their new gains, and so they entered the door to Floor 55. Fluffy white clouds and blue skies greeted Arkaziel, Werylin, and Aetheria. Despite the fluffy appearance of the clouds, they were very solid and surrounded the party on all sides except one.

Aetheria sighed, while Arkaziel tried to take a bite of the clouds.

"Regular mazes are bad enough, but did we have to add a y-axis to make things even worse?" Aetheria complained to the sky. Internally, she didn't really mind it, but on some level, she felt complaints about simple things might make the Administrators feel good about themselves.

"Just regular clouds, not marshmallows," Arkaziel noted with sadness.

"Are clouds often marshmallows?" Werylin inquired with a touch of disbelief.

"Only once so far. Aetheria stuffed the marshmallow generator into her soul. It's why she's so fluffy and nice." Arkaziel winked at the aqua-haired woman with the words.

"If you're a wonderful cat, I'll whip some marshmallow out for you later. I've almost finished my retrofit on the Mellow Mallow, but it needs a better name and the ability to fly a bit faster." Aetheria felt that if you had a flying castle, it should go over fifteen kilometers per hour.

They had no choice but to move forward. The first break in the tunnel of clouds came a few minutes later. The white, fluffy clouds ended abruptly and opened to the azure sky. Great gusts of alternating wind currents shot through the opening and led to several different cloud tunnels across the gap.

"We should stick together," Werylin opined, while the other two stared at the multiple options the currents led to.

"Hold on." Aetheria held up her hand, and five birds made of ice appeared above her hand. She tossed them into the air currents each time they shifted, and let her senses follow the constructs to get a feel for which of the tunnels should be their target and which currents led to which option.

"Why don't you just use air?" Werylin tilted his head slightly, curiosity overcoming politeness.

"My wind affinity is still pretty terrible, even with the ambrosial fruits. If we find a few more gardens, I could raise it up higher, but there were suspiciously few wind-aspected fruits in the garden we visited." Aetheria shrugged. "So, I substitute a lot when it comes to air."

Werylin nodded, but Aetheria could see the confusion writ large on his face.

"How am I trash at air while I have the Primordial Flame of Aetherius? No clue. And it looks like none of the paths are dead ends. Who's feeling lucky?"

As if on cue, Arkaziel lifted a claw to point at the second highest ledge.

"On my mark, jump." Flurries of snowflakes drifted into the wind currents. Once the right air stream appeared, Aetheria said "now" and leaped into the air.

For a moment it felt like the wind wouldn't pick her up and carry her, but she'd only fallen a few centimeters before the air launched her up to the next tunnel. Aetheria landed in the next opening, and moments later Arkaziel and Werylin arrived.

"I wonder if we can cheat the maze by traveling the gaps." Arkaziel's yellow eyes sparkled with mischief.

"Already tried it, buddy. My bird exploded when it went to the top. Seems like they've winnowed out the cheating over the years." Aetheria grinned, amused they had both thought of the same thing.

"Are there no enemies?" Werylin looked down at his second and newest sword.

"Not that I've scouted yet."

So the three walked through the maze, jumping on air currents every time they came to what would be an intersection in normal mazes. After days of traversing the clouds, in yet another same-ish cloud tunnel, the trio finally arrived in a large spherical chamber. The room contained a table with a single key and three large treasure chests.

"I'm not a fan of the arbitrariness of this level." Aetheria frowned.

"Open the third chest. Something about it is calling to me," Werylin muttered.

"All three just smell like boredom to me." Arkaziel yawned.

"Oh sure, make me open the chests. Whatever shall I do if they explode?" Aetheria's red eyes rolled with her words, but she grabbed the key and opened the third chest as Werylin had asked. Heavy air pressure suddenly pressed down on all three; Aetheria managed to remain standing, but Werylin was forced down enough one of his knees hit the cloud floor. Arkaziel, like Aetheria, seemed impervious to the pressure.

A vortex of wind shot into the air, and where no being had stood moments ago a nine-meter-tall hazy blue humanoid now floated. The elemental being radiated power; Aetheria estimated the creature to be early Tier Four.

"I am called Mistralis. Defeat me, and I shall grant you a boon."

"What kind of boon?" Arkaziel and Aetheria asked simultaneously.

"To the victor, I shall give one of my own mangoes."

Arkaziel laughed.

"That's a wind affinity increaser, Aetheria."

"Sweet. Alright, let's rumble, I guess."

Previously calm, the air in the room churned and swirled into a vortex. Werylin's swords both cleared their scabbards, and the swordsman danced around Arkaziel and Aetheria. Harmonious Tempest and the new wakizashi both moved unerringly as the elf deflected hardened gusts of air away from his companions.

"It has been ages since I've seen an elf dance for me." Mistralis's amusement failed to anger Werylin, who maintained the rhythmic moves of his protective dance.

Aetheria's experience told her that you did not fight fire with fire. Especially when air was her weakest affinity. Instead, she lifted a finger, and five pillars of red etheric ice rose from the clouds around the party. She shaped each pillar with soft and smooth edges, the roundness forcing the wind to alter its paths subtly.

"You think round pieces of ice will stop my winds?" Mistralis scoffed, insulted.

"No, not at all." Aetheria smiled, but Werylin's dance of defense had changed. The elf now had breathing room between each parry and deflection, thanks to the slight alterations of wind currents.

"Shadow Spire!" From the shadows of each pillar arose darkness. An inky black substance climbed into the air to form a web of connected shadows above the pillars, then climbed up into the air to form a tower of darkness.

"Mere shadows cannot touch the wind." Mistralis seemed unconcerned by the structure of shadows and instead conjured a new vortex of wind inside the pillars. Aetheria couldn't help but notice that the elemental lord had targeted Arkaziel and not her. Arkaziel had assumed a small draconic form, only double Aetheria's size. Currently, he had a dark aura surrounding him, and his yellow eyes were focused in concentration on the attack he was shaping.

Aetheria's arm elongated, and her fist plunged into the vortex as it formed. Although terrible winds ripped at her hand, the pain was minimal. The nascent vortex barely broke through her skin or drew blood. Still, she had no intention of letting it form all the way.

"Etherfrost Nova." Instead of centering the spell on herself, Aetheria directed the flare of Ethereal frost to expand inside of the vortex. The energy that powered the vortex was frozen by the pulse of power, and then consumed by Aetheria as it broke down into raw power.

"Checkmate." Arkaziel laughed madly.

The spire above them, strangely, cast twelve shadows across the spherical room. Shadows convulsed up the webbing of her ice pillars, and then the shadow spire seemed to become real, tangible, and more solid than the surrounding clouds. The very tip of the spire changed into a deep purple, and then a vibrant indigo beam fired from the spire to strike Mistralis.

"Ahaha . . . ha-ah-ahh—"

Laughter at the idea of mere shadows hurting the elemental turned to halted cries of pain.

"Pentagram Pillar." Aetheria lifted her hand, and five red etheric pillars rose around the wind lord, and the temperature between the posts around him dropped quickly. In seconds the whole chamber had dropped dozens of degrees, just from the leaked ambient cold inside the pillars.

"S-s-t-t-o-p. Y-iee-l . . . " The arrogance previously on display faded, and Aetheria dismissed the pillars. The chamber remained frigid.

"I'll take my mango now, thanks."

Three fruits appeared before Aetheria.

"In respect of your power, I shall also give you this." The elemental recovered quickly once he was no longer under assault by the shadow spire or ridiculous subzero temperatures.

A small gem also appeared with the mangoes. It radiated a strong and powerful wind attribute to her Ethereal Sight, far more than any of the wind cores or gems she had collected in the tower so far. A small smirk appeared on her lips as an idea struck her.

"Hey, Ark, can we fashion this into something that'd let someone fly even better?"

"Probably. It's wind, so that'd make sense. Did you learn more enchanting when I was napping?"

"Nope, but next town we'll find an enchanter. I've got a great idea."

Werylin and Arkaziel both looked slightly dubious about her smile and suddenly energetic tone.

"Elfling, how did you block my wind blades? That attack alone has defeated countless Cultivators." Mistralis wanted an answer from Werylin.

"Your wind cutters all follow the same pattern, even when you try to make it appear random. If you harmonize with the universe, such tricks are very easy to see through."

Mistralis scoffed at the elf, then vanished. In his place, the door to Floor 56 appeared.

"How'd you really do it?" Aetheria wondered.

"With a name like Harmonious Tempest, do you really think my blade wouldn't let me see through weather phenomena?" Werylin scoffed in imitation of Mistralis, then smirked.

"Anyone want one of these mangoes?" Aetheria looked at the other two.

"Go ahead; I don't sully myself with elemental magic." Arkaziel harrumphed.

Werylin just shook his head, but he did have a question. "Why were your shadows purple, Arkaziel?"

Aetheria had also wondered that.

"Oh, you want to know my secret?"

CHAPTER 12

Crystal Caverns

Arkaziel never told them what the reason for the purple light was. The jerk just left Werylin and Aetheria hanging in curiosity. The StarMane derived sadistic pleasure from not telling them, too—Aetheria could feel it through their empathic bond. So, when Arkaziel hopped onto her shoulder, she just happened to have a wet hand when she petted him. *Vengeance is mine, feline!*

When the trio appeared on Floor 56, it was in a familiar place. They appeared on the disused path leading into Gladia's cottage outside of Raven's Hollow.

"How often are we supposed to get repeats?" Aetheria asked Arkaziel, while she studied the state of the cottage. The building had no signs of habitation. From the thick dust on the welcome mat to the abandoned feeling the building radiated, clearly, it had been some time since their departure.

Arkaziel, grumpy and with a still-wet head, didn't answer her beyond a noncommittal grunt that Aetheria took for *who knows?*

"You've been here before?" Werylin seemed surprised.

"Yeah, we solved a bit of a problem with some redcaps and orcs trying to destroy the local settlement, and we freed the spirit of an alchemist they'd bound as a skeletal slave to help them increase their combat readiness."

While Aetheria spoke, Arkaziel's golden eyes flared, and his twilight duplicates wandered through the cottage. By the time she'd finished her brief description of the events of their last visit, he'd already scouted the cottage.

"No one's been here for some time, and anything of use is long gone. Let's head to Raven's Hollow. Maybe the kids we saved last time will still be around."

The trio opted to walk toward the settlement rather than fly. It gave Aetheria an opportunity to stock up on reagents and let them get a sense of the wildlife and other changes. The path to Raven's Hollow took slightly less time than on their last visit. New, heavy stone walls surrounded the settlement now, and it had grown to nearly twice its previous size. Old buildings had been renovated, restored, and showed a pride of ownership. Renovations and new buildings alike bespoke a healthy citizenry capable of infrastructure expansion and upkeep.

A pair of sentries stood at the gate. The two watched with anxiety as the elf and human walked out of the forest. As the party approached the gate, one guard argued with the other about if Aetheria's hair was blue or green, and if it glowed. By the time Werylin and Aetheria stopped ten feet from the guards, Aetheria could see the facial features of both guards. One was an older man in his thirties or forties while the other guard looked to be twenty-something.

"Holy hell, an elf?!" the younger guard exclaimed in surprise, and the older guard's eyes finally left Aetheria to examine the purple-haired and lavender-eyed Werylin. Werylin looked like an anime character if you asked Aetheria. He wore little in the way of armor, just loose and flowing clothing, and his katana and wakizashi rested on his hip. The elf wore his hair in a ponytail similar to Aetheria's, and while femininely gorgeous, Werylin's eyes were those of a very ancient being. When the younger guard stared into Werylin's eyes for just a few seconds too long, it left him with goosebumps, and his expression shifted from curious to almost scared.

"Excuse the new kid. Not a lot of high tier Cultivators pass through the Hollow, and almost never through this gate. Although, when I was his age, Cody and Mabel brought a certain Cultivator through this gate, too." The older man winked at Aetheria. He had streaks of gray visible in his temples and bangs, but with the names of the kids she'd escorted last time, Aetheria placed him after a few moments of thought.

"Hello, Tad." Aetheria offered a smile.

"I thought that was you, Miss Aetheria. Mabel has been sure you'd show up any time now for the last two months once the Crystal Creep started." The familiarity and fondness of the way Tad said Mabel's name put a smile on Aetheria's face, and the way those red eyes looked at the guard made him shuffle his feet a little. "I've done right by Mabel as best I can, ma'am. Hopefully you don't . . . "

Aetheria held a hand up to stop Tad from continuing.

"Who someone ends up with is their business. As long as you are treating her well, I hope you're both very happy. If you aren't, well, I guess I might feed you to my cat."

"Meow." Arkaziel made the cutest, most precious meow in contrast to Aetheria's threat of the yellow-eyed feline feasting on the guard. Aetheria had never felt so betrayed before.

+*I'm not a prop!*+

~*Since when do you not want to eat people?*~ Aetheria wanted to scoff at Ark but maintained a smile despite their telepathic conversation.

+*It could happen. Theoretically. Oh fine, I am hungry now that you mention it.*+

Werylin coughed and entered the conversation. "What is this Crystal Creep you mentioned?"

"How have you made it here without hearing about it?" The young guard gave them all suspicious looks.

"It's the talk of the kingdom," Tad said. "We found the crystal caves on the frontier just four years ago. For the first three years, it brought us a lot of attention. Money, caravans, adventurers, crafters. Then the miners and adventurers quit coming back to Raven's Hollow. Six months ago, the king's elite adventurers went into the caverns. They never came back. About two months ago, the crystal started expanding out of the caves—and it keeps spreading. Two weeks ago, it was half a kilometer from the frontier gate. Yesterday it was two meters from the gate." Tad spit to the side of the road with the words.

"Your settlement seems to be cursed with invasive things. First a plague, now crystallization. I don't suppose there have been any orc or redcap sightings in the area?" Aetheria pondered aloud before she shook her head. "May we enter town? I'd like to talk to whoever is in charge now. It seems I'll be helping you again."

"Go on in, Lady Aetheria. The entry fee has been waived for anyone who has come to help out." Tad gestured to the open gate behind him.

After a short exploration of the bigger and better town of Raven's Hollow, the trio ended up in a lavish office in the town hall. With reinvigorated purpose apparently came political changes, as the town was now administrated by a nobleman from the capital, Lord Andross. Mabel, now the lord's secretary, ushered them into the room where an average-looking man looked at them disparagingly.

"Ugh. Really? Common riffraff answer our calls for heroes now?" Lord Andross muttered, just loud enough to ensure that the people who entered the room could hear. Mabel's eyes widened, and she looked about to intervene with the lord when Aetheria simply unsealed her aura. The snowflakes half-materialized in the air, while the man visibly sunk in his seat from the invisible pressure of her unveiled presence. Andross tried to overcome it, and struggled to keep his dignity by remaining upright and back straight. Each second of her unveiled aura pushed the man just a little deeper into his seat, made his skin just that little bit paler. Anxiety and fear crept into Andross's gaze, all while Aetheria stared the man down.

"This is Werylin Amaryllis, former head of House Amaryllis and once Imperator of the Elder Forest. My lovely companion"—Aetheria scratched Arkaziel under the chin with his introduction—"is Arkaziel, son of Azrael, a StarMane who previously saved this village. I, meanwhile, am Aetheria, acknowledged daughter of Aetherius and Nyx. Also called the Etherfrost Asura. If our assistance is too humble for your liking, we shall take our leave."

Andross didn't speak. In fact, he had went entirely pale during the introduction, and at some point thought had vanished from his eyes. A few seconds of silence ended when the nobleman's face hit the desk. Mabel started to move to check on him, when Werylin shook his head and laughed.

"Your lord is fine, lass. He fainted. No doubt a mixture of Aetheria's aura, Arkaziel's malicious gaze, and my own scowling. The obvious displeasure of three Cultivators of our progress was too much for his unrefined soul to withstand." Werylin did not bother to hide his amusement at the situation.

"I'm so sorry, Lady Aetheria. Should I rouse him, or fetch a doctor?" Mabel looked slightly panicked, perhaps afraid she would be blamed for this by Andross, or that his impropriety would reflect badly on Raven's Hollow.

"Nothing to worry about, Mabel. No need for a doctor; he's just out of it. He'll wake up on his own, eventually. I hear you are married to Tad? Congratulations! Young love is so sweet; I'm very happy for you. It's too bad you can't just enjoy these moments, but I'll take care of it all for you. Tad gave us the gist of the Crystal Creep, so if you can show us on a map where these crystal caves are, we'll head there and see what we can make of it."

"I could just eat him." Arkaziel, out of character, spoke despite Mabel's presence.

"No. Well, maybe. Is this guy a good lord other than being a pretentious jackass?" Aetheria asked Mabel.

"He's skilled at administration of the town," Mabel said, avoiding the question.

"Whatever. I'll leave him to be your problem, then. You'll have to save your appetite for whatever we're going to fight next, Ark. So. Crystal caves?" Aetheria reiterated, and Mabel sifted through the things on Andross's desk until she found a map of the area. Blue had been used to shade in the territories affected by the spread of the crystal.

"Alright, thanks, Mabel. We'll be on our way, then." Aetheria turned to lead the way out of the room when Arkaziel spoke again, looking at Mabel.

"If you change your mind about having that guy as a lord, I'm still willing to eat him."

Aetheria bonked Ark on the head. "Quit being a bad influence."

Aetheria, still annoyed, transformed into an Etherfrost Dragon outside the city hall. Citizens scattered at the appearance of a thirty-meter-long dragon in the center of town. Once Werylin and Arkaziel hopped onto her neck and she jumped into the air, her size increased even more. She didn't quite rival Arkaziel in his true form, but she easily measured over fifty meters.

"Leave it to a nobleman to piss off a dragon." Werylin seemed amused at it all.

"Did being dead for thousands of years make you immune to being slighted?" Arkaziel asked curiously.

"It mellowed me out. When I was Imperator, I would have had his tongue cut out, cooked, and fed back to him. Even in my days before politicking, when I traveled as a minstrel, I would have engineered some great fall for someone who spoke to me like that. Lady Oizys fosters misfortune for all, after all." The elf raised his shoulders in a tired shrug. "Now, I see the hand of misery in these things, and so feel less hostility toward those who slight me."

Aetheria, flying them, spoke in a rumbling draconic voice. "Doesn't that line of thought reduce the impact of free will and abdicate responsibility of action to nebulous gods who can't directly control you?"

"We're literally inside a god-made dimensional tower, where everyone we meet is of questionable origination. Are these people not existing solely at the mercy of the gods for purposes they aren't even aware of?"

"If the gods are actually gods, couldn't they do anything they can in these towers in the real world?" Aetheria countered.

"Maybe. We'll have to revisit this discussion when we have discerned the truth of the towers. Arguing over conjecture alone is quite pointless. Besides, the caves are right down there." Werylin had spotted the source of the expansive crystallization of the frontier just before Aetheria did. Moments later, they landed on a sheet of ice created by Aetheria to quarantine and cover the crystal. Each analyzed the glittering material with their own abilities.

"Oh yeah, this is going to be fun." Arkaziel laughed.

"Sarcastic fun or real fun?" Aetheria couldn't tell.

"Real fun. Ever heard of a crystal collective?"

CHAPTER 13

Crystal Collective

No, I've never heard of a crystal collective. What is it?"

"It's a living crystal with a hive mind. The more it spreads, the more powerful it becomes. Not just magically, either, but in all areas. The growth starts out small. Usually, a sentient creature or monster is the point of infection, and then it becomes the den of the original creature, until finally it spreads out into the wider world. The collective's growth is exponential, and with as much territory as it already has, it is going to be powerful. This thing could be dangerous even to us," Arkaziel answered smugly.

"So, do we need to worry about being infected by the crystal?" Werylin inspected the expansive plain of crystal that spread out from the cave and went in all directions.

"Possibly. It shouldn't pierce a powerful Cultivator's aura or body without some trickery, but let me cast a spell before we head in."

"It's nice to see you two getting along so well." Arkaziel rarely offered to buff others, in Aetheria's experience. Aetheria smiled at both of them while Arkaziel scratched a claw through the air and then bright light engulfed the three of them. When the brilliant effect faded, each of the three shimmered just a little.

"If it gains strength through expansion, shouldn't we destroy some of this crystal field before we go inside its domain?" Werylin gestured to the expansive fields of beautiful, if dangerous, crystal.

"If you want to play it safe, yeah. The stronger it is, the better meal it would be, though." Arkaziel's tone and eyes pleaded with them to not weaken the creature.

Aetheria and the elf laughed.

"Can you leave one of your duplicates out here to rampage if we need to weaken the main collective?"

Arkaziel nodded at Aetheria's inquiry and summoned his three duplicates to leave outside the caves.

"They should be able to handle destroying a lot, if it comes to it."

With that, the trio entered the cave. The crystal underfoot seemed like any normal crystal initially, but with every step on it, lights flickered inside of the crystal. At a mere half kilometer into the tunnel, the walls, roof, and floors of the cave had become a dazzling light show. Everything they walked past had become unmoving crystal, from bats to cave lizards, to mushrooms and lichen.

"Oh. Crystal rat," Ark said, while he poked at a crystalized rat the size of a dog. When his claw tapped the rat, it shattered into dust. "Oops."

"I thought this stuff would be stronger? Where's the security? They sent adventurers here before, and there's nothing attacking us."

"Sure, there is. The pulsing lights are a hypnosis attack. I've been disrupting their spell this whole time. I'm sure if you didn't have a defense against the hypnosis, it would make you fight your companions or lead you to submit to crystallization. Then the primary host consumes you to grow stronger, and when it's done, there's nothing left but brittle crystal like that rat." Arkaziel seemed to have some respect for the method.

"So it cultivates like you do, by eating everything," Werylin deadpanned.

"It is efficient. Grandpa once left a collective to grow for a few decades, just to come back and eat it. He said it saved him a month's worth of eating."

"Speaking of the adventurers . . . " Aetheria pointed at humanoid crystal shapes ahead of them. "Can we reverse it at all?"

Both Arkaziel and Werylin tried several spells to no effect. Purification, Restoration, Healing, none of it worked. In fact, the crystalline lattice that had consumed them seemed to absorb the spells before they could reach the latent life of the adventurers. *Or there's no life left for the spells to target.*

"Will the crystal revert once we kill the primary host?" Aetheria refrained from touching the statues, in case it consumed them as it had the rat.

"Ugh. I do not know. It is possible, but they may already be hollowed out. Guess we'll find out after we kill the host. Look alive, incoming." While Arkaziel spoke, strands of darkness spread out from his paw. The strands wove together into a wall seconds before a blast of a high-intensity light beam reflected down the cave. The opaque wall of darkness absorbed most of the light attack, and what little it failed to block bounced down the way they had come. Aetheria couldn't help but notice with each contact against crystal the beams grew stronger.

With a wave of Aetheria's hand, an opaque wall of ice rose behind them to seal the cave.

"I don't really want to get hit from behind by that laser." She answered the unspoken question in the other two's eyes.

"What's a little high-intensity light between friends?" Ark chimed in.

"We've reached the hive center." Werylin pointed ahead.

The pulses of light had grown so intense that discerning where the walls of the cavern were had become problematic. Without Ethereal Sight, Aetheria wasn't sure how Werylin could even tell, but it occurred to her that the elf probably had his own type of sight power. It seemed like the sort of ability most Cultivators probably would develop.

Werylin was right, though. The cavern opened into an enormous chamber, easily larger than a football field. Stalactites filled the top of the chamber. Many of them glowed with an inner light that made Aetheria a little nervous, the same gut feeling she got when approaching traps. She did not have long to dwell upon the differences of the glowing stalactites versus the dull, vibrating stalagmites on the cave floor. Instead, her eyes focused on the first moving creature they had found in the cave.

A tall figure of gleaming, luminescent crystals filled the chamber. Light refracted off its shimmering body into gorgeous displays of color. The creature possessed four heads, each a masterwork of crystalline beauty. Each serpentine head had a strange, jagged crystal crown upon it, and hungry red light illuminated its sharp, translucent teeth. Delicate scales covered the body of the hydra, giving the creature the appearance of a masterpiece. Despite its solid crystal form, the hydra moved with a surprising grace and fluidity, all while light danced across its body hypnotically.

"Hey, you overgrown geode! Your mom was a paperweight! You're about as scary as a chandelier, and half as bright!" Aetheria tested out taunting in real life, even as she triggered her teleport. In a flare of multihued chaos, she appeared next to the crystal hydra and delivered a punch into its front right leg. Aetheria let the flow of power from Frostfire emerge from her soul aperture. From there, the Ethereal power filled her to capacity and charged her Ethereal physiology to the maximum, while she also increased her density and borrowed extra mass from her repository to her punching hand.

Small chips of crystal flaked off the hydra, not even full scales, but the punch created a few small fissures in the transparent creature's leg. Fissures that already mended themselves, but Aetheria delivered a second punch to the same location, adding even more damage to the creature and sending more chipped crystal into the air. Each punch sent shockwaves of pain through Aetheria's hands, but the damage she caused to the hydra exceeded the damage she took from striking it.

"Gimme!"

Tendrils of darkness rose from Aetheria's shadow to pass through the body of the hydra. The tendrils were wispy and not a physical attack; instead they appeared to be a variation of Arkaziel's Devouring Darkness. The hydra lost some of its internal light with each pass through of the incorporeal tendrils.

Werylin blurred and appeared behind the hydra. Werylin used a sword-draw attack reminiscent of more than a few anime. Harmonious Tempest left a golden afterimage in the air seconds after the katana had already been returned to its sheath. Crystal seemed no match for the legendary sword, as the hydra's tail hung in the air for a second. The golden energy of his strike flowed into the removed tail, then it fell to the crystalline floor and shattered into thousands of pieces.

"I always hated tail strikes." Werylin's serious tone came at odds with the slight smirk on his lips.

The hydra roared from two of its four heads, and the delicate-looking scales on its back were shot as projectiles. It forced Werylin to defend himself in a flurry of parries, while Arkaziel used even more tendrils of darkness to consume the shards that shot through the air at him. Aetheria let the ones that came her direction almost hit her, then shifted them into her repository at the last second. That they went, she hoped, meant they weren't invasive, but for now she quarantined the scales.

Aetheria counterattacked with another combo of strikes fueled by the Primordial Flame of Ymir. The power of the frost giant invigorated the power of her physical blows and imparted even more cold to the Etherfrost Asura's strikes. Large chunks of crystal flew with each blow, as well as a dust cloud of powdered crystal. The Flame of Ymir seemed to fortify her fists as well, reducing the stress of punching such a dense creature.

The eyes on one of the hydra's heads began to glow, and another high-intensity laser shot across the chamber toward Arkaziel, who just opened his mouth and sucked the light into his stomach with a deep breath. After, he burped. Two of the hydra heads began a game of cat and mouse with Aetheria, with her dodging between blows, and them trying to bite her to death.

Fresh off the defensive from the scales attack, Werylin leaped onto the back of the hydra and thrust his new wakizashi in between the overlapping scales. It took an incredible amount of finesse to pierce the hydra's hide, but the elf managed, despite all the movement of the angry beast. With half the shorter blade thrust into the crystalline hide, Werylin's figure glowed with a golden haze.

"Fracture!"

Aetheria expected to see some kind of golden glow, but a strange darkness spread inside of the hydra's back. Something about its crystal lattices changed with that darkness. Whatever the nature of the attack was, she didn't understand it, especially when Werylin pushed down even further on the hilt and jagged breaks appeared. The elf then pulled the blade off and danced out of the counterattacks two of the hydra's heads delivered. A solid third of the hydra's back shattered and crumbled when the fractures had quit spreading.

Arkaziel did not engage beyond the continued tendrils that sapped the light out of the crystalline hydra.

"I've met glass windows tougher than you!" Aetheria shouted at the heads to try to get their attention. When that failed, she materialized spears of ice and flung them at the heads. The spears sent miniature fractures through the beautiful crystal but didn't pierce the creature. In response, all four heads of the hydra roared. Attuned to the roar, all the crystal of the chamber emitted a bright light that shined into the hydra. The lights bounced off the scales and reflected around the chamber, but no longer was it light. Instead, the contact with the hydra had shifted the composition of the attack.

Fire, lightning, wind, and ice attacked all three of the Cultivators. Ice was no problem for Aetheria, but Arkaziel and Werylin didn't share her near immunity. Aetheria's aura snuffed out the flames in half of the room, removing most of that concern as well. Lightning, none of the three had a resistance against. Multiple bolts of electricity struck Aetheria, making her hair stand on end and temporarily stunning her, but doing little actual damage to her.

Arkaziel and Werylin reacted to the attacks differently. Arkaziel raised a shield of darkness that held off the fire, but the wind and lightning pierced through to leave scorch marks and minor cuts across his scales. None of the wind blades possessed the strength to do more than superficially pierce his draconic scales.

Werylin had drawn both of his blades and batted attacks aside as if they were sword thrusts to be parried. Somehow, that actually worked, but there were too many attacks for him to deflect them all. Small patches of purple hair burned, a bit of frostbite burned on his arms after ice pierced his flesh, and then he spasmed when a lightning bolt struck him. Lucky for him, all four of the hydra's heads had gone to try to eat Aetheria while she too was stunned.

CHAPTER 14

Crystal Calamity

Pain, Aetheria's frenemy, accompanied the lightning bolts. Most attacks she could simply endure or shrug off, but fighting higher tier monsters had started to show the folly of tanking damage. Not that it was the damage she had a problem with. The paralysis that accompanied the lightning was the real problem, but she shook that off quickly. In fact, she broke free of the paralysis much quicker than her two companions, but she couldn't pinpoint whether this was due to her Flames, or one of her pieces of equipment.

Still, she didn't break free before one of the hydra's heads bit off one of her legs, and another took her left arm. Aetheria altered her shape to a ball, and bounced out of the way of the other two biting heads before they could take off her own head or torso. Once she ricocheted off the wall and got some distance, she returned to humanoid form, but not human. Aetheria's skin had become the red diamond of the Luxentian race, and her fingers had become long, dangerous talons. At the cost of a fruit from Cryostrialis, her limbs immediately regenerated.

"You're going to have to do better than that," Aetheria snarled at the hydra, then shouted to Arkaziel, "Light me up, buddy."

Claws and biting heads once more assaulted Aetheria, but she fought defensively now, parrying the claws and dodging bites. Each bite she dodged earned the hydra a stab from her talons into its face before she resituated herself. This kind of fight always reminded her of games where you had to time blocks to launch devastating counterattacks. Afraid the hydra would target the other two, Aetheria maximized the power of her domain to slow and hinder the hydra. Hoarfrost formed along its legs, and the hydra's movements slowed significantly.

Intense light flared from Arkaziel, bathing the Luxentian Aetheria in light that she hungrily absorbed. This pushed the relative power of her Luxentian body into approximately Tier Four, like the hydra. The difference in her counterattacks significantly increased, with her roughly thirty-centimeter-long talons slicing through the crystal scales of the hydra like butter.

The new damage slowed the healing of the hydra's tail and the section of its back. If she maintained her current output, it would still be a long fight ahead of them.

Werylin, free from the paralysis, circled the hydra while he hummed under his breath. Whatever attack the elf swordsman planned to make clearly took buildup of some sort. Aetheria maintained her attempt at tanking.

~Jump when I say jump.~

Arkaziel warned her telepathically. If not for the warning, she would not have noticed the increased intensity of the shadows beneath herself and the hydra. The tendrils that had attacked and leached from the hydra since the start of the fight continued their assault, but something bigger seemed to be on the way.

~Jump!~

Aetheria did as instructed, jumping up, and her pillars of ice rose with her. This allowed her to hop between pillars and maintain mobility, since she wasn't sure what kind of attack Arkaziel unleashed.

Tentacles thicker than her body rose from the shadows and wrapped around the hydra. There were nine tentacles, and together they seemed to be able to overpower the hydra. In fact, they pulled the hydra down to the ground and entangled it. The hydra took to thrashing with all of its weight, but the tentacles held it tight.

"Blades of Harmonious Resonance!" Werylin lightly tapped his two blades together, before flashing in to attack the ensnared hydra. When the wakizashi touched Harmonious Tempest, both took on a powerful golden aura, and their images vibrated slightly to the naked eye. With the buff on his weapons and a stationary target, Werylin danced through multiple steps of an extremely beautiful sword dance. The way the elf flowed between slashes and thrusts was breathtaking, and Aetheria found herself distracted from the fight. The elf's blades cut easily through the crystal, although Aetheria noticed that there were far more crystal chips thrown off than a slashing cut should produce. *Is that like vibroknife buff?*

Aetheria's distraction cost her: one of the heads broke free of the tentacles and tried to bite her. In this Luxentian form, still empowered with Arkaziel's light, the teeth only scratched her diamond skin, but the pain was still considerable. She took the opportunity to elongate her left arm while the hydra tried to chew her, and stab it through the creature's left eye and mince its brains with her long talons, even as extreme cold radiated from her hand, and the life-draining Flame of Nyx sucked at the life force of the hydra.

"Stage 2!" Werylin murmured. Aetheria wondered if she needed to know about these stages; was there going to be a friendly fire wide-scale attack? She hoped the elf remembered that he hadn't shown this attack before.

She needn't have worried.

Apparently, the second step of the Blades of Harmonious Resonance was akin to the ever popular spin attack. What game didn't have a whirlwind, cyclone, or spinning attack, right? Apparently, the elves had adopted it into their blade dance, and with every twirl Werylin's blades unleashed even more devastation upon the hydra.

"Cripes, how'd you do that?" Aetheria felt shock when Werylin, still spinning, somehow blurred up the hydra's back and unleashed a multitude of attacks against all of the hydra's necks. The head she had impaled the brain of was the first to shatter and disintegrate. To prevent the other three heads from going for Werylin, she flung a swarm of icicles at the heads to pull their attention. Not that Werylin seemed to need the help: with Aetheria's domain slowing the ensnared hydra, the elf nimbly dodged each attack while he cleaved the crystalline necks to pieces.

"Snack time!" Arkaziel shouted from the back row, and opened his mouth wide and mimed biting the air before him. A shadowy replica of his head emerged from the shadows under the hydra, and while no physical damage occurred as a result of the attack, the inner light of the hydra had dimmed to almost nothing, and its regeneration stopped entirely. Even with the afterimage of Arkaziel's attack gone, the inner light of the creature weakened by the second.

"Just die." Aetheria's talons slid into the thickly scaled area where the necks met, and she ripped at the last of the creature's essence with the Primordial Flame of Nyx.

The hydra stopped moving. Then a cracking sound filled the air, and the crystalline hydra, walls, ceiling, and floor all fragmented. Crystalline fractures ran everywhere. The previously lustrous crystals went dull, the inner light extinguished, and then in a sound reminiscent of ice floes breaking, the crystal shattered and became dust. Nothing remained of the hive creature, and its expansive field of crystal went with it.

A treasure chest in the room's corner drew the attention of all three.

"It is locked," Werylin declared after a failed attempt to open it.

"Let me." Aetheria's fingers pressed against the keyhole, and her pointer finger flowed into the mechanism to reshape and allow her to open the chest. The chest opened under her ministrations, revealing only two objects.

"May I have that stone? Unless I'm wrong, that is a Stone of Harmonic Echoes. I could build my core around such an item, and it would increase the power of my Words of Creation and sense of harmony." Werylin looked exceptionally serious. *Guess the pretty rock is incredibly valuable. Who'd have guessed?*

"Go for it." Aetheria had no use for it.

"It is pointless to me. We beast Cultivators do not form a core as you humanoids do." Arkaziel's yellow eyes were focused on the other item in the chest, though.

"I would like that ingot." Ark sniffed the air a few times, then tried to hide his salivation.

"What is it?" Aetheria asked, even as she picked it up and handed it to the dragon.

"Twilight Steel. It enhances light and dark powers, and if you can use both, increases the power of any twilight power you use. Its durability is roughly equivalent to mithril, but I can always eat some raw adamantite to increase the endurance later."

Arkaziel lifted the ore to his jaw and chewed. And chewed some more. Apparently, digesting and absorbing ores took longer than chewing a whole wad of gum. It was disconcerting to watch anyone chew metal, and the sounds of Arkaziel's unbreakable teeth rending metal sent shivers down Aetheria's spine. Nails on a chalkboard would have been a vastly preferable sound.

"All the crystal fields are gone." Arkaziel spoke around his full mouth, words punctuated by the harsh sounds of teeth and metal at war.

"Don't talk with your mouth full, Ark," Aetheria hissed at him, and the cat sulked to the corner of the room to poke at the walls. Perhaps the StarMane was looking for more ores?

"Aetheria, could we camp here for a day or two? I believe I am ready to cross over to Tier Four, now that I have the foundation for my core." Werylin had been absorbed in the examination of the Stone of Harmonic Echoes this whole time.

"Sure, no problem. Is there anything else that could help you out? I've got a lot of stuff in my repository." Aetheria considered "always offer a helping hand to your friends" to be a great rule to live by.

"Actually, I believe you mentioned your ability to mimic the affinity of any object you place in your repository, yes?"

"Yeah, I can do that. What do you have in mind?"

Werylin pulled the wakizashi off his belt and tossed it to Aetheria.

"Can you feel its affinity?"

The weapon vanished into her repository, and Aetheria tilted her head.

"Yeah, yeah, I can feel its affinity all right." *Chaos.*

"Harmony is a fantastic affinity. If you could use the wakizashi to generate an overabundance of the surrounding energy while I shape the Stone and form my core, that would be very helpful."

"Sure. You seem pretty confident about making your core with just some energy and one item. Wouldn't waiting and using more stuff make a stronger core?" The occasional painful shriek of dragon tooth and metal still filled the air. Aetheria barely stopped herself from telling Ark to chew faster.

"I've made a core before. They destroyed my first core when they sentenced me to become a guardian. The remnants of it are still within me, so if I combine enough energy, this stone, and the fragments of my original, I am certain to create a high-end core."

"Wait, you can go backward in cultivation?"

"Yes. If you cannot meet the requirements of a tier. The destruction of your inner world or of your Cultivator's core will push you backward. It is also exceptionally painful, and can kill one on its own."

"Alright. Let's do this." Aetheria synchronized her affinity to the weapon, and her aura took on a golden glow. *Guess this proves me right. Chaos and order are a sliding scale, two extremes of the same power. Werylin's harmony seems to be ever so slightly closer to order, but otherwise near the middle of the spectrum.*

"I can't generate mana, so you'll have to settle for harmony-attuned Aether. Hope you've learned to deal with it!" Aetheria grinned. Rather than absorbing the ambient Aether, she pulled vast quantities from her repository and aspected it to match the affinity of the wakizashi, before she exuded the raw harmonic Aether into the air. To her Ethereal Sight the air seemed to almost thicken, as if Werylin were swimming in a pool of aetheric energy.

"Just how much energy can you project?" The elf gave her a questioning look.

"I'm drawing it from my inner world, which seems to have the same nearly unlimited tides of Aether and Nether that the real world does. My only bottleneck with it is my rank once I get beefier meridians . . ." Aetheria trailed off at the slightly horrified look on the elf's face.

"You're ridiculous." Werylin laughed, then settled into a meditative pose.

"Good luck. Don't blow up, but if you do, Ark will heal you."

"Do you blow up frequently?"

"Every time I rank up."

"Normal Cultivators don't blow up, Aetheria."

CHAPTER 15

The Hall of Mirrors

Watching someone else build a Cultivator core is much more boring than I thought," Aetheria said, offering her take on the ongoing process Werylin worked on. She continued to generate large amounts of the attuned order of the wakizashi for the elf.

"It is much tamer when people aren't melting, reshaping, exploding, and randomly turning into other people," Arkaziel agreed.

"Wait, I melt and shapeshift while I'm tiering up? You've never mentioned that."

"Didn't seem important."

Aetheria gave Arkaziel a flat stare. The cat stared back at her equally flat. Silence reigned in the cave. Both laughed at the same time after ten minutes of silence.

"You can go hunt for a while, Ark. This might take a while."

In fact, it took four days until a sensation of harmony and golden light enveloped Werylin and lit the chamber. When it finished, Werylin's hair had shifted from purple to contain more shades of blue, which resulted in a more violet hue, and the elf's formerly lavender eyes had become silver. Werylin did not appear to have undergone any other physical alterations beyond.

"That was exhausting. Thank you for providing the ambient power, Aetheria." Werylin gave her a tired but genuinely thankful look.

"Do you not suffer a blowback for tiering up?" Aetheria frowned.

"I did. It was much nastier than the blowback I endured the first time I did this. I believe that my time as an undead left me with enough Nether contamination that the spiritual cleansing was very painful."

"So it was just spiritual and mental pain? No bones reshaping or anything like that?" Aetheria felt cheated.

"I felt some physical discomfort with the incorporation of Aetherial physiology. It was pale in comparison to the mental toll. I told you before, ordinary people do not explode or suffer the sort of blowback you've described." Werylin shook his head.

"Ordinary? You were an elf king, and seem pretty elite to me."

"Imperator, not king. As for elite, perhaps. I am no Asura, though. Even discarding the time in which I was a spirit, I am significantly older than you are. Much of my combat capabilities come from Harmonious Tempest. Regardless, I have broken through to Tier Four." Werylin stretched out, and Aetheria tossed him his wakizashi again.

"Arkaziel is waiting at the cottage for us," Aetheria said. "The doorway to the next floor is there. He already let the villagers know we'd taken care of the problem. They offered us some minor rewards, gold, and a feast. Ark ate it all."

"Even the gold?"

"Even the gold. He says it makes his eyes brighter."

"Now then, allow me to transport us there." Werylin touched her shoulder, and pale white light with golden notes enveloped the two. After the flash of light, they reappeared outside of the cottage. "I can only go to places I've been, and I'll have to test out my maximum range. I missed being able to teleport."

"I'm looking forward to longer-range teleports myself."

"Took you two long enough." Arkaziel lay in front of the doorway, bathed in sunlight.

"Tallyho!" Aetheria laughed and dived through the doorway.

The brief darkness of teleportation and nothing faded, and Aetheria emerged in a dimly lit small chamber. Mirrors lined all of the walls, and the other two did not appear with her. She counted to one hundred, and they still hadn't arrived.

~You out there, buddy?~

+Yes. This might be a difficult floor for you and your unresolved issues. The mirrors will project your fears and desires into reality. Be on your guard; I'll see you at the floor-master's chamber.+

On the bright side, she could still communicate with Arkaziel. The terse response from the StarMane left her with the impression that he needed to focus on his own desires. *Oh man, can a murder cat even make it through a trial of their own desires and fears used against them? That's like, the absolute worst thing a narcissist could be subjected to.*

Rather than immediately look for the door to the next room, Aetheria walked up to one of the mirrors and examined her image. Initially, it was an honest reflection of her that captured even her glowing red eyes and glimmering aqua hair. Then the reflection morphed slightly; red eyes turned blue, as they'd been when she first reincarnated.

"Why do you keep the scary red eyes, me? It only takes a thought to change your eye color."

While the words sank in, Aetheria wondered if she actually sounded like that much of a Karen.

"I like the red. It matches my coat, and even if I change it to blue, the weight of the Ethereal will still be carried in my gaze unsettling most people I look at. Or are you the fashionista reflection? Maybe I should go with heterochromia?" One of Aetheria's eyes changed from red to blue while she blinked.

"Oh, I'm definitely the fashionista reflection. You are one of the most versatile shapeshifters around, and you spend all of your time like that." The fashionista stepped out of the mirror. She no longer matched Aetheria's wardrobe, but instead wore black lace-up boots, stockings, and a knee-length black dress. Instead of the scarf Aetheria favored, the fashionista wore a choker. "You can literally change yourself with less effort than it takes to drink water, and you can't be bothered to liven things up a little?"

"Change for change's sake isn't that important to me."

"For Pete's sake, girl, you're an immortal Asura with the power of Primordials! Live a little. You've got the sparkle princess hair, the divine glowing eyes, and an aura thick enough to give Tier Two Cultivators a heart attack. Flaunt it!"

"Maybe I'm a little conservative with using my power, especially for trivial things like changing my appearance. How's that a bad thing?"

Fashionista had her wardrobe again.

"Let's see. First we've got the coat that covers you from neck to ankles, but wait, there's more. You wear a scarf, no matter the temperature, to hide just that little bit extra of skin. And the fingerless gloves, really? Isn't that just a little ridiculous for someone who can turn to diamond? Afraid of getting a little dirt on your hands? The only thing you are missing is a big hat or hood to hide your face, and you'd be the most defended person around who isn't in full body armor."

Aetheria stared flatly at her reflection.

"And?"

"What do you mean, and? What kind of defective person runs around with look-at-me hair and eyes, while everything else about them says 'don't look at me!'? You've got issues, girl."

"Yes, yes I do. If this is supposed to make me feel bad, you're coming at this from the very wrong angle. Yes, I'm self-conscious, even though I can change every single physical thing about me. I've no interest in becoming a chameleon that just constantly changes to please those around her."

Fashionista clapped mockingly.

"You are just afraid that if you change, people still might still reject you. If they dislike you despite your physical transformations then it's not your appearance that's flawed—it's your personality."

Aetheria held her tongue for a few moments, then laughed and nodded.

"That is actually fair. So, what, this is the Hall of Therapy Mirrors?"

Fashionista faded away when Aetheria acknowledged she was right, leaving her alone in a room with just ordinary reflections in the mirrors again. One of the mirrors shifted into the wall, revealing a passageway out of the room.

"That wasn't so bad." Nonplussed, Aetheria wandered down the hallway to the next chamber of mirrors. The process repeated itself, except it was not her own reflection that stepped out of the mirror. Instead, it was Aoibhe, in all her glory. She stood at the same height as Aetheria, six feet tall, with long, glorious legs covered in black stockings. A purple dress flattered Aoibhe's full figure, and the blonde's beautiful gold eyes peered at her from under the brim of the tall witch's hat she frequently wore. Her yellow-to-orange angelic wings flared behind her dramatically and contrasted beautifully with the black and purples of her wardrobe. Even this imitation of her soul-bonded partner filled her with emotion, awoke desire, and Aetheria found herself sending warmth through the connection between their souls.

Not that it would be received by the reflection, but the loneliness of being separated from Aoibhe hit her like a truck sending a Japanese salaryman into an isekai adventure. The friendship, and occasionally frenemyship, with Arkaziel had been enough to sustain her sanity through the floors, but this was the woman she longed to spend time with.

"Looking beautiful, Aoibhe-reflection. What's your spiel going to be?" Aetheria hardened her heart and prepared for some truly vile things to be said to her.

"Are you aware of how strong you are, Daughter of Aetherius and Nyx, sole inheritor of the Flame of Khaos?" The Nephilim tilted her head to the side to study Aetheria with those words.

"Is this going to be one of those 'live up to your potential' speeches? I'm strong, and keep getting stronger. I don't have a benchmark, but Arkaziel seems to be pretty close to me in power."

Aoibhe's reflection laughed mockingly, and Aetheria squirmed at how unpleasant it felt.

"The closest benchmark you have is a StarMane. Not just any StarMane, but an Ethereal StarMane that consumed the essence of its clutch mate before insects could, giving it the strength of any two others. No wonder the gods had me seduce and bind your soul to me. Can't have a truly immortal being with that much power running totally free." Aoibhe's reflection rolled her eyes and gave Aetheria a put-upon look.

"Oh, didn't you know that Aetherius set up our meeting? Even the Primordials who birthed you have made contingencies to deal with you."

Aetheria decided the smirk looked much better on Aoibhe's face than the contemptuous looks.

"You might be reaching a bit there. You think Primordials are afraid of me? Me? Really? My progress through this tower hasn't made me feel like a god should be afraid of me."

The mocking laughter her answer generated felt like a stab in the gut.

"Poor little dear one. You are immortal, a true honest-to-goodness immortal. Nothing can kill you now, not even Aetherius or Nyx. Of course, they're afraid of you, especially the ones who weren't involved in your creation. How do you think the Overgod feels about someone outside even his power? I bet Aetherius got quite the scolding for that . . ."

Aetheria's lips compressed into a thin line. The best, most damaging lies, were ones based on some measure of truth. Did she believe that Aetherius arranged the meeting with Aoibhe? Yes. Did she think it was with those kinds of intentions? No. *Pete just wanted to set me up with a hottie who's totally my type.*

"If I'm so powerful then why doesn't Oizys just abdicate Grief, instead of having to deal with me?"

"These ancient gods aren't always smart. Nyx's children are overwhelmed by their nature, and don't see the forest for the trees. If they did, Grief would never have devolved so badly, because falls are always the best after a rise. Nice deflection from immortality."

Dammit.

"I'm just supposed to take a reflection of my significant other's word that I'm totally immortal? Not really the best source of information. Has it been hinted at? A little. Seems ridiculous that Aetherius or Nyx would go so out of their way to make me immortal if it's such a rare and threatening thing to even gods."

"Have any of the gods you met struck you as infallible? All knowing? Omnipotent? They're powerful, sure, but they aren't all seeing and all knowing. They're fallible, like your world's Greek gods. They have deep flaws of character and have a preponderance to whims. So, you should ask yourself, Aesca, just what whim are you fulfilling for Aetherius, Nyx, and Khaos?"

The replica of Aoibhe vanished then. Aetheria didn't feel good about it, like she had with the fashionista. After all, there was no such thing as a free lunch.

CHAPTER 16

Mirror, Mirror

The unsettling question was one that had come up before, of course. Just what was she to these gods whom she was acting on behalf of? Did the liberation of Grief even highly factor into the plans of the Primordials, or was it a convenient song and dance? Aetheria had not even hit the two-thirds mark on the first tower of ten, and already her power had entered realms beyond her imagination at the start of all of this. How powerful would she be after ten?

If the plan went that way, they wouldn't make me aware of it inside of their own tower. This is just another mind game by an Administrator to make me waver.

Mirrors shifted to reveal another passageway. As expected, she found herself in another chamber of mirrors.

This time the mirrors revealed a reflection of a man. His clothes were fine, a mixture of a nobleman's finery and light armor. The pallid man had a rapier at his hip, and an arrow pierced one eye. It took Aetheria a few seconds to recall the name of the man: Benedict. He had died on one of the earliest floors of the tower. The delay left a sense of guilt that she did not immediately put a name to one of those who had died in front of her in the tower.

"It's been a while, daughter of Aetherius."

"Hello, Benedict."

"You remember me? I'm impressed. I'd have been more impressed if you hadn't taken an arrow and if you had fought to protect me, but I guess we can't have everything we want, now can we? After all, it was my own companion who slew me, not an enemy."

"Apologies probably mean very little, but I'm sorry I failed you."

"Death and rebirth are an endless cycle. I will live again, and again, and again."

"You sound awfully morose about that."

"There is no end to the cycle. There is no opting out. The long sought-after immortality is a lie; even gods die and are reborn. You should know, you killed your namesake."

Aetheria's eyes narrowed at the specter of the dead duelist.

"There is no higher realm at the end of the Winding Way, nor are there lower realms to ascend to ours from. There are only adjacent realms, full of more suffering. The burden of existence is without purpose or reward."

"That's very nihilistic of you. You found no meaning at all in your life?"

"Life itself, emotional investment, soul ties, the yearning of the flesh. These are all rose-colored lenses. When those are removed there is only the inescapable torture of continued existence."

"If you feel that way, how about I free you from the mortal coil?"

The ghost laughed.

"You don't have that power."

Aetheria held her right hand aloft. First, red energy played over her extended hand as she allowed as much power as her meridians could withstand to flow from Frostfire, through her soul aperture, into her hand. Then Aetheria awoke the Flame of Khaos, and the energy took on the multicolored aspects of the goddess.

"What is that?"

"Game over," Aetheria whispered softly and shattered the image before her.

Aetheria thought she caught a look of bliss upon the ghost's features before it vanished.

A new reflection stepped from the mirror. Herself.

"What did you just do, me?"

"Khaos is so much more than what I thought she was."

"You aren't making sense."

"Clearly you don't understand. Do you want me to explain it to you?" Aetheria smiled patronizingly at the reflection of herself, who nodded.

"Every system has a state made up of multiple properties, obviously. Time, distance, forces. So obviously there are going to be some hidden ones that aren't within the realm of mortals or gods. Opting out of the cycle appears to be one of those properties that only Khaos can access. You probably should not have gotten too curious though, Administrator."

The Administrator's form flickered as her reflection became hazy. It made Aetheria remember the hazy reception of the old broadcast television during storms, and how mad her father would get when he couldn't watch a Vikings game. The reflection was gone when it ended. No one replaced it. No Overgod appeared to lecture her, no Aetherius, no Khaos, no Chronos. Instead, she simply *knew* she needed to be careful with this particular power. *I wonder if they just deleted that Admin? I'll have to ask Pete next time I see him.*

The Overgod(s?) had split Ethereal power into Aether and Nether to limit the threat to reality by the Ethereal. Modification of the values of a system could lead to system failure, and Aetheria felt the power of Khaos represented a larger threat to existence than the Ethereal. Had they provided Aetheria with the means to destroy existence? Within her mind, the Flame of Khaos had locked itself into the final form of Tier Three, and she was certain it would enter the fourth tier along with her when she managed to construct her core.

Aetheria laughed a little. She hadn't even had to drain chaotic energies or order energies to empower it this time; she'd simply had to use it on a deeper level. Overcomplication could easily hinder anyone, yet it seemed using the Primordial Flames on a deeper level could empower them as well. *If the Flame of Khaos is Primordial.*

The mirrors shifted once more, allowing Aetheria to stride down another tunnel. At the end of the tunnel lay a chamber of ice. Unlike the other chambers, the mirrors in this particular chamber had all been obscured by sheets of ice, and upon a frozen throne sat another version of herself.

"Why hello, me."

"Hello, Aetheria."

"What are we going to chat about this time?"

"Your path, of course. You've started to take the winding part of the Ways a little too seriously."

"Ah. So what is it you want me to abandon?" Aetheria asked herself a little flippantly, fully expecting the reflection to answer Khaos or the like.

"I don't care what you drop or pursue. You are all over the place right now, trying to fulfill too many roles. Are you a brawler, or a ranged caster? Are you a defender or a striker? Versatility to fulfill multiple roles is not a bad thing, but you have not thrown yourself in to master anything. You jump from new toy to new toy like a child. You are not far from forging your core, and while you can evolve and upgrade a core, reforging it entirely could destroy even us."

"I've got a lot of options. It's a good idea to explore them before committing to something; look how we felt about being a Librarian by the time we died. Just because I punch a lot of people and monsters, usually in the face, it doesn't make me a brawler or a monk. I'm all in on freezing, though. That resonates with me in a way I can't deny."

The Aetheria on the throne barked a laugh.

"Oh please, we both know punching fools in the throat is every bit a part of us as cold and ice are."

Aetheria walked around the room, examining the creation of the sheets of ice, the throne, the sculptures. A globe of ice caught her attention particularly, and she managed to copy a replica of it to her storage on the down-low.

"Sure, that's true. I always threatened to throat punch people back on Earth. A little immature, sure, but I never did follow up on that threat before I died."

"My biggest regret," both Aetherias said, then sighed together.

"Okay, me. What would you do in my shoes?"

The Aetheria on the throne smirked.

"That's not how this conversation goes, me. I'll lead you by the nose a little though. Let's think about your strengths. Immortality, near instant regeneration, shapeshifting, freezing, speed." Queen Aetheria ticked off a finger with each word.

"I'm not that fast. Werylin is quicker than me."

"Are you complaining because an elf is more agile than you? Not just an ordinary elf either, but a vaunted war hero with thousands of times more experience than you? Check your ego."

Aetheria grimaced before she nodded.

"You have a point. So, what are my weaknesses?"

"You are impatient, like to be the Big Damn Hero far too much, and lack mastery of your toolkit. You don't know how to best use your arsenal because it expanded too fast.

"Learning to be a Cultivator in a tower is kind of a shitty experience."

"You'd rather have spent decades learning tiny variations of the same thing and being spoon-fed concepts by teachers who can't brave the Winding Ways, and just follow preplanned routes?"

"Are those the only two options?"

"No. There are other options, but walking the Winding Way or the established routes are the two most common."

"So how do I fix my deficiencies?"

"With hard work. Unless you want to let me take over for you? No? Then you are stuck with the hard work option. Stop going with whatever ability is the most convenient and start working toward your goals. If you just keep walking on any path in front of you, you'll get lost on the Winding Way. You need to visualize your goal and walk toward it."

"What path did you end up on?"

"I named my path the Path of the Timeless Glacier. It worked, for a while, until it didn't. Time is a poor focus for us."

"I could've told you that. Got caught up with Chronos in your timeline?"

"Yes. I drank that bottle of alcohol he gave us; he implied some things that weren't accurate for *me*, and that was that."

"Not going to warn me off time?"

"I just did. You'll do what you'll do, you stubborn bitch. If you commit to something, do it sober."

Aetheria laughed, and the queen reflection joined her after a few moments.

"Thanks for the advice. By the way, can I get another bottle of booze?"

The figure on the throne frowned at her, its form rippling into that of Chronos.

"When did you figure it out?"

"When you called me a bitch. That wasn't self-loathing inflected in the word. You did a remarkable impression of me, though. I'm guessing you looked just far enough into the future to pick your words? The ice also gave it away. The reflections inside the mirrors are still visible, barely, and are all locked in time."

Time personified laughed.

"Good catch. You did well with Khaos's gift, but you have work to do. After you become an Ethereal Scion I shall visit you again and grant you my Flame. You aren't ready for another Transcendent Flame yet."

"HAH! I knew Khaos wasn't a Primordial. So you two are Transcendant? Is there something beyond that?"

Chronos didn't answer Aetheria; he just smiled. She could almost hear him whisper "yes" through his closed mouth, though. Maybe that was her imagination running wild.

"Did you seriously visit me just to tell me to work harder and revisit the basics?"

"Oh yes, that was definitely my goal." Chronos rolled his eyes before he tossed her something. It was a black leather collar with a moon on it. "For my favorite kitten."

With that, Chronos vanished. The ice sheets and throne went with him, and Aetheria was left to deal with another reflection of herself that harped on about how she had to choose between paths. It was obnoxious after Chronos had led her down the same topics, and had done so much more eloquently. An hour later, she found herself in a small room with Arkaziel and Werylin, and the door to Floor 58 awaited them.

CHAPTER 17

Skygarden

When the darkness of teleportation faded, the trio found themselves on a large fluffy cloud. Strangely, trees, bushes, flowers, and other plant life grew from the cloud as if that were a completely normal thing. The sweet scent of ambrosial fruit filled the air, and the fruits on the plants all shimmered with an inner radiance. Each of the trio fought to contain drool.

A powerful presence pressed upon them, but none of the three could identify its source.

"Do you think it's a trap?" Werylin inquired of the other two. His silver eyes scanned the skies, and he even peered over the edge of the cloud to look down.

The garden somehow disrupted Aetheria's Ethereal Sight, but an important factor still revealed itself to her.

"There are massive winds between all of the gardens." Aetheria gestured. A stream of snowflakes materialized from her hand and drifted on a small gust of wind. At the end of the garden the stream split into thirds. Those that went over the glass bridge to the next cloud were fine, but the two groups that went around the bridge into the sky were pulled into vortexes of air currents. The not-so-fragile snowflakes were destroyed entirely within seconds.

"How durable were those snowflakes?" Arkaziel asked from beside what looked like a blueberry bush.

"Tougher than mithril." Aetheria grimaced.

A single twilight cat appeared, and Arkaziel sent it upward. The tallest plant on their cloud was a tree with peach-like fruit. Aetheria estimated it to be maybe eight meters tall. Without warning, less than a meter above the tree, winds ripped the duplicate to pieces in an instant. Arkaziel's yellow eyes narrowed.

"I think I'll stay on the ground."

The other two laughed at the flatness in Ark's voice.

"So, no flying, a hugely powerful presence, and a series of bridges between clouds that look to only have one or two paths. Can you see the exit on the far platform?" Werylin squinted at the far distant platform.

"I see it, but bad news. Teleportation is blocked here." Arkaziel hissed under his breath. "What kind of sadistic asshole set up this garden? It is a conspiracy against yours truly. No flying, no teleportation. Next you're going to tell me there'll be a whole patch of . . . StarMane . . . Mint . . ." Arkaziel trailed off when he saw a patch of bushy mint on the next garden. Drool immediately leaked from his mouth, and the cat stared in awe.

"This is definitely a trap." Aetheria sighed. Even her mouth watered a little with the raw need that filled her empathic bond with Arkaziel.

"Without a doubt. Nonetheless, the bounty of this garden could provide even more benefit to us than the ambrosial fruits you previously obtained. Look carefully. Many of these trees have evolved." Werylin gestured to a plum tree. "That one is Tier Four. I can feel a Tier Six two platforms ahead."

Aetheria grinned at the open desire in Werylin's voice.

Arkaziel remained strangely silent. Drool escaped his mouth, and the feline's eyes remained locked on the patch of StarMane Mint on the next cloud.

"So just sightseeing is out of the question, because why wouldn't we live the pirate's life for me? Cast Haste on all of us, Werylin, and you two head for that bridge. I'll swipe the plum, and everything else I can, and we'll haul ass." A halo of ice formed behind Aetheria as she spoke, and her hair shifted to white, her ears elongated, and her reflexes increased to match her elven body.

"You make quite the elven beauty, Aetheria, but red eyes on an elf are quite disturbing. Haste!" The spell took effect, and Arkaziel roused from his stupor.

"Do. Not. Miss. The. StarMane. Mint!" Ark told his minion with an absolute command.

"Get moving." Aetheria rolled her eyes and moved to brush a finger along the trunk of the plum tree. No calamity befell them from a mere touch. Aetheria, being Aetheria, shifted the entire plum tree into her repository. A sudden sense of pressure struck her hard enough to make her knees weaken for a brief moment, before the Flames within her blocked the outside influence. *I guess that's what my aura probably feels like to most people.* A deep roar shook the heavens, and the presence solidified beneath the sky gardens. Yet it closed rapidly.

Tendrils of ice shot from the halo behind her toward other plants as she hauled ass to the bridge. Whenever a tendril got within two meters of a plant, it disappeared into her repository. *This might work!*

Aetheria made it to the first bridge before the garden's guardian rose into view. The guardian was a green dragon, covered in vines and moss. It was much larger than Arkaziel's draconic form, easily over one hundred meters long. Worse, its unrestrained woken aura far exceeded the presence they had felt before. In its hibernation the dragon had felt like a Tier Five beast, but now that it had been roused, its aura was that of a sixth-tier beast.

"For Pete's sake. Run, you idiots!" Aetheria's tendril touched the first cloud as a test as she tried to shunt the whole cloud and the plants she had missed into her repository. It worked, to her surprise, and the dragon who had just landed on it fell unexpectedly.

None of the trio wasted the time to gape at the dragon as it lost precious seconds to regain altitude and fight the surges of wind currents. *No flying here, if a Tier Six dragon has to struggle with the wind.*

Once she crossed the glass bridge to the next garden, Aetheria sent her tendrils out to claim the plants. Werylin and Arkaziel were already to the next bridge, although she couldn't help but note that Arkaziel had swiped a few leaves of the StarMane Mint and chewed them while he ran.

- Take the left bridge on the next platform; I'll go right. Grab the most important stuff you can. -

The bridges all ended at the same final cloud, but there were four paths total by Aetheria's counting. There was, unfortunately, no way she could see that they would be able to acquire everything in this place. Yet even a single Tier Four or Five ambrosial fruit was a treasure beyond anything they had acquired previously. The temptation to throw caution aside and aim for a full sweep was great, but if one of them got caught by the dragon they would be dead.

"That was quite the trick, small one." The voice of the dragon shook the heavens, and temporarily deafened Aetheria.

Aetheria summoned a slew of large rocks, stored ice walls, and other large objects from her repository. With the ice tendrils as exit points, she yoinked the second garden into her repository and pelted the once-again-falling dragon with objects. None of them so much as left a scratch on the dragon. Even the hardened Ethereal walls of ice that had been strengthened by a decade of fighting demons shattered against the dragon's hide. Not even a single blemish marred the dragon's perfect green scales.

The move bought her a precious few moments to draw even more power into her body and sprint across the third garden. *There's no way he's going to fall for the same trick again. Unless he's been lobotomized to be a gardener, which he speaks far too well for, he's going to either strafe me or go ahead of me, next.*

True to her expectations, the dragon landed on the cloud ahead of her, the fourth platform since the start. It drew itself up majestically, and Aetheria felt a flicker of fear and intimidation travel through her, before the mental protection of the Flames safeguarded her mind.

"Very impressive. Few have managed to steal such bounty from me, but you have lost, little elf. Surrender to me, and I shall let you live."

Aetheria smiled as multicolored Flames surrounded her elven body.

"I'll take my chances!" Then she teleported, and the power of the Transcendent Flame of Khaos allowed Aetheria to break through the limitation on teleportation. She reappeared on the next bridge, and the fourth platform vanished under the dragon. A shocked screech escaped the majestic green dragon before it plummeted into the winds, and Aetheria dumped even more crap after the dragon. Hundreds of demonic weapons, more huge chunks of ice, ten of the large fruits off Cryostrialis, and an entire building from the Lost City of Atlanta.

"Oooh, yummy." The green dragon had caught the fruits of Cryostrialis, and flapped in place while it popped the Aetheria-sized fruits into its mouth like Aetheria would popcorn chicken. *I miss popcorn chicken.* The dragon hadn't even shook off the building, it had just ignored it entirely. *Talk about demotivating.*

The seventh platform beckoned to the Etherfrost Asura as she darted over the fifth platform. The end of the fifth had two bridges, one of which led directly to the seventh. She doubted teleportation would surprise the dragon again. The left sixth garden contained a Tier Five tree as the highest, while the right contained a Tier Six tree. Aetheria started across the bridge to the left platform, and true to her expectations the dragon landed on it and glared at her.

"The game is over now, little Asura." The green dragon inhaled, and then exhaled a stream of caustic force. Aetheria vanished in a burst of multicolor power, but she did not appear on the left platform at all. Instead, she appeared on the right bridge, while the left platform and bridge vanished into her repository, and the dragon fell. On a hunch, Aetheria also materialized a few of the Tier One and Two plants to drop onto the dragon.

The dragon cursed, and caught each of the precious plants. It even went so far as to create small new clouds to put the plants onto. With a smirk, Aetheria closed the distance to the last platform, tossing the least valuable plants at the dragon to keep it occupied.

"Come on, Aetheria! We're going through."

Werylin and Arkaziel jumped through the exit door, and seconds later Aetheria tossed one last plant at the dragon.

"I will have my revenge, Asura! We will meet again!"

Aetheria gave the dragon a big smile and an energetic wave.

"Sure will! I'd be happy to fight you when we are on equal footing!"

Then she stepped through the doorway to Floor 59, and after a brief stint of darkness, Aetheria found herself sitting at a wooden table. Before her was a plate of popcorn chicken and a mug of beer. Werylin sat to her left, and Arkaziel in humanoid form sat to her right. Opposite Aetheria sat a handsome young elf that Aetheria recognized.

"G-g-great-Grandpa?" The elf blinked repeatedly at Werylin, then eyed Aetheria, who still bore the appearance of a white-haired elf. "Who's your traveling companion, sire? Something about her aura makes me hurt."

"I go to the little girl's room and you give my food and beer to a stranger, Tasmin? Such a poor brother you are," Ithyrra, the lovely blonde druidess, exclaimed while she gave Aetheria a dirty look. It clicked then, that neither Werylin nor Arkaziel had food or beer in front of them. Aetheria's features flowed into her normal form, and she winked at Ithyrra.

"Sorry, I didn't mean to steal your beer. The popcorn chicken, however, I did mean to steal."

"Lady Aetheria!" the druidess exclaimed, while her brother also exclaimed the name in a very different tone. Apparently, he hadn't forgotten the crotch punch.

CHAPTER 18

Consolidation

The city of Concordance lay between the elven forest of Amaryllia and the beastkin nation of Primevellis. Concordance had grown into a powerful trade city over the years, with multiple trade routes connecting to other kingdoms. Until semirecent changes with their human neighbors, it had been one of the few places for other races to acquire elven trade goods and artisanry. Ithyrra and Tasmin had come on a quest to seek out some lore and items to help Tasmin break into Tier Three on the new path he had undertaken after the slightly embarrassing tale of Aetheria removing his Nether curse and his shift toward Aether cultivation.

Tasmin and Werylin now shared the distinction of being elves with access to Aether, which gave the elder Amaryllis something to bond over with his great-grandson. After a meal and a few beers, the current plan was for Werylin to join the two young elves and assist them in Tasmin's growth. Arkaziel had opted to join the trio, under the pretense that someone had to eat whatever they ended up killing. Aetheria suspected it more likely the cat wanted the druid to tell him how to grow more StarMane Mint. Apparently, the vaunted genetic memories of StarManes didn't contain much botany.

Left alone, and totally not just avoiding the awkwardness between herself and Ithyrra, Aetheria had pulled the Mellow Mallow from her repository. The small floating castle could barely be called a skykeep, but what it lacked in size it made up for in aesthetic and adorability. The small garden courtyard provided a serene place free of all distractions. She could focus without fear of disturbance.

First on Aetheria's agenda came the metal globe she had received. The replica she had copied of the one on display by Chronos took her some time to mimic. The liquid metal-like surface of the globe altered with slight pressure from her fingers. It felt like finger painting a non-Newtonian fluid. It took her most of an afternoon to transition the globe from resemblance of Grief into a replica of Arcadia. While Aetheria enjoyed artistic endeavors, discerning the path from A to B felt more like a mystery than art.

Once she managed to make the ice replica and the metal match, the sphere hardened. A golden inner glow illuminated the metal sphere, a blindingly bright prime meridian. Nothing further happened until she touched the line, and the metal shell disintegrated. In its place a detailed 3-D schematic of light-given substance came into view. A foreign presence brushed against her mind, and names, details, and other information became available to her via the now-annotated schematic, all in Ath, the divine language.

For the first time since her reincarnation, Aetheria had access to what felt like an augmented reality menu. Unfortunately, it was limited only to the schematic before her, but it still put a smile on her face. Overall, the design for the core before her seemed relatively straightforward. The annotated notes showed places where decisions could be made, but the greatest takeaway of the core wasn't that it bolstered power. The primary function of most cultivation cores, according to the books Aetheria had, was energy gathering and retention. Thanks to Frostfire, her Ethereal Sun and Origin Gate, she had the ability to draw unlimited power from the Origin, and thanks to Cryostrialis, a world tree in her repository, she had immense energy retention capabilities.

The base framework of the core before Aetheria was called an autopotency core, and its simplicity belied its power. Like her ability to employ cold as a concept, the autopotency core functioned on conceptual levels. Construction was something she could do that day, but Aetheria was determined to go through every annotation on the schematic and tweak things as much as possible before she created it. Why? Because it still had some of the holdovers of a normal Cultivator, and Aetheria wasn't that.

Her meridians were, and always would be, the limitation upon which her ability to employ Ethereal power bottlenecked. This schematic did not have anything to help with that problem, but one of the books they had obtained previously detailed a subcore modification that amplified meridian growth. *But Aetheria, why not just damage your meridians and let them instantly heal? Thanks for asking, me. It hurts like all hell, and I'm not a masochist.*

A second massive question loomed in her mind. Strength or speed. Werylin's speed and agility filled Aetheria with jealousy, while she had never batted an eye at the superior physical power of dragons, giants, or monsters. So, she opted for speed. She could always gain more strength via shapeshifting, but there seemed to be upper limits on obtaining more speed via physical shapeshifting.

Elemental, or conceptual, alignment didn't even need to be asked. Cold, or freezing, had been and remained the path she wanted to walk. Sure, being able to teleport via Khaos was fun, but the powers of Khaos only interested her in their ability to enhance her skills with cold. *Maybe that's why she gave me her Flame to begin with, because I had no interest in making it part of my primary path? In fact, none of the Primordial Flames really reflect my path either, I need to find out at what stage I can consider merging the Flames. The cold associated with Nyx's Flame fits my path slightly more than Ymir's, but neither is perfect.*

But Flames aren't the now subject.

Construction of the autopotency core could be completed entirely within her repository. It was, in fact, required to be forged within her soul, out of her very essence. The schematic detailed the process of creating soulsteel, a metallicized version of one's essence. *If I remember right, Aoibhe has soulsteel armor and a staff.*

The process was straightforward: visualize the object to be constructed, push your essence into the proper shape, then imbue it with the energy of your choice until transubstantiation occurs. Straightforward did not mean simple or easy. Aetheria dimly felt the passage of time while she slowly built up enough soulsteel to forge the elaborate pieces of the core. Aetheria risked damage to her soul by forging it into soulsteel and a single slipup could be fatal. The longer she worked, the more intense the fear of failure or self-injury grew. For whatever reason, her regeneration seemed to apply to her soul, which she discovered when a small error caused her to temporarily lose the sense of hearing and the problem fixed itself. When the last pieces were fit together like a jigsaw puzzle, the sphere flew into the sky of her repository, where it drew torrents of Ethereal power from Frostfire.

Initially, Aetheria counted the seconds as the core absorbed more and more Ethereal energy with no end in sight. When she passed one thousand seconds, she stopped counting. For minutes, she stared up into the current night sky, marveling at the beauty of the world's two moons.

Lub-dub. Lub-dub. Lub-dub.

The core came to life in time with her heart. With an anxious swallow, Aetheria pulled the core through her soul aperture and into her chest. This part of the process, thankfully, went of its own volition. She still had to control her thoughts and body, though, so the core could take its proper place. In the midst of her heartbeat, which matched the core's own, the flesh and blood heart vanished, and in its place now beat the cultivation core. She knew its name, too.

Ethereal power pushed through her body, her meridians expanded, and she had a new awareness of her own body. How or why the core improved her shapeshifting Aetheria didn't quite understand, but what she did understand was that her Etherfrost Flash Core of Autopotency had been forged successfully.

~Brace yourself, Etherfrost Asura.~ The mental whispers of Themis, Gatekeeper of the Origin, emerged into her soul from Frostfire.

Aetheria pushed her eyes shut, and quietly slipped a "Gosh darnit, not again!" out before tides of power flowed from the Origin into her soul, and from her soul into her body. It still felt unfair that Werylin hadn't had to suffer any type of blowback like this.

To Aetheria's suddenly super-sensitive eyes, the dim light of evening became a retina-searing radiance, the ever-present tides of Aether flowing through the air suddenly blistered her throat, the faint flow of Nether froze her blood, and the soft grass of the courtyard ruptured her skin with the briefest of touches. *Sensory overload, close your eyes. Focus on the lub-dub of our new core.*

Emotions and fatigue filled Aetheria's essence. How could one be fatigued with the equivalent of multiple fusion reactors' worth of power flooding their body? Easily, it turned out. The unstoppable currents of power that flowed through her expanding meridians required her to clamp down with all of her mind. She needed to slow and blunt the damage uncontrolled energy wracked upon her mortal vessel. The damage would heal, was healing even now, but if her physical condition deteriorated too much, a cataclysmic chain reaction of energies could be unleashed.

A soft, cool hand pressed against Aetheria's forehead.

"You can do this. Focus."

It was like Aetheria's soul was straining to hold Lake Superior in a few cobbled together soulsteel cups. She could do this, though. The human soul remained inviolable, regeneration buoyed her body, and she was an Asura. Saturation occurred, and hundreds of what she compared to storm drains opened in her pathways. Like every other time she had ranked up, pre-established dominos filled with redirected power and then one by one began to fall. An overly elaborate Rube Goldberg design set off within her, as previously unknown subspaces activated, but Aetheria had no chance to glimpse the magic and technology within herself.

I used to wonder how monks found the courage to self-immolate.

Here she was, willingly embracing the powers that were shattering her bones, rupturing her organs, squeezing her eyes until they burst. Around her the air turned to absolute zero. The stones and garden of the Mellow Mallow disintegrated, but she forced the castle back into her repository before it could suffer too much collateral damage. Instead, the air froze under her into a shelf. The hand on her head pressed stronger against her forehead, and comforting words were whispered into her ear. Night's hand was cold, but compared to Aetheria, it was an inferno—and yet it reassured her.

Even when her limbs exploded, re-formed, exploded again, transitioned into tendrils of ice, flared into diamond, and then bubbled into iced tea, that hand stayed pressed against her forehead, another held her shoulder, and soft words of encouragement whispered into her ear. Aetheria rode out the waves of transformative pain, until Helios started his ascent and Selene her descent, and the pain stopped.

Aetheria laughed for a good minute, before her companion finally spoke up.

"That looked painful." Nyx sat down next to Aetheria and stroked the human's multicolored hair.

"Yeah . . . it was rough." Aetheria shifted, laid her head in Nyx's lap. "Thanks, Callie."

"You've done well. Chronos overplayed his hand. All he needed to teach you was the soulsteel technique. You'd have figured out the rest of the core on your own, given a little more time. You still vastly outdid the basic design he and Aetherius cobbled together in that globe. How does it feel to be an Ethereal Scion?"

How does it feel? Aetheria almost laughed, but she let her mind wander over how she felt, beyond the exhaustion and strain on body and soul. The intuitive senses of her body had improved, and the fingers of her left hand had each become a different color of gemstone. Dawn's burgeoning light briefly illuminated her fingers before they returned to flesh.

"Awesome, I think. Even with the fatigue I can feel the differences, and I'm already on the path to recovery. I'll credit that to this amazing lap, though." Aetheria smiled fondly at Nyx, who still stroked her red-and-blue hair. Each time Nyx stroked Aetheria's hair, the red strands turned back to aqua blue.

"You did fantastic, Aes. You built a very different core than I anticipated."

"I suppose it'd be more normal for someone with my affinities to lean in to being a fortress, but I just had no interest in going that way. Now I can say zoom, zoom, zoom to myself all the time."

"I remember that commercial."

CHAPTER 19

The Orc-ening

I hate to interrupt you, Aetheria, but the elves summoned a big bad guy complete with an army; we could use you.~

Arkaziel's telepathic sending displayed an uncommon urgency. A mental vision of their location accompanied the telepathic SOS, then Aetheria felt a light wrap around her. Shadows and darkness crawled across her skin for a nanosecond that seemed to stretch on for eternity, and then shadows ejected the aqua-haired Asura. Her boots crushed, shattered rock underneath her, and Aetheria's abnormally heightened perceptions allowed her to study the scene before her.

At sixty-five meters long, Arkaziel's draconic-feline form dominated the top of a rocky hill. Two of the elves, Ithyrra and Tasmin, sheltered before Arkaziel's chest.

"Since when can you summon me?" Aetheria demanded of the dragon.

"A master can always summon his minions." The *duh* went unsaid, but the contemptuousness of Arkaziel's response summed up every cat Aetheria had ever met in her life.

To their rear rose sharp mountains, and before them swelled a series of rocky hills. To their left, a vast river fed by mountain waterfalls with high cliffs provided a natural safeguard. Swarms of enemies charged from an opposing hill, and funneled up the front hill where Werylin defended a natural bottleneck in a rocky passage. Those who attempted to circumvent the bottleneck via rough terrain on the right were sniped by the siblings' magic.

Arkaziel fended off both siege weapons and magic spells from a tall, brown-skinned figure on the opposite hill. Arkaziel still teetered on the edge of the fourth tier, and this enemy radiated a power in the middle of the fourth tier, which explained the scorch marks and minor injuries Ark suffered. Werylin seemed to be in much better condition, but he was holding back a literal army of orcs. The bulk of the army was Tier Two, and exceptionally weak compared to her companions. The orcs were on the same level as Werylin's great-grandchildren, though, and Ithyrra and Tasmin sent spell after spell to reduce the numbers of the army.

With a burst of rainbow-hued energy, Aetheria appeared behind the enemy mage on their command line. The moment Aetheria appeared, quite a few things happened simultaneously. Aetheria released an Etherfrost Nova, and the surrounding orcs who were lower tier froze completely and crumbled to dust, while the orc mage only had small patches of frost on his brown skin. Aetheria's teleport triggered contingency spells; a fireball exploded, centered on herself. The flames tickled her skin, extinguished by the massive flux of cold generated from her nova. Dozens of weapons reached for her before Aetheria's nova annihilated every living thing in ten meters, except for her and the mage.

"Who the hell are you?" The orc mage snarled, and a burst of fire from his hand exploded toward Aetheria with the strength of dragon's breath.

Aetheria sidestepped the fire; her new baseline physiology easily allowed her to dodge and outmaneuver the flames and mage both. Ice coalesced around her fist, and before the mage could swear about missing her, she shoved her gloved fingers into the orc's stomach. Ice covered the orc's abdomen, and spikes of ice spread into his body. Or that was what should have happened. Instead, the ice fizzled and exploded in a spray of steam that forced Aetheria back two steps.

"Ice can never win against the Skull Flame of Salazaar!"

Before Aetheria could ask who the hell Salazaar was, a nearby corpse's skull flew into the air and burst into flames. The flesh and organic bits burned off in a flurry of flames, and the fire in the empty sockets looked demonic to Aetheria.

Darkness swirled around Aetheria as she empowered her aura with the Primordial Flame of Nyx. Hungry night leached the heat from the skull, stole the flames from the skull's eyes, and then the still hungry darkness crept toward the shadow of the orc, who sputtered at the loss of its familiar demon.

"Looks like you can't keep it up." Aetheria closed the distance between them with what looked like a single step, and then her arm blurred. Ice materialized over her knuckles on her punching hand. The blow to the head delivered so much force the orc tumbled head over feet. A flash of flames sent him back to appear before Aetheria, and he exploded in a ring of fire.

"Mm." Aetheria sighed at the orc's failure to learn; the dark aspects of her aura consumed the ring of fire before it touched her. She contemptuously stepped closer, but when she swung her fist again, suddenly another orc stood where the mage had previously. This one was high Tier Four, held a shield and an axe, and exuded the battle-hardened killing intent of a warrior.

In fact, the counterattack came when Aetheria reeled at the unexpected concussion of fist to shield, and an axe deftly severed her right arm at the elbow.

"Wow, that barely hurt. That's a sharp axe." Blood sprayed from her wound for only the tiniest of seconds, before blood and flesh reconnected midway between the stump of her arm and the falling forearm. The muscles and tendons reconnected before the arm had fallen halfway to the ground. Aetheria took a step back to recenter her posture and took stock of where the mage went. The appearance of three twilight duplicates of Arkaziel on the next hill answered that for her.

~I can keep him entertained for a few minutes.~

Aetheria definitely took note that Arkaziel didn't claim he'd eat him, only keep the higher tiered enemy occupied. Maybe Arkaziel wasn't completely narcissistic?

"Doesn't look like I cut you hard enough," the orc warrior hissed.

The orc who faced off against her possessed elaborate armor, an axe inscribed with strange glyphs, and eyes that promised a quick death to opponents. They stepped to meet one another again. Aetheria's hand flared into diamond talons at the last moment, and she ripped deep gouges into the shield—but a magical field deflected her initial attack. When her attack petered out against the shield, the orc put more force behind it and slammed the shield into her right side. She took the blow full-on, used the momentum to spin her body, and drove a diamond spike from her elbow through the orc's helmet.

"Freeze," Aetheria commanded, and another Etherfrost Nova exploded from the spike that impaled the orc's head.

"Inferno Strike!" the orc exclaimed, and the spike at the center of the haft of the axe stabbed into her gut, flared red, and warmth filled Aetheria. Frost spread across the orc's skin. One eye froze solid, but still the warrior moved. Still, his killing intent burrowed under her skin with a promise of death even at the cost of his own life.

"Earth-shak-er . . . Cleave."

The orc growled out syllable after syllable, raised a hand one last time, and swung the axe down at Aetheria's shoulder while its shield slammed into her torso with just enough force to destabilize her entire posture. If she were a normal person. Instead, a third leg slipped from her hip to steady her, while her left hand slammed up after the shield impact to send it flying from his hands. Aetheria teleported out of the way of the overhead axe attack. She appeared in a flash of multicolored flames that appeared before and behind the orc. The telegraphed attack missed, and the axe-head plunged into the ground. Aetheria's diamond taloned hand plunged into his undefended back.

The orc's corpse fell to the ground and broke into hundreds of frozen pieces.

"I'm loving being an Ethereal Scion." Aetheria flicked the blood from her long taloned hand. "I felt powerful before, but this is another level."

Daylight wavered; darkness descended. For a brief moment, Aetheria wondered if Nyx had arrived to say something she had forgotten, but this wasn't Nyx. Arkaziel had absorbed all localized light, and he then released it in explosive projectiles. He created hundreds of light bolts, and each exploded with enough power to easily destroy clusters of ten rank-and-file orcs. It was the epitome of overkill, and Ithyrra and Tasmin looked a little shocked at the cataclysm unleashed by Arkaziel's annoyance.

The orcs routed. Not that many survived the apocalyptic light attack Arkaziel unleashed. The siblings picked off a few solitary retreating enemies.

"The mage teleported away," Arkaziel hissed when Aetheria made it back to the others.

"I wondered why you went full artillery mode. So what the heck happened here, guys?"

"You have entered the fourth tier. Congratulations. Your growth seems to have been quite explosive." Werylin congratulated Aetheria with a smile and the twinkle in his eye of a natural politician.

"Great-grandpa activated the stele across the way, and it summoned all these orcs!" Tasmin tattled on Werylin. Werylin just shrugged his shoulders, as if fighting armies of orcs was par for the course.

"How'd some pretty pillars summon an army of orcs? Seems odd," Aetheria questioned the others while she examined the far clusters of stelae on the far hill with telescopic vision.

Arkaziel had returned to his small black house cat shape and jumped up to make himself comfortable across Aetheria's shoulder.

"The orcs appear to have been waiting in ambush for someone to open the way to the other side of that portal. It would explain the eagerness of the half orc to sell us the information back in town; no doubt he was affiliated with this clan and directing gullible fools to open the gate for them. Their leader and his guard went through while the plebs and mage bought them time." Arkaziel's anger had already vanished, and his feline eyes were filled with anticipation.

"Alright, so what's on the other side of the portal? Cookies and milk, I'm sure." Aetheria found herself salivating at the mere idea of a cookie. *Maybe the next city will have a skilled baker.*

"An ancient fortress dedicated to Aetherius lies on the other side, with trials and treasure galore. The story we picked up in town was that you can obtain the Blessing of Aetherius at the temple by undergoing trials, and if you do well enough you can even obtain access to a treasure trove of light and sky magics." Arkaziel's greed for anything related to his own magic knew no limits, and his eyes shone with dreams of loot.

Aetheria did not press about Werylin's gung ho decisions that had started the battle. Instead she gestured to the still-open portal.

"Let's go; no point in letting the competition get ahead of us. Arkaziel, Werylin, buff up our young friends and let's get through the portal."

Werylin immediately cast three spells, one after another: Haste, Courage, and Shield. Arkaziel only cast a single spell, a life protection magic called Second Chance.

I should really learn a few useful spells myself; I don't contribute anything in terms of buffs.

The portal remained open, tantalizing them with its promised treasures and knowledge. "Why do a bunch of orcs want to get into a temple of Aetherius anyway? That part just doesn't make much sense," Aetheria said.

"To reconsecrate it to their god, who would get a major power boost from stealing from a Primordial like Aetherius," Arkaziel answered without any delay. "Plus, treasure is always useful."

"I, personally, love the sound of treasure. I'll go through first, if I don't tell you to follow after a ten count, come through spells blazing." Aetheria jumped through the portal and came out the other side in a small park. Clouds drifted across the city at "ground level," which made the case for yet another flying city. Clouds or flying cities were not enough to drop Aetheria's jaw anymore.

No, what astonished Aetheria was that she recognized this city! There were subtle changes, like not being underground in a cave, but the crystalline lattice structures, the serene beauty of the city's layout, and the infusion of Aether and Nether into everything made very clear this was some kind of sister city to Nova Azura, city of the Aetherials.

CHAPTER 20

Pax Azura

I*t's safe to come through. ~*

The two orcs left to guard the portal lay frozen and shattered on the cobblestones. Their corpses, a forgotten afterthought, had been discarded from her attention in favor of the most breathtaking city that Aetheria had ever seen. Before her lay a city in sparkling blue crystal. No, it wasn't blue crystal—the city had taken on the hues of the blue sky and fluffy clouds.

Unlike Nova Azura, this city dwelt in the clouds instead of a dark, dank cave.

Eagerness bubbled to the surface of Aetheria's thoughts, despite a feeling of serenity that had settled over her. The serenity, while enjoyable, felt hollow to Aetheria. For some reason her eyes were drawn toward a towering crystal structure at the center of the city. To her Ethereal Sight, pulses of energy radiated outward from the large tower with regular timing. Artificial serenity? No wonder it felt hollow.

Arkaziel, Werylin, Tasmin, and Ithyrra stepped into the beautiful city, which brought Aetheria's attention back to the crystal that floated above the platform the portal had formed on. Nearby pedestals contained plaques written in Ath.

Aetheria read the plaque to her companions. "The Azure Altar marks the first established structure of Pax Azura. The blue crystal connects to a global network of similar altars and allows instantaneous travel to anywhere within the network."

Of Aetheria's companions, only Werylin seemed to be put off by the hollow nature of harmony the tower cast over the area. At least, that is what she took his slight grimace to mean.

"So, we are looking for a temple of Aetherius. I believe we're looking for that building there." Aetheria pointed toward a structure made of four parts. Said building lay halfway between the crystal tower and their current location. The base of the temple was a tall central spire that rose high into the sky, and circling the spire were three inverse pyramids. To her Ethereal Sight it had the highest concentrations of Aether in the city, but the real giveaway was the familiar resonance with the Primordial Flame of Aetherius the building possessed.

"Then that's where we go. Maybe we can still beat the big orc there?" Ithyrra readied her staff for combat.

"Everything here is tied to Aether. How powerful were the Aetherials?" Tasmin's eyes darted between the temple Aetheria had gestured to and the strange tower in the center of the city.

"Their city on Grief was very similar to this, although it was subterranean, so Nova Azura had a higher concentration of Nether. Same architecture and building styles, although we're seeing fewer domes here. Similar to Nova Azura I'm not seeing many defensive structures, and I'll be a little surprised if there are any serious armories. The Aetherials seem to have been dedicated to peace, and fell back on their overwhelming affinity to Aether and Nether when diplomacy failed. Maybe they had laser swords."

"Why would they have laser swords? Laser swords seem highly ineffective." Werylin looked confused.

"Just something from my old world; don't worry about it. Aoibhe said I might be able to crack the knowledge orbs I obtained in Nova Azura in the fourth tier, but she was just throwing a shot in the dark, I think. Still, if we have time after taking care of this orc, I'd like to explore the city fully. Might be some clues here that would help me unlock the secrets of the Aetherials."

Arkaziel hopped onto Aetheria's shoulder in his small black house cat form.

"Most intelligent species view the Aetherials and other demigod-like races as bad luck, you know. Getting caught up in the whims of the gods inevitably leads to turmoil and sorrow." Arkaziel finished his warning by pointedly licking the back of his left paw.

"Quit trying to intimidate the kids. They know you're a StarMane, we all do, Mr. I Was Created by a Drunk God." Aetheria bopped Arkaziel on the nose.

"He's not wrong, actually. StarManes, Aetherials, Titans, and the other children of the Primordials all historically represent a tumultuous experience for mortal races when encountered. Look at the two of you, sweeping up a poor once-minstrel into a quest to defeat Misery." Werylin's phrasing of their quest did make Aetheria wonder about the sanity of their goal. *Can you even defeat Primordial gods? They're literally the concept, right? So how do you defeat Misery? Do I climb ten towers, then give her a hug after I punch her in the throat?*

"Oh, you poor old elf. Are you feeling the strain of your advanced age? Have one of these; it'll make you feel better." Aetheria flourished her hand dramatically and summoned a Tier Four golden apple from her repository. She tossed it to the minstrel, before she summoned a few more fruits, one for each member of the party and the siblings, who she tossed Tier Two fruit to, despite the brief flood of annoyance that filled her empathic bond to Arkaziel.

"I can't be the only one who finds these fruits basically being pudding inside weird, right?" Tasmin inquired. The golden apple Aetheria had tossed Tasmin was a lower quality version of the one she tossed to Werylin, and in addition to the physiological effects like extended lifespan, promotion of healing, and meridian growth, they increased one's Aether affinity.

"At least yours doesn't have fuzz all over it," Ithyrra grumbled, her small belt knife working diligently to free the succulent fruit from its brown, fuzzy protection.

"I'm *pretty* sure that one is plant affinity," Aetheria murmured, before she flourished her hand again to conjure her own fruit. For herself, Aetheria had decided on a black plum with deep red flesh, and a sweetness that led her to eat so fast that the fruit left dark red stains around her mouth, as if she were a vampire feasting upon blood. The plum held affinity to Nether, she was fairly certain, as the Primordial Flame of Nyx resonated with the fruit and gained a dramatic boost in strength.

"How are the plants doing after being transplanted?" Arkaziel asked between bites of dark, robust grapes known as Shadowberries.

"They're still alive, so there's a chance they'll produce more fruit down the road. I've tried to maintain their original planting. Nothing has died, but only the Aether and Nether aspected plants are really doing well. Some color changes . . . I think exposure to Frostfire is mutating them?" Aetheria finished lamely, with a not at all potentially disturbing conjecture.

"Alright, we've had our snacks. Let's get that orc." Werylin dusted his hands against his thighs. "After all, Aetheria looks like she ate his subordinates. Let's capitalize on that."

"Quit trying to move in on my gig, Aetheria. I do the eating around here." Arkaziel huffed at her, then his rough tongue cleaned one of her cheeks.

"Holy cows, Ark! Does your tongue double as an adamantite grater?" Aetheria rubbed at her cheek, surprised at the fact it had hurt quite so much.

"Uh. Yes? Adamantite lollypops are one of my favorite sweets. Those plums are tasty. I want one next time."

"Enough of the gags; let's catch the orc. It'd be best if we wiped them out before undergoing any trials in the temple. Getting ambushed is much less fun than doing the ambushing." Werylin's serious voice cut through the friendly ribbing and drew the whole party's attention to the seemingly peaceful wide avenues of Pax Azura.

"I'll take lead, Werylin you're on rearguard, Ark stays with the twins." Aetheria's voice dropped into business mode easily, and in moments the group repositioned. She set their pace to a fast walk. Little in the way of disturbances had been left to mark the passage of the orcs.

"How many of them even made it through the portal?"

"I counted ten, including the two you killed by the portal. All were at least Tier Three," Ithyrra answered, then pointed ahead. "I can sense three living beings ahead, in that garden to the right."

"Their actual leader was Tier Five, and the mage who escaped no doubt made it through the portal, too." Werylin's voice carried softly to the party. Aetheria had to wonder how he cast his voice like that, quiet, yet clearly audible. Magic? Skill? Maybe the minstrel had a history as a ventriloquist? *Don't laugh, don't laugh.*

"Ouch. Sucks to be them." Aetheria winced with the words.

Inside the eerie garden, three orcs had been bound by thick ivy against a single large tree. The vines tightened by the second, and the bark of the tree had already grown up to at least each of their knees.

"Let's not got in there. The trees don't feel evil, but they will attack us if we go in. Apparently it's been a very long time since they had any nourishment other than rain water." Ithyrra's wariness of the garden seemed quite fair to Aetheria. The trees emitted a Tier Four aura, twice that of the druidess's rank.

"So that's five down, five or six more to account for." Arkaziel did not seem deterred or cowed by people-eating trees.

~After we take care of the orcs let's take care of these trees, too. They might push me into Tier Four.~

Aetheria simply nodded at Arkaziel's telepathic sending.

The rest of their voyage to the temple passed unremarkably, until a block before the temple they caught sight of the orc mage. The mage did not dash toward the temple, but instead toward the spire at the city's center. In fact, the temple looked sealed still, with no signs of anyone having gone near it. After a brief discussion, they decided to follow the mage toward the Tower of Hollow Harmony.

"Ten life signs ahead," Ithyrra hissed quietly.

Aetheria wanted to sigh. The area around the tower and its energy pulses lit up like a second sun to her Ethereal Sight. Goosebumps formed on the back of her arms and neck. Something, or someone, had activated a relic of unimaginable power ahead.

"I want you two to stay back and snipe off people as best you can. Ark, you are on artillery and keeping them out of the crossfire, Werylin we're on the front lines. Whatever is happening is bad, so go big to start out with." While Aetheria spoke, a small pillar of ice arose, detailing the area ahead of them she could discern via her expanded senses. The courtyard before the pulsing tower contained eight life signs that she could detect, despite Ithyrra saying ten.

"Let me start the fight, then." Werylin stared at the position of the enemies marked by Aetheria, drew Harmonious Tempest, and walked quietly toward the corner of the building they had hid behind. Golden electrical charges flared to life around the elf and his katana, and as he stepped around the corner he exclaimed the words that unleashed hell.

"Stormstrike Symphony!"

The sky darkened before the searing radiance of lightning filled everyone's vision. Five thick bolts of lightning struck into the courtyard, and four humanoid figures were utterly obliterated. When the last bolt hit a large figure underneath a large blue crystal, it simply seemed to stay and connect the ground of Pax Azura to the sky above. Then the lightning dissipated, absorbed by the crystal above an orc with a Tier Five aura.

"Oh look at that, it's the elves' vaunted hero, the fallen Imperator." The orc laughed, lifted a hand, and the bolt of lightning emerged from the crystal above him to shoot at Werylin. Just before impact, as the elf's hair began to stand, Aetheria stepped in front of him and froze the lightning bolt. Even as the energy froze, she stashed it into her repository.

"It's not polite to regift. Know Mr. Tusky, Werylin?"

"Tribal chief. Vorgar the Vulgar, third Chieftain of the Green Tide. Whether he reincarnates or just is so generic no one can tell the difference between orcs is quite the mystery." Werylin's answer to Aetheria bordered on useless, but a history between them definitely explained the harsh look the minstrel had.

"No paladin will save you this time, elf!" The blue crystal above Vorgar shone with a dangerous glint, before energy flowed out of it. That energy took the form of a transparent green humanoid woman. The elemental clearly radiated air energy, and before Aetheria could cry out at finally seeing a sylph, the woman raised a hand, and three massive tornadoes formed between the orcs and their enemies.

"I didn't plan to spend today fighting a tornado." Aetheria sighed.

CHAPTER 21

Vorgar the Vulgar

Three colossal tornadoes bore down on the party at the command of the Sylph. With the young elves' presence, they couldn't risk letting any attacks from the Tier Five orc hit them, or they would need another phoenix heart and feathers.

"Wipe out the support and keep the kids safe; I'll keep the Sylph and Vorgar occupied."

Aetheria stepped forward three steps and expanded her domain to cover ten meters to her sides and front. With her tiered-up physiology, more energy than ever flowed through her soul aperture into her body, her capacity to hold Ethereal power in each cell had doubled from her capabilities just yesterday, and thicker meridians meant she could dump more energy, and faster, into her body.

Aetheria raised her left arm to about shoulder height, and used her hand as a focus to direct the Primordial Flame of Ymir and the Primordial Flame of Aetherius before her. Gusts of wind picked up behind her and shot toward the tornadoes. The gusts carried with them an instantaneously generated blizzard. A whiteout blocked the world before her, even as pillars of ice rose in the path of tornadoes.

"Brrrr. How do you hang around with Lady Aetheria and not wear a winter coat all the time, Gramps?" Ithyrra asked the older elf, and Aetheria had to bite her lip to maintain composure.

"I'm not done yet. Keep watching."

Aetheria's right hand pointed to the sky, and she bent the tides of red Ethereal energy to her will, combined them with the Primordial Flame of Ymir and the Primordial Flame of Thalassa, to construct a huge ball of ice in the sky, obscured from Vorgar and the Sylph by the whiteout she'd created. The tornadoes had lost all forward momentum against the unending winter, and with each second lost a little bit of their rotational force and power.

"I didn't know you could fight a Sylph that way." Werylin seemed impressed.

"It's just a minor elemental lady. She could've just teleported over and killed it, more efficient and less likely to give the kids frostbite." Arkaziel disparaged the method Aetheria had chosen, but Aetheria could feel the envy in their bond. He hated it when people did things he couldn't.

~I'm shattering the winds now. Be ready to leap through and eat the Sylph, Ark.~

+Aye, aye, Captain.+

"The blizzard is about to drop. You're on guard duty, old man." Arkaziel had altered his form to his draconic-feline appearance, and had grown to about five meters long. The moment the tornadoes lost their cohesion the blizzard stopped, and Arkaziel took a running jump through where one of the pillars had been. The green elemental had no time to look shocked, as the StarMane came through the whiteout conditions and bit her. Again, and again, until there was nothing left of the elemental besides a few glowing spectral bits on Arkaziel's snout.

The head of Vorgar the Vulgar's axe crashed into Aetheria's hand just centimeters in front of Arkaziel's head. The StarMane looked shocked to have been imperiled, and saved, without even having time to react in any way. Arkaziel opted to sink into the shadows. He reappeared next to Werylin in a guarded stance.

+How'd you block that, Aetheria? I didn't even see you or him move.+

~I'm Tier Four now, remember? I'll explain in a bit.~

Aetheria had not blocked the axe without a cost. The ice she had armored her palm with had shattered, and even at her densest she hadn't been able to stop the blade without it piercing her hand a solid inch. The bleeding ceased the moment she pulled her hand free, and Vorgar smirked at her, idly caressing the haft of his axe.

"Not bad, for a human. This might be fun. Don't disappoint me like that poor excuse for a warrior behind you. Elves make terrible warriors." Vorgar opted for a slow approach to Aetheria. His will honed into murderous intent meant to intimidate her. It failed to sway Aetheria in any way, beyond nervousness about fighting someone a full tier above her.

"I'll make sure your tombstone mentions that you asked for it." Aetheria's voice remained flat with the delivery of words, and she activated her new Cultivator's core. *Lub-dub. Lub-dub.* Her heartbeat felt overwhelmingly loud as she activated the Flash aspect of her Etherfrost Flash Core. A loud buzzing sound filled her mind, like the noise electronics made when pushed to perform—coil whine. Did Aetheria speed up, did time slow down, or was it a combination of the two? From her perspective time slowed down to a standstill.

Even Vorgar moved in slow motion now that she had entered Flash. Aetheria stepped into melee with the orc, and unleashed a flurry of slashes with her Luxentian talons. She delivered a total of twenty strikes, stepped backward, strafed to the side, and unleashed another flurry of assaults on his unprotected backside.

Lub-dub.

The strain on her body felt like nothing she had experienced before. The rush of speed compared to the rest of existence barely moving was a strange kind of high, like a rush of adrenaline and endorphins at once, mixed with a feeling of supreme capability. When Aetheria stepped back from the ambush attack, she blurred to a stop in front of her companions, and the world slammed back to normal. She still had gas in the tank, but just that tiny bit of Flash had exhausted her significantly.

Blood shot from Vorgar in fountains, while forty wounds appeared across his body. None were individually deep, but combined they were significant. The orc's thick skin had been difficult to pierce even with the talons, a damning reminder of the difference in their rank.

Vorgar laughed madly. The orc's eyes shone red, and his killing intent exceeded anything Aetheria had experienced before. *Berserker!*

Orcs appeared in a swarm behind the chieftain, brought forth from his inner world. While the majority of them were weaklings at Tier Two, there were a smattering of Tier Three and Four elites within the roughly one hundred orcs Vorgar had summoned.

~Ark!~

Aetheria raised her hand, and a nova of Etherfrost burst forth. The blast held a multicolored radiance of the Transcendent Flame of Khaos, and even Vorgar couldn't ignore it entirely when it struck him. Patches of frost appeared on the berserk orc's skin, before his own frozen blood formed spikes to stab him internally. While this mostly just angered Vorgar, those he had summoned suffered far worse. If he were not controlled by bloodlust maybe he would've protected his troops, but instead the wave of power passed through the lower rank orcs unhindered. Layers of unbreakable ice (to a Tier Two) formed over joints; icicles formed in their mouths, gagging them; and the ground turned into an ice rink.

Darkness enveloped the battlefield. The bright blue of the crystal above Vorgar and the aqua beacon of Aetheria's hair and ruby eyes were the only sources of light not dimmed, before light returned to reveal a terrifying black and white sphere of twilight power in Arkaziel's jaw. His jaw opened, and he exhaled. A thick beam of annihilation passed through the forces around the berserk orc. Each orc killed by the beam became a pitch-black negative energy spirit that then turned on its surviving brethren. The ranks behind Vorgar who survived the dragon's breath were not the lucky ones.

His subordinates mowed down like wheat pushed the already berserk Vorgar past the limits of rage. The ice that barely restrained him shattered without him even moving. Even at a distance of twenty meters between him and Aetheria, slashes suddenly appeared, healed, and appeared again on her skin.

"That's no domain. That's just his killing intent. We need to take him out, now!" The blade of Werylin's Harmonious Tempest flickered deftly before the elf, deflecting the slashes created from pure intent away from Aetheria and himself.

"Any idea on how to—oh shit!" Vorgar had leaped through the air, and landed with a shockwave that pushed Aetheria back a dozen meters, interrupting her words. The orc didn't wait for her to recover but charged straight to her and swung his axe wildly. In the depths of rage, what the orc lost in wits he made up for in strength, speed, and durability. Each generated wind projectiles, and even after she dodged them, the wind slashes changed trajectory and sped toward her back.

"Ope! Let me sneak by you." Aetheria dodged past Werylin, whose deft parry work protected himself and his descendants, then leaped into the air and changed her shape. Four paws the size of limos crashed into the ground when she landed. She had abandoned humanoid form in favor of an Etherfrost Dragon, and her tier-up showed. The ice-blue scales that covered her body shone with an intensity they previously had not. The intensity of her presence, and mass, were such that the entire floating city shuddered just a little when she landed.

Vorgar's wild swings could not miss a target as large as Aetheria's Etherfrost Dragon form. The rage-filled orc embedded his axe deep into her left foreleg, eliciting a roar of pain from Aetheria. She had anticipated taking a few hits with this strategy, but anticipating pain and experiencing it were two different things. No matter how often she got hurt, she knew she'd heal from it, but it still hurt. A lot.

Etherfrost Flash!

Aetheria activated her core again. The world froze around her, and her Cultivator's core pulled power through her soul aperture in a previously unmatched quantity, to the point it strained her soul. No wonder she couldn't maintain this level of exertion for long. So much power flowed through her draconic form that excess energy bled into the air from her body, and wisps of blue and red Ethereal power were carried in the wind.

Aetheria did not get fancy. Her new and improved aura as a Tier Four Etherfrost Dragon was impressive, but with her core and affinities added into the mix, it came close to the cold she had created when she tiered up. She summoned the Primordial Flames of Nyx and Ymir on her right paw, and stomped down on Vorgar. Repeatedly. When her paw came away after the fifth one, she exhaled a breath attack that disintegrated the ground around the Vulgar orc.

+I'll finish him!+

Arkaziel's telepathic sending pulled Aetheria out of her own mini-rampage, and she hopped backward, returning to human form as she disengaged her core. She had a lot of work to do if she wanted to freely use her core's abilities for more than a couple of seconds at a time.

Arkaziel darted in when Aetheria retreated. Vorgar had taken a lot of damage, but broken limbs were going to heal all too soon without intervention. Intervention Arkaziel provided, when the cat plunged spears of darkness into the orc's already open wounds, rooted around inside of the fleshy bag of the orc's body, and then shoved a hand into the orc to pull out his core, which Arkaziel proceeded to gulp down without chewing, and then he did the same to the orc.

"Ew!"

Aetheria was not the only one to exclaim her disgust. Ithyrra, Tasmin, and Werylin all echoed her.

Arkaziel didn't care. In fact, the cat purred, then stretched out like he might take a nap.

"Oh, wow. I got to eat his inner world. I feel totally satisfied, like I just completed the first step of my life's work. His core was tasty, in a decadent and primal way. Like when you eat hearts and livers." Arkaziel let out a big yawn and closed his eyes.

"Go take your trials, I'm going to nap." Arkaziel seemed to expect to be obeyed, so when Aetheria picked up his house-cat-sized form and carried him, he hissed a little before he decided this was acceptable.

CHAPTER 22

The Boring City

Days passed while Aetheria waited for the trio of elves to finish up with the temple. Unlike Nova Azura, Pax Azura had been raided times beyond count. Its immense bookshelves had been looted, its indexes stolen, its treasures plundered. Even the secret rooms she found in the library had been ransacked. Fortunately, she found some intact treatises in the administration building, which also happened to be the same building that fired the pulses of harmony. Unfortunately, they were full of nearly useless information about censuses, governing principles, and a massive thesis on waste management.

While Aetheria and Arkaziel awaited the elves, the cat broke into the fourth tier. The digestion of Vorgar and the Sylph had pushed Arkaziel through the final bit he had been short, and the proud cat declared himself a beast emperor after a nap on the fifth day.

On the sixth day they grew bored of sifting through looted buildings and entered the temple of Aetherius. They left multiple notes for the elves, in case they did not make up the head start the elves had on them.

Aetheria found the trial to be a joke. The first four levels of the trial were basic Aether control, which took less time to do than it did for her to walk to the next trial. In fact, all of the trials were very basic, and for kicks she started to complete them with Nether or just her regular ice affinities, and surprisingly the challenges still counted as completed. Which didn't make a lot of sense to her, until she considered the fact that maybe some Aetherials gained access only to Aether or Nether, or perhaps the temple was for all races, and its conditions of completion were suitably broad and general?

It gave her some confidence that Ithyrra would be able to complete the trials, at least.

The final trial proved interesting, though. Aetheria sat in a comfortable chair while the projection asked her questions. The projection had blue skin, red hair, purple eyes, and wore a priestess's vestments with incredibly bountiful cleavage on display, topped off with a lab coat, for some reason.

"Why do you use Aether?"

"I mostly use Ethereal energy these days."

"*Why do you use Aether?*" the projection asked again, as if Aetheria hadn't answered anything.

"I use it when I need some holy aspects, I guess."

"*Do you possess a genuine belief in the power and teachings of Aetherius?*"

"Well, he is my adopted father, so yeah."

The projection stopped responding. Aetheria waited. After an hour, a projection of an Administrator appeared.

"Your cat ate the trial core. You may either teleport yourself out, or follow the trail you took to reach here. Our apologies." Before Aetheria could question the projection, it vanished.

"Of course he did. Dammit, Ark." Aetheria teleported back to the outside to find the elves lounging around in the middle of the promenade. As an Ethereal Scion, her teleportation range had increased considerably.

"Did all three of you succeed?" Her words drew the elves out of their own meditations, and Werylin actually appeared to be surprised by her sudden appearance.

"Yes, the tests were relatively easy. It felt condescending, really. All three of us have been blessed by Aetherius now. I gained fuller access to Aether, and a deeply increased wind affinity." Werylin brushed a finger through the air and a small, neon-blue, aetheric dust devil appeared and bounced around until it dissipated naturally.

"I gained access to holy light." Tasmin's declaration was short, but those six words were full of pride.

"The obnoxious blue lady talked to me like I was a toddler. I got a bit snippy with her, but they still gave me a blessing that boosted my storm affinity, and she taught me some interesting weather spells. If she weren't a projection, I think she would've hit on me." The blonde druidess laughed.

A large dragon-shaped shadow fell over them, and then a tiny black cat dropped onto Aetheria's shoulder.

"I didn't interrupt anyone's boons, did I?" Arkaziel asked while his claws extended into Aetheria's shoulder, and he made an elaborate show of getting himself comfortable.

"No, all three of us reached our goals," Werylin answered with a shake of his head.

"You interrupted mine, you jerk! I was talking to the projection lady, then the system crashed. What the heck, Ark?" Aetheria pretended to be more upset about it than she was.

"Ooops. Sorry. The projection said I couldn't have a blessing, since I'm a StarMane. We got into an argument about how racist that is, and she agreed. So she offered me her life as recompense, and showed me the way to the temple core. I figured you were long done, if I had already finished such an easy trial and took a twenty-minute walk to the core to boot." Arkaziel rebuffed her mock offense with mock sincerity.

Two people with an empathic and telepathic bond fake arguing seemed to bore the elves, who hadn't been that interested in the scenario to begin with.

"Alright, this town is now mine, in the name of Aetheria, Looter of Flying Cities." That was the only warning Aetheria gave the others, before the whole city vanished inside of her repository, and everyone fell, but within a hundred meters or so, they all ended up safely on the back of a large Etherfrost Dragon. So ended the adventure on Floor 59. Once they dropped the twins off at the town and said their goodbyes, which were still really awkward for Aetheria and Ithyrra, they proceeded on to Floor 60.

The trio appeared in a portal room. Similar rooms, separated by transparent glass, extended to either side. Each of these square rooms were identical. Black marble floors, white luminescent crystal ceiling, glass walls on three sides, and a portal on the fourth wall. A sign hung on the wall opposite the portal, that read "Please wait for the attendant before exiting your arrival room."

"Oh man, this is SubterraNaut!" Arkaziel's claws dug into Aetheria's shoulder in testament to his excitedness.

"One of your ancestors passed through here?" Werylin asked while he examined the equivalent of an entry port. "With that name, it is subterranean?"

"You know it." Arkaziel answered both questions at once. "They've got a bit more technology here, kind of like your world, Aetheria, but lots of magic, too. Big-time interdimensional trade city, since SubterraNaut is a massive creature that burrows infinitely through the earth. It's a beast sovereign, so even its excrement is a valuable commodity."

Arkaziel's explanation of the creature got cut short by the arrival of their attendant with a tablet and a clipboard. The attendant brushed a badge against the other side of the door, and the door swung open for them to enter.

"Welcome to SubterraNaut, travelers. Let's see here, intelligent cat, an elf, and oh my, are you perchance Aetherius's challenger and daughter, the Etherfrost Asura, Aetheria?" The tablet device the man had displayed information about each of them. Most of it was wrong, of course, since it thought Arkaziel was just an intelligent cat.

"I am indeed Aetheria," she answered with a half-contained laugh. She was on the fence about knowledge of her identity spreading throughout all of existence being a good or bad thing.

"When you exit the chamber, the Ritual of Arrival will commence. Our Chief Executive will surely be interested in meeting with you during your stay, doubly so if the commotion of the arrival wakes our beloved Naut from his nap. As a Very Important Person I will guide you through customs, and escort you to an inn befitting your station. Unless you know anyone within our fair city or have prearranged accommodations?"

Aetheria could feel the proverbial high society closing in around her all too quickly, but Werylin took the lead with the attendant as if he were her steward. *I bet he had a steward when he was the Imperator.*

Werylin fielded the customs and the attendant's other queries, which only increased after they left the glass room and the gongs of celebration at the arrival of a challenger swept the city. The process went more smoothly with the charming elf acting as a wall between others and Aetheria to get the bureaucratic necessities handled, which included a meeting with the Chief Executive in two days, a license to both buy and sell in the city, and a visa for the three which lasted for a year and could be renewed for a mere five thousand gold.

Either Aetheria's reputation had grown significantly, or their Chief Executive had an ulterior motive upon the reception of a new challenger. While the attendant finished the last of their paperwork, he looked shocked at a pop-up on his tablet, and informed them, "You've been accorded loan of Embershaper Manor for the duration of your stay, one of the premiere estates lent to the most influential of Very Important People."

~Ark, do you know who this city belongs to, Creator-wise?~

+Gaia. Maybe. Thirty percent sure.+

Aetheria chose to ignore Arkaziel's guess.

+Kidding, kidding. It was created by Vulcan. The giant worm eats earth forever, producing all sorts of refined materials for the people inside it. Leave it to a crafter to make a living city that refines crafting materials for you.+

The clean marble rooms and technology on display did not make her think of Vulcan.

"That's very kind of your government. Please pass on my thanks." Aetheria tried to convey sincerity with a soft smile, but the attendant just squirmed under her gaze. *Probably creeped out by the Light of the Origin, no need to take a blow to my self-esteem.*

An alert dinged on the attendant's tablet, and the awkwardness did not last long, thanks to the arrival of their chariot. No horses pulled the chariot, which resembled a limousine to Aetheria.

"No need to be concerned. Our chariots are completely safe. They are self-driving, although this one has a living driver to help facilitate your needs during your stay with us. Please enjoy your time with Naut, and remember, while we do not forbid fighting, we do ask all Cultivators to avoid causing damage to Naut. You are obligated to do your best to ensure a minimalization of collateral damage." The last, the attendant said with a touch of humor. Even Tier Four Cultivators were unlikely to be able to scratch a Tier Six on accident, even from the inside.

+That warning isn't for show. They charge you for all damage you cause.+

"This way, lady challenger, sirs." Their chariot driver was a stout dwarf with a glorious red beard separated into three braids, and a mustache that likewise ended in braids, which drooped down to rest with the beard braids. He wore an immaculate suit with long tails.

"I am Sebastian Embershard. Welcome to SubterraNaut."

Inside, the vehicle reminded Aetheria of cars enough to be eerily familiar, though the fact that the sky was worm innards unsettled her. It certainly didn't help foster a sense of safety, or cleanliness.

Arkaziel hated the car ride. He shifted in annoyance on Aetheria's lap the whole way.

"I'm hungry!"

Aetheria and Werylin rolled their eyes at the StarMane, but their temporary manservant laughed and nodded toward the manor after opening the door.

"If you'll follow me, good lady and lords, the house chef has already been notified of your arrival, and after a light lunch I shall give you a guided tour of the estate. Shall I arrange visitation to the next auction, or any specific merchants?"

Aetheria's eyes lit up, and her right hand tingled just a little.

CHAPTER 23

Preparations and Capital

Aetheria could really get used to the life of luxury. Embershaper Manor was a beautiful three-story building. About two-thirds of its exterior walls were beautifully designed glass, while the other third was composite mixed materials. She had been expecting a dour estate for some tired noble, but they'd given her a modern styled mansion any Earth oligarch would be happy to call their first or second home.

The first day of their stay in the manor had gone smoothly, and ended in one of Aetheria's favorite luxuries, a hot bath. Sure, she had a bathtub in her repository and could conjure water and heat, but neither Arkaziel nor Werylin seemed to understand her desire for baths. *At least Arkaziel has an excuse; he's a cat. What's Werylin's excuse?*

The next morning, after a delightful breakfast, the trio split up to tackle their to-do list. Werylin had been tasked with information gathering. The attendant had mentioned Naut had an issue, and Aetheria wanted to know what it was before their meeting with the Chief Executive. Arkaziel's task was to gather crafting and alchemical ingredients, as well as to round out the pantry in Aetheria's repository. The cat had muttered something about gourmet spices before he left the manor in human form. Aetheria's responsibility was to sell off some of their loot, get estimates on some of the items they were willing to sell, and otherwise prepare for the next auction.

Sebastian had insisted on chauffeuring Aetheria around Naut, which simplified the logistics of her trips. The dwarf butler knew all the reputable, and disreputable, merchants, bankers, and various collectors in the worm city. Her interest in finding out about the items she had for sale or trade waned throughout the tedium of inspection and analysis for each of said items. No, she didn't care that the orcish axe had been made from some corrupted orichalcum, nor did she particularly want to listen to the art appraiser wax poetic about some of the elvish paintings she'd decided to sell from the Mellow Mallow.

What she did care about was that by the time ringing bells announced noon, she had managed to sell off six million gold pieces worth of junk from her repository and had gotten a quivering old alchemist to label one of her fifth-tier ambrosial fruits as priceless. Hard currency could be augmented with barter items, but you needed to have a rough idea as to value if you wanted to interrupt an auction with a barter bid. Apparently, while a valid tactic to slow down bids, it was frowned upon if done more than once by a bidding party, and the auctioneer would fine you if you dramatically overestimated the value of an item. *Sounds like a racket to me. I'm just supposed to trust some auctioneer to be impartial and not try to make a buck off me because he can?*

While the trio had succeeded so far, Werylin had seemed greatly relieved to be in a place with access to crafters and vendors of (hopefully) sufficient skill to create equipment on their level. Werylin himself had only a few enchanted items after his rebirth, Arkaziel generally didn't use gear, and Aetheria just relied on raw power and immortality. With equipment to reinforce their abilities, their battle capability could skyrocket. Which meant parting with some of their exotic treasures, reagents, and accumulated wealth, and also scouting crafters. Maybe Aetheria should have done this sooner for herself, but her baseline capabilities needed exploration. In fact, she wasn't certain she had realized half of her current potential.

Sebastian parked the vehicle before a building with an obsidian façade.

"Are you sure you wish to meet with Hin Ton, Lady Aetheria?" the serious dwarf asked when she stepped into the street and examined the dark building before them.

"You say he's the best crafter in Naut to work with darkness and night. That means he's my man. Why the consternation?" Aetheria wore her usual adventuring outfit, which was a strong contrast to the elaborate tailed coat that the butler wore.

"There are few of the fae in Naut, Lady Aetheria, and fewer still of the shadow fae. While the stance of Naut is to accept all without prejudice, many find the shadow fae to be difficult to trust. I have allowed my bias to color my words. Forget that I said anything, Lady Aetheria." Surely, the dour butler did not whisper "But be on your guard" under his breath after he reprimanded himself.

The parlor of the obsidian-clad building was dimly lit. A girl Aetheria judged to be thirteen sat at a reception desk playing with what looked suspiciously like a smartphone. The young woman ignored the pair until Aetheria stopped just before the desk, at which point she looked up and greeted them with a smile.

"Welcome to Ton Crafters. Do you have an appointment?"

Aetheria had been wrong. She was no teenager. When her eyes met the girl's eyes, she saw the age and power there. Despite looking like a teenager, the woman was a third tier Cultivator, and probably older than Aetheria. *She looks mostly human, other than the pale skin, the black sclera, and slightly elongated ears.*

"Yes, it should be under the name Aetheria."

"Let's see, you're to meet with . . . Oh, Hin Ton. I'll take you back to see him now." Most people probably did not get to go straight into a meeting with the clan elder; her increased renown had proven useful so far.

The back halls were even gloomier than the entrance, but Aetheria had Ethereal Sight to fall back on in the dark hallways. Well, that and the illumination provided by her hair and eyes. Portraits of clan elders lined the walls, interspersed with depictions of previous masterworks created by the famed shadow artisans. The silver glint to the eyes of the secretary and the butler were similar. *Do dwarves and shadow fae have some kind of dark or night vision?*

Here you are, Lady Aetheria. Your butler may wait in the outer study; Grandpa Hin only sees the client themselves, no attendants."

A raised hand stopped Sebastian from protesting.

"That's fine, thank you . . . ?" Embarrassment crossed Aetheria's face, realizing she didn't know the woman's name. The shadow fae looked embarrassed herself.

"I forgot to introduce myself. My apologies. I am called Xian. Shall we have tea while your lady goes about her business, Sebastian?" Xian asked the dwarf in a playful tone. Obviously, this wasn't the first time the butler had brought a VIP here. Aetheria left the two to chitchat in the study, and entered the main office.

Hin Ton's office was beautiful if a bit two note. The shelves, desk, and chairs were all crafted of a dark hardwood that seemed to hold the essence of shadow itself. The few light sources in the room were muted, and located to accentuate the darkness rather than banish it. The shelves full of books piqued her curiosity, but she couldn't recognize the language on the bindings.

"Lady Aetheria, it is an honor to meet a daughter of the divine Aetherius. Welcome to my humble studio."

Hin had the appearance of an emo teenage boy back on Earth. Pale skin, black-accented makeup, a thin build that almost had the grace of an elf, and the same black-on-black eyes that Xian had. The artisan wore a comfortable-looking robe that seemed a mix between a bathrobe and a wizard's robe, and had a plushness that made her think of velour.

"It's an honor to meet you as well; you come most highly recommended." Not for the first time, Aetheria bemoaned the lack of pre-scripted dialogue choices in scenarios like this. She just had to push through, and rely on her connections, status, and power to counteract any faux pas she made.

Hin gestured to a set of chairs that faced one another, with a coffee table between them. Tea and snacks had been set out. Otherwise only a notepad lay on the table, on Hin's side.

"Please, sit. What can I do for you? It is rare for one of lineage to light to come to us of darkness."

Aetheria smiled and let the Primordial Flame of Nyx flicker through her aura and around her body for a few brief moments. Once she got the slight widening of eyes reaction she expected, she let the power disperse.

"I myself am of a mixed lineage, as you can see. I wanted to commission a few items from your clan, one for myself, and potentially two for my bonded companion. If possible, I would like to aid the process by providing Nyx's touch to the items."

"My apologies, the informants did not mention your relation to Nyx." Given the annoyance in the man's voice, Aetheria suspected said informants were going to catch an earful for that omission.

"Your requests seem reasonable. Let us get down to the details on what you need from the pieces of equipment, and what we can and cannot do." Hin rubbed his hands together and got the notepad ready. When she described what she wanted, and that one of the items was a twilight item, the fae looked surprised, but once she said she'd be happy to pay for any outside expertise they needed outside of normal, the problems all smoothed out. Still, it was over an hour before she escaped.

Aetheria had to endure a similar routine twice more, once with an artisan who specialized in frost, and the other with one who worked on the principles of elven harmony. The latter refused to commit to any commissions until they met Werylin. An annoying requirement, but they explained a need to match item to wielder in-person. A minor delay at worst. Unfortunately, the sole Ethereal crafter in all of Naut refused to meet with her, with no reason for refusal given.

Over breakfast next morning the three reviewed their progress. The next auction was to be held in seven days, so they had more time to prepare and deal with local craftspeople than they initially thought. Arkaziel had managed to raise upwards of ten million gold the previous day, which made Aetheria suspect the StarMane had been using his genetic memories to gather both useful and valuable items on their path so far. Werylin, the former head of House Amaryllis and one time Elven Imperator, was ironically the poorest of the trio. Aetheria gave him some items to sell off, including a few lower tier ambrosial fruits. Sebastian had also provided Werylin contact with a few elves in the city which might prove useful.

Aetheria herself had her meeting with the Chief Executive of SubterraNaut, which involved traveling to another section of Naut. The sleek, futuristic designed city was not the only section of SubterraNaut. Naut itself was a worm, and no one had ever successfully plotted its full length. Each section of Naut consisted of approximately one hundred and twenty square kilometers, and gravity drew toward the outside of the worm. Due to the size and anatomy of Naut, one could not see the opposite side of the segment, but Aetheria's head swam to think that everything would be literally upside down over there, from her perspective.

In fact, it didn't seem possible by the normal laws of physics. Naut had been designed by a god, though, so natural laws being subverted wasn't shocking.

Nonetheless, travel between segments seemed anticlimactic to Aetheria.

"These gates take close to a hundred years to make," Sebastian told her. "Temporary gates can be made in a week, but over time Naut will destroy them. As powerful as Naut is, it is only by Vulcan's blessing we can gain access to a new segment. Outside the six cultivated segments, it gets dangerous. Naut doesn't recognize us as welcome in the others, so his immune system will attack you out in the wilds. Then there are the parasites, diseases, and assorted hangers-on—people Naut ate who managed to escape his digestive tract over the years. Few of us leave the safety of the civilized segments."

"Is that a . . . traffic light?" The vehicle had stopped, and when she looked to see why, a familiar red light proved to be the answer.

"Yes. The arrival sector doesn't have them, very few large vehicles like the manor's in segment one. The administration segment, or two, is where the conglomerates, guilds, and government set up shop, so much more vehicle traffic and less pedestrians. Both have transit stations, though. We will reach the Executive Retreat in five minutes, Lady Aetheria."

"Why are there crowds around that building?"

One of the large structures that reminded her of a glass bank back on Earth had quite a large crowd with signs around it. Most of the languages on the signs were not ones Aetheria knew.

"Protesting the newest segment opening. Since Naut stopped moving a week after they opened the last temporary gate, people are blaming the Infrastructure Association for the current situation."

CHAPTER 24

Astrum Nexus

Six hours after Aetheria entered the Chief Executive's office, she arrived at the temporary gate to segment seven in an armored people carrier. The men and women on duty here were armed with a mixture of martial weapons, guns, and magical technology. As much as Aetheria wanted to examine what looked like a mini gun made from wands, she had been hired to scout the new segment.

A weaselfolk man in the brown uniform of Naut approached her. He looked shocked that the Chief Executive had sent a single person.

"Welcome to the cursed gate, Lady Asura. You've been cleared already, so go through whenever you want. We don't recommend taking any vehicles—they tend to attract problems more than help." The laughter when he called it the cursed gate seemed out of place to Aetheria, but she supposed he was being glib.

"I'll head through now, thanks." Aetheria walked toward the gate. On this side of the segment Naut's flesh had been covered with other materials, which made the bare worm flesh of the segment wall even more out of place.

Aetheria felt that the disconnect between appearance and reality only grew the more one ascended the tiers. If she went full-out with everything she had, it wasn't likely she'd do much more than scratch the segment walls. It made the metal gate even more impressive: the ritual and technology to create them were proprietary secrets from Vulcan himself. *Can rituals exceed your tier? I'll have to research that. Maybe it's a property of divine rituals?*

Arkaziel and Werylin had been given other tasks to do, so she couldn't ask them. Aetheria had given Arkaziel even more goods from her repository to sell, while Werylin had assumed the duty of wrangling crafters. The next auction was in six-and-a-half days; the boys would handle the auction in case she hadn't returned by then. *I hope Arkaziel doesn't blow our fortune on a snack.*

The black metal gate looked cursed.

"Is it supposed to look like this?"

"Yes, ma'am, that's how the temporary gates look. After the permeance rituals they take on the silver look the other gates all have." The weaselfolk man had followed her and answered her inquiry.

"Creepy." Aetheria laughed, then walked up to the black metal of the gate. The access key she had been given worked, and the door slid open with a rumble.

"If you happen to see someone who looks like me, but whiter in her fur, please bring her back. We've lost thirty-two people to reconnaissance so far."

"I'll keep my eyes open and bring back anyone I can." Aetheria hid the grimace, and instead offered the worried officer what she hoped was an encouraging smile.

"Here I go; wish me luck."

Aetheria walked through the black door, and it sealed shut once she was clear.

The new segment looked nothing like the furnished, built-up segments of SubterraNaut. This segment was wild, and the ground and ceiling were the same flesh as the segment walls. There were minute traces of soil here and there, but clearly the ground of previous segments had been artificially constructed. No lighting had been placed here—the only light came from pools of phosphorescent liquid or herself. In the far distance a red, flickering glow that danced like fire, drew her attention. Her Ethereal Sight revealed this place to be a treasure trove of crafting ingredients.

Alright. Might as well help myself to some Tier Six materials while I head for the red glow.

Nothing dangerous had shown itself, but she was next to the gate. There was no sign of the missing scouts yet. With minimal soil, tracking was out. If she got within twenty meters of a scout and they still had their locator, the small handheld device they'd given her would lead her to it. If something had eaten or destroyed the locators, though, the device would be useless.

Her first step made a terrible squelch on the worm flesh. She grimaced in displeasure, then recommitted to see this through. The faster she got this done, the faster she could have a bath and go to an auction. She wasn't about to miss the experience of an auction in an interdimensional trade city.

The glowing pools of liquid were highly concentrated with power. When she passed each, she got just close enough to transfer them into her repository. Nothing fought her; no strange creatures jumped out. She encountered three of the scout vehicles after a half hour of jogging. No damage was evident, but when she went to start them the ignition failed on all three. None of the systems on the vehicles functioned at all.

A quick check of the scanning device she had been given showed it too had lost power.

"Fun. I'm glad I'm not relying on a flashlight."

Aetheria gestured, and three white-blue orbs of ice shimmered into existence. Individually the three orbs provided light equivalent to a 60-watt bulb, and she commanded them to float slightly above her head, where they rotated in a slow orbit. Light was only their secondary purpose.

More pools of secretions, the occasional tree or shrub, was all Aetheria saw as she jogged toward the red glow. The Chief Executive had assured her there was the possibility of monsters, parasites, and other strange phenomena inside unexplored segments. Yet after two hours of jogging, and kilometers of travel, she hadn't seen anything of interest.

Two hours later she approached the red glow. It was a fire. Two fires, actually. One was a massive bonfire with tiny shapes arranged around it. The other red glow came from a forge, where a large figure worked. Said figure was about two meters tall, and to her Ethereal Sight he might as well been composed entirely of aetheric flames.

The small figures around the bonfire were the missing scouts or . . . memorial statues for the scouts? Each was made of metal, not flesh.

"They'll be fine when we've concluded our business." The two-meter-tall man spoke in a confident, deep voice. "I lack the means to properly entertain mortals."

"You are Vulcan?"

"Yes, I am Vulcan, and you are Aetheria. Grab that hammer and work the forge with me. I am told you learned the craft in Solace, and that you can make soulsteel. Create two ingots of that size." Vulcan gestured to an ingot of adamantite that lay casually atop the forge.

"Are we forging something together?" Aetheria couldn't keep the confusion out of her question, but she began the process of creating soulsteel ingots within her repository.

"Chronos *commissioned* me to build you a weapon." Vulcan's tone had layers to it that Aetheria didn't quite grasp. Was Vulcan angry, proud, or annoyed? Probably all three.

"A weapon? I usually fight barehanded."

"The soulsteel will reveal what is needed, don't worry."

Don't worry. Words that immediately filled Aetheria with worry, but she could always just not use it or melt it back into her soul if the result wasn't something that fit her.

Two ingots dropped next to Vulcan. At first glance it looked nothing like metal, but transparent ice. It even radiated cold enough to make Vulcan shiver, and the forge fires to waver for a few moments, but then the forge grew hotter, as if it had been insulted by its momentary weakness to the cold.

"Quickly done, that. You do not appear to be lessened by the creation either. Did you already have them made?" Vulcan eyed her with a hint of respect, but it was marginal at best.

"No, I just made them. Why? I haven't experienced a lessening or weakening when using soulsteel before?"

"You are human, but not. The Primordial Flames you carry mark your soul as an anomaly to begin with. No human has ever carried more than two Primordial Flames without imploding. *Pop. Boom.*" The mental image of a human just imploding into a super bouncing ball filled Aetheria's imagination when Vulcan made the *pop* sound.

The details of the vision were clear, to the point she was fairly sure he'd used a sending of mental imagery via the sound, somehow. Of course, the *boom* followed when the bouncing ball exploded in a shower of gore.

"Yeah, that's me. The nonhuman human. So how do we do this? I've only forged soulsteel inside myself, never in the physical."

"The same way we work all metal. Hammers." Vulcan seemed to share her love of sarcasm. "You have two Divine Orbs, I'm told. I suggest you use them here."

Aetheria looked lost. "If I have two Divine Orbs, you might need to be a little more specific about it? I don't know what you mean."

"Aether and Nether aspected. You took them from Nova Azura?" Vulcan shook his head.

"Oh. These." Two gemstones appeared in her hands.

"Still locked, even. That's probably for the best; I can refashion the locks to work as information limiters."

"I won't lose all the information contained in them?" Aetheria had worried, for a moment, that Vulcan had lied about who hired him.

"No. Not unless you are terrible with a hammer, but Durgan was once my apprentice, until Aetherius lured him away from me."

Aetheria hefted the hammer that the God of Fire had gestured to before and gave it a few trial swings through the air.

"Guess it's time to find out."

The sound of hammering filled the air. Vulcan worked much the way Durgan had in Solace, and he spoke only the minimal words needed to convey his instructions. They had been hammering for an hour, when Vulcan laughed wildly and looked at Aetheria as if she were insane.

"What kind of soul do you have, lass? We'll start the imbuement soon. Two flames per bracelet."

"Bracelet? I thought we were forging a weapon?"

"Oh, it will be a weapon. A very interesting weapon. Better start thinking of names. If you can think of a better name than I can, I'll add a blessing of my own."

Aetheria laughed but said nothing. She wasn't sure how to respond to that. It was a nice offer, after all, but Vulcan's fire was the opposite of her cold. She didn't understand how that would work.

Sure enough, they forged two bracelets, rings, and then spent what felt like a year forging chain mesh gloves. The finished item consisted of a ring, mesh glove, and a bracelet for each hand. The left glove held the broken-down Nether orb interwoven with the mesh, and the bracelet held the Primordial Flame of Nyx and Ymir. The right glove had the Aether orb, and the bracelet held the Primordial Flame of Aetherius and Thalassa.

The right ring held the Transcendent Flame of Khaos, and the left, thanks to a strange clock Vulcan had pulled out of his pocket, held the Transcendent Flame of Chronos. Symmetry in aspect and power were very important, according to Vulcan.

However, Aetheria's lack of an internal Flame of Chronos made it the odd Flame out in terms of symmetry.

"So, what are you going to name them?"

"Astrum Nexus. There's a lot going on with these."

Aetheria didn't have to deal with the difficulty of getting them on; she simply touched them, and then they reappeared properly equipped. They were already bound to her soul, having been forged out of the soulsteel she had made. The gems all shone with dim external light, and the soulsteel had retained its transparent blue-ice appearance, even after being heated and forged. The rings each bore a single word in the divine language, Ath, that shimmered to her Ethereal Sight. The left said *Time*, the right said *Chaos*.

Vulcan thumbed his chin for a moment, then nodded.

"Normally one would name each, but they do form one greater whole. Very well. Be blessed by your creator, Vulcan approves of you."

Vulcan touched the gloves with those words, and a power settled over Aetheria. She had no idea what the power was, of course.

"Don't suppose you'll tell me what the blessing does?"

"It's more fun when you figure it out on your own. Now take the mortals and go back to the city. Once I depart, the parasites will emerge. If you use Astrum Nexus, you'll make it to the gate before I finish packing the forge." Vulcan smirked.

Aetheria quickly shifted the scouts into her repository and waved at Vulcan.

"Thanks for letting me work with you. It was educational."

Then Aetheria ran.

CHAPTER 25

Auction

While Aetheria would have loved to test out her new weapons, she didn't want to risk getting pulled into fights with enemies that could be a higher tier than herself, when she had people's loved ones depending on her. On paper, she was immortal and could survive anything. There are a lot of things you can do to tie up immortals for a very long time, especially if said immortal is weaker than you are. So, Aetheria activated her flash core. When she did so, the inscription of time on her left ring glowed, and the energy drain her super-speed mode took was reduced significantly.

The sustainability of Flash Mode had increased so much she reached the temporary gate before fatigue forced her to deactivate it.

Aetheria hummed a certain Proclaimers song while she fiddled with the passcode to open the gate. Whatever no-power trick Vulcan used had not harmed the key, and the door opened as it should have. A small, paranoid part of her mind had been afraid this had all been a trap, a ruse to lock her down in a place she couldn't escape. It seemed like the thing a goddess who literally represented Misery would do, but instead the weaselfolk officer from before saluted her. His eyes widened as the world on the other side of the door flashed and filled with monsters, before the door sealed shut.

"What in Vulcan's name was all of that?"

Aetheria let out a breath, happy she'd avoided fighting Tier Five worms.

"Ironic you should mention him. He was out there. Nice guy. You might want to call your medics over."

The scouts, still encased in metal, appeared around Aetheria. While she examined them a new sensation filled her mind. Something akin to an augmented reality tooltip popped up on each of the metal-encased scouts. It said *Status: Metal Cocoon of Protection—A devote prayer to Vulcan will remove this effect.*

"Oh my gooses," Aetheria exclaimed while she rubbed her hands together excitedly. *Did he give me an AR display? A system? What is this?*

Other people did not show status effects. Instead, it seemed to be related to crafting and items. When she looked at her boots she instinctively knew they were

Nidhogg's Fury, and their marginal abilities. Other knowledge also filled her mind, such as how to upgrade the boots, the logic behind why they had been crafted the way they had, and how to repair and maintain them. Whatever blessing Vulcan had given her, it seemed exceptionally useful.

"Lady Aetheria, where did the scouts come from?" the weasel-man asked in bewilderment. "And why are they metal?"

"It's a protective blessing from Vulcan. A devout believer praying to Vulcan will end the protection. How long was I gone?"

"Six days."

"Sorry to save and dash, but I've got an engagement to make. Please update the Chief Executive on what happened, and I'd avoid going through that door. All the baddies are back." Multicolored flames exploded around Aetheria when she finished speaking, and she reappeared in the room she had been using in Embershaper Manor.

~Ark, have you and Werylin left yet?~

+We're getting ready now; meet us out front. Sebastian is pulling the car around.+

While a real shower would be ideal, an impromptu summoned wall of water to walk through and shapeshifting to different clothes would have to suffice for the short term. *I don't miss worrying about that kind of stuff so much. Shapeshifting is amazing.*

When Aetheria stepped out of the door to join Werylin and Arkaziel she whistled. Both had acquired new outfits in the time she'd been gone. Arkaziel wore a dark blue suit with a golden glitter design that evoked scales on the lapels. It contrasted his dark skin and yellow eyes excellently. Werylin, always handsome, wore elaborate braids in his violet hair, and he wore a dark blue twin-tailed coat. Both of the men had incorporated blue into their outfits, and it put a little smirk on her lips.

"Did you plan to wear something else if I didn't make it back in time?"

Arkaziel puffed out his chest, but Werylin spoke first.

"Yes, we had fallback options prepared if you didn't make it back."

"Did you manage to get any idea on what kind of goods would be on the block?"

"No, the auctioneer's guild doesn't share that information with outsiders. If you did well on the mission for the Chief Executive, maybe they'll change their tune next time, but we're going in blind on this." Werylin shrugged.

"Some of those who are selling things off let slip there are some armor and accessories going up. Apparently challengers are known for having more money than sense." Arkaziel's eyes sparkled, and his smirk annoyed Aetheria.

The trio had time to make a brief plan, and went through their singular and combined funds, and what was the highest priority. Not long after their review, the limo pulled into the VIP line at the auction house. It looked more like a theater, in Aetheria's mind, but the large building had been built with an eye toward aesthetic rather than function. There was no fanfare outside the establishment, just people exiting vehicles and entering in an orderly manner. The three followed others' example, and once at the door were led to a private balcony by an attendant. Each of the three had their own bidding number, and corresponding paddles waited for them.

"If you need anything, I will be close by. Press that button there if you have any questions or need anything." The attendant seemed nice enough, but Aetheria didn't pay her much attention. Instead, she tried to glimpse a peek at the others in nearby balconies, or down in the normal seats. With her Ethereal Sight she was able to see clearly through most of the wards and identification masks, but a few outliers had privacy wards greater than her perception.

The balcony had fine synthetic sofas for them to relax on, and several tablets that displayed the itinerary for the auction. No similar information seemed to be made available to those in the lower seating.

"Oh, Werylin, look at item number three." Aetheria was shocked, and a moment later, so was Werylin.

"If the item lives up to its name . . . " The elf trailed off, no doubt wondering if he'd brought enough gold.

"Ladies and gentlemen, the auction will now begin. Now, as a reminder of the rules, all bids will be treated as an incremental increase of one hundred gold per bid by default. The bid adjustment on your paddle should be used if you wish to use a different amount. Remember, the default bid increase is reset after a bid."

The establishment was dark, with only the stage, auctioneer, and assistants in full light. A massive screen covered the whole back wall above the stage, so anyone could have a detailed view of items or the stage regardless of where they sat.

"There's a demigod or two here, Aetheria. I sense there are a few people in Tier Five as well. We may wish to mingle afterward, if you want to have a glimpse of the factions that rule the universe."

"They all climbed towers?" Aetheria scoffed a little, then frowned when Arkaziel shook his head.

"If you've cleared a tower you gain access to the ability to purchase teleportation tokens. They don't work inside of the tower, but you can access the trade cities with them from the greater universe. Very handy for sect elders to help boost their elite fledglings before sending them into a tower."

"That sounds handy. We'll talk more later." Aetheria shushed Arkaziel as they brought out the first item. All three of them laughed, because it was one of the items they had brought to auction.

"Here we have an Ambrosial Dragon Fruit. It has been certified to be a Tier Four fruit. This Dragon Fruit will bolster your fire affinity, lifespan, purify your body of toxins, and a whole host of other remarkable effects associated with the veritable food of the gods."

Bidding exploded. Within minutes the bid war had reached ten million gold, and the contest between the two holdouts raged on. One had tight concealment around their identity, aura, and appearance. The other person bidding against the unknown party was a dragonoid race with red scales, and a Tier Five aura that was poorly concealed.

The bidding stalled at twenty million. Apparently even the incredibly wealthy had not thought to bring more than that much hard coin. The uptick on each bid had dropped to ten gold coins, and this carried on for minutes. Aetheria's tablet lit up with a ding, and a prompt asked her if she would accept a barter in addition to the money. The item name was there, but no description of what it was, except an estimated value of ten million. She hit "Yes," and watched the auctioneer bang his gavel.

"Sold! Twenty-three million and three hundred thousand gold and the Wyrmheart Talisman, thank you, #213."

The next item passed quickly; a Tier Three staff that sold for half a million gold.

"Next we have the Verseblade's Aetherweave Resonance. A storied armor from the realm of Arcadia. A remnant of the ancient Sylvan tradition in the belief in the power of the Words of Creation. Bidding will start at two hundred and fifty thousand gold coins."

This third item looked like Japanese clothing instead of fantasy armor. In fact, Aetheria felt very certain she was looking at a hakama. Between the katana and the wakizashi, if Werylin wore that armor there was no way in which she could avoid having a serious conversation about Earth's Japan with the elf. When her eyes fell upon it, unlike the fruit, she got an augmented reality pop-up about the item.

"Buy that," Aetheria hissed at the elf.

Werylin's silver eyes had lit up at the description and look of the clothing.

The bidding went up quickly to a million gold, but it became apparent quickly that Werylin got caught in bidding against one other person. There were enough private balconies and boxes that she couldn't sense them all. Despite her best attempts to discern who Werylin was bidding against, Aetheria didn't find the elf's opponent.

"Four million, going once . . ." The item was sold to Werylin.

"My apologies, once-Imperator. I would not have driven the price up so had I known I was bidding against an acquaintance." The soft voice belonged to the projection of a green-skinned naked woman, that had appeared within the balcony.

"It's fine, Deirdre. It is well worth the money. After all, there's far more wealth in being an attendant to an Asura than there ever was in being the Imperator." Werylin, somehow, resisted the beauty of the dryad. Aetheria had a very hard time not staring, until it felt a little too much like crossing a line that she didn't want to.

"You, a mere attendant? To whom? Ahh. The human with the power of Khaos, I see. Visit any of our enclaves, Werylin. You have been missed." The dryad was kind to Werylin, and left giving Aetheria a knowing smirk before the projection vanished.

"At least I won the armor. Why were you so insistent I buy it? It is up my alley, suspiciously so if Dierdre is here, but, and beg my pardon, since when do you know much about armor?"

"Don't let her off with the old I-read-it-in-a-book excuse," Arkaziel helpfully chirped.

"Oh well. I ran into Vulcan on that mission, he gave me a blessing, and now I just know things about some items. We have the material to upgrade that armor, already."

"I could almost kiss you, Aetheria." Werylin grinned.

"Shush. This next auction I might go all in on." Arkaziel commanded silence from his minions.

"Is that . . . ?"

"Yes, it's a fishing pole and tackle box." Arkaziel nodded sagely, and raw hunger lit his face.

CHAPTER 26

The Chest

Aetheria refrained from asking Arkaziel a whole litany of questions that crossed her mind. Why did a shapeshifting dragon-cat need a fishing pole? Since when did he limit himself to catching one fish at a time? Why spend time angling when he could just use Devouring Darkness to catch entire schools of fish at a time? It did not make any sense to her; Arkaziel was lazy and gluttonous. Nor did he respect his prey. She and Werylin watched in silence as their companion spent seven hundred and fifty thousand gold pieces on a tackle box and a fishing pole.

"I won!" the capricious StarMane cheered, then frowned when the other two showed no enthusiasm for his victory.

"Good job?" Aetheria smiled and patted him on the head. This gesture felt very awkward to her, given Arkaziel's current form as a tall human.

"Now, here we have a unique book of poetry by the previous governor of the City of Verses." the auctioneer continued. The book gave her no indications of its contents through her new Vulcan-gifted senses. The description made it sound entirely mundane, and no one bid on it until Aetheria felt pity and matched the opening bid of a thousand gold coins. She won without contest. *What is the City of Verses, anyway?*

A series of duds followed, with only one or two people even bothering to bid at all.

"Lot ten is sure to excite! Fresh from the forges of Master Aventinus is a new entry in the dancing sword series!" There were murmurs of appreciation and applause throughout the ground seating. When Aetheria finally caught a glimpse of the sword, it didn't seem that spectacular. It was solidly a Tier Two weapon that could fight on its own to protect the wielder. It did not have many upgrade options according to her new boon, which she had taken to calling Forge Insight.

"Why's it going for so much?" Aetheria asked her companions, as the bidding crossed two million gold and continued to climb sharply.

"It's a masterwork sword. Aventinus is one of the best swordsmiths in Naut. A weapon like that given to a disciple in the first tier would make their ascent into second and third tier much smoother. It could also do the opposite, though, and produce a paper tiger swordsman who has failed to elevate their skills due to overreliance on the automated weapon. The best use for it, I think, would be to give it to a mage." Werylin offered his take on why the sword had value.

It is a power leveling item? Aetheria laughed a little when the sword sold for eight million gold.

"Behold! A mysterious item said to have been plucked from the Shores of Chaos! What is in this locked chest? Who knows! How do you open it? We don't have a clue. Is it worth even a single copper, or all of the gold in Naut? It's a mystery to us. Bidding starts at ten gold."

Forge Insight told her nothing about the chest. Her senses told her nothing about the chest. Yet as Aetheria gazed at it, an incredible sense of longing filled her. A desire to hold it, open it, and be reunited with what was inside overtook her so strongly she started to shake.

"Are you okay, Blue?" Arkaziel asked meaningfully. Had her emotions bled into their empathic bond?

"Uh." It was all Aetheria could say, but she bid on the chest, again and again.

"Why are you bidding on a clear money trap," Werylin asked.

The goosebumps slowly faded. Aetheria could only compare the brief experience to an aura prior to a migraine: her ability to speak, think, and feel had been impacted. It had not been a mental attack, or a migraine, though, it had emanated from Origin into her soul. Additionally, she noticed the other two had moved a little away from her. Her earrings, Ocean's Serenity, were extremely cold to the touch. So much so that they had radiated enough cold to make the other two uncomfortable. *Did the effects fade because the earrings dampened the emotions from whoever is behind the Origin?*

"I'm in my right mind. It might be a curiosity trap, but it might hold answers to some very pressing questions for me." Aetheria continued to bid while she spoke. Every time she looked at the chest on the stage, she felt a small resurgence of the longing for the chest.

"What are the Shores of Chaos?" Aetheria wondered aloud.

"It is another dimension. I don't know if it is like the towers, an overlapping realm like the astral, or a higher plane like the Origin. It's just the Shores of Chaos." Arkaziel shrugged after his explanation.

"It is said that to reach the sixth tier on a path involving the Words of Creation requires traversing the Shores of Chaos, but I know no more than Arkaziel." Werylin frowned.

"Sold! For two million gold." Even the auctioneer seemed shocked that someone would pay so much for a chest they might not even be able to open, and if they could, might contain anything from a sealed monstrous god to someone's favorite sandwich. Aetheria felt a little unsure about spending so much money on it as well, but money was meant to be spent, right?

Aetheria spaced out after the next series of items were again for lower tier interests.

"This next item has been flagged by our establishment as being of dubious origination and quality. The seller claims this ribbon to have been used as the hair tie of a silver dragon, and that it has fantastical properties for beast Cultivators. This is all unverified, so bid accordingly."

Arkaziel's eyes narrowed.

"Silver dragon my ass."

"Recognize it?" Aetheria watched as no one bid on it, until some lesser bids started on the common seats.

"I do." Arkaziel didn't expound on that, but the grimness in his voice told Aetheria this had something to do with genetic memories, not something that had occurred since his hatching.

The bidding petered out at twenty thousand, when Arkaziel entered. When he pushed it up to seventy-five thousand his opponent dropped out of the bidding, but then another bidder drove the price up. Someone on one of the balconies Aetheria could only partially sense drove the price up to a half million before they let Arkaziel win.

"Idiots." Arkaziel shook his head and smirked after he won. "I would have paid all of our gold pieces for that."

"Why?" Werylin and Aetheria asked simultaneously.

"You'll see! Oh yes, you'll see." Arkaziel rubbed his hands together like a supervillain and laughed happily. It creeped Aetheria out a bit. "I'm just happy; be happy for me."

Only Arkaziel could make a plea like "be happy for me" sound like a royal command mixed with the implication a good friend would be happy for him, all at the same time.

The rest of the items were uninteresting, until the second to last item came up.

"A tome by one of the Primordials! Written in their divine language, sealed by a Primordial lock, it could be the work of a lifetime to unlock and decipher!" Aetheria almost choked with laughter at that statement. She and Arkaziel both spoke and read Ath, while the Primordial lock could be opened with the use of any Primordial Flame. At least, that's what Forge Insight told her when she studied the book. It certainly looked divine, with its golden cover, adamantite bindings and lock, and a one-word title in Ath: *Flames*.

"Bidding shall start at three million gold."

Bids flew in, although people were playing it relatively safe in terms of increments of ten thousand. Aetheria bid occasionally, while she hit the button to summon the attendant.

"How can I assist you?"

Bidding had crossed five million.

"I would like to offer a barter bid. One of my previously cleared items, the Tier Six Ambrosial Lemon of Wind." Aetheria handed the attendant the paperwork with the analysis.

"Of course, Lady Aetheria. Let me enter this into the system right now."

The attendant pulled a tablet out, scanned a barcode, and then spoke into a smartphone-looking device. The current bid had already broke twelve million. On stage, the auctioneer's face suddenly paled at what appeared on his screen.

"We have a barter bid!" he exclaimed, to the sound of boos from the floor crowd. "Now, now, this one has already been estimated, and its estimate is priceless!" A shock went through the auction hall, while Aetheria grinned to herself. Sure, the ambrosial fruits were valuable, but they could only be used once, albeit by anyone.

"Are there any counteroffers?"

Silence reigned. Agitation radiated from a few of the balconies, especially from the ones which belonged to the demigods. Furious negotiation may have been occurring in those rooms, but ultimately no one made a counteroffer.

"Sold! Now, we come to the final item for the night."

"Was it worth it? None of us really care about wind, but still, we only have a few of the Tier Six fruits." Werylin did not seem offended, merely curious.

"Err. I suppose I should have asked you two before I did that. Yes, it was worth it. The book's title is *Flames*. If Primordials keep coming out of the woodwork to give me their Flames, there has to be a reason for it, right? Chronos all but promised me his down the road, too. I have a copy of it in my gloves, but it's different using a copy held in the Astrum Nexus than it is the ones in my soul."

"When he gave you my leather necklace?" Arkaziel tapped the moon attached to the leather collar around his neck. He insisted it was a necklace, not a collar, even though it very clearly was the kind of collar a cat would wear back on Earth.

"Yeah. Although he imbued some into my new weapon."

The other two gave her a disbelieving look.

"Our final item for the day is a Tier Five ambrosial fruit . . ." the auctioneer continued, as the audience gasped and cooed. Everyone on the balconies already knew it was coming, thanks to the schedule provided. Perhaps Aetheria could thank the schedule for the lack of competition for the book?

"Just wait until next auction when they do the lemon. Let's head down to receive our items and deliver the lemon." Bids on the apricot had already reached twenty million when they left the balcony, and the attendant escorted them to the VIP offices.

A very out-of-place man in loose pants and a simple shirt waited to meet Arkaziel.

"You the one who purchased my rod and kit?" He extended a hand, and surprisingly, Arkaziel extended his own and shook it.

"Of course, Glaucus. I'll treat it with the respect it is due. I intend to fish up Pontus and eat him."

"Ugh. You're just as bad as your father was. But good luck, I guess. Even I wouldn't try to catch a crab with a fishing rod." The fisher, or Glaucus, shook his head, but seemed to realize the level of narcissistic delusion he was dealing with. "Good luck, I suppose."

The man vanished.

"Care to explain?" Aetheria arched a brow.

"Minor god of fishing; he and Dad have history."

While their paperwork was being written up, other auction attendants funneled into the VIP offices, along with a lot of very well-dressed, self-important people, none of whom were the kind of people who liked to wait.

"You there!" A brash young man with white hair, blue eyes, and the touch of divinity afforded by Aether, spoke to Aetheria and her group. "Your presence offends me; depart so that I may conclude my business in a timely manner. After all, I just spent forty-two million gold. Flee from the presence of divine Aeroth!" The prideful declaration, the stance, the muddied but still divine aura, it all made Aetheria want to slap the man, but instead she smiled.

"No. I don't think we will."

What looked like steam came out of the demigod's ears.

"How dare you!"

CHAPTER 27

Arrogant Young Master

It wasn't really steam that wafted off the demigod before them, of course. From what Aetheria could tell with Ethereal Sight it was holy (Aether) energy manifested through the godling's aura. It might intimidate a first tier Cultivator, maybe even a second tier, but anyone on the third tier of their path and beyond had surpassed tricks like that. She noticed something else while she stared at the demigod, though: she could see his Divine Flame with Ethereal Sight.

It was a nearly transparent Flame. Light, airy, insubstantial, and frankly it struck Aetheria as something of a letdown that the first Flame she identified in another person would be such a flimsy thing. Distracted by her discovery she nearly failed to notice that Aeroth had stepped forward and his hand was flying toward her face. She activated her domain, and the godling's hand suddenly slowed. To others it must look like Aeroth's hand suddenly fought against a strong current, and then the godling was overpowered, all forward momentum with his slap lost. He frowned.

Aetheria reviewed the rules of the auction house in her mind. Assault was forbidden, so she couldn't strike the idiot, even in self-defense. There were any number of things she could do that skirted the letter of the rules, but the spirit of them meant not annihilating this arrogant jerk, which she really wanted to do. Humiliation would have to suffice.

"If you wish, Lady Aetheria, you may invoke Rule 3, subclause C, to refuse sale of your item to this . . . customer." The attendant they had been provided, Aetheria thought her name to be Arissa, had stepped in while Aetheria mulled her options.

Aeroth had not yet recovered from the shock of his absolute failure to strike a stupid mortal at the hands of a mere domain.

"Which one is subclause C, again?" Werylin asked the attendant helpfully.

"That clause specifies clients shall not attempt to directly interfere with the seller of an item they sold at auction. Since you sold the fruit that Mr. Aeroth won the bid for, this would qualify, to say nothing of the numerous other violations he nearly committed before being stopped by the lady challenger's fantastic use of a domain."

A lightbulb turned on above Aeroth's head. Sadly, he had the situational awareness of a rock and ignored everything else going on around him, even his attendant and friend who tried to get him to back off.

"*You* sold my fruit? Do you have more?" Hunger filled Aeroth's eyes.

"Obviously we do. We have an entire orchard. You don't?" Arkaziel stepped in helpfully, one of his hands resting on Aetheria's shoulder, a predatory smile on his lips. The demigod-eater also radiated hunger, and although his human form lacked fangs, he still conveyed the impression he possessed razor-sharp teeth.

"Offer them to me as a gift, and I shall forget this shameful encounter ever happened."

Aetheria laughed. She didn't mean to; it was just so absurd she couldn't help it. *How do you deal with someone this delusional? They aren't going to learn.*

"Ah, yes, demigods. Always eager to remind us *mortals* of our places, eager to steal and eat up resources we earned, while declaring it only your due." A voice as frigid as Aetheria's domain cut the tension in the room. The man who spoke appeared to be in his forties, but she knew an Old Man Voice when she heard one. He exuded a powerful presence, but the details of it were tightly concealed. This was the first person, a self-proclaimed mortal, that she had met who could control their aura to the degree she and Arkaziel could.

"Who do you think you are talking to! I am Aeroth, grandchild of Ouranos!" The demigod had not learned to take hints.

Arkaziel licked his lips, and if he had a tail at the moment, Aetheria knew it would swoosh back and forth.

The frigid-voiced man scoffed at the demigod. In contrast with the demigod's flashy outfit, the man wore a simple yet exceptionally well-made black robe and a floppy hat. Comfortable shoes peeked out underneath the hem of the robes. If he carried a gnarly stick she wouldn't even question it if he called himself Old Man the Black, or whatever his name was.

"I know full well who I am talking to. That is Aetheria, favored daughter of Aetherius and Nyx, bearer of the Flame of Khaos. At her side, ready to devour you, is the son of the God Eater, eager to prove he is the successor to that great voracious hero. Their third companion once held the interest of Hecate as the preeminent Speaker of his youth, before becoming a storied Imperator of the Elves of Grief." The frigid voice warmed only in regard to Aetheria's party, but his word choices left no doubt that the man had a dim view of gods that did not seem to translate to the Primordials.

"I . . ." Aeroth sputtered a little.

"As for me, as your friend tried to tell you before he ran away, I'm just an old man with a grudge against the tyranny of gods." The man smirked, but his attempt at mystery was ruined by his companion, a younger man of third tier.

"Lord Siegfried! That's far too humble of an introduction for the leader of Celestial Wardens!"

If the introduction of Aetheria and her party had humbled Aeroth, the name Siegfried and whoever the Celestial Wardens were made the demigod pale.

"Just apologize and go, Aeroth, before I make a spectacle." Siegfried's voice remained frigid.

"My deepest apologies for causing this disturbance." Aeroth fled to a different line.

"I've never seen someone that arrogant run that fast. Thank you for interceding, I didn't want to get myself kicked out of here by going overboard." Aetheria offered a hand to Siegfried and couldn't suppress a giggle when he kissed the back of her hand. He was almost her height, well built, with icy gray eyes and blonde hair.

"The pleasure is mine, Lady Aetheria. When you have finished your business with Grief, you should visit us in the Celestial Wardens. We could help one another reach our goals. A pleasure to meet you, as well, son of Azrael." Siegfried smiled, but it was a dismissal, except he was the one who left to another line.

Arissa coughed to get their attention, and guided them through the paperwork with another clerk. Aetheria only paid scant attention to the paperwork, but Werylin, as her steward, stepped in valiantly.

~Who are the Celestial Wardens?~

+A group led by a bunch of ancient monsters, like Siegfried there. They fight the tyranny of the gods, and police them. They are one of the few really big factions that like StarManes, especially Dad, because he makes it a habit of eating gods. Unfortunately for all of us, gods just get reincorporated. Maybe the new version is better than the old, maybe they are worse. More to eat, but impossible to stop.+

~Are you sure about that? Aetherius and Nyx both have made it sound like my immortality is different from theirs.~

Aetheria recalled the floor that was a future vision, where she had founded the Aetherium and made the gods her enemies. *Am I actually on a path of conflict with multiple gods, beyond just Oizys? Why would the Primordials want me to topple their children?*

After the party collected their shares of the sales and claimed their new items, they returned to Embershaper Manor and spent the evening with their loot. The poetry book Aetheria bought she gave to Werylin, as it pertained to the Words of Creation. The chest she couldn't quite get to open. The lock kept almost opening, but reset itself just before opening each time. When she was close to throwing the chest through a wall in frustration, Sebastian arrived to give her a box delivered by a courier from the Chief Executive.

"I believe it is your pay for a successful mission," the dwarf butler commented, before he went back to his duties.

"Oh, he came through after all." Aetheria laughed as she plucked a token out of the box. There was a small purse of coins, but the only thing that truly mattered to her was the token. It glowed brightly to her Ethereal Sight, as it should, since it was a highly concentrated magical spell given physical form. If she broke the token with an item, it would transfer the enchantment it contained to the item. There were more elaborate ways to use the token than that, though. Thanks to the knowledge imparted by Forge Insight she now knew she could weave the token into the creation of a brand-new item to amplify the effect.

Almost none of her clothing had any real enchantments. The clothing Aetherius had given her to start out had served her well, but it held no special powers. All that she had originally considered enchantments were properties of her own shapeshifting.

Could she make a soulsteel scarf? Maybe there were variations of soulsteel, like soulsilk? *I can't imagine everyone who forges something out of their soul wants to wear actual armor. What if I materialize Ethereal energy?*

~Hey, Ark, are there crafting materials made from pure energy?~

+Yeah, all the elements and most other specialties have their own version. Aether has Aetherweave, then there's Netherweave, and Etherium. Like soulsteel the quality of the material is based on the creator. Why?+

~I'm working on a new scarf. ~

+Why not just buy one?+

~I got the enchantment already, and it's pretty straightforward. I needed a break from the box, and we have at least another week until the crafters we hired are done with the other gear.~

+Good luck?+

~ Thanks. Is there something comparable to soulsteel, but cloth?~

+Spiritweave.+

Arkaziel's input saved her a significant amount of time. Simply knowing something was possible made things easier to succeed at. The real question she had to answer now was should she make her scarf from Spiritweave or Etherium? When she made trial Etherium she found it to be a metal, when she tried to make cloth her Forge Insight told her it was Etherweave.

Etherium seemed weaker than soulsteel, and the same went for spiritweave and Etherweave. Why? She assumed it correlated to the changes wrought on her soul by the Primordials and herself. Whatever the reason, her soul hit outside of its weight class by a large margin, to the point that even the amazing power of Etherium paled in comparison. When the clocks of the manor indicated dawn had arrived, she was the proud creator of a new scarf.

"I dub you my Spiritward Scarf," Aetheria proclaimed, while she stroked the soft fabric woven of her own soul. It required no binding, being part of her soul already, and its colors and appearance shifted with a mere thought just like her own flesh did. The enchantment token provided by the Chief Executive had been an effect called Hexproof, which provided near total immunity to hexes and curses. Combined with the scarf's materials, the results appeared fantastic. Forge Insight had no information on how she could have made it better, or could upgrade it.

That's a good sign, right?

Aetheria went to find Arkaziel to do some sightseeing. Once their other orders were done, they'd leave Naut, regardless of whether she managed to open the stupid box from the Shores of Chaos or not. With that thought, Aetheria nearly doubled over in the hallway at the rise of panic and desperate need for the contents of the box that flared from the Origin.

Alright, alright, I'll try the dumb box again after I have some time to think of a new way to open it! Stop it with the neediness!

CHAPTER 28

From the Shores of Chaos

Aetheria dreamed of a place she had never been. The unending tides of Ether marked the location of this dream as somewhere inside the Origin. What she had thought of as an endless expanse of red gave way to violet, and then to an aqua blue the same shade as her hair color. The tides of power in this blue place moved in precise patterns. The power pulled her deeper.

From depths Aetheria couldn't gauge rose a single mountain spire. Beyond the colossal mountain only ice could be found. Nothing moved past that mountain, not time, not even the blue Ethereal power. If there were variances beyond that wall of ice, she didn't know, as an unseen hand tugged her away from the wall of ultimate, perfectly frozen order.

Aetheria drifted back the way she had come through the blue, violet, and finally back to red tides. Her journey unnerved her. Until she saw the ice and mountain, she had thought the Origin to be devoid of physicality. She continued the strange journey, not that she seemed to have any ability to alter her path. If this was her dream, she couldn't shapeshift or call forth her powers in it. Finally, red gave way to orange.

A beach rose from the depths. Its sand started out a pristine beige that quickly gave way to garish mixtures that hurt the eyes. Every color of the spectrum could be found on the beach her feet touched down upon. A yellow ocean lapped against the hideous multicolored beach. Its tides were unpredictable, and matter spewed from it whenever the tides crashed against the sand. A sword here, a car there . . . had that been a spaceship she glimpsed farther down? Each construction of matter turned to the same yellow as the tides, glittered as light, and then transformed into something new.

This process seemed to be the only constant here, the transformative power of chaos rebirthed and re-formed everything from a muddy yellow tide. Aetheria assumed that this place was the Shores of Chaos. Like the field of ice, this yellow ocean of infinite possibility provided an impassible obstacle that her dream did not venture into. Her forward momentum had stopped on the beach, and her gaze was forced down. This body had sizable breasts, large golden wings, and male genitalia, but no other details struck her beyond blonde hair.

The left hand of her dream-host picked up a clump of sand, formed it into a ball, and threw it into the yellow waves. It bobbed under the water, and re-emerged as Earth, before it vanished in a burst of radiance that blinded her.

Then Aetheria woke up.

"The hell?" Aetheria grumbled about the dream, before she wiped sweat off her body. Her sheets were soaked from excessive sweat, and scattered all over the bed from undue movements in her sleep. The warm water of a shower refreshed her, helped her bring her thoughts into focus, and allowed her to talk to herself without feeling odd. *Who doesn't talk to themselves in the shower?*

"Who would that even have been? Is it even something that exists in mythology as I knew it on Earth? Let's go over what I know. Whoever it was, they traversed the Origin from two extremes I didn't even know existed in it. They did not interact with the icy side at all, but played on the beach and made a planet. I'm also assuming that's the Shores of Chaos. I . . . I'm just babbling and repeating things I already know." Aetheria let a large sigh escape her as she attempted to take on the form of the mysterious figure. The large golden wings barely fit in the suddenly cramped shower.

"That was dumb." The water on her skin froze and shattered against the floor of the shower. Aetheria didn't bother with towels anymore, and after she stepped out of the shower her clothes formed around her body. She continued to the study connected to her bedroom. The chest she bought dropped from her repository onto a heavy wooden desk, which she then sat at.

When they left Naut, she would miss this place. The manor was beautiful, had working plumbing, beautiful architecture, amazing décor, and even Sebastian's overly proper ways held a charm of their own. If it had coffee, it might be the perfect place, despite being built inside of a colossal worm. That part still weirded Aetheria out.

"Wait. Arkaziel said the Shores are another dimension, but my dream made it seem like they were part of the Origin." Which was wrong?

"What kind of madman would go dumpster diving on the Shores of Chaos? A few million gold coins doesn't seem to be worth any journey there." The back of her neck itched a little, and Aetheria felt suspicious. This whole situation stank of a conspiracy to her, a setup, by someone who wanted this item to end up in her hands. Someone who knew she had a connection to the Origin. Which put the list of culprits of any type of setup to be one of the people's powers embodied in the Astrum Nexus, unless the culprit was the gold-winged planet creator?

The chest itself was made from a white metal Aetheria couldn't identify. Forge Insight told her nothing about the item. Apparently, things from the Shores of Chaos transcended the knowledge of Vulcan's gift, or potentially even Vulcan himself. Golden scrollwork adorned the chest, and visually there was no lock upon the thing at all. To Ethereal Sight, a series of interlocking constructs flowed in changing patterns and locked the chest tight.

Aetheria's dream had gone from order to chaos; perhaps she needed to take the chest from chaos to order? What if the lock wasn't meant to be solved, but needed to be transfigured? With this idea in mind, she tried to freeze the lock into a state of ultimate order, where the pattern would lock into place. She transitioned the lock several times back and forth, and on the fourth try she locked the pattern in the correct phase.

"Who the hell is Phanes?" The correct pattern ended up being a name written in Ath, the divine language. Then the strange chaos chest emitted a clicking sound. Aetheria's fingertip pushed against the lid—the white metal felt cool and comforting against her skin—and on smooth hinges it opened upward. Only two objects filled the large chest, neither very large.

The first item had the shape of a torch. Its outer layers were made of crystalized Ethereal energy, while its interior pulsed and flowed in strange patterns. Although small on the outside, the compression and intensity of the power within the crystal staggered Aetheria's senses and blinded her when she looked at it with Ethereal Sight. With her regular vision it merely looked like a crystal torch illuminated from within. When she touched it all the Flames within her flared slightly in resonance, but it didn't strengthen the Flames in any way she could discern. The higher ranking the Flame, the more it danced.

Like the chest, the crystal torch seemed beyond the capabilities of Forge Insight to offer Aetheria any knowledge about the torch. "Why would you give me a torch?" she asked the room and the air itself, but no answers were anywhere to be had. She touched the torch one more time, before she shifted it into her repository. Until she knew what it had been created for, or what its intended use was, it could remain quarantined. Perhaps its use would become evident down the road?

A pouch made from Etherweave remained within the chest. When Aetheria untied the drawstrings, she found it filled with dirt. She let her fingers run through the soil, and on some level she knew this small bag of dirt had come from Earth. Memories, forgotten sensations, old smells, and fond flavors filled her mind, before she retied the pouch and sent it into her repository to join the torch.

Soon she would have to start focusing on the expansion of her repository into a full-fledged world if she ever wanted to join the ranks of Tier Five or be on the same level as Aoibhe. A surge of determination filled her. She would be able to stand as her love's equal next time they saw each other, or damn close to it.

With the two items removed, the chest seemed to be empty, but then Aetheria noticed something off. The inside of the chest was much shallower than it should be. After some poking, prodding, and shapeshifting her fingertips repeatedly, she managed to catch the false bottom and pull it up. Three items lay underneath the false bottom. Two were identical, large yellow feathers like the ones the dream had shown. They radiated a concentration of power that felt unnerving. Without knowing what their aspects were, or purpose could be, she felt it best to dump them into her repository. Hopefully she wasn't taking something into herself she would regret.

The other item resembled a heart, the romanticized ones, not the actual shape of a human heart. Unlike the torch with its yellowed cast that hinted to the Shores of

Chaos, this crystalized item had been fashioned from the normal red Ethereal energy, although its core contained a blue cast to it. When Aetheria's finger touched it, she felt a minor connection form in her mind, and a voice reached from what felt like a very far distance to her.

"How far have you come?" The voice was masculine, one she wasn't familiar with, and spoke in Ath.

"I'm a fourth tier Cultivator on the Ethereal Path."

"That's not what I asked. How far have you come? It is a hard question to answer, isn't it?"

"Who are you; are you Phanes?" It had been the name on the chest, so it seemed like a safe leading question.

"I was Phanes. Unlike other gods, I will become less upon resurrection, and my death is inevitable."

"Why are you sending me a message?" Aetheria didn't know if she was speaking across time or speaking to the equivalent of a recording.

"I was the first, or so I thought. I lured Chronos, Khaos, and Ananke here, so that I could escape from the vessel I used to cross the Origin. They made towers and enshrined my creation with permanence, but they are bound. Trapped here just as I was trapped in the Astral Crawler. I regret that. Yet by their hands did they forge the chains that hold them—they can't blame me! The guilt makes it hard to love, the responsibility makes it impossible to atone."

Aetheria's lips compressed. Phanes did not exactly answer her question, but what he revealed intrigued her, nonetheless. She could do without the emo narrative.

"The advantage of being, at least temporarily, the Sovereign of All, God of the Gods, Ruler of Rulers, Tyrant of Existence, the Overgod, are manifold. Those who follow me will not be as benevolent, and so I have seeded contingencies into place. To hear me, you must meet the prerequisites I set forth."

Aetheria remained silent, waiting for Phanes to continue.

"Patience is good. Love is better. When you have mastered love, cast your mind into the crystal heart."

"Does how powerful I am matter, or just mastery of love?"

"The towers corrupted the Great Cycle. Permanence traps the turning of the wheel, makes a mockery of our plans, and makes liberation from the Samsara impossible. With love, you could restore the ability to transcend the cycle." The connection ended there. Had that even been an answer to her question? No, not even slightly. Had they even talked at all? Some of his answers had felt like direct responses to her questions, but maybe that was coincidental?

"Why did it feel like he meant death instead of love?"

CHAPTER 29

Treetop Trial

The last few days of the trio's time in Naut sped by. They split up and acquired things they might need: alchemical supplies, food provisions, weapons, armor, and even musical instruments. They went out of their way to spend most of their money—it would be another thirty levels, Floor 90, before they reached another trade city. In fifteen levels they would take on the three-quarter boss of the tower, and then at one hundred they would take on the final challenge of the Tower of Aetherius. Until they hit the road, though, they were closer to halfway than to three-quarters.

When the day came, Sebastian drove them to the departure gate. Aetheria thought she saw tears in the old dwarf's eyes when they separated from him and went to the rune gate.

"Alright, you two got your heads on? It's time for challenges and trials again." Aetheria didn't appear that different from before, nor did Arkaziel. Sure, he wore a collar that a moon dangled from, and his thickening mane in cat form had a small band tied in it now, but those were his only changes. Werylin, meanwhile, had entirely new armor, new accessories, and a storage ring full of who knew what.

"I'm ready to eat some prey. Farm-bred food just doesn't have the same satisfying crunch to it." Arkaziel's yellow eyes were excited to hunt.

Werylin nodded solemnly. "I am ready to traverse the final third of the tower. Few are those who beat a tower, fewer still those who beat the Tower of Aetherius. Let's add our names to the list, and then do it all again. And again, and again, and again, and then five more times, hey?" Werylin laughed, and they all stepped onto the rune gate, and vanished from Naut.

They appeared in a beautiful grove of trees. Unfamiliar silver-green leaves filled Aetheria's vision. Winding paths surrounded by bushes and other vegetation ran through the trees, and the soft sounds of birds, small animals, the wind through the leaves, and the babbling of a brook added a serene feeling. The forest felt peaceful, despite the presence of numerous Cultivators in the vicinity. No one radiated harmful intentions, let alone even wary ones.

Werylin seemed least disturbed by the situation. Arkaziel wore a hangdog look, like someone had stolen his hopes and dreams.

"Eternias." Arkaziel sighed.

"Which is?" Aetheria arched a brow at the depressed cat, even as he took his smallest feline form and curled up on her shoulder.

"A lovey-dovey nature commune dedicated to harmony. It's a place of mental and spiritual challenges. Self-improvement, that kind of crap. Not a lot of murder and devouring of prey in these woods," Arkaziel whined.

"That's not entirely true, friend cat." An elf had stepped from around the winding path to address them. "There is more than enough game to go around, so long as one hunts in harmony with the grove. Perhaps you come on the tides of fate. There are more nuisances than usual as of late to be taken care of in the wild paths." While his facial features had the same elven cast as Werylin's, little else was the same. This elf had green hair, a body that displayed a lot of tattoos on barely hidden flesh, and muscles that seemed more in line with an orc than an elf.

"Careful, friends, though it looks like a jungle we are hundreds of feet in the air. Eternias is the name of the world tree we live on." The smile and repeated use of the word *friend* put Aetheria on her guard. *I've been in the tower long enough to be suspicious of anyone who seems too friendly.*

+*This guy is going to skin you and wear an Aetheria mask.*+

~*They are a little overly friendly, aren't they?*~

Arkaziel shared her distrust, which Aetheria felt meant she should give him the benefit of the doubt.

"So, what is it you all do in this world tree?" Werylin inquired of the green-haired guide, who now led them along winding paths toward the village. "I am Werylin Amaryllis, and my companions are the Lady Aetheria and her bondmate, Arkaziel."

"Well met. I am called Thorn. We seek harmony with earth and sky, and Eternias is the bridge for us between the two. You are not the only outsiders here. Did you come in answer to the call of the priestess?"

"We were called here by the needs of others." Aetheria spoke before Werylin could, but the elf caught on to her track.

"We did not answer your priestess's call specifically, but we have been summoned nonetheless." Werylin expounded on Aetheria's answer.

"I see. You are all quite powerful. Is one of you perhaps a hero?" Thorn seemed certain, which followed, since natives could innately sense Aetheria's status as a challenger.

"I am a challenger, yes." Aetheria did not offer any extra details. So far, any time another climber had appeared outside of trade cities, it meant conflict loomed ahead. If it could be avoided, excellent, but if not, best to limit knowledge for now. If they offered who she was the challenger for, or her "lineage" to Aetherius and Nyx, it would potentially identify her. Her reputation had preceded her into Naut, but that could have been a fluke.

Aetheria's slightly ambiguous and standoffish nature led to a collapse of discourse. Silence reigned until the party emerged from winding paths onto a more open area. The bark of the world tree was revealed here, and glimpses of higher branches allowed the scale of the tree to truly sink in. She estimated the clearing to cover a square kilometer, but distances were difficult to keep sorted with the massive branches of the world tree defying normal scales to begin with.

"Here we are, Arborhaven. You are welcome among us. If you come in answer to the priestess, her temple is the tall building to the right there. The inns may or may not have openings; if not, the priestess or I can arrange for you to lodge with someone. Just ask for Thorn at the inn." With a wave that seemed part salute, Thorn walked off toward a building with no sign, but the appearance of a store.

"Let's go meet the priestess, and we'll figure out our plan of action from there?" Aetheria checked if the other two were on the same wavelength. Werylin nodded his agreement, and Arkaziel snored his agreement from Aetheria's shoulder.

Whoever designed the temple had done so while drunk. The elements of the sky and earthy nature were merged without subtlety or skill. The architect had simply split the building in half, with the left half being dedicated to Aetherius and the right half to Gaia. Reflective surfaces, sharp angles, and a spire that climbed twice the height of the right side of the temple almost captured the essence of the Primordial of the Upper Sky, but it felt hollow and empty to Aetheria. Even the randomly affixed glowing crystals did not help improve the atmosphere.

Gaia's side felt equally hollow. The right side had gaps in its walls. The old, weathered wood made a poor exterior product, while the rough-hewn stone had not been cut well, and large gaps remained. Perhaps the openings were meant to symbolize an idea, such that nature finds a way, but it just looked awful and reminded Aetheria of the buildings in a certain post-apocalyptic FPS RPG. *If this is supposed to be aesthetically pleasing, it's lost on me.*

Inside, the architectural mishmash grew worse. Where sky and ground met revealed itself to be a place of jagged edges and chaotic, ill-fitting surfaces. In the center of the temple a woman in simple robes knelt before statues of the two Primordials. Each statue seemed to ignore the other, despite the fact their hands each cupped half of an orb. Unlike the temple itself, the orb had a very weak divine presence. The statue failed to convey any sort of harmony or cooperation between the two, and the orb had been nearly depleted of power.

The priestess, so enveloped in her task, did not notice them until Werylin finally coughed dramatically after a few minutes.

"Oh, what's this, do we have some . . . oh my." The priestess had the appearance of a twenty-something human woman, and she stared at Aetheria with one blue eye and one green eye.

"Has divine Aetherius sent us even more heroes in our time of need? Gaia's champions prepare for the task of restoring the Orb of Warding, as do the druids. It only follows the Lord of the Skies would send a group, too. Welcome, welcome, I am Aeris Skysong; welcome to Arborhaven."

Aetheria eyed the woman, the statues, and rolled her own eyes in annoyance before she gestured. She flared the Primordial Flame of Aetherius and tapped the fields of Aether around her and inside of her. This allowed her to pull massive quantities of highly concentrated holy power that, with the slight assistance of the transformative power of the Transcendent Flame of Khaos and the knowledge provided by the boon of Vulcan, she used to empower the orb to its original state in less than a minute.

Tears of joy filled the eyes of Aeris.

"Oh my! To think you could restore the orb on your own, without the need to journey to the sacred places." The priestess seemed to be truly shocked. "Who are you?"

"Leaving, that's who. Give our regards to the other two groups." Aetheria could not contain her victorious grin, while Werylin struggled to suppress a smile. They left the stunned priestess before her hideous altar, and outside slipped around the side of the building where Aetheria summoned the gateway to the next floor.

"This is what we call cheesing it." Aetheria laughed, pleased with herself. Arkaziel, still asleep, meowed for her to quit making so much noise, and bopped her in the face with his tail.

Werylin frowned. Rather than disapproval it was concern that radiated from the somber elf.

"Aren't the Tower Administrators going to retaliate for subversion of the challenge?"

Aetheria shook her head.

"Aetherius himself approved of our brand of problem solving. The last Admin to lodge a complaint got eaten by Ark. He said something about the Admins needing to remember what they were doing and getting too focused on their own scenarios. We aren't here to be actors in an Administrator's play, we're here to climb the tower and claim our prizes. We may have to revise that approach with the next tower, but for now it's acceptable."

"We've got thirty-eight more floors to get through. Let's go."

Behind them, the disjointed, ugly temple radiated holy power in powerful waves, marking the resurgence of Aeris Skysong's power.

CHAPTER 30

Wicked Currents

Floor 62 had no sign of the ground below them. The trio appeared on a transparent platform that was lifting them. Unpredictable gusts of wind hit the platform, shifting its balance, and altering its upward trajectory. A few minutes of yelling over the constant wind later, and they managed to achieve a sustained balance.

Arkaziel sent his twilight duplicates off to inspect the islands that floated above them in the sky.

"Sky without any ground underneath feels quite unnatural," Werylin murmured.

"I thought that at first, too, but then I realized it gives you a lot of time to make corrections if you screw up. Even without flying, it gives you time to catch an updraft, cast a spell, whatever, that a more immediate ground doesn't. I'm sure it's a climber advantage to have impossibly large fall space." Aetheria's opinion got a nod from Arkaziel.

"That is one way to look at it. Everything does have a reason, I suppose." Werylin did not sound convinced.

"Everything does have a reason, maybe, but in the tower it is open to debate if the reason is game theory, Administrator whim, or the personality of Aetherius himself made manifest. On paper, challenges like these seem difficult, challenging, sometimes strange. The more our powers grow, the more we make a mockery of challenges, though. This most certainly isn't the original purpose of the towers." Aetheria shook her head, but she was certain of that. Whatever the original purpose was, it had ended up being a trap of some sort. Phanes had been very insistent she should not create a tower of her own.

"The first island is a small lake, lots of fish, a dock, a cabin. Scenic and empty. The second island is a small elf village, although they're very tanned and have wings. The third island is, oh, the door to the next level." Arkaziel sounded surprised at how quickly he had found the gateway—surprised and disappointed. "Well then, shall we jump on Aetheria's back and fly to the exit?"

Aetheria snorted, bopped Arkaziel on the nose, and spoke before he or Werylin could pile on her. "No need." Multicolored flames engulfed the platform, and they and the platform reappeared on the highest of the floating islands.

"That was new. When did you figure out taking more than yourself?" Arkaziel easily adapted to the teleportation method Aetheria employed.

Werylin, however, had paled and vomited to the side.

"Sorry, Werylin. Didn't realize you might have problems with it." Aetheria watched the elf in concern, even as he tried to regain control of his stomach.

"The nature of your teleportation is counter to my own nature. It might be best that you and I avoid teleporting one another, unless necessary." Werylin grimaced after he finished wiping his face with a handkerchief.

"Which makes me the teleport master of the group. I will only charge a small fee per teleport. A planet to be fed to me later, perhaps." Arkaziel stretched lazily atop Aetheria's shoulder. "I'll even use light instead of darkness, so you don't get manhandled by the shadow beasts."

"Shadow beasts?" Aetheria asked with slight alarm.

"The dark dimensions are full of nasty stuff. Tentacles, shadow beasts, ancient horrors waiting to consume reality, and a surprisingly high number of fae. You really don't want to be stuck interacting with the dark fae. It's all 'give us your name' this, 'trade us your power' that, while they try and screw you over. Swindlers, the lot of them." Arkaziel harrumphed, then went back to grooming himself.

"We can test if your teleport makes me sick later, Werylin. I don't think it will, though. I haven't shown any aversion to harmony or order, even when wielding the power of Khaos." Maybe Aetheria could change the way she did it, so Werylin wouldn't get sick? She knew ice teleportation worked, it just felt weird to step through ice. Perhaps she could figure out a way to teleport via ice that didn't rely upon portals.

The portal to the next floor stood before them, and the only challenge on the way through it was sidestepping Werylin's mess.

On Floor 63 they appeared in a maze. The walls were made of transparent, turbulent wind, and the moment they appeared Aetheria felt disoriented. No matter how she altered her physiology via shapeshifting she couldn't block out the disorienting effects of the floor. Her Flames failed to protect her, so it wasn't mental. Her hexproof scarf failed to block it, so it wasn't a curse. Ocean's Serenity had no effect on it, so it wasn't emotional. Or it was one of those things, and the Administrators had simply chosen to overwrite her defenses, because screw you that's why.

Aetheria grimaced and tried to adjust to the disorientation of the maze.

"This is going to be awful." Werylin voiced her feelings on the matter. His skin had a greenish tint to it. How much had he eaten this morning? Aetheria didn't want to get vomited on.

"I believe the climber parlance for floors like this one is meat grinder." Arkaziel unleashed a mighty yawn. The feline kept his eyes closed and gave no indication he might get off her shoulder anytime soon.

Ethereal Sight did not help. Apparently, the flesh-rending winds that made up the walls didn't count as magic and were just normal wind. Aetheria couldn't help but feel that this seemed like payback for their rapid ascent on the last floor. Rather than frowning or cursing, Aetheria extended her hand, and filled the room with a thin fog. The eddies and currents of the invisible walls were almost completely visible this way.

"This should work, unless one of you has a better idea?"

"Good job, Aetheria. Can we do anything about the disorientation?" The green continued to rise in Werylin's complexion.

"I can't. Even my regeneration isn't helping me against it at all, or if it is, not by much."

"I found something," Arkaziel told them with a literal cat-ate-the-canary look.

"Is it a cure to the disorientation?" Aetheria and Werylin asked simultaneously, hopefully.

"Better! Maintain the fog; I'll lead the way." Arkaziel's excitement proved to be contagious, the other two momentarily forgetting their distress. The StarMane hopped off Aetheria's shoulder and took on a two-meter-long draconic form. He also sent one of his clones ahead of him by a few paces. The current room had multiple exits. Arkaziel chose the only one that ascended. The path, like the walls, was only visible due to Aetheria's fog.

"Not going to tell us where we are going?" Aetheria kept a close eye out for traps, but the concentration only made her vertigo worse.

They entered another room. Like the last, it had dozens of exit points. Again, Arkaziel had them ascend up a sharp incline. In the next room, Arkaziel led them to descend, and they descended again at the next room, where the walls abruptly shifted from wind to rock. Despite the changes, Arkaziel led them unerringly down a path only he could see. He took them left, then right at the next intersection, then left, then right.

The rooms changed once again, and they found themselves in a room with only two exits other than the door they had entered from. One marked *A,* one marked *B.* Arkaziel led them down the metal tubed tunnel of *B,* and they emerged into a room that looked identical, with *A* and *B* tubes. This time Arkaziel led them down *A.*

When they emerged from the tunnel, their disorientation faded. Before them were five different portals. No symbology was present, no labels, nothing at all that marked one door as different from the other four.

"What is this?" Werylin did not bother to hide the excitement and confusion from his voice.

Arkaziel's smirk grew wider.

"It's a shortcut. Sometimes you can find them in the towers. Thanks to Mom I knew about this one. When she came through here, she used the second door, and it took them up two floors. There are five doors, so the best I can guess is it's either a one-to-five floor shortcut, or a two-to-ten shortcut. Doesn't eliminate that it's totally random, I guess, which throws any supposition out the window."

"Who's feeling lucky?" Aetheria asked.

Both of the boys looked at her. She looked at them. No one spoke.

After three minutes of the stare-off, Aetheria sighed deeply and walked toward the portals.

"You both suck."

There was nothing to go by. Even the frames of the portals were identical.

"There's three of us, let's go with number three."

No one opposed, so Aetheria walked through the third door. Darkness enveloped her, and the sensation of teleportation lasted longer than it usually did between floors. When the duration of nothingness verged on troublesome, panic about to rise, the world returned to color and physicality.

The trio appeared on a raised platform. Before them stairs descended, then a long straight hall went on for quite a distance to a raised altar on the far side. The floor looked like white foam, or a marshmallow. When Aetheria hopped down the stairs to poke at the white material, it moved and swirled. It was a deep, thick fog. When she pulled her hand back, she faced some resistance to the act, and she had to fight to unstick herself from the material.

"You missed the sign, Aetheria," Arkaziel chided from the top of the stairs, before he coughed and read the notice aloud.

"Welcome to Floor Sixty-Nine. None of your abilities will work here. Purge yourself of negative emotions and cross the hall to the altar. Those who succeed shall be rewarded." Arkaziel laughed, and an edge of hysteria or mania could be felt through their empathic bond.

"Having a Negative Nancy kind of day, Ark?"

"Some of us are predisposed toward certain emotions, Blue." The dragon heaved a sigh, before he shifted the color of his scales to white.

"White looks very majestic on you, Arkaziel." Werylin, ever the diplomat, sought brownie points with the draconic cat.

"Twilight and darkness are more to my tastes, but this challenge is all about light and positive energy. I can master my base instincts for the duration of crossing one ridiculous hall." Arkaziel's attempt to psych himself up did not pay off. His first step into the white fog saw the material thicken and glob around his front paw. The more he fought it, the denser and stickier it grew. Within seconds, his paw couldn't even move.

"I hate this," Arkaziel whined, then closed his eyes to master his emotions.

Aetheria petted his head softly and sent reassurance and love through their empathic bond.

"I'm pretty sure Aunt Lyrazea died in a trap like this," Arkaziel groaned.

Werylin casually walked past the other two and crossed toward the far hall. The fog did not slow him down at all. The elf made it a quarter of the way down the hall before the fog transformed and captured him.

"Smugness is apparently a negative emotion. Who knew?" the elf called back to them.

CHAPTER 31

Sticky Floor

Aetheria matched her pace to Arkaziel's in their journey across the sticky hall of doom. Any time any of them started to do too well with positive thoughts, outside influences tried to push their thoughts down other paths. She was certain this was done by the power of the Administrators, as these invasive thoughts managed to whisper past the mental protection provided by her Flames. Arkaziel never heard those whispers—he struggled with positivity all on his own.

Werylin made it halfway down the hall before Arkaziel had even made it a tenth of the way. The slow progress and substandard performance left Arkaziel a mass of nerves, his mood turning darker by the second to Aetheria's observation in their bond. The final straw came when the back end of the hallway disintegrated into nothing.

"I need your help, Aetheria." Arkaziel hissed the words.

"You always have my help, buddy. What do I need to do?"

"Remember my clutch mate? That I ate the essence of before the insects could?"

"Yeah, no. Wait, yeah." Aetheria corrected herself. She remembered it all right, it had been one of the things that disturbed her regarding her cat.

"Well, his essence hasn't been fully consumed, so that's the source of the negative emotions I'm dealing with. I need you to reach through our bond, hold the little jerk down, and let me finish the job."

Aetheria couldn't help but feel that he was asking her to murder someone.

"No time to screw around right now, Aetheria. The hallway is disintegrating, and if I don't finish him off and consolidate my mind quickly, I'm going with it."

"Fine. Do it." Aetheria felt through their bond, and indeed, there was a third presence in it now. Arkaziel must have concealed it before. She focused her mental attention to ensnare the weaker presence within Arkaziel. Weaker being a relative term—somehow, the remains of the sibling had gained ranks and power like Arkaziel. Had the StarMane been fighting his own sibling this whole time without letting on?

If they had access to their normal powers, this would likely have been harder. Instead, the scenario allowed Aetheria and Arkaziel to harness their will as weapons. The only method of defense the bodiless sibling had was to try to resist their combined will. Despite her expectations Arkaziel repeatedly failed to unleash decimating attacks, and he kept pulling his punches. Realization came to her. Arkaziel asked her for help, yes, but he had been coy about the real problem.

Do I have a sign on my back that says PLEASE, ASK ME ABOUT MY FREE MERCY KILLING POLICY?

"Oh, just merge then, you dumb twins." Aetheria ceased her participation in the mental wrestling match. It seemed to be pointless, and a massive waste of time. "Just accept each other. You were always meant to be together as twins, so just take that a step further."

The unnamed essence stopped its struggle.

Arkaziel's mind opened to the other, and as much as Aetheria could tell the two reconciled into some kind of mental meld. The darker emotions grew subdued within their empathic bond, until something like surprised happiness filled Arkaziel's side of it all. Aetheria could no longer sense the third presence, but she had never sensed it before this incident either.

In the minutes it had taken another ten feet of hallway had disintegrated.

"Haha, I can move now!" Arkaziel cackled madly and dashed down the hall. Periodically, he was slowed for a few seconds, but they crossed the halfway point well before the disintegration of the floor had even reached the quarter way point.

"Conquer your inner demons?" Werylin inquired when the trio had caught up to one another.

"You could say that. You could also say I'm the greatest, and the closest of the three of us to reaching Tier Five," Arkaziel crowed, but the fog didn't lock him down for arrogance or smugness. Perhaps it was genuine happiness, filtered by Arkaziel's personality, and therefore exempt? She didn't make the rules here, but whoever made the rules played incredibly fast and loose with them. Did other towers have more organization, stricter rules, maybe even augmented reality menus? *A girl can dream.*

After the halfway point the whispers stepped up their game. Aetheria heard the voices of her mother, father, Aoibhe, Arkaziel's unnamed sibling, and multiple old acquaintances emerge from the fog. The only voice that tugged at her heartstrings enough to even muddy her steps with the thickening mists was Aoibhe's. The Nephilim continued to have a monopoly and stranglehold over her heart that could not be stopped. Yet Aetheria refused to yield or be seduced by the whispers of her love. The only path to Aoibhe lay forward. She had to reach greater heights in the Tower of Aetherius and on the Ethereal Path if she was to be reunited with Aoibhe.

Not that the occasional whisper of Arkaziel's unnamed sibling didn't cause her more than a few stumbles into sticky territory. The whole scenario there felt very weird, and she wasn't sure what a correct resolution could even look like, or what possibilities had existed. She and Arkaziel had both taken things into themselves without fully comprehending the consequences.

For Aetheria, the rest of the trial passed quickly. Werylin and Arkaziel had more sour faces when they reached the altar at the end of the hallway. Clearly, the two boys had taken more than a few points of psychic damage and trauma along the way. To fit in, she sat down and let out a large sigh.

"You succeeded. You may choose between the Luminary Lantern or Joyful Jester's Cap."

The disembodied voice sounded bored, and no information about either item was forthcoming.

"Going to tell us anything about them?" Silence was the only answer to Werylin's questions.

Since they weren't going to get clarification they opted to go for the Luminary Lantern. It sounded potentially useful, while a jester's cap seemed like the sort of thing none of them would wear, no matter how good or powerful it might be. After all, this wasn't a game, Aetheria wasn't going to run around dressed like an insane person for a few minor gains. The Etherfrost Asura had more pride than that, but her incredible power also gave her the luxury to not desperately seek another scrap of new power at every opportunity.

The door to the next floor appeared along with the lantern. Forge Insight proved to be a useful boon yet again as she examined the artifact. It had a few abilities, relating to illuminating the most positive outcome in a situation, revealing hidden threats—physical or emotional—and the ability to absorb and dispel negative energy and replace it with a sense of hope. It struck her as the kind of item that either helped a lot or was completely useless. Time would tell which it would be.

"Do you need some time to consolidate, Ark?"

"Yes, that would be good. I'd like to finish the job and make sure we aren't going to have a reoccurring problem on our hands," Arkaziel answered decisively, before he moved over to the side of the altar. Fish appeared in his hands, and he ate while he theoretically worked on cementing the conjoining of his sibling to himself.

"What do you actually plan to do when you're done with the quest to displace Oizys?" Werylin asked.

"Wander the universe? Figure it out as I go. Maybe have some children. I never did that when I was back on Earth."

"You're an Asura, Aetheria. If you displace Oizys you'll be making a lot of friends and enemies. Climbers who beat a single tower are rare. Beat ten? Everyone will want to learn from you or learn by fighting against you."

"The moment Nyx and Aetherius declared me their daughter, I made a lot of enemies. Overwhelming power seems the answer to most problems, especially if you don't get caught up by the rules. I've been told very clearly *not* to become a god and *not* to make a tower. I suggest you follow the same guidelines. Figured out any happily-ever-after plans of your own?"

"I think re-establishing the Elven Empire might be on my to-do list, but by then, maybe I'll be content to be in the shadows while someone else stands in the light. Ruling is a lot of work, and none of it is very fun if you take the art of ruling seriously."

"Sounds like a downer. Themis didn't get why I didn't want a faction, planet, or any of that crap. Chronos, Khaos, and Phanes seem to have ulterior motives for me that go beyond Nyx and Aetherius. I don't know how much wiggle room I have to fight their plans, or if I even need to fight their plans, so I've mostly focused on progressing through the tower and summoning Aoibhe as soon as I break through into Tier Five."

"It'd be a lot easier if they were just straight with you, wouldn't it?"

"Maybe. They understand a lot of things I haven't experienced yet. Maybe some discussions are waiting until I have more of that context. Or maybe they're just trillion-year-old ancient beings beyond my scope of understanding using me for their benefit? All I know is that Pete and Callie were my friends and adopted parental figures before this started. The tower has thrown questioning of their intentions at me a few times now."

Aetheria shrugged, then looked more intently at Werylin.

"What's it like being alive again, after so long dead?"

"It's slowly faded from my memory, the years in the tomb. The living mind is antithetical to the undead mind, perhaps? Maybe it is my path of harmony with the universe? Or perhaps it is the growing Flame of Aetherius in my mind that banishes such things, in order to heal. I have heard that Flames of the Primordial quality protect the minds of those who bear them."

"It is very possible. I've been able to shrug off most psychic stuff without even knowing it happened, thanks to my Flames. I've got a book on the Flames if you want, or I can try to guide you through using the Flame of Aetherius once you think you're ready. Our Paths are about as dissimilar as they come, though."

"Superficially, yes. We both follow combat-focused paths. Yours as a brawler, mine as a swordsman. You seek embodiment in cold, and I in harmony."

Aetheria held up her hand and shook her head.

"I don't think I'd say that's truly accurate. You try to embody harmony? I don't really try to embody anything."

Werylin looked surprised.

"You *are* cold, Aetheria. The water, the ice, that is superfluous. You are the strongest vanguard I have ever heard a story of, full stop, and you embody all the traits of cold that I can think of. You emit a chill that slows and preserves all around you. You isolate and control battlefields, while emitting a calm strength that bolsters your allies. No matter what environment we fight in, you bring order to it, and death's cool release to your enemies. Snow and ice are crisp, clean, and symbolize purity or a new start without old tracks."

Werylin frowned.

"Do you not seek to emulate anything when you focus on gains?"

"Not so much. I could use your help with harmonizing with my new weapon, though." Aetheria raised her hands to show off Astrum Nexus. Her fingers brushed the crystals woven into the mesh around her palm. "These contain all the knowledge of Nova Azura. If I can properly attune to them, I should have access to the knowledge contained inside, according to Vulcan."

Werylin's eyes bugged out in a most unattractive way.

"Vulcan, as in the God of the Forge? You skipped a few stages in hiring crafters, Aetheria, you don't just jump to the end."

"He came to me, commissioned by Chronos. See what I mean about their plans?"

Werylin didn't take his eyes off the Astrum Nexus, and the elf laughed in shock.

"That's Chronos's sigil. Khaos. Aetherius. Nyx. Thalassa. Ymir. You don't even have a Flame from Chronos, but he infused your weapon with his power? Have you tried to use it yet? Time is said to be a tricky mistress."

"I haven't. Little worried about messing things up there. So, I've only considered expanding my cold through it, to slow down time. Maybe that's why my flash core got so much more efficient now that I have it?"

Werylin rolled his eyes, and the two stared at one another in awkward silence until Arkaziel finally indicated he was ready to go to Floor 70.

CHAPTER 32

Dance-Off

On Floor 70 the trio appeared within a cave. The smooth walls of the cavern were embedded with crystal light sconces mounted between elaborate tapestries, each detailing the moves of different dances. There were also shelves filled by books with titles like *Waltzing Wombats: An Unconventional Guide, Break Dancing with a Broken Heart,* and of course Aetheria's instant favorite, *Robot Rhapsody: Bring Down the House While Dancing Emotionlessly.*

"This seems more like a torture room than a challenge." Arkaziel hissed at the tapestries and dance books, before he jumped onto a bookshelf and curled up for a nap.

"Guess it's just the two of us then," Werylin commented dryly when Arkaziel fell promptly asleep. "Do you know how to dance, Aetheria?"

"I had some lessons from Selenthe about dancing while in Solace, but I'd say I'm still a novice at best. How about you?" Aetheria couldn't hide the slight smile at the lessons from the dark and sultry Selenthe. She had been very keen on trying to seduce Aetheria and had taken her failures at seduction as a personal attack.

"I preferred to play the music rather than dance to it, but yes, you can't be part of the nobility without knowing your way around a ball. If that will help with what is depicted in these, I'm not sure."

The large cavern had only one exit. Aetheria took a peek up the stone stairs to see the peak of a mountain. Upon a large outcropping of crystal sat a bird she had never seen before. It looked like a ten-meter-tall bald eagle with bolts of lightning that continuously danced along its wings. The bird was massive, majestic, and above all, gave off an aura of judgment on all that dared to come before it. As if it sensed someone watching it, the thunderbird let loose a massive caw and bolts of lightning filled the darkness beyond it, followed by huge booms of thunder. Aetheria scurried back to the cavern.

"Well, I'm pretty sure that's our dance judge out there. Big old bird with lightning bolts for wing accessories. Mid-to-high Tier Five, so fighting it might be a risk." Aetheria didn't feel like it was beyond their capabilities, but Arkaziel and Werylin were not immortal, so risk management still needed to be considered.

Werylin snuck up the stairs to peek for himself. Thunder shook the cavern, and the elf hurried back down the stairs. No hint of anxiety marred his pretty face; instead the elf displayed a brave grin.

"I shall start practicing now. I suggest we check each of the tapestries and books for any clues to appeasement of the thunderbird. He does not seem like a lenient judge."

"How'd you know it was a male?"

"You didn't see the plumage? Female thunderbirds do not have the golden markings on their wings."

"First time I've seen a thunderbird before, guess I missed it."

"Your original world really didn't have beast kings like the thunderbird?"

"Nope, just some old myths. I'm not sure why you and Ark have such a hard time with the concept of a world without monsters, cultivation, or magic, just science and humanity."

"Sounds awful." Werylin gave Aetheria a sympathetic pat on the shoulder, then started his quest to search the room for clues.

"It wasn't *that* bad."

Werylin enmeshed himself in the tapestries and books, while Aetheria pulled a hammock out of her repository, then lazed in it as it swung between two poles of ice. Before long Arkaziel woke up, migrated to her chest, then went back to sleep while he got pets. To all outward appearances they napped peacefully, despite the offended glare Werylin directed at them for ignoring his attempt at delegation.

Aetheria's attention had shifted inwardly, through herself and her soul aperture into her repository. The pouch of dirt from Earth was there, and she let her mind run over the mix of dirt and rocks. Could she use such a small sample to expand into the basis of her inner world? Did she even need to form an inner world the way real worlds were formed? Did it need a core, a mantle, and a crust? Were inner worlds spheres, or were they just planes like in some cultivation books she'd read? If they were just sort of flat planes it seemed like that might simplify things, but it would also complicate her ability to imagine and visualize.

After some consideration, Aetheria decided she preferred the spherical world concept. The logical place to start the creation of a world would be its core, but she had a different idea. She spread the pouch of earth around the base of Cryostrialis, and then pushed Ethereal power into the dirt. As much as she would like to claim intuitive understanding of her soul-space, the tingles in her hands made her suspect the Aetherial knowledge stored within Astrum Nexus filtered into her mind naturally. *I wish I knew how that worked.*

The vault of knowledge, interwoven into icelike mesh, looked gorgeous on her hands. Intuitive understanding seemed great, but it created a problem for Aetheria. Without a way to differentiate what was instinct versus what was Aetherial knowledge, she could easily end up dealing with problems of her own creation like she had with the Origin gateway in her soul. Admittedly, it hadn't been that much of a disaster yet, but she couldn't shake the idea it would be a real problem at the worst possible time. Worse, she still had no idea who or what lay on the other side of the Origin. The only intelligence she had ever sensed in that place was Themis, who occasionally stopped by for a chat.

From the visions and oral history Aetheria had learned, Chronos, Khaos, and Ananke had crossed the Origin to create this new universe. Phanes claimed to have lured them here, to be freed from what he called the Astral Crawler. The Astral Crawler sounded an awful lot like a spaceship-type vessel to her—maybe he'd lost power and needed saving? Either way, Chronos, Khaos, and Ananke had come from outside of the Origin. It was a medium through which they had passed in hopes of ascension to a higher realm. Phanes, on the other hand, was more of a mystery. Sure, he had been trapped in the mysterious Astral Crawler while crossing the Origin, but where did he come from?

What happened to Ananke? She's the only one of the four I haven't encountered in some fashion. I suppose it is in the nature of one called inevitability to have a sense of timing.

Aetheria gave a small laugh after a minute. A small part of her had thought that by creating the perfect "ah-ha" moment in her mental dialogue perhaps Ananke would summon herself, but it didn't happen. Arkaziel bopped her in the face with his tail in retaliation for the laugh that disturbed his slumber.

For now, though, she had no avenues to explore with the Transcendents, so Aetheria pushed the thoughts about them and their mystery to the side. While her thoughts had diverged, she had managed to create a few acres of earthen soil around one side of Cryostrialis. The progression was going faster than she thought it might. It would take a long time to build an entire world this way, but she didn't plan to use this method alone. The core needed to be made, and from there she felt it would go faster. *It always goes faster when you are building on something else, right?*

Werylin drew Aetheria's attention away from introspection. The elf practiced moves with a grace that filled her with envy. Yes, she could become an elf, yes, she was faster than him with her flash core, but the way the elf moved captivated her. Perhaps such grace came with time? The younger elves she had seen certainly didn't share Werylin's fluid grace. Even without his blades drawn, the steps Werylin moved through reminded her of his fighting style. It wasn't an innately elven thing, but a result of his blade style and a life of practice. *Would it be uncouth to ask if the centuries spent as a specter helped with that fluidity? Probably.*

Aetheria's eyes felt heavy. Her breathing slowed. Arkaziel's cute little snores and warmth, combined with the rocking of the hammock lulled her to sleep. She dreamed of water, mud, and a terrible mess that just wouldn't come clean. For some reason a snake and an egg were in the muddy mess with her. She played with the snake, who really liked to lick the gem fragments woven into the Astrum Nexus. When the egg cracked open all the mud and water vanished and a bright, terrifying light emerged from the egg. The snake hid inside of her coat from the tyrannical light.

"Aetheria, wake up." Werylin's voice pulled Aetheria from the dream to awareness.

"What's up?" Aetheria rubbed at her eyes and focused to wake up quickly.

"I've got the routine down, I believe. Shall we head up and see if I pass muster or if it's a fight on our hands?"

"Oh cripes, I'm so sorry, Werylin! You asked us to look at the tapestries and we both just totally spaced out and didn't help at all." Writ large in eyes and tone, Aetheria's genuine panic at inadvertently shirking work triggered a temperature drop from Ocean's Serenity. "Forgive me, that won't happen again."

"You're forgiven, Aetheria. It takes time for new team dynamics to form. Aw. He's awfully cute for a world eater."

Werylin's comment drew Aetheria's attention to Arkaziel. The cat had managed to position himself against her side. His head rested against her shoulder, while the rest of his feline body remained hidden in her coat.

"He is a cutie. Wake up, Ark!" It took four rounds of head pats to wake the beast.

"I left specific instructions to not wake me up, didn't I?" The feline lifted his head to look at Werylin then at Aetheria. "Why are you both staring at me like that? It's creepy."

"You were being cute." Aetheria couldn't resist and stroked Arkaziel's head until he purred.

It only took a few moments for the baleful yellow eyes to refocus on the two humanoids again.

"Why'd you wake me up?"

Werylin twirled, struck a pose, and exclaimed, "It's time to dance!"

Aetheria choked on laughter, which seemed to improve Arkaziel's mood.

"I bet that sounded more heroic in your head," Aetheria said.

"It did. Dramatic, heroic, with a mix of seductive. I got caught up and forgot who my audience was." Werylin's deadpan delivery of the last bit left the other two in laughter.

"Seriously, though, it is time to dance and/or fight a thunderbird. Let's go."

"Think of the fried chicken we could make out of a thunderbird. I'm just saying, maybe peace was never an option?" Arkaziel floated a new strategy as they climbed the stairs.

"That's an interesting point he makes. Didn't someone tell us eating higher tier beast kings helps you advance?" When Aetheria spoke the party stopped on the stairs. They did not really have a choice, since she led the way and Arkaziel lazed on her shoulders. The stairs were too narrow for Werylin to step around her when she stopped to talk.

"I've never heard that. I've heard they taste divine, of course, but wouldn't the real gains be from defeating an extremely difficult foe?" Werylin almost managed to keep his annoyance out of his voice.

"Well, it's true for me. Beast Cultivator, remember? And Blue here can cultivate by eating if she takes on a beast king form. Quit glaring, elf. We'll do it your way, do your song and dance. If it works, it works, if not, it's eating time." Arkaziel sulked when no one else jumped on his eat-the-powerful-bird bandwagon.

"Do you need me to hum some music or anything while you perform?" Aetheria resumed the trek up the stairs, but asked the final question before they reached the door.

"Thank you, but no. I've got this covered. *Play.*" Werylin pulled a flute and a lyre from his storage ring, and when commanded to play, they floated into the air behind him and did exactly that. Aetheria pushed the door to the mountain peak open as the instruments started an unfamiliar song.

CHAPTER 33

Dancing King

Lightning crashed in the distance when the door opened. It illuminated the large thunderbird who sat upon a rock perch, where it watched the large flat rock area that made up the dance floor. When the echoes of thunder faded, the sounds of Werylin's flute and lyre filled the void. The violet-haired elf bowed to the thunderbird, then sauntered into the middle of the dance floor.

The music grew tense. Werylin pulled into himself so much that he seemed to become less. Then he exploded into motion. The depths and tides of emotions he had experienced, the feelings of the path he had walked were amplified and made manifest around him. Wisps of spirits formed, and the spirit lights added another dimension to his performance.

The dance started with freedom. A bird soared high in the sky, a child explored a garden, a man hunted the most dangerous game, women. Tension, a life shattered, shackles formed of responsibilities held Werylin in place. The music changed, and his arms swung and shifted in mimicry of swordplay. The music slowed; each note hung in the air with deliberation. The rhythm increased, and then fell, creating the rising and falling fortunes of a terrible war. The graceful sweep of his arms through the air spread red spirit lights that fully evoked the spilling of blood. Frantic leaps, fluid twirls with flashes of blue spirit light hinted at defense and protection of allies.

The dramatic tension in Werylin's silver eyes exposed the toll of leadership.

The music changed into a haunting melody, and all of Werylin's movements altered. It evoked a sense of damnation within Aetheria, as if she had been sentenced for past misdeeds. A crescendo hit, and an explosion of green spirit light represented the transformation into a specter. The swordsman's unnatural grace perfectly conveyed the insubstantial nature of torment. Each gesture at the heavens and hells conveyed his repentance, his desire to be redeemed, the desperate need for forgiveness. Delicate sways and ghostly spins portrayed sorrow and desire for amends.

Then the instruments wove a new element into the threads of the performance. Hope. Flashes of blue from the spirit lights illuminated a rough human form. It was vague, but it was undeniably meant to be Aetheria. The illusion patted Werylin on the head, and the instruments swelled to a new height. Werylin's intensity increased, before illusionary fire spilled everywhere, and from the darkness and through fire he jumped, to dance in a pillar of light. Sorrow vanished from his face, replaced by triumph.

Then a new emotion dominated the dance. Werylin radiated a newfound sense of adventure. His leaps boundless, his spins ecstatic, his footwork echoing a change in the heavens themselves. The elf bowed once more, to the thunderbird and to Aetheria and Arkaziel as well, as the echoes of his dance filled the observer's eyes and hearts.

Aetheria brushed the back of her hand against her eyes, and frozen tears fell to the ground. The tiny ice crystals created a strangely loud sound when they shattered against the mountain. The loud sound broke the silence that lingered in the aftermath of the emotional dance.

"You danced from the heart, little elf. One of the best performances I have seen in years. I especially liked the themes of sacrifice, the tolls of leadership, regret for decisions made from emotion, and the light that brought you back from the darkness." The thunderbird's voice filled the mountaintop. No doubt anyone farther down the mountain would only hear thunder, not words. "Indeed, there is always the possibility of redemption. In thanks for sharing so heavily of yourself with me, I shall share with you, little elf."

A bolt of lightning struck the empty space between Werylin and the thunderbird. When the afterimage of such a bright impact vanished, it revealed a cloak made of blue and purple feathers. Werylin quickly moved to pick it up and examine the cloak. His previous cloak had not been so grand as this new one, but the new one matched the Sylvan armor he had acquired in Naut. *For a Cultivator focused on order, he sure ends up with a lot of storm associations.*

"Thank you for this amazing gift, great one. I will treasure it."

"Haha. As well you should, little one. Wear the Mantle of Stormbringer with pride!"

Stormbringer then turned his gaze to Aetheria and Arkaziel.

"Protect this one well, Etherfrost Asura, and eat his enemies before they eat him, little God Eater."

"I'm not little!" Arkaziel hissed from his spot in Aetheria's arms, where he had cuddled up in the form of a small house cat.

"You are in the form of a small cat, Ark. Not everyone automatically knows how big you actually are." Aetheria wondered how big Arkaziel's true form was. He could become massive, but so could she. How much was shapeshifting, and how much was real? Which was real? The mighty dragon, or the lithe cat?

"We will keep him safe." Aetheria followed up with a promise to the thunderbird.

A lightning bolt fell from the sky, but it froze just before striking Werylin. The bolt vanished into Aetheria's repository.

"Thank you for keeping your test strike within the realm of my ability to stop." Aetheria spoke through a strained smile. She had barely managed to freeze it in time. Stormbringer had not held back much at all. *Birds are jerks, just like cats.*

"Of course. Feel free to use the bolt to strike down an enemy." Stormbringer granted magnanimously. *Yep, jerks. It is already in my repository; you don't get a say.*

Stormbringer vanished in a flash of even more lightning. In his absence a storm formed in the skies above, and the clouds rapidly changed from peaceful to dangerous. They wasted no time and moved through the portal to the next floor.

The trio appeared on a platform in space. Floor 71 consisted of a circular platform with a radius of twenty meters. At the center of the platform floated a burning sphere of pure, concentrated Aether. Beyond the platform crawled forces that, while composed of Nether, were of a different variety than the cold hungry power of Nyx. This strangely flavored Nether flowed and gathered into its own concentrations.

"Why don't I recognize this type of Nether?" Aetheria asked the other two, while Arkaziel hopped off her shoulder to curl up underneath the blaze of concentrated Aether. A powerful aura of light surrounded Arkaziel, and the ball of Aether grew in intensity.

"Good idea, Ark." Aetheria dropped a few Ethereal fruits from storage to help keep the cat powered up.

"It is Void Nether, Aetheria. Nothingness, Emptiness, and Nonexistence are its traits. Some say it is the origin from which our universe came and will return to at the end of time." Werylin stared at the darkness beyond their platform with a frown. The darkness seemed to shake the elf in some fundamental way that it didn't Aetheria and Arkaziel.

The stronger that the sphere of Aether grew, the larger the clusters of Nether grew.

Aetheria raised her left hand. The fragments of the Nether crystal woven through Astrum Nexus glimmered in resonance, and a pulse of recognition flowed from essence of Nyx, while the essence of Ymir also recognized this void as antithetical to itself. The Nether past the platform reacted like a beehive hit by a rock. Agitation, erratic movement, sudden and strange shifts in form.

"Mine." Aetheria vocalized her intention, and the Primordial Flame of Nyx within Astrum Nexus and within her burned dark and intense. The Nether grew more and more agitated, but streams of power were pulled from the gathered clumps and pulled to Aetheria's hand, where they were devoured mercilessly. The other clumps of Nether around the platform shot around the platform to reinforce the concentration she attacked. The flow of power she stole from the Nether diminished but did not stop.

Voices filled her mind. A cacophony of nihilism, a chittering of madness, a hundred voices clamored for her to accept the Void and give her power to it. It was inevitable, after all; all power ended there at some point.

Ocean's Serenity formed tiny icicles from the effort of regulating her emotions, but other than goosebumps Aetheria stared at the dark tendrils at the edge of the light with determination in her eyes.

"I have it on good authority you weren't first."

Aetheria's right hand clenched, and a rainbow-hued inferno surrounded her. The addition of the Transcendent Flame of Khaos from Astrum Nexus with the

Flame inside of Aetheria had increased her ability to wield the power of Khaos significantly.

"As someone trying to sort out the truth from the lies, it is just beyond annoying to have all of you gods, embodiments, forces, and whatever's bragging to me about how you are somehow better than the others, the first, the best, or the end. It's obnoxious."

The stream of Nether being ripped out of the Void increased beyond what it had been originally. Even with all of the chthonic force or entity gathering together, it couldn't resist being devoured. At the same time, Arkaziel had continued enhancing the sphere of Aether, and it had already increased in size to take up half the platform. Its holy light made the Void smoke.

"We were first; we will be last."

The Nether form had been pulled onto the platform by Aetheria's drain attack, and the proximity to the divine Aether burned even more of the darkness away to reveal disturbing figures underneath the flows of Nether. They looked like insectoids, a mix between a mantis and a cockroach, with black exoskeletons. Their pitch-black eyes hungered for the end of everything. Aetheria felt her stomach churn while she examined them.

A flash of Werylin's katana beheaded one of the strange insects, which caused the other three to screech with such intensity Werylin fell to the platform, hands over his long ears.

Aetheria smiled savagely as she ripped the last of the Nether from them, then froze the insects until they shattered into nothing.

"Does anyone know what those were?" Aetheria asked while she helped Werylin back to his feet.

"Not a clue." Werylin shook his head and looked at the fragments of ice with disgust. "They made me feel . . . terror? Existential dread?"

Arkaziel's tail lazily thumped the platform repeatedly until the other two looked at him. He still lay under the ever-growing sphere of divine Aether, its light growing by the second.

"We StarManes have heard legends of creatures like that. They seep through the Void, from somewhere else, and want to turn our universe into a void like theirs. They might not have been lying, Aetheria. If they come from a suitably different place, maybe they were the first? Or they're just arrogant pricks. You kicked four of their asses solo, Aetheria, so how tough could they be?"

Aetheria frowned. That felt like the kind of statement that would eventually return to haunt them.

CHAPTER 34

The Vortex of Voices

The doorway to the next floor formed only when the sphere of Aether covered the whole platform, at which point it exploded like a balloon and showered them in confetti. The door to the next floor appeared as they finished plucking the confetti off themselves.

Floor 72 started in one of Aetheria's least favorite ways. She appeared on a small platform. The hiss of wind pushed tides of sand through the air, which reduced visibility to nothing. On the wind she could hear whispers in a multitude of voices. Unlike the voices of the void insects, these whispered directions on how to make it through the maze. Well, some did. Others just ridiculed her.

First things first, Aetheria tried to take control of the winds. Air was one of her worst affinities, even after eating a number of air affinity increasing fruits. Her attempts to manipulate the winds went nowhere. Her efforts created eddies in the gusts and nothing more. Her next idea involved creation of a few ice walls to stop the winds. The sand just went through the ice wall, and a moment later the wall crumbled. Annoyed, Aetheria flared an Aetherflame Nova. Surely fire would melt the sand and cause at least a little clear area?

Nope. The sand seemed to be completely immune to everything she threw at it. Ice, cold, fire, wind, water, chaos, time . . . nothing she did mattered.

"That's not going to work." One of the voices laughed.

"Oh, it might, she should keep trying," another taunted.

"What if she eats the sand?" another inquired.

Aetheria took slow, deep breaths to calm herself.

The voices clearly played a role in this challenge, as far as she could tell. Unless her absorption of the Void Nether had corrupted her mind? A brush of her fingers against Ocean's Serenity showed the earrings were still normal temperature, not the frigid temperatures they reached when they fought external influences.

"Oh, look how cute she is, in a sandstorm and checking her earrings!" A familiar voice mocked Aetheria. Her own. She opened her mouth to retort but no sound came forth. They had stolen her voice from her! Indignation and anger flared through her mind, so intense Ocean's Serenity chilled her skin a little, while the artifact smoothed out the abrupt surge of emotions.

Annoyed at the theft and the uselessness of her usual tools, she drew deeply of Ethereal power within herself and expanded it outward as a new domain.

"I always knew you weren't the brightest human, but now you're just throwing energy around in a temper tantrum?" Arkaziel's voice taunted her.

"Now, now, maybe she has a plan? Her plans are always so amazing." Werylin's voice riposted with more sarcasm than Aetheria had ever heard the elf use before.

Aetheria ignored the voices and fashioned herself a new domain. She tapped the Transcendent Flame of Khaos, the Primordial Flame of Ymir, and the Primordial Flame of Thalassa for this creation. The Flames of Thalassa and Ymir were mixed to add creation and water to the mix, while the Flame of Khaos should allow her to break the rules. With the domain extended to ten meters, she activated it. Spheres of water popped into existence. These spheres managed to catch the rule-breaking sand. Before long the ground, previously bare stone, lay heavy with sand.

The maze before Aetheria held no challenge once she could see. She made quick work of the maze and found herself before a door at the end of the maze. It tried to bar her way, but a single punch destroyed it. She admired the way ice formed around her fist when she punched like a gauntlet. She didn't like to overuse the word *love*, but she legitimately loved Astrum Nexus already.

Aetheria entered a spherical room. The acoustics of the chamber were odd, and the sounds of wind, sand, and thousands of voices reverberated in a deeply unsettling way. Goosebumps popped up on her arms, the hair on the back of her neck stood, and her stomach felt queasy.

"So the little Asura wants to play with the Lord of Voices? How adorable. I'll tell you what, if you ask for your voice back, I'll give it to you! Ahahaha."

Aetheria decided she really didn't care for this trial. Did she sound that obnoxious when she tried to be clever? She decided there and then she would make this self-proclaimed Lord of Voices suffer for the temerity of using her own voice to mock her. Multihued spheres of water appeared in the air to catch the dust, only to explode and get the stone floor of the chamber wet.

"Sorry, but this is my lair, no domains but my own!"

The Lord of Voices didn't appear to be able to collapse her domain, only negate its function. Perhaps the Flame of Khaos prevented its total annulment? She retained the domain; there seemed to be a chance she could make it work once the Lord of Voices got pushed to the defensive.

Aetheria launched herself toward the whirlwind form of the Lord of Voices. An explosion of sound erupted in front of her, and a sonic scream from hell hit her point-blank in the face. The force of the explosion of sound sent her flying like a doll thrown by an angry toddler. She slammed into the outer wall of the chamber with enough force to send cracks through the stone walls.

"That looked like it hurt. Did it hurt? Your regeneration is depriving me of watching you bleed."

Another explosion of sound erupted to her left, and then to her right. Again, Aetheria flew through the air, and just before she hit the ground another explosion of sound sent her flying again. The continued explosions annoyed her more than they hurt her, but she had lost all forward momentum and couldn't escape the cycle of explosions. The next explosion in the chain didn't come, however, and she slammed into the ground and rolled. Surprised, she looked up to see Werylin had entered the room.

"Oh-ho. Two on one? You know, the doors were meant to let you all gather and challenge me at once, but no patience, no patience! Oh, whatever will the swordsman whose powers are all keyed to speaking the Words of Creation ever do to me?" The Lord of Voices mocked Werylin, who didn't seem the least bit perturbed as he drew Harmonious Tempest and advanced on the lord.

Aetheria and Werylin made eye contact. They charged. Raucous explosions of sound sent both through the air. Werylin, somehow, managed to dodge the explosion of sound and appeared in front of the Lord of Voices. Harmonious Tempest flashed through the whirlwind, the runes on the katana flared brightly, and a voice not Werylin's said "Harmonious Cascade" to the shock of the Lord of Voices.

From her position against a wall, Aetheria witnessed the golden lightning of the Imperator of Order crash into the whirlwind. Chunks of something resembling glass formed when the lightning struck the Voice, and a terrible shriek exploded outward. Even Werylin couldn't dodge a nova attack, and slammed against the wall. Aetheria, only a few steps away from the wall she'd just hit, found herself flung into the wall again.

"Your tenacity shall be rewarded with death. I will keep your voices as my due. Few indeed manage to hurt me." The whirlwind accelerated its rotation: first the air pulled in toward it, then Aetheria and Werylin both felt the pull toward the center of the room.

Amid this drama, another section of the wall exploded, and Arkaziel walked into the chamber. The StarMane had taken on a form like a lion. Unfortunately, his dramatic entry left him also at the mercy of the inescapable draw to the center of the room. The look of triumph on his face quickly turned to confusion, then to anger. Tentacles of shadow rose from the ground across the room, but Aetheria didn't understand their purpose until the tentacles grasped the trio to fight the suction.

"Hemorrhage!" another voice that was not Werylin's exclaimed, and the Lord of Voices shuddered. Hundreds of voices cried out in pain, and then thousands. Blood leaked from Aetheria's ears. The crescendo showed no sign of ending anytime soon.

Aetheria activated her flash core, triggered the Transcendent Flame of Chronos to increase the potency, and also activated the Transcendent Flame of Khaos in her right hand. The room seemed to be frozen in time while she blurred past the sand to the whirlwind itself and snapped her multihued right thumb and middle finger.

Snap.

An explosion of sound erupted from her hand, aimed at the vortex. Rules were meant to be broken when Khaos entered the picture. The frequency and intensity of the sound waves struck the Lord of Voices and counteracted its own.

Aetheria tapped her foot, bored, while she waited for her attack to finish off the defenses of the creature within the whirlwind. An eternity later, the winds stopped completely to reveal a small creature the size of a Yorkshire terrier. It looked like an imp, but slightly cuter, although its vivid blue eyes were every bit as cruel as those of an imp.

Aetheria ended Flash Mode, and the world slammed into relatively normal speed around her.

The creature begged for its life immediately. "Don't kill me, don't kill me! It's just my job, you know!"

Werylin and Arkaziel joined Aetheria, who stood with palpable menace above the fae creature. Her right hand still flared with the multihued power of Khaos.

"Why shouldn't I?" Aetheria asked, then smiled when she realized her voice had returned.

The fae creature stuttered, then looked up to Werylin. Surely the elf with Sylvan armor would save it?

Chomp.

Arkaziel licked his lips and swallowed.

"Oh, tasty."

"Ark! You should chew your food! The last thing we need is some gremlin making a nest in your stomach because you were too lazy to chew your food." Aetheria let out a loud sigh, but she felt a little thankful that Arkaziel had handled the execution.

"Definitely. That was a type of Sylph, I believe. Very stubborn and lingering."

Arkaziel burped. A cacophony of voices shot out of his mouth and dissipated into the Ether.

"Never mind. Remind me to never get eaten by a StarMane, I don't want to go through anything that digests a Sylph that fast." Werylin shook his head in disbelief.

"You're a good seed, Werylin, I'd never eat you."

+Elves don't have enough meat on their bones to be more than an appetizer.+

~Bad kitty! Bad!~

Aetheria coughed and jerked her thumb toward the doorway that appeared.

"Floor Seventy-Three. We're getting close to the three-quarter boss. Make sure you test out all your new equipment before we hit the boss floor."

+Hey, Blue, what does this collar Chronos had you give me do, anyway? I can't figure it out.+

CHAPTER 35

Ciphers

Aetheria stared long and hard at Arkaziel.

~*So it's a collar now, is it?* ~

The cat's yellow eyes stared back at her red eyes.

+*I misspoke. My leather pendant, do you know what it does?*+

Aetheria thumbed her chin and examined the collar. She hadn't actually paid it any attention since she had gained the Forge Insight ability. She really ought to review all of their equipment with it, in case they were missing out on any hidden capabilities of their gear.

~*Let's see here. It has a name: Aeon Eclipse. It looks like its abilities won't activate until you bind it to your soul. It increases the efficiency of your consumption of energy and creatures, and . . . Oh, that's not good.* ~

Arkaziel practically twitched when Aetheria trailed off. His tail swayed back and forth with extra gusto, and with every millisecond she kept the cat hanging, he grew more and more agitated. She talked again just before he nearly lost his patience.

~*Your lovely creator god seems to like the cut of your jib, Ark. It speeds up the charge on your Eclipse attacks and generates extra shadows in areas that have passed through there within the last day when you need more shadows than are present. If you hit Tier Five, it will upgrade with you, but I can't tell what it'll do at that point.* ~

+*Chronos must love me! That's all super amazing. Let me bind this real quick, then let's jump into the next floor! That shadow part sounds really useful, actually. Combined with my own abilities I can spy on the last day anywhere I go!*+

~*I doubt Chronos meant you to be a peeping Tom, Arkaziel.* ~

+*What's a peeping Tom?*+

~*A pervert who invades people's privacy.* ~

+*I am a pervert. Why, remember that cat-girl? I—*+

~*Nope. We are not having that conversation, Ark. What you do on your time is your business, and I'm very happy for you if you enjoy it, but I don't want to know.* ~

+*Does this mean I'm not going to get juicy details about you and the witch?*+

~No, no you won't be getting juicy details. Anyone who tries to spy on us will find out the meaning of absolute zero.~

+Sounds cold.+

Eventually, the trio made it through the portal to Floor 73. They appeared on a hilltop inside of a series of stones that formed a five-pointed star, with them and a statue atop a large plinth at the center. The enormous statue of an attractive male angel dominated the plinth, and he held a large scroll that flowed all the way to the ground. The words upon it were written in Ath.

"Oh no, not again, am I having a stroke?" Aetheria asked her companions.

"Nope, it's complete gibberish to me. Excellent artistry on the runes of Primeval Sylvan you rarely see, though."

"It's written in Ath, you fool, and it makes no sense." Arkaziel disagreed with Werylin.

"It's written in the viewer's primary language, Ark. I'm reading Epmpiwxi Eixmxmwx, Pmsx qi rswxpi xmrk gsqqivw wtsr xsvi rmiwigx ws xli evms lipxyvi. Which just doesn't make any sense at all." Aetheria kept observing the text from different angles, but nothing helped. She studied the words with Ethereal Sight and found nothing special about them.

"It has finally happened. We've reached a puzzle floor with ciphers." Arkaziel hissed.

"Ciphers as in writing through a code?" Werylin looked displeased.

Aetheria took a deep breath and quelled the unpleasant way her stomach swam in response to this type of puzzle. A pile of equipment fell out of her repository around them. Three chairs, some clipboards with writing utensils, and paper.

"No choice but to work it out. The faster we knock this out, the faster we're on another floor."

Arkaziel gave Aetheria the stink-eye for the chair and clipboard. When she sat on one of the chairs, the cat jumped onto her shoulder, and then on top of her head, where he slapped her in the face a few times with his tail. Only then did the clipboard from the other chair float through the air, and shadows grasped the pen to write on the paper.

"So happy you're comfortable up there, Ark," Aetheria said in a quiet voice.

"Oh yes, very comfortable. Your hair is very silky, plus my fur is absorbing the lovely glow, so it is also energizing sitting here. I should sit on your head more often." Arkaziel played dumb in his response, but Aetheria noticed his tail no longer approached her face.

The hours slipped by while each of the three doodled and played with letters and words.

"It's a shift cipher." Aetheria growled under her breath.

"What's a shift cipher," Werylin dutifully asked while Arkaziel snored on Aetheria's head.

"You shift each letter of the alphabet by the same number of spaces. Back on Earth we referred to it as a Caesar's cipher. This message is shifted four. So, the first letter of the first word, shift it back four letters in your alphabet, and then do the same for each one."

Werylin took to the information quickly, and after moment they compared answers.

The elf walked to the plinth, knocked three times, then said loudly.

"Almighty Aetherius, lift me into the airy heavens so that I might join you."

The angel statue emitted an intense glow, and when it faded the trio were in another place.

Aetheria, Arkaziel, and Werylin appeared atop a cloud with a very familiar setup. Another angel statue surrounded by a five point star, another gobbled message.

"Yld, zmw hzb: Olri lu gsv Fkkvi Hprvb, yivzm nv slfihv rnvhhv blfiw."

Aetheria spoke the gibberish aloud, while Werylin had already set to work to see if this was a shift cipher like the last. Arkaziel snored, but the other two found it better than the alternatives the cat could be up to.

"This isn't a shift cipher," Aetheria said with a laugh. It had been a slim chance the Administrators would reuse the same cipher. "Well, there's a few other somewhat basic ciphers. There are substitution ciphers, but they would need to give us at least a partial key to start from with that. It's not written in the right way to be a zigzag cipher. It could be a reverse cipher?"

Aetheria eyed the first word, reversed the letter placement, and smirked when she got an actual word. "Bow."

"Got it!" she exclaimed, and then quickly wrote out the rest of the cipher.

"Bow, and say: Lord of the Upper Skies, bring me higher into your domain." Werylin delivered the bow and message, since Arkaziel still slept atop Aetheria's head.

When the teleportation effect faded, this time the trio found themselves before a statue of Aetherius. It radiated divine power, and the flows of Aether in this place were exceptionally dense. While they watched, a tablet appeared before the statue, with a five-by-five grid on it. Only the first row had letters in it.

MAGIC

A series of letter pairs were displayed below the grid.

GD UF DS CT XE MY BG FX PT QD ND XG TG SE

"Oh god, this is college all over again." Aetheria groaned loudly when she saw the grid.

"So, not an easy one," Werylin asked with a chuckle.

"No. I sort of recognize this one, though. Give me a few minutes to remember how it works."

Aetheria wrote on the tablet with the provided piece of chalk to finish the grid.

MAGIC

BDEFH

K L N O P
Q R S T U
V W X Y Z

"I am not a fan of ciphers, I have decided," Werylin declared with narrowed eyes and a scowl.

"You didn't use them as Imperator or during the war?"

"No. We had magic for secure communications. Why would we rely on something this asinine to relay a message?"

Magic seemed a lot easier to Aetheria, too.

"Could we just cast a spell to solve this?"

Werylin laughed, then thought about it, before he cracked his neck and chanted.

"The answer is: Aetherius, give me your blessing."

Nothing happened.

"What a crock. Not going to give it to us unless we break our brains on this? Okay, so I think we have to break the letters into pairs, then there's rules to what you do. If I remember right it's same row goes left, same column goes above, and something like . . ." Aetheria trailed off as a ding sounded.

"Guess they're giving it to us as close enough."

"Lucky us." Sarcasm dripped from Aetheria's words, but truthfully she felt thankful. The last rule of playfair ciphers dangled out of her memory, but the Administrator had saved her from having to struggle to recall it.

A blue ephemeral light illuminated all three of them. Aetheria noted the relief, the loss of tension, and a general increase in strength flowed through her body with the strange light. Arkaziel actually woke up, looked around, and hopped onto the ground to examine the statue.

"Oh cute, it's a playfair cipher with magic as a keyword. Let's see, it says 'Aetherius, give me your blessing'."

Aetheria and Werylin stared daggers at the cat.

"You guys didn't struggle with this one too long, did you? I was just like, really tired. You know how sometimes you just need sixteen hours of sleep? No? Guys? Why are you both glaring at the statue of Aetherius, isn't that sacrilege? Better knock it off. Oh look! The door to Floor 74! Let's go!" Arkaziel bolted through the portal to the next floor while Werylin and Aetheria exchanged looks.

"I'm dumping him into a lake next time we find one."

"Can't you just make a lake? A really big one?"

"I can; good point."

"How did you make it through half of a tower with him?"

Aetheria grinned at Werylin's question.

"Honestly? It wasn't so bad. Ark knows when to scale it back. He pushes the boundaries without crossing them, most of the time. Like everyone, he misjudges. His heart is in the right place, I think. He's a surprisingly emotional kitty, but you'd never know that if you weren't in a psychic bond with him."

"You are an odd person, Aetheria. The worshippers of Eros have a saying: a soft heart is strengthened by love, a hard heart is weakened by it. You are very softhearted for an Asura."

"Glad to hear it. My homework this year is to master love."

Werylin gave her an odd look before he walked through the portal.

CHAPTER 36

Interrogation

The room had no light. The only illumination came from Aetheria herself. Dim red light cast from her eyes, and aqua radiance sparkled from her hair, to reveal she had appeared in an oblong sphere. The walls were constructed of an unfamiliar white crystal that she couldn't scratch, not even with a super-hard shard of ice or a diamond talon. *Administrator trickery.*

The thought acted like a summons.

"What is your name?" The voice came from all directions and none, omnipresent and creepy. A feminine voice, bored and following protocol like every bureaucrat she had ever met in her life.

"Aetheria," she answered.

"No surname?"

"Not yet."

"Occupation?"

"Tower Climber," Aetheria answered a little uncertainly.

"Is that a question or an answer?" Aetheria could hear the arched eyebrow of the questioner, the annoyance at an uncertain answer.

"An answer, sorry. Tower Climber is my current occupation." It had, in fact, made her fairly wealthy. She didn't know anyone else with multiple flying cities in their pocket, but she didn't know that many people either, so maybe she wasn't that rich.

"Age?"

Silence. Aetheria couldn't offer much of an answer there. Was she supposed to include her time as Aesca in that? How long had she been in the tower? Did she include the twenty years of stasis while her body exploded?

"I don't know."

"That's more common than you'd expect," the feminine voice answered with surprising sympathy.

"Do you know?"

"I've always taken the stance of rounding to the nearest fifty, so let's call you fifty."

Aetheria nodded. Her estimates of how long she had been in the tower were close, then.

"Why are none of your companions your own race?"

Aetheria felt the question like a slap in the face. Perhaps it was the tone the woman asked it with?

"Uh, well. I haven't met many people who could survive the climb with me, and race wasn't really that important of a factor?"

"You did not like your own race much in your original world."

"Look, people are difficult. What race someone is doesn't change that. People judge, they jump to conclusions, they intentionally misunderstand what you say to make a point. There are a lot of people who just want to make their point, and everything else be damned. That's not a purely human characteristic from what I've seen on the city floors, but a trait that spans all people. So no, I wasn't the biggest fan of people on Earth, or I wouldn't have spent so much time escaping in video games, anime, and books."

"So you don't like people?"

"I like *some* people."

"Do you think something is wrong with you?"

"Yes."

"What's wrong with you?"

"I don't know. Does labeling it accomplish anything?"

"It accomplishes me filling in the blank on the document."

"Of course, sorry to inconvenience your completion of my interrogation document. How about we just write mental illness?"

"What type of mental illness?"

"How big is the blank?"

"As big as it needs to be."

"Let's see. There's the depression, that's been a lifelong struggle. Self-image."

"Expound on that, please."

"Self-image? Look, what teenage girl doesn't fight with appearance issues on Earth? I came out of it with a better understanding of nutrition and dietary needs."

"As a shapeshifter, you can look like anything."

"I wasn't always a shapeshifter. Those don't exist on Earth."

"My apologies, that's not documented here."

"So, as a shapeshifter, why do you stick so strongly to the same basic appearance?"

"This is Aetheria."

"What does that mean?"

"Aetheria was a persona I made up for video games. Tall, lithe, bright, sexy, and badass. She was my avatar for over two decades, while I wasn't any of those things except tall. So, when I think me, I think this."

"So, do you think of yourself as human? Glowing hair and eyes are not intrinsically human traits. In fact, nothing about you resembles a human, except your soul."

"Isn't that the most important thing?"

"Souls change over time. A human soul today could be a squirrel, elf, or gnome soul in the next cycle. The wheel turns ever on, and a new part is picked with each life. It is a stretch to call your soul human, with how much reshaping your *parents* did."

"You avoided my question there. Aren't souls the most important thing?"

A long, drawn-out silence.

"I suppose you could say that. You could also say that they are not. Like your urge to dispel some of your personal responsibility onto a neurological divergence, souls both are of primary importance and none at all."

"How does that work?"

"Very few souls ever escape the cycle of existence. The Samsara has greedy hands, so while souls are recast, reshaped, recycled, very few manage to break free of the endless cycle to make their own way. Those souls find their way *elsewhere*."

"You aren't an Administrator, are you?"

"No. No, I am not."

"Who are you, then?"

"Juno."

"Hi, Juno. So, who decides what happens to souls?"

"Gods."

"Not one specific god, or one type of god, just . . . gods?"

"Correct. Don't ask me what sorts the souls, but they are sent to the towers. We may use those sent to us as we wish, in the tower or on one of the planets within our domain in physical reality."

"Were you supposed to tell me that?"

"You stand outside of most rules, thanks to being freed from the Samsara. Still, maybe don't spread it around?"

"When a god dies, does it get sent to someone else's tower, or its own?"

"Fantastic question. Who knows? Our re-formations just appear, sometimes right away, sometimes after delays. Only slight differences, subtle wrongness, give away any change has happened. We ourselves don't recognize anything has changed, beyond a gap in our memories. Some of us have died significantly more often than others."

"Do so few souls escape the Samsara because you gods are jealous of your own eternal prison?"

"Possible. It's an onerous process, you know. Even Nyx and Aetherius had to cash in much to achieve it just for you, and Nyx once held the Divine Scepter and reigned as the Overgod after Phanes's death. Helping enlighten even one soul is more than most gods could do within their means."

"There's a lot you aren't telling me there."

"Astute, but yes. There are things I can't tell even you. The rules of the Overgod are absolute."

"So why you, and why me?"

"Call it my maternal instinct? Or perhaps I wanted to assess whether you are a threat, an ally, or a nonfactor. You consort with the oldest of Primordials and other dangerous figures, and ascend to the heights of power faster than a newborn demigod. Chronos even paid my son to forge a weapon for you. The ancients haven't moved like this since ages long gone. Even I have taken notice."

"And what has your meeting with me inclined you to think?" Aetheria didn't restrain her curiosity. She had answered the goddess's questions honestly as she had been able, and hopefully Juno would return the favor.

"I have a number of theories. At first, I thought Nyx sought the Divine Scepter once again, but Aetherius continued his involvement and pulled Thalassa and Ymir into the mix. Ymir, barbarian though he is, is ancient and powerful. My curiosity was truly piqued when he gave you his Flame and you survived. Then Khaos and Chronos themselves got involved, which is simply unprecedented. Most modern gods don't even know those two retain sapience. Popular opinion holds they had both devolved and/or no longer hold interest in the universe."

"So, that made me revise my opinions. Nyx, glorious though she is, pales in comparison to those two ancient horrors. I believe they intend to push you to ascension to a higher realm. What I don't understand is whether they intend to somehow stow away when you escape this realm for a higher, or if the act of your ascension would somehow cause a chain reaction that I am ignorant of."

"Can't help you there. You have more ideas of what they want than I do. I also think, maybe, you're seeing unity where there is self-interest?"

Juno's laughter had a hint of something dangerous to it, and it made Aetheria deeply uncomfortable.

"You are being set up for something, child. I do not see the endgame, but the pieces are on the board. A dual-souled StarMane, one of the few remaining scions of the Speakers of Creation, then there's the daughter of Belial being your soul-bound partner."

"Belial?" Aetheria couldn't help but be surprised. Aoibhe had never mentioned her father's name, beyond the fact he had been a corrupt and terrible fallen angel. That would be a discussion saved for their reunion when it came, but there were probably reasons for it, even if she was sad that Aoibhe hadn't told her. Some powerful beings could hear their name, no matter where it was said. Perhaps Belial could be one of those beings? Or Aoibhe carried shame for such a dark relation. Aetheria sent pulses of love through the connection in their soul.

"Angel. Demon. Divine punisher and demonic torturer. His roles vary, but he is evil in all incarnations."

"We had a Belial in mythology of my world. Juno, too, for that matter."

"Existence is a wide, confusing tapestry."

Juno failed to rise to the bait. Aetheria had really hoped to get one of these gods to spill the beans on how the crazy intermixed theologies melded together, instead of just saying the equivalent of "oh that's interesting."

"Have I passed your interrogation then, Juno?"

"You have answered my questions admirably. You are far too modest, naive, and guileless to be a true immortal. May the heartache caused by your naiveite be minimal, Aetheria."

"That's not at all ominous. I'm not your enemy, am I?" To the former Minnesotan, the idea of direct conflict with individuals still felt unnatural and disturbing to Aetheria. Even with three quarters of a tower behind her, the realities of a world or universe of conflict had not fully taken root in her mind. Fighting monsters, demons, and undead had never driven the point home, and most of the sentient humanoids she'd been forced into conflict with had been arguably evil.

"No, but I would not call you an ally either."

Juno spoke no further.

Somewhere between an hour or two later, Aetheria lost track of time. While building up her inner world, cracks formed in the egg around her. A flare of light later and she stood on a stage with a crab-man at a podium. On the other side of the crab-man a bingo popper spun balls.

"There you are, Aetheria! Let's go. Mission accomplished." Arkaziel hopped onto the stage, then onto her shoulder. Werylin waited at the base of the stage, which the crab-man shooed her toward so he could get back to running a game.

"What'd I miss," Aetheria questioned. She gave Arkaziel a good pet and cuddle.

"We had to play bingo to free you from the ball. I do not like this game." Werylin's hard stare at the ball conveyed the depths of his disdain for the game. "Why would you willingly play a game that you cannot influence?"

"You are looking at it all wrong. It is a game for socializing with other people. You barely pay attention, drink some beer, eat some chips, and have a good time. Don't elves have a game like that?"

"No. If we wanted to socialize in that way, we would just socialize without the pretext," Werylin declared haughtily, defending elven superiority.

"Says the race that invented the game Stars of Fate."

Arkaziel's retort left Werylin incoherent and muttering. Aetheria and the cat stared at the minstrel until he regained his composure. The portal to the next floor had formed in the back corner of the bingo hall.

"Well, not as many combat trials as I would have liked, but let's fight the second to last boss, shall we?" Werylin asked when he regained his composure.

"We should figure out a battle cry."

CHAPTER 37

To the Death

Aetheria, Arkaziel, and Werylin appeared on a rather large sky island. The island had no inclines, no animals, no vegetation even. The gray clouds that marked where the island ended had the appearance of smoke more than clouds. A strange dome of energy appeared over them, blocking out vision and any other senses.

Arkaziel piped up. "They're building the arena now, so that no side gets a home court advantage."

"The Administrators have never bothered with that kind of move before. Why now?" Aetheria questioned with a frown. The first two large bosses had seen them thrown into the den or home turf of incredible monsters. Ocean's Serenity chilled against her skin as the artifact calmed her.

"Are we fighting actual people?" Werylin bit his lower lip slightly. The elf stroked the hilt of his katana while he pondered the nature of their opponents to come. Aetheria couldn't detect any consternation within the elf about facing humanoid opponents instead of beasts, but Werylin had spent a century fighting a single war. It would stand to reason he had fewer qualms about fighting humanoids than Aetheria.

"Werylin, once the dome drops, cast Haste. Ark, pulse the shadows of the entire island, locate any hostiles. This might be more than a two-sided fight for all we know. I'll cover you both." A thrill had risen within Aetheria. The same rush that she felt when new arenas or Player vs. Player scenarios were released for Eldest Fantasy Wars Online filled her now. The air practically vibrated around her in response to the excited tension she had no way to release.

"Focus, Aetheria. Your red streaks are showing, and one of your eyes went blue."

As Arkaziel said, the nervous energy had wound Aetheria up enough that the physical changes her last tier-up had wrought upon her were on prominent display. She didn't bother to hide them again. With how anxious and jittery she felt, it seemed inevitable she'd revert to her newest truest self.

"Go!"

The voice rang through their ears and minds. The energy dome dissipated.

"Haste!" Werylin buffed the trio.

Every shadow Aetheria could see squirmed briefly.

"Four enemies, quarter of a mile away. They're splitting into two groups of two." Arkaziel followed Aetheria's directives without complaint, surprisingly. "One of them did something like I did with the shadows, with light. I faked our presence over in that ravine. It seems like they're intending to flank the ravine. Ambush?"

"Ambush," Werylin and Aetheria agreed.

The sky darkened. A lightning bolt descended from the heavens, but Aetheria froze it and stored the enormous bolt of electricity.

"I don't think they fell for it, Ark." The flatness of Aetheria's voice was such that it could convert the weak minded to being a flat-earther.

"Incoming!" Arkaziel had no time to retort. Two figures shot toward their location.

The first wore only a pair of white shorts, and otherwise the man looked like he belonged at a bodybuilding contest. Which he would win. His hair was dark blue, and he wielded a lightning bolt in his hand as if he were Zeus. He had almost no equipment on, beyond a bracelet on his left arm. He emitted a strong Tier Four aura, which he made no effort to hide or restrain. Aetheria dubbed him Bolt. *He's going all out from start to finish.*

The second wore chainmail, carried an axe, and flew by his command of powerful winds. Like his companion, he emitted a powerful fourth-tier aura with no effort to restrain or hide it. Oddly, none of his equipment bore magic of its own; it was all just standard, if well-made, equipment. The axe made her think of Thor a little bit, but this guy didn't quite give her Thor vibes. So, she called him Stormy.

~ *Full out, help me take down Stormy.* ~

+ *Who?* +

~ *Axe man!* ~

The sky darkened more than either of their opponents managed with their storms as Arkaziel formed an eclipse faster than ever before.

Aetheria sprang forward, and suddenly there were two of her, one made of ice. The one made of ice approached Bolt. With each step, a new ice creation appeared next to the ice-Aetheria. First came a dragon, then a spear turret, and then a human figure with a railgun. Bolt went from offense to defense, as spears of ice, rails, and ice breath assaulted him, to say nothing of the ice-form of Aetheria who tried to punch his glorious face in.

The real Aetheria accomplished this by activating her most powerful trick first, the Flash Mode of her cultivation core. To her the world had essentially stopped moving, so she had plenty of time to control multiple constructs. It gave Arkaziel time to get into place, before Aetheria blurred before Stormy. Her fingers shifted to diamond talons, and Astrum Nexus formed Ethereal ice into even more ferocious claws to accompany the talons.

Stormy had no defense against her first hit. Aetheria's claws and talons ripped through his ordinary armor as if it was not even there. The first strike gouged him from left shoulder to right hip, and her follow-up went the other way. Stormy still hadn't reacted yet, so she stabbed her right talons into his chest to find his core.

The dire threat to Stormy's life seemed to have pushed him past his normal limitations, but he still moved in slow motion compared to Aetheria. The blood from her first slash still hung in the air—Flash Mode combined with the power of the Transcendent Flame of Chronos in the Astrum Nexus were a truly formidable combination. She did not even bother to dodge the axe swing Stormy tried to fend her off with. Her talons clutched around his core, and with the Transcendent Flame of Khaos in both herself and the Astrum Nexus, she stole his power and life.

When she cracked open his core like an egg, the man's flesh flecked away, his hair withered, and he vanished from existence within the equivalent of a one count to her, which meant that to the others it looked like she'd appeared, and then Stormy died with blood in the air and her hand in his chest.

The massive flux of energy Aetheria stole initially tried to form itself into another Flame within her, yet it felt weaker by far than any of her Flames, so she stopped it. Instead, she pushed the power and aspects into her core, and it flushed her with strength, electricity flickering around her briefly until the core acclimated the power.

Aetheria dropped out of Flash Mode, and the world sped up around her.

~Hit the other guy if you can.~

+That was brutal, Aetheria. I love it, but I don't know how I feel about having to compete with you for eating people.+

~Don't be absurd, I didn't eat him.~

Praise and then silence were worse than an open condemnation of what she had just done to Stormy, in a way. Hadn't she set out on this journey to be a heroine?

"What the hell was that?"

"What?" Aetheria asked with an innocent look at Werylin's demand.

"That!" The elf gestured not at the spot where Stormy had died, but toward Bolt.

The dark-haired man deflected spears of ice with his lightning bolt, he blocked the dragon's ice breath with a stomp of his foot to create a shockwave of debris, and a railgun shot hit the man in the abdomen, but the wound regenerated as they watched. Ice-Aetheria boxed with him throughout all of this, and with each strike dark patches were left on the man's skin. Those healed, but slowly. Otherwise, no real damage had been done to the man.

Total eclipse struck, and darkness ate all light in the area.

Except . . . a burning radiance countered the darkness. Two radiances. One bright and pure, like the morning sun, the other flamboyant and joyous, in the full hues of a rainbow. The eclipse completely shattered, and behind Bolt appeared two figures. One female, one male.

The male looked to be related to elves at the least, with pointed ears, a slender masculine build, and a sword made of rainbows. He wore light Sylvan armor like Werylin's, but otherwise their similarities were met with just as many differences. Yet the swordsman smiled at Werylin and beckoned him to fight him with two fingers.

As if the two had entered their own sphere, they both walked off to one side of the battlefield, while the other four all looked on with expressions that varied from amused to annoyed.

The second figure had feminine curves hidden under a very modest robe. Her hair hid from view with a habit, while a veil obscured her face. Despite her attire offering no actual idea about the physical appearance of the woman, she radiated beauty in an inexplicable way that lit a minor spark of jealousy in Aetheria. Her ineffable beauty and ethereal grace, mixed with the soothing presence, seemed quite out of place on the battlefield.

"You ruined my spell!" Arkaziel boomed so loudly the floating island shook. If the cat had been in his full-sized form, perhaps that thunderous voice would have not seemed out of place, but he had taken on his house cat size and form. Even the swordsmen, about to start a duel, stared at the ridiculousness of a cat shouting at the robed woman.

The woman did not answer, beyond lifting a folding fan in one hand. She snapped it closed, and the fan became a katana.

"You taking her on, Ark? Guess that leaves you and me, Bolty."

Arkaziel vanished in a blast of shadows, while the woman vanished in a burst of radiance. Trees fell in the forest, and flashes of magic lit the island. Aetheria felt a surge of annoyance that she wouldn't be able to watch their fight. She felt certain that the maidenly woman might have been the most powerful of the four enemies.

Her reverie broke when Bolty emitted a massive nova of lightning that obliterated her ice minions, even the dragon, and the railgun sniper who had been farthest away.

"If I win, you may survive if you become my concubine," the shorts-clad lightning man offered.

"Wow. Are you that sick of living, or are you just that arrogant?"

Bolty flexed and posed at her, and Aetheria had her answer.

Aetheria appeared behind Bolty, her foot delivering a kick to his ass that sent him through trees, rocks, and most of a hill before he stopped. While she casually walked toward the hill, she pulled the multihued power of Khaos to her right hand, and the eternally hungry power of Nyx into her left hand. Bolty walked out of the hill just as she reached the base. Not a single scratch marred his skin.

"You are out of your league, little assassin. Speed might have worked on that other dolt, but you used it up on the wrong target. I am the greatest, the strongest, the best combatant—"

While he droned on, and on, Aetheria teleported again. She appeared in front of him this time, and she punched him right in the crotch with the power of Nyx. The obnoxious man flew back into the hill, shot out the other side, and came to a stop against a cliff of some obscenely durable material.

The man eventually stood up from where he had fallen, and continued as if he hadn't been interrupted at all.

"—the universe has ever seen. For I am Zeus!"

The sky rumbled ominously in response to that declaration, but Aetheria didn't react in the way that Zeus wanted. Rather than being impressed, she put her hands on her hips and scowled at him.

"I get to annihilate the God of Perverts? Oh, you are going to wish I had targeted you instead of Stormy when we're done here."

CHAPTER 38

Deicide

A cacophony of sound and light filled the sky island. The clash of blades between the swordsman and Werylin created a fast-paced percussive beat. The battle between Arkaziel and the maiden created flares of darkness, light, and twilight that would have been a huge hit at a rave. The fight between Zeus and Aetheria had the same ridiculous effects of two powerful Tier Four Cultivators deadlocked in an attempt to kill one another.

Zeus summoned lightning. Aetheria froze and stored it. Swarms of snowflakes fell upon Zeus, and each snowflake ripped at the god's skin like a buzz saw until chain lightning imploded the swarm, and the god king's wounds mended in seconds.

"Looks like we are evenly matched at energy projection," the Olympian proclaimed sourly.

Aetheria responded to that statement with a lopsided grin. Energy projection, she felt, didn't describe the conjuration arts she used with ice, but she could see the misconception on the part of Zeus.

The air between the two shimmered, rocks shattered, and pure unadulterated cold purified the air and Zeus alike. The god's skin turned blue, his eyes widened in panic as gusts of hot wind were carried in, and flares of static electricity burst all around him in a dazzling display of energy control. Zeus managed to purge the cold with hope and a prayer. Confidence returned to Zeus's face as his counter returned warmth to the air and his skin regained some color.

Aetheria reached within herself and opened the full flood gates of Frostfire, her Gateway to the Origin. Ethereal power filled her essence, and the hot winds, the bursts of static, even Zeus himself were blasted with pure cold that approached absolute zero. Aetheria closed in while hoarfrost covered Zeus and punched the god in the sternum. He shattered like a statue. His frozen flesh covered the area like a burst piñata.

Well. I guess I need to think of cold as an energy more often. That worked surprisingly well.

The shattered body of Zeus flowed like liquid into a complete whole.

"You have turned yourself into a personification of the Origin? You are no god, no Primordial, no matter how many Flames those ancient wretches have filled you with. Whatever scheme they concoct shall not be allowed to pass!"

Maybe he'd tell me what he means if I asked? Probably not.

The tiny delay between Aetheria's thoughts coincided with the delay between Zeus's largest attack yet and its realization. A bolt of lightning the size of a house struck from the heavens. The brilliant flash blinded even Zeus for a moment, and the thunderclap that followed leveled the forests and rock formations for a kilometer around on the sky island. Even Zeus found himself pushed back dozens of meters by the concussive force of the thunderclap.

When the dust settled, Aetheria stood where she had been, completely unharmed.

"Huh. I figured that might hurt, but that's all you've got?"

"How?" Zeus asked while he stared at her with immense hatred.

"I'm rubber and you're glue, now I'm going to annihilate you. Oh gosh, that was terrible."

Multihued energy burst from where Aetheria had been, and in front of Zeus. She teleported face-to-face with Zeus to deliver a sucker-punch to his pretty face. The dark-haired god flew through the air until he slammed against a pile of debris from his own last attack. When he crawled to his feet, the skin of his face still had a withered appearance and did not heal the way the previous assaults she'd landed on him did.

"What fell titan magic is this?" Zeus rubbed his cheek in horror, but the wound would not heal even when he pushed energy into it.

"I recently encountered creatures of the Void. It opened my eyes to flavors of the Ethereal I had never realized existed. It seems you don't respond well to their aspect. Do you think it's because you're a shadow copy of the real Zeus, an Olympian, or a god?" Aetheria didn't expect an answer, since the copies seemed incapable of acknowledging they were, in fact, clones.

"Consorting with the Primordials isn't enough for you, wretch? The fell offspring of the Void make even Erebus seem divine and righteous in comparison. I have stood in the gaps between and fought the tides of Voidspawn, none held magics so fell as this." Zeus spoke, and the darkness of his cheek grew.

"Oh. That's probably because I upgraded it to the Ethereal, instead of just copying it in its original Nether form. I read your little *Erotic Tales* book on the forty-ninth floor, you know. Not one of those horrible tales involved consensual love. It's a pity you're just a shadow of the real Zeus. Punishing you is pointless. You are just a *shadow* though, a pale copy that once climbed this tower a long, long time ago."

Aetheria activated Flash Mode and appeared behind Zeus. She didn't bother with talons, but the Astrum Nexus did create thin layers of ice over her knuckles with each punch she delivered to Zeus. Dark splotches covered the shorts-clad god with each contact. The god managed more of a defense than Stormy had. Every third punch Zeus managed to raise a fist to block her punches with a lightning-clad hand, but it didn't stop her. Punch after punch landed on Zeus, until finally the god fell to the ground, nearly all of his body covered in dark splotches.

"I'm surprised you can move anymore, Zeus."

Aetheria appeared over Zeus, and she disengaged Flash Mode. While Zeus tried to scramble to his feet, weakness had set in.

"Last words?"

"The Primordials started all of this. They set the stage! Why make the gods your enemies?"

"I haven't made the gods my enemies, that I know of. You are just a shadow. For what it's worth, I'm not enjoying this. You are a living *thing*, after all. So, I won't prolong this anymore. Here's my mercy."

Aetheria ignored the temptation to kick or torture Zeus more and plunged her hand into his chest. Talons of ice formed around her fingers to part the blackened skin of the previously muscular god until she found his core. Then she proceeded to devour him the way she had Stormy. First, she cracked the core, then absorbed the power. Again, a new Flame tried to form inside of her, but she resisted the Flame and only took the energy.

It disturbed Aetheria how Zeus's expressions of horror and panic felt so *real*, despite the god being a false copy made by the Administrators. The clone of Zeus no doubt came from the time in which he climbed this tower himself. She funneled the power of the shadow into further construction of her inner world. Between Stormy and Zeus, she had made a significant amount of progress toward the formation of the core of her inner world. A few more enemies of that strength, and she might be able to move on to the mantle.

It occurred to Aetheria, after brutally annihilating and consuming two gods, one of which was a powerful god, that the gods might really be afraid of her. If she were to be someone whose only motivation was power, and gods could be consumed so easily for quick gains, why wouldn't she become their enemy? Especially if the Primordials backed her. *From a public relations perspective it might be time to let Arkaziel do all the god eating from here on out.*

Zeus's lightning bolt didn't disperse with his death, so Aetheria threw it into her repository, where it immediately reacted to another item. The disturbance within her soul felt somewhat like indigestion of the soul, right between the stomach and the heart. Arcs of electricity flowed between the lightning bolt and the crystal torch of Phanes. Before she could take any action to interrupt whatever might happen the torch emitted a powerful spiritual pulse that dazed her, and then the torch sucked the lightning bolt into its crystals and went inert again.

"Uffda!"

Aetheria stared into the clouds for a few seconds while her mind recovered from the strange pulse the torch had emitted. Then she played what had happened over in her head again, and then a few more times. She had other Tier Four, and some Tier Five and a couple Tier Six items stored within her repository. Why had the torch not shown any reaction with those? Therefore, it wasn't just a matter of power. It had to be related to the type or origin of the power. The torch reacted with instant aggression toward the symbol of Zeus's power, but she couldn't know for sure if it was Zeus specifically, any Olympian, any god, or what.

If Arkaziel's or Werylin's foes were still alive, could Aetheria see if the torch reacted to other gods in similar fashion? After all, she had a pretty strong hunch Arkaziel fought against Amaterasu and Werylin faced off against a shadow of Freyr.

~You need help with her or you want to keep it one-on-one, buddy?~

+She doesn't know it yet, but I've already won. Check on Werylin before you rendezvous with me.+

Aetheria considered her options. Arkaziel would respond that way even if he were losing, but his emotional state remained calm and confident. Her companion could also summon her if he had to, so she opted to check on Werylin first. To find the elf she simply followed the sound of the clash of swords. Although Freyr's blade looked like a rainbow, it seemed to make the same sounds a normal blade would during a fight. She found the two in a hollow that had escaped the collateral damage of Zeus.

Neither Freyr nor Werylin showed any wounds, not a single cut that she could see. Each danced through sword forms in fluid, graceful motions that anyone not of Tier Four would be unable to follow. Aetheria suspected that even some on their own tier would fail to follow the speed the two swordsmen dueled at. The two paused their duel to note their observer.

"Is my opponent so weak you join against me, or are you content to observe?" Freyr asked with no hint of fear.

Aetheria didn't answer, she simply looked to Werylin. The silver-eyed elf remained composed, no sweat trickled down his brow, and none of the ruins of Harmonious Tempest had been engaged recently from what she could tell.

"I will end this in a single blow." Werylin smirked at his opponent. "I was waiting for an audience."

"False bravado will just get you killed, elf. Yet we both feel the same way. Very well, let us exchange blows one last time, before I kill you and your companion."

Werylin sheathed his blade, and Aetheria almost squealed at the sword-draw stance the elf took. Between the Sylvan hakama, the katana, the wakizashi, and the sword-draw stance, she had to remind herself that the minstrel wasn't a samurai, and he definitely wasn't one of her favorite anime characters from her youth. His sword had the edge on the proper side, after all.

Both swordsmen looked to Aetheria, who counted down. "Three. Two. One. GO!"

Freyr already had his rainbow sword in hand, while Werylin took a half step forward and drew Harmonious Tempest in a wide draw. The blade arced through the air, and in its wake glowing musical notes formed. A pulse of Werylin's killing intent formed into a blast of aura he fired from his blade toward the god, and Werylin's blade continued to move in a full arc. Freyr parried the intent lazily, took a step forward, and thrust for the still-turning elf's internal organs. Werylin pressed down on his scabbard with his left hand while he spun. The scabbard parried Freyr's blade and threw the god's balance and momentum off, and as the elf finished his spin, the still-glowing blade made its full three-hundred-and-sixty-degree sweep. A head thumped onto the ground.

"Dang. How often does that move work?" Aetheria watched as Werylin bowed to the corpse after he regained his own balance, then thrust his blade to destroy Freyr's core for good measure. Aetheria noticed the intensity of the glow on Harmonious Tempest increased significantly when it shattered Freyr's core. *Can weapons power up like beast Cultivators?*

CHAPTER 39

The Brightest Light

Werylin never answered Aetheria's question about how often that move worked. Instead, the elf went over the corpse of the god, stripping his equipment. The rainbow sword wasn't a katana like Werylin's preferred weapon, but the way he picked it up and swung it a few times left her with the idea the elf could probably use most types of swords with a high degree of skill.

"Did the other two have any useful gear on them?"

"The first guy just had generic gear for some reason. Was he handicapped because of numbers, or am I missing something? Zeus only had the lightning bolt, a bracelet, and those stylish shorts, but uhh, the lightning bolt sort of reacted to something in my inventory and it's gone now." Aetheria's sheepish explanation of the lightning bolt's fate resulted in Werylin rolling his eyes at her.

"His quick demise without a show of power did seem odd. Perhaps you simply prevented any grand shows with your preemptive annihilation. Has Arkaziel finished his opponent yet, or what is his status?"

Intense flashes of light and darkness on the other side of the island answered Werylin's question before Aetheria could. The amount of power displayed by Arkaziel and his opponent kept increasing dramatically. They kept trying to catch the other in massive attacks that failed to make a decisive hit in the fight. Aetheria and Werylin were slightly reluctant to close in on the fight, and stopped to watch momentarily on a ledge.

The sight before them differed vastly from the scene Aetheria had expected. Two gargantuan dragons wrestled with one another. The woman had become a blue water dragon, of the long and sinuous type. Arkaziel, somewhere around seventy-five meters long, was bulkier than the female dragon and about ten or fifteen meters longer than her. The ground around them writhed in unnatural shadows, shadows cast from nothing currently there. From the temporally displaced shadows emerged elongated limbs that tried to force scales from the water dragon. The blue dragon countered with pillars of light that turned into heavenly lasers.

With her Ethereal Sight, the fight looked very different to Aetheria than it did to Werylin.

"We should help him," Werylin said immediately.

"There's no need. The damage is all superficial. It looks worse than it is. Arkaziel isn't even trying to overpower her. Everything about his moves is a lie in this fight." Aetheria laughed.

"Could you explain?"

"Sure. See how that pillar of light seems to be burning his scales, and he seems to be trying to get out of it, but the blue dragon is doing everything possible to keep him in the target, including letting him run his claws around her belly? Arkaziel's like the scariest video game character ever, a pink puffball of an elder god who eats his way through everything: obstacles, enemy's attacks, *and* of course, his enemies. When I asked him earlier how it was going, he said he'd already won, his opponent just hadn't realized it yet."

"You have a great deal of confidence in him. I don't see it. The blue dragon appears to be uninjured, while Arkaziel looks much worse for the wear. His shadow tendrils aren't even succeeding in prying free her scales."

"Then just watch."

Through immense struggle the blue dragon managed to finally entangle Arkaziel a few times with her own body and hold him in place stretched horizontally. Nine pillars of light appeared, each pinpointing where only Arkaziel's body would be hit. Each of the nine pillars suddenly flared with nine magic circles. Each magic circle magnified the power of the light pillar, transforming divine light into a terrible disintegration beam.

The split second before the enhanced light touched Arkaziel's scales the world went black. Light pillars, magic circles, the radiant glow of the divine form of a goddess inside the shape of a dragon, the sun, all of it vanished into pitch-blackness. Even time seemed to slow down as the darkness feasted upon everything. From their vantage point Aetheria's own glow did not diminish, although they were within the effective range of the eclipse. Arkaziel must have exempted her.

"Here it comes."

Twilight swallowed the darkness itself in an instant. Three massive magic circles appeared, one at Arkaziel's maw, and one at each of his front claws. The form of the water dragon flaked away, and the energy-matter mixture flew into Arkaziel's maw where he swallowed again, and again. Six large gulps and Arkaziel had eaten all of the draconic form that had surrounded the female goddess. The conservatively cloaked goddess made one last feeble attack with blasts of light when Arkaziel exposed her real form, yet the magic circles at his claws easily absorbed the light attack without strain.

Then the StarMane leaned forward and with a terrible crunch, the goddess joined the ranks of gods consumed by the dragon-cat. The wounds on Arkaziel healed visibly once the conflict ended: sparks of holy light appeared with bursts at his wounds while he channeled the healing energies through his massive form.

"Here I thought those wounds were illusions. That looked painful." Aetheria admitted she'd misread the situation.

"Pain is transitory, and I did keep healing any internal damage she did to me. I've never heard of anyone having to fight a group of gods at the three-quarter mark. Usually it's another beast king with a large pack. Groups of gods in outnumbered combat are usually reserved for the last floor. We're going to have a doozy of a time at the top of the tower, aren't we?" The laughter of the dragon shook the whole sky island.

Werylin refrained from comment, but he did seem to be deep in thought.

"I thought the whole setup felt wrong. I feel like that guy I killed off the bat was supposed to be way more difficult than he was, or maybe he was supposed to play support and make the others more difficult?" Aetheria shrugged with the words.

Arkaziel's answer was a belch that shook the sky island, which continued to shake as a door to Floor 76 appeared.

"Sorry. That was a large meal. A little indigestion is to be expected. Didn't you eat yours too, Aetheria? How come you aren't full?" In the flash of movement the calamitously large dragon jumped into the air and a tiny black house cat landed on Aetheria's shoulder, where he immediately began to lick his paws and groom himself.

"I expended the energy immediately into building more of my inner world, and I also had a bit of an incident with one of the items I had stored and Zeus's lightning bolt."

"You nonbeast Cultivators sure have it rough. I just eat things and get bigger, stronger, and more badass, and thanks to my ancestors I am already intimately familiar with all the become-one-with-the-light bullshit." Arkaziel's bragging tugged at Aetheria's thoughts for a moment.

"Let's go, twenty-five more floors to go. Your attack seems to have left this place damaged, anyway."

"Oh yeah, Twilight Apocalypse will do that. I devoured every bit of energy in this area besides yours. If we were out in the real worlds, it would take years for the energy flows to recover here."

Arkaziel's words hung ominously in the air when they stepped onto Floor 76.

The brief disorientation of teleportation between floors faded, and the trio found themselves atop a hill. Around them rose twelve large, weathered stone obelisks of various sizes and styles. At the center of the stones a large metal astrolabe topped the hill and marked the center of the stone circle. The metal of the astrolabe gleamed in sunlight, and Forge Insight told Aetheria the tool had been forged from an alloy of orichalcum and scarletite, which gave it a beautiful gold and red appearance.

"Anyone know a lot about astronomy?" Aetheria asked with a grimace, before her eyes fell onto the fragments of gems woven into the Astrum Nexus.

"Not even a little bit." Werylin shook his head.

"Within my vast and profound knowledge base lie the secrets of hundreds of civilizations, science and magic, myth and legend. Surely I can figure out how to operate such a basic tool."

Arkaziel poked at one of the astrolabe's pieces with a paw a few times, and ten seconds later admitted his failure.

"I have no idea. It's a mystery for the ancients. Clearly, no one will ever figure out such a complex and ineffable machine. I'm hungry."

"You just ate a goddess."

"She was empty calories? Look, it's been ages since we left Floor 75."

"It's not even been ten minutes." Werylin entered the conversation.

"Ten minutes is a subjective eternity. Why are we having a debate about if I should be hungry or not, anyway? I am, therefore, hungry am I. I could use a nap, too. We can't do any astronomy until it's dark out anyway. Food and naps for everyone!"

"Fine." Aetheria gestured and created a level platform of ice next to the hilltop and a large multiroom tent appeared already set up. Arkaziel hopped off her shoulder to go set the table or prepare his list of demands.

Once the boys went into the tent, Aetheria remained back to fiddle with the astrolabe. While yes, she couldn't ascertain what each celestial body represented until nighttime, she could make an inventory of how many pieces there were and see if there was a pattern behind the planets, suns, and other celestial bodies. That's what logic said, anyway, but between Forge Insight showing her the names of each piece of the astrolabe and surges of knowledge from the Astrum Nexus she could figure out which pieces represented what celestial body as far as names went. She lacked sticky notes, but she did have the means to just bind a snowflake with the name of celestial object to each mark.

+*Come eat, Aetheria.*+ Arkaziel's telepathic sending intruded on Aetheria.

~*Fine, I'm coming. I think I've figured out the movements on about a third of the celestial bodies already.*~

+*They're celestial bodies, don't they just go in circles?*+

~*No. Oblongs are more common than actual circles.*~

Arkaziel's response came in the form of a wordless mental groan that made Aetheria's head vibrate a little.

"How'd you do that?" Aetheria demanded as she took a place at the table. "What's for dinner?"

Arkaziel had taken human form to set the table.

"Ondoorian leg shanks in a sauce of Mega-Oranges, a side of scalloped pordangos in cheese, and a salad of seared greens mixed with fried Pogorian bacon, tomatoes, and onions. Accompanied by a whiskey."

Aetheria thought it looked a lot like chicken legs, scalloped potatoes, and a not-very-healthy salad. It all tasted delicious, of course, but she was happy they didn't get time to sit down for meals like this that often. It felt far heavier than simply pulling energy directly into your body.

Huh. Never thought I'd reach the food is an annoyance over just passively existing on energy. Guess I'm still moving further and further from being human. Should I lament that, or celebrate it? Maybe I'll just keep ignoring it. Denial is always the most effective coping method, never fails!

CHAPTER 40

Celestial Mapping

After delicious food and a nap full of dreams of a certain Nephilim, Aetheria awoke refreshed and in a good mood. The good mood dampened slightly upon recollection she had an astronomy puzzle to solve. Arkaziel still lazed on the pillow next to her own, but he stared at her balefully with his yellow eyes.

"I'm consolidating gains. Werylin, too." Arkaziel's tone was unusually brusque, which Aetheria took as a sign of some internal work on the cat's part.

"Alright. I'll work on the astrolabe and see how far I can get on my own. You two take as long as you need. It doesn't seem like time is a factor here . . ." Aetheria trailed off and shrugged. There had been no indications of time constraints, and if the boys needed time to incorporate their gains they might be on this floor for months, potentially even a year or two.

Six months later, Aetheria lay on the grass of the hilltop next to the astrolabe. She watched the clouds as they flowed across the sky and a solitary falcon soared high above in search of prey. *I feel you, falcon, I could use some prey.*

"Hard at work, I see," Arkaziel commented, before he hopped onto her stomach and settled there.

A thick ring-bound makeshift notebook appeared above Arkaziel and bopped him on the head before it fell to the ground.

"Astrolabes are boring," Aetheria grumbled before she commenced petting Arkaziel.

"It is kind of odd that someone made one out of such precious metals." Shadow tentacles held the notebook up for Arkaziel to read. The pages flipped fast enough that Aetheria felt confident he hadn't actually read anything on the pages, but maybe StarManes were extreme speed readers?

"I'm about to disassemble the gosh darned thing. I've documented every measurement the thing can take for six months, and do you know what I've learned in that time?"

"Uh. That the solar system is working as intended?"

"No. That the solar system is rotating around this planet. Every night, each celestial object moves along the same path. Even the sun rotates around the planet!"

"I always knew I was the center of the universe." Arkaziel purred at the divine chin scritches Aetheria gave him.

"Yeah, sure. So, long story short, the astrolabe was a red herring and it has absolutely nothing to do with our task to get past this floor."

"How'd you figure that out? Can we take it? Scarletite alloyed to orichalcum should be worth a pretty penny."

"Oh, it's coming with us when it is time to go. I intend to dismantle it and separate the ores if I can. I figured out the real task a few days ago, after beating my head into the wall for months." Aetheria lazily waved a hand at one of the stone obelisks that now showed significant damage. Fractures ran through it, and debris littered the ground around it. "Literally, by the way. If you look, the obelisk has a crystal center."

"Mm. Aventurine. It's rife with Aether lattices. Is it some kind of data storage?" Arkaziel hopped off Aetheria to examine the obelisk more closely. "Why hide the crystals but leave an incredibly expensive piece of useless equipment out in the open?"

"Hiding in plain sight, obviously. The enchantments that worked on the crystal and stone were so good I couldn't even feel or see through them with Ethereal Sight, and none of my other senses picked it up either. I've only skimmed the surface of the contents of that column, but it seems to be a manual on building an inner world that truly reflects oneself. Shall we crack the rest of them open and see what the others contain?"

"I suppose so." Arkaziel's disinterested answer confused Aetheria, until she remembered that as a beast Cultivator the creation of an inner world and other major events were an intrinsic evolution created by strength and devouring of opponents. Despite the cat's lack of enthusiasm he moved to one of the obelisks and carefully ran a claw along the stone multiple times. She couldn't resist the show Arkaziel put on. He tapped the stone, ran a claw along it, tapped again, and repeated until one of his taps saw the whole stone exterior crumble to the ground to reveal a glorious lapis lazuli structure underneath.

"Are those the same claws you knead me with?" Aetheria arched a brow.

"Dragon claws are known to be able to pierce almost anything, I'll have you know. No armor in existence can protect you from the bite of a StarMane."

"Is that actually true?" Aetheria felt it wasn't.

"Within certain contexts, it's true." Arkaziel yawned to display his sharp teeth.

"You can't say something like that then not tell me what the context is. Is the context that you can bite and rend anything that's weaker than you? Because that's sort of how everything works."

"No, he's right. Dragon claws and teeth are known to be amongst the hardest, most armor-piercing materials around. There are some materials that come close, such as my star-metal blade, or divine materials, but within their current cultivation tier they stand at the precipice." Werylin talked while he walked in circles around the exposed crystal.

"See?" Arkaziel stuck his tongue out at Aetheria.

"This crystal represents instructions for a path called Journey of the Astral Tides. The inner worlds it creates resemble an astral ocean, upon which your 'worlds' follow ebbs and tides, ever on a new journey. Interesting, I don't think I've ever heard of someone making an inner world of that sort." Werylin rubbed his chin in thought.

"Well, it's not like there's a preponderance of Tier Fives wandering around Grief, is there? Makes sense you'd never have heard of it." Arkaziel viewed the ancient world ruled by the Goddess of Misery in a fairly dim light. He considered it a backwater not worth saving, but he did like to eat gods.

"You have a point there, Ark. Although you underestimate the cultural knowledge flow imparted by climbers and the towers. How many worlds have been walked by a Tier Seven Cultivator? Yet legends of them cross every world because of the towers." Werylin defended his home world as best he could.

"Alright, Ark, crack the rest of these open. Let's figure out what we've got here, see if anything is interesting to anyone. If we can copy the data, we should, if not I'll just throw them into my repository."

In addition to the Journey of the Astral Tides, they discovered eleven other paths.

The Path of Celestial Harmony sounded like it could be of interest to Werylin based on the name, but it related to a different kind of harmony. It unfortunately related more to the astrolabe type of celestial. While it did in fact involve harmony, the importance it placed on celestial phenomenon and energies would result in an inner world that had a variance of power. Sometimes it would draw from you, and other times it would provide for you. When they discerned that part, no one retained any interest in the Path of Celestial Harmony.

The Way of the Mystic Mirror didn't appeal to anyone from the outset. The inner world created by the path would reflect anything that entered it. Aetheria could not see a single use for a house of mirrors as one's inner world, but Werylin noted it had been a path popular amongst monastic traditions for a very long time, with many an old monk that used the world to force confrontations with one's inner self not just for them, but for their disciples, too.

Path of the Boundless Void, as the name suggested, involved creation of an inner cosmos devoid of worlds. Any constructs within the Void were temporary, unable to fight the consuming endless darkness of the Void. One of the more esoteric of those in the crystals, the path trained a Cultivator to master the power of creation while also accepting the futility and transient nature of all things.

Domain of the Inner Guardian focused on the creation of an impenetrable fortress within one's own soul. Within the fortress one could buoy the mind and spirit, cultivate the durability of a mountain, and draw the protective power into one's body. Aetheria thought the path sounded interesting, but it also struck her as completely redundant and pointless for her. She already had strong mental and physical defenses. It piqued her curiosity because it was the first path to explicitly call out advantages brought into physical reality from an inner world.

The Path of Bestial Harmony involved the creation of primitive, primal worlds dominated by beasts. Of course, the Cultivator needed to either create these bestial personalities by splitting off fragments of themselves or by capturing and nurturing actual beasts. It sounded like a zookeeper inner world design to Aetheria, although the idea of splitting one's mind and essence to create individual aspects outside of one's direct control struck her as a terrible idea. *Not worse than opening a gateway to the Origin in your soul, I guess, but still. Someone just really liked beasts; I dub you Path of the Furry.*

"Oh, gardening! It's almost up your alley, Aetheria." Arkaziel pointed at an emerald crystal.

Path of the Ethereal Blossoms had nothing to do with the actual Ethereal. It alluded to the meaning she knew from Earth: delicate, divine beauty. The path itself revolved around a world of orchards in which plants could be created for a myriad of power and affinity uses.

"Yeah, no. It's not at all my style. It's basically a mad scientist mixed with a gardener to make magic trees. Thanks, but no."

"These do seem to be esoteric and niche paths" Werylin said. "Still, we could format these into a tradeable data-crystal or tomes and make a pretty penny selling them. When we hit Floor Ninety we can see what the value might be, but it should be significant. Many are the Cultivators who would rather follow a proven path than risk stagnation from being unable to continue their own path." Werylin shook his head sadly at the last.

"That's a good point. We'll sell or trade them. I'm surprised you aren't at least slightly interested in the Sylvan Empowerment Path."

"I could say the same of you and the Path of the Sage's Library. Surely, you, a former librarian, would be interested in the creation of a repository of knowledge for the ages?" Werylin arched a brow at her.

"Okay, yeah, I'm sorry. That came off a little wrong. Not all elves want to live in a forest, and it was wrong of me to assume you would." Aetheria had not meant to insult or insinuate anything about Werylin or elves, but she could see how he had taken offense at the stereotype.

"You're forgiven. After all, I did read its data and intend to steal liberally to improve my own path."

"Jerk." Aetheria made a rude gesture at Werylin.

"You should see both of your faces right now. Oh hey, there's the portal to the next floor. Let's go, maybe there'll be someone to eat." Arkaziel's enthused voice broke the tension in the air. His tail whipped back and forth in excitement at the prospect of prey.

"Don't you mean something to eat?" Werylin asked with a hint of despair.

"I meant what I said," Arkaziel hissed.

CHAPTER 41

The Aurora Arena

Floor 77 started when the trio appeared in a flash of brilliance. Aetheria, Arkaziel, and Werylin appeared in the center of the floor of a large arena. Unlike most arenas they had experienced so far, this one had no gates for enemies to emerge from, which immediately sent Aetheria's mind into a paranoid spiral as she feared the possibility of being forced to fight her companions.

"Look up." Arkaziel swatted Aetheria's nose with his tail.

Aetheria still had not banished the alterations to her form. One eye remained red, and the other blue. Vibrant red still ran through her aqua hair in wild streaks. When she wore this form, the Aether crystal woven into Astrum Nexus glistened on her right hand with the same blue glow as her left eye, while the Nether crystals glimmered red on her left hand in a match to her right eye. She rather liked the unique look, but she still felt self-conscious about it. She felt like it represented her as she existed now, but some doubts lingered in her mind on whether these changes were wrought by her or by Aetherius and Nyx.

"Did you just get distracted by your reflection in my eyes?" Arkaziel hissed at Aetheria before he jumped off the top of her head to lay on her shoulder instead.

"Sorry, sorry, I'm still getting used to looking so exotic."

"You call that exotic? It's just some different colors."

"Humans from Earth don't have teal hair, and no matter what color our hair is, it certainly doesn't glow bright enough to guide Santa's sleigh with. Same with our eyes."

"Surely your auras glow?" Werylin joined the conversation.

"No auras or magic on Earth, as far as I know." Aetheria had wondered about that one a lot. If Aetherius and Nyx had been in her video-game guild, then there might have been magic on Earth, but maybe it had been hidden?

"Well, humans in other places have all sorts of hair colors, and unless you're completely devoid of magic, aura, qi, intent, or are a total impotent, you can still pull off some sparks and glows with relative ease." Arkaziel droned on happily, in love with the sound of his own voice.

"Wait, what's an impotent? No one's used that term before with me."

"An item-impotent, sometimes called a magical null, or even an enchantment-deficient person, is a person or thing who can't even manage to use magical items. It's pretty rare to find someone who can't use most magical items, but those whom magical items or artifacts won't resonate with are sad sacks. Their only hope for power is via politicking, weaponry, or technology. Worlds with low background mana can generate a lot of strange things with technology. Mom said it is just another source of power, even if it is one we don't really use." Arkaziel paused his explanation. "Whatever happened to deals with devils, extra-dimensional entities, demons, and eldritch abominations? Those are way easier than making technology."

"Look up," Werylin reminded the other two with an exasperated tone.

Above the open sky of the arena three gigantic figures radiated raw power. Thick streams of energy flowed into each of the three vaguely humanoid shapes. All three looked quite similar, but the type of energy that flowed into each one varied. The first elemental form absorbed almost pure air aspected Aether, the second absorbed light, and the third elemental absorbed holy aspects.

A hologram of a humanoid male appeared before them.

"You may choose which of the rules you wish to follow in the Aurora Arena. You may engage the Aurora Elementals three versus three, one versus one, or other similar scenarios. You will be rewarded appropriately for the difficulty of your choices, with one of you taking on all three being the most highly rewarding, and three of you versus one of the elementals as the least rewarding. Do you understand?"

"If we opt to do one versus three, will the rewards be for all of us or just the person who takes on all three?" Arkaziel asked the important questions.

"Only those who fight get rewards."

"What's the next highest reward, one versus one?" Aetheria wondered.

"Correct," the Administrator responded with a smirk.

"One versus one," the trio answered simultaneously.

"Very well." The trio vanished and reappeared in a waiting room. One entire wall of the room showed a live feed of the arena, where streams of energy still flowed into the elementals. A long table had been filled with catered food, and comfortable massage recliners waited for them.

"The first match will be Arkaziel versus the Holy Aurora," the Administrator's image declared before it vanished. The cat vanished with it to reappear in the arena.

"Whoops. Maybe we should have specified our opponents when we chose one versus one. But maybe letting them pick our opponents will help our loot?" Aetheria gnawed her lower lip while she looked to Werylin, who gave an indifferent shrug.

"It will be what it will be. Arkaziel will do fine." Werylin attempted to console Aetheria, missing that she was more worried about him than Arkaziel or herself.

"From the depths of the addled mind of Chronos we have one of the StarMane Clan, child of the infamous God Eater who's had a few pieces of gods himself. We have the dragon of prophecy, the ender of worlds, the Dragon-Cat of Apocalypse, the Twilight Bringer, Arkaziel!" Arkaziel had transformed into his draconic-feline form. Despite the almost one-hundred-meter size of Arkaziel's glorious draconic form he didn't even take up a fifth of the arena floor.

"Sanctus!" One of the elementals disappeared from above the arena, and a pillar of holy power appeared inside the arena opposite Arkaziel. The humanoid form of the elemental had a soft golden radiance that spoke of absolute strength, divine judgment, and of course, wrath.

"The embodiment of holy power, the Deliverer of Divine Wrath, Sanctus has come to smite the son of the God Eater! Let the clash begin!"

Before the embodiment of holy Aether could even move, Arkaziel opened his huge maw and roared. The ground shook from his cry, the sky vibrated, and even in the waiting room Aetheria could feel the force of the roar in her chest. She had never witnessed Arkaziel declare his superiority over an opponent so profoundly before, which felt like bravado given the elemental was Tier Five and at least half a tier ahead of her cat. The roar had carried his intent to the elemental and managed to stun the forty-meter-tall elemental.

Arkaziel shot forward in a blur of claws and a snap of jaws. His maw took massive bites of the form of the elemental while his claws ripped massive gauges into the energy being. Despite the nature of the physical attack, it did a not insignificant amount of damage to Sanctus. The bites and devouring its life force directly left a visible deformation on the neck and shoulder of the elemental, while the areas Arkaziel's claws had swiped through re-formed normally.

"I guess even dragon claws don't punch up an entire tier themselves." Werylin rubbed his chin in thought.

"His devouring worked well, though. He'll eat the elemental one way or the other. If it's made up of divine Aether, it'll be like eating a god. It might put him on the brink of Tier Five." Aetheria sighed at the idea of a Tier Five Arkaziel. It felt inevitable, but she hoped Werylin or herself beat him to Tier Five to maintain the pathetic version of humility her narcissistic cat displayed.

The stun wore off, and Sanctus punched Arkaziel in the face. Scales cracked, sparks like a fireworks display filled the arena behind Arkaziel, and the massive dragon got pushed back dozens of meters. Arkaziel left deep grooves in the floor of the arena from where his claws had dug in to keep him in place, or so Aetheria had interpreted his actions. She was wrong, though. From the black grooves Arkaziel had clawed into the stone floor arose dark tentacles made not of shadow, but of Ethereal power. He had aspected them with Dark Divinity, the highest form of Nether made manifest in the highest order of energy in existence.

The tentacles lashed out and entangled the legs of the huge elemental. Where they touched Sanctus, its holy light dimmed, while the tentacles pulsed with power as the tentacles fed.

"That's the creepiest version of his Devouring Darkness I've seen yet."

"Have you ever worried about that whole apocalypse dragon spiel the Administrator introduced him with?"

"No, well, yeah. I tell myself it's the Administrators trying to break my trust in Ark. I have a few theories about the StarManes. Maybe I'll share them sometime."

Sanctus refused to give in. Even though Arkaziel had pulled out such a devastating attack, he was still only Tier Four, fighting a Tier Five elemental. Sanctus emitted a series of pulses that repelled the tentacles, while Arkaziel summoned three twilight clones each half his size. The clones and the original lunged in on the elemental. Aetheria had expected the showdown to focus on powerful magics and ranged blasts, but it ended with tooth and claw. It took long minutes, but in the end Arkaziel stood triumphant in the arena. The new glow about Arkaziel represented the only remains Sanctus had left behind from being devoured.

"Damn," Werylin muttered.

"Jeez. That was a bit extreme," Aetheria agreed.

Cat-sized Arkaziel appeared in the waiting area, where he yawned and licked at his paws.

"That was a great meal. So sleepy." Arkaziel looked like he might not even stay awake to watch the next fight.

"Our next challenger is known as the Etherfrost Asura, Daughter of Aetherius and Nyx, Beloved of the Primordials, She Who Weaponized the Knowledge of the Aetherials, Bringer of the Deep Freeze, Aetheria!"

Aetheria appeared in the massive arena. She looked like an ant compared to how huge Arkaziel had been, and when her elemental opponent appeared opposite her, she seemed even smaller.

"Lumina! The Elemental of Light! Scourge of Darkness and Bringer of Life!"

Aetheria let out a happy sigh. Light was not an aspect she could control very well, but it also wasn't a weakness of hers. Her skin shifted to diamond, and a wicked smile crossed her lips as she took on the form of a Luxentian, one of those rare silicon-based life forms that grew more powerful the more light they were exposed to. She always felt like the Luxentians reminded her of a comic character from the '90s she couldn't remember the name of.

"Begin!"

CHAPTER 42

Lumina of Light

The elemental did not recognize the race Aetheria had shapeshifted into, which was to be expected: according to the book of unique races across the universe that Odin had given her, the Luxentian race lived in a dimension called the Far Realm. Which meant they were not a frequently seen species, but their unique abilities to absorb and process light into durability and strength made them one of her absolute favorite races to mimic. Someday, she would figure out how to alter the form to draw strength from Ethereal power, and then she'd be untouchable!

Lumina did not maintain its humanoid shape very well. It flowed like liquid, constantly changing. The elemental attacked first, its form flowing and moving with such speed that Aetheria had to focus to even be able to follow the movements with her eyes. A massive volley of light fragmented the rock floor around her, while her skin sucked the light in like a black hole. Under the cover of the artillery volley Lumina moved in to slam a massive appendage down on Aetheria. Due to the amorphous nature of Lumina she wasn't sure whether it was an arm or leg, but she lifted a tiny human hand to catch the blow.

"!!@#!!" Lumina chimed some strange melodic sounds in a tone that Aetheria interpreted as a swear word. Aetheria had blocked the massive blow and stood unharmed and bolstered by the bombardment. She reached through the Flame of Aetherius imbued into Astrum Nexus, amplified it with her own Primordial Flame of Aetherius and released a burst of energy in the form of her infrequently used Aetherflame Nova. The aqua-colored flames stuck to the malleable form of Lumina and burned like napalm; they showed no immediate signs of extinguishing.

Huh. It isn't responding in pain.

In fact, Lumina didn't seem to react to being immolated at all. While Aetheria watched, the Aetherflames dwindled across Lumina's body, and then extinguished.

"Hey, what the what? You can't just ignore fire." Aetheria huffed and stomped her foot so hard rocks flew in all directions, while she channeled Ethereal power into the shockwave with the Transcendent Flame of Khaos. Confident of its ability to defend against an opponent a whole tier lower than it, Lumina took the shockwave straight on. The elemental promptly collapsed, no longer able to maintain a humanoid form as Khaos's power caused its amorphous nature to take over completely.

"That's what you get." Aetheria smirked as her attack temporary disabled the blob. She closed the distance in a burst of speed and took a play out of Arkaziel's book. The multihued colors of the rainbow took over her aura as she fully activated the Flames of Khaos and Nyx. Khaos provided the strength to break through the defenses of the higher tier enemy, while the Flame of Nyx consumed the very life essence of the elemental.

Aetheria almost fell on her well-toned butt in shock at the amount of energy the elemental represented. Lumina did not just represent Aetherial light, but anima, or life itself. The best comparison she could think of for the sensation of feeding on Lumina was energy drinks. It reminded her of the nervous energy provided by chugging a whole can during a raid: the jittery feeling, the sickly sweet attack upon her taste buds and stomach. The sensation took her straight back to Earth. Even her Cultivator's core beat faster, and the sound of each thunderous beat filled her ears.

So, of course, Aetheria reached out and drank more. The arena spun around her. Her mind flew free and light, until a cold so intense it burned shocked her mind back to rationality. Ocean's Serenity did its job as usual, preventing her emotions from going too far astray.

"@!###!@" Lumina issued a series of melodic chimes once more in surprise that the human had shaken off the druglike effects of its nearly endless wells of anima.

Snowflakes manifested across the arena. The rock floor covered instantly in ice.

The amorphous blob of light slowed down. Crystals formed on its exterior. Even the mournful chiming sound ceased—the sudden intense cold that filled the arena had prevented Lumina from further vocalization.

"How did I freeze you? I can freeze almost anything if I can conceptualize it."

The frozen blob of light struggled. Cracks appeared in the ice that coated it. The ice repaired itself. Shafts of light broke through the ice and sent fragments in all directions. Aetheria didn't bother to dodge any; those that hit her super-dense Luxentian form vanished.

"Ohh. You have tenacity."

Another volley of energy blasted Aetheria. Multiple hues of light could be discerned from the attack, as well as multiple aspects. Fire, Life, Light, and Holy all were present within Lumina's massive energy blasts. Aetheria devoured all of it by channeling the power of the Flame of Aetherius and Nyx in the Astrum Nexus and inside herself. Her hair glowed as if it were made of pure light, her diamond skin sparkled, and her mismatched eyes unleashed light that reality itself tried to shy away from. The walls, the floor, even Werylin and Arkaziel in the waiting room shied away from the alien nature of the Light of the Origin that escaped from Aetheria's eyes.

"!@!!!@#!!" Melodic chimes escaped Lumina once again, as Aetheria's eyes focused directly upon the amorphous light elemental, and it bore the brunt of the Light of the Origin.

Aetheria shoved both hands into the luminous being, imagined herself grasping its essence, and she ripped it free and devoured it. The absorptive properties of the Flame of Aetherius were more polite about these things and were more comparable to an energy drain that could feast upon almost anything but the Ethereal. The hunger of Nyx, though, was the cold, dark, endless hunger of night. Insatiable, all encompassing, undeniable, temporarily held off at best.

A few last uncomprehending, despair-filled, melodic chimes emitted from Lumina before it ceased to exist, eaten down to the last drop of energy. The power filled Aetheria to the brim, her cells vibrated, her mind swam in unknown currents. She topped off the last of her Flames to the cap of Tier Four with the newly acquired power, and then shifted much of it through her soul aperture, into construction of her inner world. She had barely consumed a quarter of the power when she finally finished the icy core of her world.

The core glowed with an inner, ethereal blue light. It had been so infused with icy Ethereal power that it had crystalized into Ethereal ice quintessence, an exceptionally rare natural formation that bordered on transcendence of reality. The core fluctuated in such powerful cold that even time and space themselves froze near the core of her inner world. The powerful quintessence beat like her Cultivator core heart, and with each pulse it emitted flows of energy that would seep to the eventual surface of the inner world, where she could tap it or draw it into the physical world via her soul aperture.

The mantle as Aetheria imagined would be less of a physical space and more of a dreamlike realm of ice and cold. Countless layers of frost, mist, ice, snow, and pockets of air would allow for eventual ice aspected beings to empower themselves in the flow of ice-attuned energy as it flowed from the core to the surface. Even when she exhausted the energies of Lumina, she had only created thirty-seven layers of the mantle. In her trance she had not noticed that elementals had started to appear in the mantle already: ice wisps and impish elementals she didn't know the names for.

When Aetheria opened her eyes only seconds had ticked away from when she closed them despite it feeling like ages had gone by. The world flashed around her, and she appeared back in the waiting room.

"Nice job, Blue. How'd you expend all that energy so fast?"

"I think I may have accidentally activated the power of Chronos, mixed with knowledge sieved from the Aetherial gems. It felt like I spent months, no, years, forging the core and a lot of the mantle to my inner world, then suddenly I was done and only moments had gone by."

Arkaziel nodded sagely. *I wonder if he'll just agree with anything if I say Chronos willed it. Maybe that's an avenue of control I could use to temper his behavior. Every floor conquered is another floor closer to Aoibhe, and she wanted me to teach him manners. Talk about unachievable expectations. Thanks, love.*

I have total faith in you, my dear.

Warmth filled Aetheria's soul, and the Ukrainian-like accent filled her mind. The soul-connection between the witch and the Asura had continued to grow even without direct contact. The widening of their connection mostly stemmed from the growth of Aetheria's own self, in turn allowing for further growth of their bond. It had been a slow process in the years that had passed since she left Solace, in comparison to the formation of a bond between the two in person during her three years in Solace.

"Did Lumina taste good? You've got a creepy smile on your face. The buffet isn't bad. They brought in fried chicken halfway through your fight. I didn't even eat it all, so you could have some." Arkaziel gestured with a paw toward the catered food.

"Uh. Yeah, I guess Lumina tasted pretty good. It feels a little weird to think about it that way, but I made a ton of progress off consuming her. I need to stop eating enemies, though. It's going to get me a bad reputation."

Arkaziel laughed. "Aetheria, you're an Asura. It's impossible for you to have a good reputation. If you were a good person, you'd be a Deva. I swear we've talked about this before."

"Uhm. No, we haven't. Why can't Asura be good? You just said that Devas served the gods and towers, while Asuras served themselves. What's innately evil about that?"

"Devas are the divine forces of good, light, and virtue. Asura are driven by desire, ego, and ambition. Neither are necessarily evil, but depending on who you are in the cosmic tapestry of life, one group or the other might destroy your planet because it got caught in the collateral damage of their fights over who is the just party." Arkaziel didn't seem to like Devas much, even though he complimented their virtues.

"Why does your endorsement of their good and virtue sound so mocking?"

The cat laughed in amusement. "Am I evil? I serve myself."

"Is this just because the Asuras don't serve the gods, and are therefore castigated by the gods? Or is there more at play here?"

"Well, yeah, that's the origination of the views, I think. Same reason StarManes are reviled: we eat gods. They don't like that. Asura pursue their own agendas, and not the gods. They don't like that either."

"Nothing to do with the eating of planets?"

"Oh, they reviled us long before one of our kind got big enough to eat a planet. The first StarMane, Antara'Tethoril'Vodia'Dayl—"

"Get on with it; that's way too long."

"So, the first StarMane, Antara, never even got big enough to eat planets. He ate about fifteen gods, sired a ton of children, and then a whole pantheon and fleets of fanatics all came together to kill him when he tried to eat the Tower of Ares."

"He tried to eat a tower? Did it work?"

"They killed him before he could eat more than a quarter of it. Took a few centuries to repair itself, Ares did. No other StarMane has succeeded at attacking a tower proper since. The gods started hiding them better after that."

Aetheria felt a disturbing feeling grow in her gut from this conversation. Chronos, attacks on gods and towers, the eldest beings of this universe had been on the move for a very long time it seemed.

"Where'd Werylin go?" Arkaziel asked sleepily, as if he had forgotten what had occurred after all the food he'd consumed that day between the elemental and the buffet.

"Look at the screen. His fight is about to start."

CHAPTER 43

Ariael of the Upper Skies

Will the challengers go three-for-three against the champions of the Aurora Arena? Can Werylin Amaryllis, former Imperator, current steward of the Etherfrost Asura, master of the Sylvan blade dance, Speaker of the Words of Creation, and one of the rare Aetherial Elves maintain a clean sweep of victories?" The voice of the Administrator filled the arena and the waiting room.

Werylin stood calmly in the center of the arena, both of his blades still sheathed.

"Can the elf survive even a minute in the ring with ARIAEL!?" The announcer shouted the name, and the elemental descended into the arena. Ariael looked like the classic representations of a sylph, an elusive, airy, and beautiful feminine humanoid figure that shifted constantly. She seemed to only briefly ever flirt with the concept of solidifying enough to allow one to glimpse her face, which in turn made viewers try all the harder to see her. Whoever controlled the view of the display failed to capture a clear shot of the transient beauty of Ariael at every attempt.

"Ariael of the Upper Skies has descended! Will the elf be able to withstand the frosty judgment that even Boreas, God of the North Wind, is said to find aspirational? BEGIN!"

Werylin casually drew Harmonious Tempest from its sheath, but the elf held the blade in a grip Aetheria had not seen him use before. He held the blade in a reverse grip with the unedged back of the blade held parallel to his arm and the bottom of the hilt faced forward toward Ariael. His left hand remained empty. The air around Werylin vibrated. Dozens of clefs, notes, articulation marks, and accidentals sprung into existence around him, each composed of luminous energy.

The elemental took no action. Her attention seemed to be focused on the musical manifestations around Werylin with great curiosity.

+Even elementals can be suckers for a flashy show.+

~Is that all that's at play, or is there a literal charm component? ~

Arkaziel's lack of answer immediately led Aetheria to believe that he didn't know.

Spurred on by the elemental's lack of offensive moves, the symbols around Werylin doubled, then doubled again. Actual music emerged from the notes. It started with a low hum that grew into an entire symphony, gentle buildups that led to crescendos that vibrated a listener's whole body. The song started with a loneliness that Aetheria couldn't shake. Ocean's Serenity turned frigid on her ears, but even the Primordial-crafted emotion stabilizer could not fend off the dual sources of emotions that assaulted Aetheria, none of which were her own. The entity in the Origin had been stirred awake by the music of Werylin.

"So, the Debbie Downer in the Origin is back," Aetheria said in a drained and almost lifeless tone. The loneliness of the entity hit her like a tangible thing, and it left her barely able to speak through the emptiness in her soul, the utter meaningless of life. The empathic bond with Arkaziel filled with warmth when the cat tried to offer a counter to the desolation of Aetheria's emotions. Even the soul-link to Aoibhe felt more active, and for a brief moment Aetheria swore she felt the witch's hand stroke her cheek.

While both gestures were heartwarming, they were also futile. Arkaziel and Aoibhe, like Aetheria, were little more than ants before the tsunami of emotions that swept out of the Origin and into Aetheria.

The song Werylin created hit another crescendo, a joyous burst of sound, a divine gift, and the entity in the Origin suddenly shifted to happiness. Manic happiness, the highest of highs, the true purpose of existence, delight unadulterated by consequence. Images filled her mind with a cold, lonely void, then an explosion of power. The Big Bang played out in her mind, an entire universe formed from the explosion of Ethereal power that transformed into physical matter. The mind that guided the process felt unfathomable, only its emotions were comprehensible by Aetheria. Whatever the entity was, it was fundamentally different from humans in a way she couldn't access. Arkaziel was a dragon-cat, and overall, his thoughts and mind made sense to her, even if he was ridiculous and absurd.

The song shifted. The passage of time hung heavy. Arkaziel yawned repeatedly, and his eyes half closed. Aetheria felt the boredom of the entity, the tedium of time. Werylin's song managed to convey an unbearable passage of time.

That's when it happened. A discordant note that left blood trickling out of even Werylin's ears. A shrill screech of life torn asunder, of a universe plunged into the void it had spawned from. Finality, death, emptiness. The entity let out a soft gasp as if relieved of a heavy burden, and they were not very conflicted about it at all. It did not miss what it lost, but it did feel a hint of sorrow.

In the arena, the notes exploded when that awful note struck, and Werylin uttered a single word.

"Denouement."

A massive cascade spread through all the clefs, notes, and other symbols as the energy formed a black wind that swept across the arena. Ariael didn't even have a chance to fight against the black wind as it struck her airy form and disintegrated her on the spot.

"Remind me not to let Werylin sing at my wedding," Aetheria quipped to the sleepy Arkaziel.

The interest from the entity in the Origin faded when the music had ceased.

Wait! Who are you?

No answer was returned to Aetheria, not that she really expected one. Still, past interactions seemed to imply that communication was possible. *What if communication is one-way? It can only receive, not send. But then why can it send me emotions?*

With its withdrawal Aetheria's emotions once more returned to normal, and Ocean's Serenity no longer produced so much cold as a byproduct of fighting the entity's influence.

Werylin and the projection of the Administrator returned to the waiting room with Arkaziel and Aetheria in a flash of light.

"That was super impressive!" Aetheria said.

"Maybe you're a StarMane pretending to be an elf?" Arkaziel joked. At least, Aetheria thought it was a joke.

"Thank you. Denouement takes a lot out of me, but few things can withstand it."

The Administrator tapped his foot and coughed.

"Yes, yes, very impressive. You one-shot one of the Aurora Elementals. That's not happened to Ariael before. I doubt she would fall for it again. The rarity of your path is a boon, and speaking of boons . . ." Three treasure chests appeared, one before each member of the party. "Take your treasure."

The Administrator's projection vanished, and Aetheria swore she heard him huff on the way out.

Arkaziel rushed to open his chest before the other two had even moved.

"The hell is this supposed to be?" Arkaziel hissed at the opened chest. Tendrils of shadow lifted up a small charm in the shape of a rook from chess.

"It almost looks like a chess piece, but the little hook, it's definitely meant to be added to your collar, don't you think?"

"You know I don't have a collar, Aetheria. It's a leather banded pendant."

"Regardless, stylistically it even matches the moon on your collar. I mean pendant." Werylin smiled brightly after he called it a collar, which caused Arkaziel to hiss and stomp one of his paws. The careless action sent cracks through the stone floor in warning that the dragon didn't find this conversation amusing.

"Want me to put it on your band?" Aetheria asked, but even while she spoke shadowy hands affixed the charm in the shape of a tower or castle onto Arkaziel's collar. "And if you were wondering, it's called Ethereal Resonance. It deepens your connection to the Ethereal while strengthening your connection to elemental twilight. See how it's half black and half white?"

"Excellent. I am more powerful than ever! Soon worlds will be my hors d'oeuvre."

"If worlds are your snack, what's the meal?"

"Obviously I shall succeed where Antara failed." Arkaziel's eyes were filled with dreams of eating towers.

"Oh, this looks intriguing," Werylin murmured while he stared into the contents of his treasure chest. Aetheria peeked over his shoulder to see a tiny set of wind chimes sized to hang from the hilt of his sword.

"Echoing Chimes," she said. "They have two effects. First, they'll resonate and empower your Words of Creation. Additionally, they'll enhance the weapon they are tied to by increasing its qi absorption, allowing for greater control, intensity, and manifestation of your qi through the weapon."

"That is exceptionally good." Werylin seemed extremely impressed with it, but Aetheria had very little experience with weapons to comment on just how good it was.

"You did one-shot an arena boss, I guess that got you the best reward possible?"

"Real power doesn't come from a weapon." Arkaziel had definitive views on weapons in addition to positive attention for anything but himself.

"Let's see what I got." Aetheria opened her treasure chest to reveal an object bigger than the chest itself. Once the lid opened the chest shattered into kindling that littered the floor, while a large hunk of ice expanded to be revealed in its full glory.

"Why did you get an anvil made of ice? Won't it just melt if you put hot metal on it?"

"No, it won't melt. It'll never melt. It is called the Glacial Anvil of Unending Cold, and supposedly it can withstand any heat. It's a sixth-tier artifact." Aetheria frowned with her words. The tower shouldn't be giving out higher tier rewards to a lower tier Cultivator, but here they were. *Maybe the rules change for things that aren't direct combat items? Why do they want me to forge divine weapons?*

Aetheria touched the anvil and sent it into her repository. She would hold off on experiments with it until they hit another city again, *maybe*. The raw power of a Tier Six artifact would draw attention, and unlike her own aura and power, she couldn't conceal it.

"Well, maybe you can reforge that rainbow sword I picked up into something more useful."

"I can always give it a shot. Durgan didn't teach me much about katanas; he only had me make axes, hammers, and long swords."

"I know how to forge katanas," Arkaziel said, to their shock. "One of my great-uncles spent a few centuries on a sword kick. He wanted to make a blade capable of cutting a neutron star in half."

"Did he succeed?"

"He sure did! Turns out someone told him swords were just bigger chef knives, and he used his sword to dice and prepare a neutron star for a romantic dinner with his mate."

"HE ATE A NEUTRON STAR!?" Aetheria shouted.

"Yeah. I have his memories. It tasted incredible, all the electromagnetic waves, gravity, an entire galaxy compressed into one meal. Very heavy and intense flavor, but a terrible aftertaste that took a decade to go away. Their first litter of children were all very thick and heavily armored."

"I don't want to think about that, so I'm going through this shiny door to the next floor," Aetheria declared before she walked through the portal to Floor 78.

CHAPTER 44

Bring Me a Shrubbery!

The trio appeared in the middle of large fields to start on Floor 78. Two large buildings lay before them, and they were the only visible buildings for as far as any of them could see. The first building reminded Aetheria of Earth. The two-story white farmhouse looked like it had been plucked right out of any rural farm area in the Midwest of the US, down to the storm cellar entrance on the side of the house. The second building, obviously, was a big red barn. It did not have any farm machinery inside of it from what she could see from the front, so Aetheria wandered through the large open doors.

"Oh, thank goodness." Aetheria let out a large sigh of relief when she wandered into the barn. Large bags of seeds filled the first and second floor of the barn, not animals. In fact, not a single animal could be found anywhere near the farmhouse.

"No snacks, too bad. Why aren't there any tools?" Arkaziel also noticed the lack of animals.

"I'd imagine we are expected to cultivate the land and do so through our own abilities. It's a very common floor in all towers, from what I learned back in Naut. It forces one to focus on noncombat related uses of our abilities and grow in different avenues. Would a Tier Four Cultivator be bothered to work a field, grow food, or carry out manual labor unless forced?" Werylin seemed excited at the prospect of growing some wheat, unnaturally so.

"Let's examine the house, then we'll produce a list of all the types of seeds we have. From there we can make a planting guide." Aetheria gestured while she talked, and a dozen generic guard ice sculptures, each of which wielded a crossbow, formed. She gave them simple instructions. "Guard the barn."

"Afraid of bandits?"

"We have a barn full of seeds. Maybe it's valuable, maybe it's not, but no point taking risks we don't need to, right?"

The large farmhouse had all the amenities that Aetheria hoped for. From running water, indoor plumbing, a magic-powered oven, and even a properly working refrigerator, it was the most luxury they'd had since leaving Naut. There were even comfortable beds in the numerous rooms of the house, although Arkaziel still claimed her room even though there were plenty for him to have his own. *He wouldn't be a cat if he wasn't annoying me when I try to sleep.*

It took Aetheria and Werylin the better part of four hours to walk through the barn and inventory the seeds they had. Arkaziel had volunteered to scout the region from the air, but Aetheria suspected he wanted to explore the new hunting grounds around the farm. As long as he at least took note of the lay of the land and any nearby nests, lairs, villages, or other locations of interest, it meant the inventory of the barn went smoother without him. Besides, she could always take a few flights around the territory later to make sure Arkaziel's stomach hadn't missed anything.

Upon inventory the group realized they had a rather large task before them. They had been given a significant number of seeds, and some were not fast growers. Aetheria had arranged her list by aspect, as an Administrator seemed to set up the challenge based upon aspects the group used.

For harmony imbued planets they had Grapes of Unity, Balance Barley, and Synchrony Soy. All of the crops were mild psychoactives that increased peace of mind, unity, or general tranquility and understanding. On top of that, they slightly increased one's affinity to harmony. The increase was negligible overall, but if one spent a few hundred years eating meals cooked with the crops the effects would add up.

For ice crops they had Glacial Garlic, Permafrost Peppers, literal Iceberg Lettuce, and Snowflake Spinach. All of the ice crops, like the harmony ones, gave the tiniest of boosts to ice affinity when eaten, but mostly were used for their psychoactive components to assist vision questing. The Permafrost Peppers, in particular, were said to be fantastic for those who endeavored down the path of Frostfire. Not everyone had Aetheria's cheat-like Primordial level affinities, and in fact very few people had such ridiculous affinities as the blue-and-red-haired Cultivator. There was a single crop of the water element, Aquifer Asparagus, that could provide one with enough water to last a few days in a single stalk. Said water also happened to be quite psychoactive, and was only suitable for extended secluded sessions of cultivation.

The Administrator's cruel sense of humor left them with the largest number of crops carrying Arkaziel's aspects. In the light category they had Sunburst Sunflowers, the seeds of which, when opened, literally exploded with optimism and positivity in the form of gas that you could inhale. Then there were the Dawnbreaker Dates, Radiant Raspberries, Luminous Lemons, and of course Bright Broccolini, which improved one's darkvision permanently, albeit in the tiniest of increments.

If that were not enough, they also had to deal with the darkness aspected crops. Eclipse Eggplants, Duskshade Tomatoes, Twilight Tatoes, and Moonlight Mushrooms. These were all going to require the construction of a dark environment to grow in, and the Duskshade Tomatoes and Eclipse Eggplants both exuded a poisonous gas until they flowered. At their current cultivation tiers, the gas would not harm them, but it would irritate their eyes and skin.

Arkaziel's recon showed they had no neighbors, and very little prey. In fact, the lack of prey animals could seriously hamper the long-term success of the floor—if Arkaziel grew too bored and turned toward *helping*, things could go sideways very quickly.

The first night Aetheria stayed up late while she mapped out the fields and structures to use for the darkness aspected crops, when she realized something. Many of the crops they were to grow attracted ravenous monsters. Duskshade Tomatoes were infamous for being irresistible to a creature known as an Umbral Beast. They were chimera-like, ever-changing, and only ever appeared in the darkness. They absolutely loved Duskshade Tomatoes.

It wasn't the only crop that drew strange creatures.

The Grapes of Unity drew a pest known as the Harmonious Hummingbird Dragon, well-known for their iridescent scales, shimmering wings . . . and being the carrier of a terrific plague. Glacial Garlic, meanwhile, attracted a type of yeti that used the garlic crop to extend their reach into warmer climates. The yeti frequently turned to violence to acquire the garlic when their own stockpiles ran short, which was often, given the yeti's terrible knowledge of agriculture. The list kept going with elementals, gryphons, pixies, and even nymphs.

What had, at first, seemed like an obnoxious floor for busy work that would at least allow them ample time to work on their cultivation revealed itself to be rife with creatures that could be handfuls on their own. Who knew what else the Administrators had cooked up to sabotage them, because why play fair?

The next morning, they sat down and discussed their options.

". . . and so, that's the situation. We probably don't have months of peaceful farming ahead of us, but months of pest extermination and fruit and vegetable thieves to wipe out." Aetheria had finished explaining her view of the situation as she saw it.

"Some of this seems entirely preventable. We can redraw the fields to incorporate natural wards. With your ability to create permanent ice we can easily mass-produce barrier posts, and I can lay down Sylvan magics to gently nudge creatures to find another place to be. We'll still have quite a few intruders, I imagine, but we can take care of those, too. We have summons, constructs, duplicates, and you two both have long-range attacks." Werylin's confidence and faith in their abilities likewise lifted the emotions of the other two.

"I suppose. I did make a lot of constructs back on that demon floor; I should be able to do the same here. Why don't you handle the layout and design of the fields, Werylin. I'll start producing ice constructs and turrets to place around the farm, while Arkaziel thinks up a way to shorten the crop cycles with his light and darkness."

"What? Why do I have to do that? The elves are the ones who use nature magic."

"Do you not know how?"

"Of course, I know how! I'm the greatest Twilight Dragon in existence. Anyone who says otherwise is just jealous. It'll be a simple matter to increase the growing cycle for most of these plants by using zone magic, it's just so dreadfully *boring*."

"You can have Werylin's job of designing the fields and defenses instead, if you like?"

"I'll make plants go grow, grow, grow. You two had better keep up with me, and the plants. I'll have crops growing in days."

"Maybe a little more conservative than that? Let's aim for a month for our first crops. It would be unfortunate to grow everything and have a deluge of monsters appear at once," Werylin said.

"Fine." Arkaziel almost hissed the words. Aetheria could almost see the visions of a tasty monster-tide snack dance above Arkaziel's head.

Thus the days of their farming quest went. Aetheria split her time between creation of defensive constructs and management of ice-oxen to plow the fields; Arkaziel worked on erecting a multitude of different zones for light and darkness spells. Some overlapped multiple fields, others focused only on a tiny patch. Arkaziel proved exceptionally adept at the creation of barrier posts. Once he created one, he could brand the same symbols into dozens in a minute. The downside to barrier posts were that they could be destroyed and then walked over, but the flare they sent up would draw attention from the farmhouse.

Werylin, once Imperator of an Elven Empire, proved to retain at the least passing familiarity with agricultural operations. Once the fields were laid out, the defenses and magics erected, the elf wandered from field to field constructing what he called terrorcrows, an upgraded fae version of scarecrows. The name intrigued Aetheria, but after one look at sackcloth-headed figures she felt immensely let down. Apparently the magic behind them only worked on creatures designated as pests, so they were exceptionally unimpressive.

Their nights were a mixture of sleep, cultivation, and commiseration. Aetheria set up the Glacial Anvil of Unending Cold and worked on reforging the rainbow sword into a katana under the guidance of Arkaziel. Who constantly bitched about how the makeshift smithy next to the barn was cold, and how he needed a snack to warm up. Aetheria created a bed of fire for the cat after the four hundredth comment about how the smithy felt too chilly. Arkaziel had been terribly offended at her mundane flames, and made shadow flames to rest in, instead.

"Have you thought about how you're going to make a scabbard for the blade?"

"I have, actually! I'm going to shape the scabbard out of some world tree wood I still have in my repository, then I'll trim and adorn it to match whatever style Werylin picks. If he wants to enchant the scabbard I can help with that, too, but I feel like you two know more enchanting than I do. Regardless, yes, I've put thought into it all."

A *whoosh* sounded outside the smithy, and then light bloomed through the window, followed by a loud *boom* like thunder.

"There goes one of the barrier posts." Arkaziel flexed his claws and was out the door before Aetheria had even put her work away.

~*Let me know if you have it handled before I even get out there.* ~ Aetheria enjoyed the telepathic bond's uses, especially if it saved her cleaning up the smithy for no reason.

+*That's not going to be a problem. It's a full monster tide.*+

CHAPTER 45

On Deadly Ground

The idyllic fields around the farmhouse had transformed into a battleground. Death cries filled the night by the time Aetheria made it out of the farmhouse and into the air. She didn't even need to look in any direction to sense that her turret constructs were firing continuously. She'd used the same design as the ones she'd employed in the arena with the demons, only this version fired foot-long spears of ice with a jagged tip. Despite the dozens of turrets, the defensive perimeter had already fallen in two spots. The second barrier post breach created the same massive flare and explosive thunder the first had.

A strange sensation brushed against Aetheria's mind, and a fresh voice joined the telepathic bond she shared with Arkaziel.

=*What an odd sensation. I have the breach to the north covered for now. The grapes are the breach location up here. Insect enemies.*=

+*I pulled Werylin in.*+

~*I didn't know you could do that.*~ Telepathic communication saved time, but more importantly, it provided a crisp and clear medium to communicate with that didn't require physical hearing, vicinity, and had very minimal risk of being overheard or intercepted by enemies.

+*What can't I do? I'm amazing. I've got the southwest breach. The perimeter around the shade plants building is holding well. It's like an all-I-can-eat buffet thanks to the dumb insects just funneling in a few dozen at a time.*+

~*Well, I guess I'll try something fun.*~

Aetheria's form provided a significant amount of light in the night sky, but the glow of her eyes and hair were proportional to her human size and the amount of energy she broadcast, which were minimal. At least, until her body rippled into the form of a seventy-five-meter-long Ethereal ice dragon. The night filled with the pale blue-white light of her draconic form, and the intensity of the light she cast surpassed the light of the full moon in the sky. She raised her head to the sky and unleashed a bellow that shook the earth, toppled a few unsteady trees, and temporarily paused the tide of insects in their attempt to breach the farm.

+Showoff.+ Arkaziel seemed amused at her choice of forms for the fight. The StarMane had no issue with her taking on the form of the Ethereal ice dragon ever since she won him first place on the racer leaderboard, but if she took any other dragon form or even thought of shapeshifting into a StarMane, he got extremely irritated. *I suppose that's fair. I'd be weirded out if he shapeshifted into a woman who looked like I do, and there's the whole Chronos-made-StarManes religious aspect.*

Aetheria drew in a deep breath before she strafed over the gathering tide to the north. Once she had positioned herself a good hundred yards past Werylin's defensive spot, and had enough distance from the fields, she exhaled. Her breath emerged like an inverse flamethrower: anything even remotely touched by the breath attack froze, then shattered. The insects chittered, but were trapped in waves so dense there was no chance of escape. If this were a video game, her vision would be filled by thousands of small denominations of experience gains, but she gained nothing from these kills, not even satisfaction. Beyond the novelty of draconic might, this fight didn't matter.

+My duplicates are doing the same down here in the south. Once you've given Werylin space, focus on more defenses, please.+

Aetheria nearly died of shock when Arkaziel said please. Since when did the cat ever use the word *please* when commanding one of his minions? Realization dawned slowly. *Oh. I'm a dragon. The moment I go back to a human it'll be more imperious commands, right? Right.*

Nonetheless, Arkaziel was right. Aetheria had created a large gap for Werylin, and so she returned to human form and dropped down behind the elf. Three pillars of ice rose, each one with a different turret. One fell into the traditional ice spear chucker category, another mimicked the frost dragon breath, and the third snowflake-like chakrams that shattered like fragmentation grenades when they made impact. While she thought about what other aid she could offer Werylin, another barrier post exploded to the east side of the fields.

~I'll handle that one. You've got at least a minute left before the tide reaches you again. Werylin, repair the broken post if you can.~

=I already have a replacement ready; I've got another ten in my storage ring. I thought it best to keep an opening rather than let the insects form another entrance. I'll be ready to place a new post the moment another post goes down.=

The elf's logic made sense to Aetheria. With the sheer tide of enemies there were going to be breaches, so if they controlled the breaches, it reduced the chances of more breaks in their defensive perimeter. Maybe. It really depended on the type of intelligence behind the tide of enemies. If they were nearly mindless, it should work quite well. If they had any sort of tactical or strategic intelligence behind their actions, it wouldn't hold up. The absolute worst-case scenario would be that the enemies were controlled by an Administrator. Administrators played with cheat codes, after all.

Aetheria appeared in the newest breach with a flare of multicolored energies. The energies of Khaos disintegrated the bugs who had swarmed into the breach, and immediately thereafter Aetheria's domain filled the area. Insects that swarmed toward her all froze in place as her domain took effect, while she casually gestured, and spears of ice took the insects that got past her to hell. It only took three volleys of projectiles to annihilate the insects that had gotten into the field.

The sound of shattered ice drew her attention back to the swarm. Aetheria's domain couldn't keep up with the sheer number of insects before her, it seemed like. When she turned Ethereal Sight upon the swarm, she realized no flaw with her domain had allowed the insects to break free. A linkage had formed between the insects that previously had not been there. The stronger that linkage grew, the more ineffective her domain grew. She watched with interest but did not stand idle. Pillars of ice rose along the perimeter with multiple turrets atop them.

+ The insects are acting weird now. +

= The composition of the swarm has changed here. They're growing larger. =

~ Some kind of linkage formed between them over here. Uh. Literally. ~

Aetheria blinked confusion from her eyes. Two mantis-like enemies stepped into one another and melded into one creature. The tide of pressing insects repeated the process everywhere she looked, and in each instance a different kind of multilimbed, bigger horror emerged. Unfortunately the reaction did not stop there. Bigger, nastier, awfuller-looking insects flowed into each, and then the process repeated.

"No! No damned creepy crawlies!" Aetheria yelled at the night before she sent waves of power before her with the Transcendent Flame of Khaos. She bound the power with the intent for the fusing to fall apart, disintegrate, or backfire. Instead, the creatures absorbed the waves of chaotic power into themselves and with each merge suddenly each creature gained new affinities and aspects.

"Oh cripes."

~ Things are changing down here real fast. Watch out for adaptation to your attacks. ~

Aetheria's body rippled. Her skin changed to teal, super-dense impenetrable scales, and her features morphed to those of a dragonoid. She ran a mental checklist: tail, talons, wings, breath attack. Then she darted forward to commence a campaign of carnage, and alternation of her attacks, including changing the type of her breath attack with each exhale. She had access to a very large variety of energy types thanks to the ability to mimic any affinity within her repository. The insects still went down comparatively easily, but the time per kill had gone up. From whole hordes wiped out with a single attack to multiple attacks to kill a single evolved amalgamation.

A strange pulse of energy filled the night sky, and night turned to day briefly. The insects all fell to the ground in a mess of a goo. Goo that flowed into a massive ball in the sky. When Aetheria threw pulses of cold, ice spears, flame, even gusts of wind, the goo somehow evaded, absorbed, or reflected each attack.

+ Looks like we've got a boss fight incoming. +

= It certainly looks that way. Should we regroup? =

Before Aetheria could add her two cents to the conversation the massive form of Arkaziel shot into the sky to unleash a twilight breath attack on the coalescing ball of goo. The mixed element attack pierced through the outer layer of goo and struck a force field, where it sputtered out and died. Moments later the ball of goo exploded outward and revealed the massive form of a cockroach on a similar scale to that of Arkaziel's draconic size

~Barf. I hate cockroaches; they're so nasty. Any insights, Ark?~

+Armored scales, adaptive defenses, regeneration, flight, and I bet it has a spit attack. Most likely it'll have minions, or lesser versions of itself, too.+

=You two go fight that thing in the air; I'll repair the barrier posts. They will still protect the crops from aerial attacks if I repair them, within reason. Good luck!= Werylin sounded entirely too cheery about not fighting the cockroach for Aetheria's liking.

Arkaziel flew in to fight the cockroach physically. Shockingly the moment Arkaziel entered physical range, the cockroach managed to grasp and throw the StarMane with such force he sailed off into the night, before a flare of teleportation returned the dragon to the fight.

+It's ridiculously strong and fast.+

Aetheria took that as her cue to activate Flash Mode and teleport onto the cockroach's back. That part of her plan worked, but once she appeared on the cockroach, its exoskeleton was not what she expected at all. Instead of something incredibly dense, it was still gooey and fluid. The exoskeleton tried to ensnare her feet. With her immense speed she moved before it could constrict her, but each step on the cockroach's exoskeleton seemed to fatigue her, and the energy-use of Flash Mode had skyrocketed to a higher cost than before she had acquired Astrum Nexus.

Time seemed to be limited, so Aetheria pulled massive quantities of Ethereal power from Frostfire into her fists and into the Astrum Nexus. The sigils for Nyx, Ymir, Thalassa, and Khaos all lit up as she also activated those Flames within herself. She interlocked her fists above her head, and slammed both hands down onto the back of the cockroach's exoskeleton with all the might her shapeshifting Ethereal Scion body could generate. The blow struck like a meteor, and the cockroach dropped dozens of meters in the air, bounced off the barrier protecting the fields, and crashed into untamed nature.

Aetheria fell from its back in the chaos of her attack. The barrier didn't stop her, so she crashed into one of the fields.

"Oh, the Radiant Raspberries are pretty." Aetheria reached up to pluck one of the fruits and pop it into her mouth. The tartness and sweetness filled her mouth, while warmth and airy lightness filled her stomach. Her teal scales glowed with a slightly brighter inner light.

"Neat."

+Quit lollygagging and buy me another minute while I prepare a spell.+

~Yes, m'lord.~ Arkaziel wouldn't get the orcish voice Aetheria used from an old real time strategy game, but that didn't matter. It amused her.

Aetheria and the cockroach shot up into the air at the same time. The exoskeleton she had struck had already regenerated.

"Always seems so unfair when others do that."

Aetheria summoned the power of her core and focused on one idea. *Kali Ma!*

CHAPTER 46

Heartbreaker

Aetheria had been reluctant to call upon the full power of her Cultivator's core ever since she created the thing. When hoary old Primordials provided someone with the basic schematics and understanding of a unique core like they had done for her, she had felt it best not to jump in too quickly. The Primordials retained, or perhaps never possessed in the first place, a concept of proportional power. The gooey colossal cockroach represented a fight she just wanted over, though, and so she activated the full power of her core.

When Aetheria activated Flash Mode, the secondary component of her core, the first few beats of her core usually felt loud and reverberated throughout her body. When she activated the full functionality, it felt like a gong went off inside her chest, and each beat of her core continued to feel like a beat of that massive gong. Images filled her mind of ancient technology activated for the first time in eons, dust filling the imaginary air. Then her body flooded with a strange sensation.

Aetheria and power were no strangers. Ever since her reincarnation power had been her constant companion. Others had to strain and reach for it, but she simply breathed it in or let it flow into her from her own Origin Gate that couldn't be closed. This sensation wasn't the usual flood of power—it had a different flavor. If the raw Ethereal power she usually employed was a fine wine, then this variant of power represented a brandy. Subtle, smooth, complex, robust, and luxurious, but more than anything it felt elegant.

"Authority."

The whispered words originated from Aetheria's occasional friend, Gatekeeper of the Origin, Themis. Time had stopped according to her perceptions in the real world—neither herself nor her enemy moved, so Aetheria focused on her visitor. She projected an avatar into her inner world, and Themis generated one. They talked before Frostfire, the Ethereal Sun and Origin Gate inside her soul. Themis chose the visage that filled courtrooms on Earth. A blindfolded woman who held scales.

"What is authority?" Such a simple question seemed like it might be rhetorical, but Aetheria recognized that the specifics and definitions mattered in this conversation.

"Authority is the power to make, alter, and enforce the rules, yes? Yours is self-authority. It is in the name of your core, you know."

"I just sort of assumed the autopotency name represented an embellishment to sound grander, like enhancements on my abilities."

"Aetherius and Chronos do not make a habit of overstating, exaggeration, or embellishment. Subtlety is also not within their capability, or you would have been given just enough knowledge to create soul-materials and maybe hints at how to construct an authority core. At least you limited the core to yourself. Even you would have suffered if you reached for a full authority core."

"Definitely." Aetheria tasted ashes for a moment, her stomach churned, and numbness dominated her mind. She had not made those alterations with full understanding. She had wanted to increase her shapeshifting and internal power control. Themis had casually revealed how little of her core Aetheria understood, when she had thought she comprehended all of the ideas behind it. How badly would a full authority core have gone for her if she had not made those modifications?

"Enjoy the cockroach." Themis vanished into Frostfire.

Aetheria felt the deep desire to slap Aetherius and Chronos, and herself. She had dramatically misunderstood some of the concepts in the core designs, failed to comprehend the dangers, and walked along humming a jaunty tune thinking she was so clever.

Time unfroze, and the cockroach spit acid at Aetheria. The acid froze and disintegrated when it got within a meter of her, and she turned eyes filled with anger upon the bug. *How do I use authority?*

Intent seemed like it should be a vital component of authority, so Aetheria focused on the visualization of her desires and filled it with intent to become reality. She visualized her scaled dragonoid form as immune to the entangling gooey nature of the cockroach. Thick leathery wings strained against the air and sent her hurtling through sky to crash into the exoskeleton of the cockroach. She imagined the talons of her hands as a suppressant force to the amorphous nature of the bug, then struck with all her strength to rip a hole into its exterior. The goopy exoskeleton parted like butter, and roiled and burned like acid. It struggled to regenerate, which caused the cockroach to emit a terrible hiss and a massive cloud of corrosive mist.

Aetheria didn't hang around for the mist to reach her. She dove into the breach and created a vortex of razor snowflakes to cut the flesh and goo of the cockroach. What came next involved a certain level of detachment for her. She needed to visualize and maintain the will and intent for her snowflakes and attacks to allow her to cut her way through the insides of the cockroach, while also not allowing how ridiculously disgusting it was to force her to throw up. She let the raw power of the monster's core draw her in and paid minimal attention to the flesh and organs she passed. Any damage she inflicted now was just an extra bonus on the way to the core.

Time felt slow, and Aetheria reached a mental count of 153 before she severed yet another protective layer and breached the core chamber of the giant cockroach.

The thick, awful smelling, slimy membranes of the cockroach were no match for her authority. The chamber assaulted her with disgust in every manner it could, no senses spared. The air even tasted awful, like rotting meat full of maggots seasoned with bile and cigarette butts. The bile may or may not have been her own; she couldn't be sure.

At the center of the chamber a dark crystal core beat with malevolence, and Aetheria felt mental attacks rebound off her mental defenses. Again and again, the core attacked her mind until it realized it couldn't pierce the immense defenses provided by the equipment, her Flames, and the strength of her own will.

"Time to die." The razor-sharp snowflakes orbiting her shot out across the chamber, but rebounded off an invisible barrier around the monster's core. A flash of annoyance surged within her, but she tromped across the large chamber to assault the barrier with one of her talons. The barrier shattered, and no matter how hard the cockroach tried it couldn't re-form the defense.

"What are you?"

"Your guess is as good as mine at this point," Aetheria answered the core with a grimace. Even its voice hurt her—it sounded like someone squeezing Styrofoam, and forced goosebumps to rise on her skin and a horrible shudder to pass through her body. It did not stop her advance.

+Incoming!+

~Gods dammit, Ark, I'm at the core and about to crush it!~

Aetheria could not see the attack, per se, but she could visualize it based on the immense spikes of energy that occurred in the sky above them. A magic circle had completed, activated, and a pillar of powerful light struck the cockroach. Its adaptive physiology struggled to fight the burn of the light, but the continuous beams of power burned so intensely it lost tons of mass by the second. Unending divine light burned the cockroach, rapidly burning away all matter until only the core chamber remained.

"Looks like Arkaziel's going to eat you. Good luck with that." Aetheria offered a warning to its fate, before a flare of rainbow-hued energy erupted around her and she appeared at the field near Werylin.

Shortly after, the light momentarily weakened when a black hand shot out of the magic circle, grasped the monster core, and fed it into one of Arkaziel's shadow mouths. The magic circle faded from the sky, and in moments the peace of night resumed around the farm. Then a massive belch shook the world, the earth roiled, clouds dispersed, and birds flew into the sky in alarm.

+That was one dense meal.+

=Pardon you, Ark. I think you collapsed your potato shed.=

+Noooo!+

The large StarMane flew toward his potato shed, while Werylin and Aetheria languidly walked that way. When they got there the cat sat dejectedly on the broken shed.

"No survivors," Arkaziel moaned forlornly to his companions.

"Ugh. None? The clear criteria might require at least a few. Can you salvage some with magic, Werylin?" Aetheria poked at the remains of the shed.

"Hmm. In a bit of a roundabout matter, yes. Could you create an ice replica of the shed as it used to be, Aetheria? The more accurate you make it, the more effective my magic will be."

"Oh. It looked like *this*." Arkaziel waved a claw through the air, and the light warped to create an almost perfect illusion of the potato shed before the cataclysmic belch annihilated it.

"If only your manners were as good as your memory, we wouldn't have to deal with this." Aetheria couldn't resist chiding Arkaziel as if he were a child, but his illusion reduced the difficulty in replication of the shed to almost nothing.

From there Werylin inscribed a couple of sigils into the shattered building and the replica, then cast a delayed transference. The delay required Aetheria to invoke the power of Chronos from the Astrum Nexus. When they had all the preparations done, Werylin activated it all with a single word.

"*Transfer.*" The shed went back to its former state, as did the potatoes inside of it, while the ice shed shattered, fragmented, and otherwise got obliterated in place of the actual shed and its crops.

"That's a great party trick. Thank you, pal." Arkaziel went above and beyond in a show of appreciation, uttering the rarest of words to ever be said by a StarMane. The other two came out of the daze of shock to find Arkaziel had already wandered off to find a napping spot to digest the monster core.

"Did he actually thank me?"

"Unless I hallucinated it, yes. Maybe it was an illusion, and the real him was already napping?" Aetheria considered the possibilities.

"Probably. I'm going to finish mending all the fences and perform some accelerated growth rituals. The quicker we're off this level the better."

"Agreed. Thank you, Werylin. I'll be in the smithy if you need anything. I think I've got the details figured out on reforging the rainbow sword. Don't rush the crops too much. I'd like at least another week of preparations before we ascend. Arkaziel said the difficulty spikes once we hit Floor Eighty, so we should be prepared."

The elf laughed, then gestured at the sky.

"I think we're prepared already, honestly. The two of you defy everything I know about what kind of strength a Cultivator of our tier should possess."

"Feeling left out?"

"Slightly. With my skills and equipment, I would be welcome among most climbing teams, no questions asked, but I always feel a step behind you two."

"The ability to destroy your enemies isn't the only purpose in life, is it? You bring a lot of skills to the table that neither Arkaziel nor I possess. Look at Ark, all the knowledge of his clan from genetic memories, and still, he's mostly just a walking disaster. I guess I'm no better now that I've got the knowledge of the Aetherials." Aetheria laughed and petted the crystals embedded into her gloves.

"Maybe your spirit representation is a StarMane?" Werylin teased her, then fled across the fields as icy weapons appeared out of nowhere to menace him.

"Not funny!"

CHAPTER 47

Stormshimmer

Crops, even magically sped up crops, grew slowly. It took Aetheria two weeks after the incident with the cockroach to finish the project on the rainbow sword. The crops had still not finished growing by that time. She called Werylin to the smithy, and when the elf entered he stared at the sheathed weapon that lay upon the frozen anvil with palpable anticipation.

"I took the liberty of naming the blade in Ath. It translates to Stormshimmer in Sylvan. When you draw it, you'll see why. Give it an appropriate name in Sylvan; only you need to know what its name is in Ath."

Werylin's slender fingers longed to brush against the newly wrapped hilt of the katana, or at least that's how Aetheria interpreted the way his digits danced in the empty air. He restrained himself and examined the sheath and hilt with only his eyes.

"I made the hilt out of world tree wood, just like the scabbard. It is still unenchanted, so we'll need to figure out what enchantments you want in it, or if you want to do the enchanting yourself or hire someone more capable than me. The leather for the hilt wrap is from a species of gryphon called a Sunset Gryphon. I don't really know how much of the color variation comes from the gryphon versus how much comes from the processing, but it came highly recommended in Naut. Go ahead, draw the blade." Aetheria gestured at the frozen anvil encouragingly.

Like the first boy approaching the first girl at a school dance, Werylin approached the anvil with trepidation and anxiety before he finally grasped the hilt. Shivers from proximity to the anvil wracked his body, before he stepped back a few meters and slowly unsheathed the blade. A multitude of sparks filled the air, each a different color of the rainbow. Even when Werylin just held the blade still, sparks continued to shoot into the air.

"It is beyond beautiful." Werylin complimented the shining blade while he tested its balance.

"Yes," Aetheria agreed. The blade measured eighty centimeters from point to guard, and while it appeared to be composed of flowing light, its hardness and durability exceeded that of adamantine. It was very solid, and any opponent who disregarded the blade as a trick of lights or energy would risk their own weapons in a direct trade of blows.

"Do I need to worry about it breaking?"

"No. It will immediately heal if you break it. Let me show you." Aetheria held a hand out, and Werylin gave her the katana with a worried expression on his face. She gave him a reassuring smile before she gripped the blade in both hands and strained her muscles. A shattering sound filled the smithy as the blade of light fragmented into a hundred tiny shards, shards that then flowed back into the shape of the blade and melded back together into a singular undamaged piece.

Aetheria handed the blade back to Werylin with only a minor self-satisfied smirk to show her pride in the blade.

"How did you manage that?" Werylin examined the blade, astounded.

"I used the Flame of Khaos to set the default state of the blade, then arranged the laws that governed the chromatic alloy to always flow into their natural state when not currently in it. It was a learning experience, and I'm sure there might be a better way to do it, but this way the blade never weakens. It will always be as strong as after I reforged it, and since it's an alloy of prismsteel and adamantine, it shouldn't break too often."

"Wait, you just broke adamantine barehanded?" Werylin blinked, then tried to flex the blade himself. He couldn't even make the blade bend in the slightest. "Just how strong are you, Aetheria? You never showed that kind of strength before."

Red flushed Aetheria's cheeks, and she shrugged.

"Well, I activated my core for real in the fight with the cockroach."

"And?"

"And I can't turn it off now." Embarrassment and shame kept her voice soft, and a little elusive.

"Do I dare ask what your core does? I thought your lightning speed was your core effect."

"Ah. No, that's the secondary power." Aetheria grimaced when she admitted that, especially when Werylin's eyes widened, and he swore under his breath.

"So the primary function of your core is what, superstrength to go with your superspeed? Total invulnerability? Reality warping?"

"Well, are you familiar with the concept of self-mastery?"

"That's the entire point of cultivation, Aetheria. You absorb energy to increase your potential, until you have reached the pinnacle and are your best, most powerful, and ideally immortal, self. Mind, body, and soul."

"Yeah, sure, I guess. Well, I'm a shapeshifter, and I wanted my core to focus on helping me enhance that. Maybe it was a bit of a translation error, but do you know what *authority* is?"

"I feel you aren't quite talking about the legal authority a ruler has. Perhaps more like the authority a god has over their primary world?" Werylin shrugged hopelessly.

"Actually, that might be a great comparison. Maybe. This part didn't come with an instruction book, and Themis ran off before I could interrogate her fully. The effective answer is I have a lot of control over myself now. Strength, speed, perception, how things do or do not affect me . . ." Aetheria shrugged and trailed off. Silence hung for a few seconds before she spoke again. "So yeah, I'm apparently even more of a cheat than I thought, but hey, at least it is not reality warping?"

Werylin stared at her flatly, then looked at the katana.

"So, I shouldn't need to worry about it breaking. Is there anything else about it I should know?"

"If you channel Aether through it, it will emerge as beams of light. Very intense beams of light, proportional to the energy you channel."

"Thank you, Aetheria." Werylin bowed to her, then secured the blade to his hip underneath Harmonious Tempest.

"You're welcome." Aetheria watched Werylin wander out of the smithy, and once the elf made it some distance away, her smile fell into a frown. Their entire dynamic had just changed at the end of that conversation. *Can I blame him? I'm not a normal person. Maybe I shouldn't even pretend to be? What can't I do now, if I set my mind to it? Arkaziel is as monstrously abnormal as I am, and with our soul-bind, I'm fairly certain he's been affected by my own impossible growth. Will Aoibhe have been infected, too, or will she look at me like Werylin just did, in disbelief and recognition that she cannot keep up?*

"I hope not, lover mine. I miss you." Aetheria whispered the words to the wind and felt an abnormal gust brush a single tear off her cheek.

I miss you too, my dearest.

The exchanges had been happening more frequently. How long until they could communicate at will, like she and Arkaziel could? Aetheria desperately looked forward to that day but felt it would come after their reunion instead of before it. She had no reason to distrust Aoibhe, or doubt her, yet self-consciousness reared its ugly head frequently because of the separation the tower forced upon them. One could not even measure the distance between floors, and the odd nature of temporal flows could mean that although decades had passed for Aetheria since she left Solace, mere months could have passed for Aoibhe. Malleable reality led to strange scenarios.

With Aetheria's only project in the working stages done, she packed up the anvil and smithy. It took almost no time for her to walk through the area and for item after item to vanish into her repository, where it appeared in the same order it had been while in use.

Over the next few days each of the group spent their days in a mixture of self-improvement and farming. Werylin spread his time between practice with Stormshimmer, where he alternated between single and dual wield with Harmonious Tempest. The Sylvan artifact seemed to react to Stormshimmer, and spat minute arcs of lightning whenever Stormshimmer created bursts of light. The flashy nature of the swords looked appropriate to the vibrant design and color of the Sylvan hakama Werylin wore. Aetheria also noticed that Werylin worked more frequently with his declarations with the Words of Creation than he usually did, as if the elf were attempting to make up lost ground.

Arkaziel, being Arkaziel, seemed to do nothing at all. The StarMane always gave the illusion of sloth, but Aetheria had learned to see through some of his defense mechanisms. He spent his time cooking, working on a technique he called Twilight Inversion, and fostering growth among the darkness and light aspected plants. All of the plants benefited from exposure to his empowered light, but after two weeks he had worked out how to turn his duplicates into mobile grow lights and happily delegated the grunt work to the energy constructs. He claimed it took only a marginal amount of concentration to run all three simultaneously.

Aetheria herself spent most of her days working on impulse, thought, and emotion control. When your belief in something, especially yourself, directly impacted reality, confidence became a weapon. At first, she tried to incorporate it into simultaneous control of shapeshifting, but that complicated everything and diminished both her authority and her fine control over shapeshifting. Physical strength and speed were both basic alterations for her authority and shapeshifting, so she had to separate and identify the differences between the two. Shapeshifting allowed her to alter her form completely, gave her control over material, muscle density, weight, and volume. Self-authority allowed her to do the same things, but it also allowed her to simply will herself to be stronger. How? Screw you, it just worked, that's how.

The more Aetheria played with exercising authority, the more it felt like the early days of learning to control her shapeshifting. The technical executions were different, but it boiled down to the same way she controlled energy. Visualize, impose her will and intent, and don't sweat the details. Broad general control could be achieved relatively easily with that rough method and cut down on her randomly flying, gaining mass, or the intensity of her hair's glow ramping up to blinding when she got distracted by how nice it looked out of the corner of her eye. She even toyed with the idea of plant growth accelerating anywhere she walked in the fields, like the Green Man from a novel she'd read once. While that did work, it produced really inconsistent results with one plant growing to full size while its neighbor would grow to a behemoth four times its usual size.

Perhaps it had something to do with nature, and Aetheria's personality not really aligning with flowers growing to make her smile? That's what she chalked it up to for now. The variability and sporadic outcomes of manipulations of self-authority had almost everything to do with her subconscious mind, and so she struggled with it constantly, to the point of forgoing any other form of training while they remained on the farm.

Four months after they appeared on the floor, they started harvesting crops, and at the eight-month mark, they finally harvested the last crop: Luminous Lemons. The radiant, shining yellow fruit smelled beyond amazing, and plucking them from the trees completed the challenge of Floor 78. Each of the three released a relieved sigh when the doorway to the next floor opened.

"Floor complete. Let's loot all our hard work!" Arkaziel demanded, and that's how Aetheria ended up with even more piles of fruits and vegetables in her repository.

CHAPTER 48

Sir Loin the First

oo."

"Mooo."

"Moo."

The sounds of a herd of cattle filled the ears of Aetheria, Arkaziel, and Werylin as they appeared on Floor 79. Indeed, they appeared in a large pasture that sprawled as far as they could see, and the only living animals beyond themselves were hundreds of thousands of cows. Large, long-haired, adorable, and many long-horned, cows. On Earth, Aetheria would have said they were Scottish Highland cattle, or a breed quite similar to them. Unless the Administrators were pulling from her old world again, though, they could be called anything in the wider universe.

"Floof cows!" Arkaziel exclaimed. He had attempted to conceal his excitement at seeing the cows, but failed so poorly the cattle must either taste fantastic or be a fantastic crafting material.

"What is a floof cow?" Werylin asked with preemptive regret written all over his face.

"It's one of the most delicious animals in all of existence. They're found only rarely in any of the towers. I've never heard of such a large spawn of floof cows ever happening to another group of climbers. A herd of twenty here, fifty there, sure, but there must be thousands. This is the mother lode!"

"Moooooo."

One of the nearest cows emitted a bellow that sounded angry. The call repeated throughout the herd. Hundreds of previously docile-looking cows turned baleful eyes upon the house cat.

"I think they're calling you out, Ark." Aetheria laughed at the preposterous idea.

The golden vertical feline eyes of the StarMane raked over the endless pastures of floof cows, and the cat licked his lips.

"That's fine. I'll fight them all, at the same time, even."

"Mooooooooooo. Your challenge is udderly ridi-cow-lous," a deep voice answered.

Arkaziel's challenge, as one of the nearby floof cows stood upright, towering over its nearby herd mates and the climbers.

"Wow, you're tall. Hi, I'm Aetheria, that's Werylin, and the cat is Arkaziel. Who are you?" Aetheria put her best smile forward, but this felt weird now. You weren't supposed to eat sentient things, right? Sure, they did it all the time, but it still felt weird.

"I am Sir Loin the First, King of Grazelandia!" The large, long-haired bull snorted angrily with his name, not even slightly mollified by Aetheria's attempts at friendliness. It reminded her of documentaries where prey just knew a predator lay in wait.

"Prepare thyself, cat, for you shall face the combined might of the Moo-rine Corps of Grazelandia! To hooves, brothers and sisters! For Grazelandia! Oh, you two can watch." Two pillars of lights descended from the heavens, and Aetheria and Werylin vanished into the clouds. Their senses shifted, and they reappeared as misty projections near Arkaziel.

"Sorry, Ark, looks like we're just spectators on this one," Aetheria said sweetly, but the cat and cows showed no sign of having heard her. Even Werylin's projection didn't say anything to her, the cows, or Arkaziel, which made her suspect if she wanted to be heard she'd need to talk telepathically.

~You got this, little buddy?~

+Oh please, it's just a bunch of walking hamburgers. They don't stand a chance against me. Better prepare a large space to store floof cows in your repository for me.+

"Oh, I'm prepared, believe me. Last chance for all of your people to just line up for the slaughterhouse. I hate to risk damaging your hides or those delicious flanks. I'll even show your people mercy and leave one in ten of you alive if you submit to my hunger now." Arkaziel's view of generosity and mercy angered the king, who lifted his head and bellowed in anger. Across the seemingly endless pastures other cows lifted their heads and mooed back. One after another the cows lumbered onto their hind legs and weapons appeared in the hooves of the shaggy, long-haired cows. Every cow she looked at had a slightly different weapon. Polearms, spears, halberds, one-handed swords, two-handed swords, flails, maces, axes, nunchucks; Aetheria even saw one cow with sais.

The most surreal thing, the thing that drew Aetheria's gaze again and again, had to be the way that the cows held the weapons. Somehow, their hooves just touched the weapon and like magic they stuck to the hooves of the bovines. *Okay, that's just weird. How'd they make the weapons in the first place? Someone had to have helped them, at some point, assuming it isn't magic. Objects don't just stick to a hoof without magic or something. I guess it could be some kind of innate telekinetic power?*

"Bullrush!" Sir Loin, King of Grazelandia screamed the words. The king's fighting spirit erupted from him like a volcano, and an angry red aura visibly manifested when the king charged Arkaziel. Loin moved with alacrity that seemed impossible for a bovine on two legs, and he swiped a mighty two-handed great sword for Arkaziel's tiny cat form. Arkaziel lazily jumped into the air, dodged the strike, and with a casual flick of his tail sent the cow's crown tumbling into the press of the herd. The terrible crunch of delicate metalwork crushed under hooves filled the air.

"My crown! You fiend, that crown was an heirloom!" The great sword swung with rage-enhanced alacrity, yet Arkaziel casually dodged each swing of the great sword, the arrows and bolts volleyed from long-ranged cows, and stabs from others in the herd. The cat defied physics with casual disregard. Arkaziel landed on swinging weapons to jump to the next weapon, and when caught in the air he flattened like a pancake cat then popped back to full three dimensions. He even wrapped his tail around one swinging weapon to use its momentum to pull him out of the way of attacks.

Then Arkaziel started to attack. A casual swipe of his left paw sent a dozen black spikes through the air. Each one pierced a bovine in the center of the head, and twelve cows fell over, dead. In response to this, Sir Loin emitted a sad dirge-like bellow. The king and his thousands-strong herd shimmered into invisibility as mist swept the endless pasture. Aetheria could still see the bovines through her Ethereal Sight, so she imagined Arkaziel would not be as hindered by this move as Sir Loin would have hoped.

The herd launched dozens of attacks at Arkaziel from invisibility, but he continued his ridiculous dodges, and his yellow feline eyes gleamed with the sadistic predatory joy Aetheria had witnessed in every cat she'd ever met.

"If we're using magic . . ." Arkaziel ignored the fact he'd used magic first, and with a cackle he exhaled a blast of dark mists opposite Sir Loin's position. The blast of darkness drained the life from the grass and vegetation in addition to the bovines it passed through, and left a pile of corpses behind the twenty meter cone.

"DESPOILER!" Sir Loin's shout captured the anger and despair of the cow leader, and in response to the life-devouring attack his massive horns lit with energy. Pulses of energy formed an orb that glowed and grew larger by the millisecond. With her Ethereal Sight, Aetheria could see it was a lightning aspected attack, and indeed when it stopped increasing in size, the sky rumbled. Bolts of lightning descended, each one seeking the small black cat.

"Moo!"

"Mooo!"

"DIE!"

Arkaziel dodged lightning bolts. The insane cat defied the laws of physics to not be where the attacks landed. The glow that surrounded his eclipse collar made Aetheria wonder if he had unlocked some time aspected ability from Chronos that allowed him to dodge actual lightning bolts, but the longer she watched him dance the more she realized it was just feline grace and skill, combined with a mind full of the experience and skills of his ancestors. The final lightning bolt looked to clip Arkaziel, but when the brilliance faded, no damage could be seen on the cat.

"You seared one of my whiskers!"

Aetheria squinted to see that, yes, one of the whiskers on his right side had in fact gotten slightly shorter. Not even a centimeter shorter!

"King Cud!" Sir Loin opened his mighty maw and spit a volley of saliva and grass at friend and foe alike. Nearby cows gained a green glimmering forcefield, while the single wad of cud that hit Arkaziel sizzled and burned like acid before the grassy saliva mixture disappeared into shadows.

Arkaziel inhaled, and he didn't stop. Like a vacuum he sucked down the air, and the shadows of cows were drawn into his tiny little house-cat-sized mouth. Shadow after shadow got sucked into his mouth, and only the king's shadow seemed capable of resisting.

"He stole our shadows!"

"It's the moo-pocalypse!"

"What kind of fiend milks our shadows?"

Darkness exploded outward from Arkaziel. All of the shadows he had swallowed emerged, and like a stampede the shadows flowed over the herd. Wherever they passed a cow they made use of their shadow weapons to strike single lethal hits. Even Arkaziel's shadowy attacks were prioritizing leaving the hides and flesh of the bovines intact. The tide of shadows spread outward and flowed over large swathes of the horde. Thousands of cows fell to their own shadows and shadowy weapons.

The king's great sword swung for Arkaziel while he controlled the shadows, and four solitary strands of fur drifted on the breeze in the aftermath, and a single drop of StarMane blood. A wicked look filled Arkaziel's eyes, and in their empathic bond, Aetheria could feel the surge of pure wrath rise in her bondmate.

In a blur of movement Arkaziel hopped onto Sir Loin's meaty shoulder and slashed with his tiny claws. Instead of a minor wound, the bovine king's head fell to the ground, cut cleanly off in a single swipe. Arkaziel then opened his mouth comically large and ate Sir Loin's still-standing body in one massive gulp, and then ate his head in a second smaller bite.

A half hour later the three stood in the eerily quiet pasture. No corpses remained on the life-drained soil of Grazelandia. Aetheria noticed one of the gems from the shattered crown of Sir Loin, and picked up the emerald to examine it. She was no gem cutter, but to her eye it looked to be a fine cut, and it had a relatively high magic storage capacity, so she pocketed it.

Arkaziel licked at his paws and groomed his fur.

"Are we done here? What even was this?" Werylin seemed unsettled by the cow genocide. In the far distances floof cows still wandered Grazelandia, but Arkaziel had purged tens of thousands of their brethren. Despite that, they seemed infinite in this strange floor of the tower.

"Yes. We'll make a killing on Floor Ninety. Not that anyone can take that many floofies at once. We'll have to sell them in lots over time, if I don't eat them all before then. I guess one of the Administrators wanted to get on my good side, so they gave me an all-I-could-eat buffet. I even left some alive!"

"Yes, how noble of you." Aetheria rolled her eyes at Arkaziel. With her knowledge of his emotions via the empathic bond, she knew it had been boredom not mercy that had saved the rest of the floof cows.

"Should we roast one, or twenty more, cows and have a nice feast before we go to Floor Eighty?" Arkaziel's eyes glimmered, and his mouth watered at the thought of more delicious floof cow.

"I could eat." Aetheria shrugged.

"I've lost my appetite." Werylin's distressed look and voice canceled the feast.

"Let's get moo-ving." Aetheria smiled brightly with the words, and the other two groaned.

CHAPTER 49

The Return of Rick

When the disorientation of teleportation faded, the trio found themselves in a sky-box. The room had no doors, dark wood paneling, and one wall made of glass that showed a dark, dusty, cobweb-filled dungeon with worn stone walls and floors. A cat bed lay in the corner of the room, which Arkaziel immediately claimed for a short nap, leaving Aetheria and Werylin to handle whatever challenge the floor provided.

The projection of a humanoid form with an indistinct face appeared on the window. Aetheria idly wondered if anonymity was the standard for Administrators, or if those who had shown themselves boldly and then paid the price or made it onto the party's hit list were more representative of typical Administrator behavior. Her stomach churned a little; she took these appearances to mean they were going to demand something that would make her angry or vengeful.

"Welcome to the Crypt of the Wishmaker, your eightieth-floor challenge. You will be taking on the role of Dungeon Masters, with full control of the traps, monsters, defenses, and environments of the crypt. Your objective is to prevent the adventurers from reaching the center of the crypt. Fail and you get sent back to Floor 50."

"The hell? Fifty?" Aetheria hissed at the projection of the Administrator.

"A thirty-floor penalty does seem extreme."

"Your thought on the fairness of the rewards or punishments tied to levels is immaterial. You have been given the challenge. Whether you pass or fail is up to you."

"Wait, do we have to kill the adventurers, or can we just disable them?"

"Repel or kill them, they must be taken off the board. Good luck."

The image of the indistinct face vanished, replaced with the map of the Crypt of the Wishmaker. A timer ticked down in the bottom right of the glass wall—no, it was a screen, not a wall! They had ten minutes until the challenge started.

"How do we control things?" Werylin did not have the experience Aetheria had with an entire genre of video games like this. That experience did not prepare her for the sensations that accompanied her touching the screen. Suddenly she could feel the entire crypt like a second body, and dozens of options appeared in augmented reality style menus.

"Touch the screen. Our control options are organized by categories. Traps, environmental, monsters, direct magic, and . . . well, you can read."

While Aetheria spoke she generated trip wires, flame traps, surprise guillotines, and floor drops.

"Is there not a resource system at play here? Seems kind of unbalanced."

"It's drawing the power from us," Werylin said. "When I placed those four goblins it pulled mana from me."

"Oh." When Aetheria placed her next trap she felt the slight pull of power from her personal stores. The amount barely registered to her, and replenished immediately from her direct connection to the Origin. *No wonder they're sending us back to Floor 50 if we fail. I'm a living cheat.*

The doors to the Crypt of the Wishmaker unsealed, and light spilled into the dark stone corridors. Four adventurers stared into the ominous death trap before them. The first held a torch in one hand and a dagger in the other. He was handsome but vaguely familiar. Above his head a name appeared, and Aetheria laughed.

"It's Rick! Rick the Trapmaster! Oh man, they want me to kill poor Rick? Maybe I can just repel him."

"You know this man, this Rick?"

"He was on one of our earlier floors. We had to resurrect him after he got killed by a mummy."

"Aetheria traded our treasure for his life." Half asleep, Arkaziel joined the conversation. The cat remained bitter over the loss of loot, but not so bitter he didn't immediately resume snoring.

Alongside Rick stood an elf, a half elf, and a snake woman. The elf had the name Arilyn the Atrocious above her head. Aetheria assumed the woman to be some kind of magic user based on the light armor and plethora of occult paraphernalia strapped everywhere upon her. The half elf's name showed as Torran the Torrid. Torran's bulky robes and gender-neutral hairstyle and appearance left Aetheria completely uncertain if they were male or female, whereas the gender of the snake woman seemed quite obvious. Her name was Wendra, and the lamia's clothes left very little to the imagination. *A sexy snake lady? What the heck, snakes aren't supposed to be sexy!*

"Do lamia have any special powers?" Aetheria wondered aloud.

"Not that I know of." Werylin seemed more interested in the elves. "Let's repel Torran if we can. I suspect they are from my clan."

"Roger dodger." Aetheria gave Werylin the thumbs-up, then focused on the adventurers.

"Alright ladies, we made it through the Maze of Modo, the Tunnel of Terror, and the Den of Depravity. I'm still not okay with the way you used me in the Den of Depravity, but here we are! The Crypt of the Wishmaker. The cure for your affliction lies at the heart of this death trap, Wendra. Excited?"

"Of course, I'm excited, you nincompoop. If we don't die horrifically, I'll be a human again!" The lamia rolled her eyes at the grand declarations of Rick.

"If we succeed, maybe you should quit having intercourse with gods?" Arilyn the Atrocious had an acerbic tone, and Wendra looked as if she'd been punched.

"Enough, Arilyn. You know full well Wendra was seduced, not the other way around. Blaming the victim is boorish at best, and despicable at worst. Don't let your appellation apply to your personality as well as your magic." Torran's voice followed their appearance, androgynous and enticing.

"Shh. We're being watched." Rick lifted a finger to his lips.

"I sense nothing." Arilyn disagreed with Rick, her eyes alight with a sickly green energy as she scanned the crypt entrance.

"The hairs standing on the back of my neck don't lie." Rick shrugged and began the descent down the stone stairs that lead into the crypt itself. After a moment's silence the other three followed Rick down the stairs. The first chamber of the tomb consisted of a massive statue. The face and overall appearance of the god had been worn; all that could be discerned was the iconography of death.

"I rather like the sound of phase spiders," Werylin said to Aetheria moments before four blue-white arachnids walked through one of the stone walls. Only the first of the spiders emerged at ground level, drawing the attention of the four.

"It's not alone!" Rick shouted and waved his torch at the spider, while Wendra moved up to support him. The lamia wielded a massive two-handed great sword that appeared to be made of moonlight. The weapon actually hit the transparent spider, which shocked the arachnid. While it reeled in shock from the first blow, a blast of toxic green energy struck the spider, hurled by Arilyn. The green energy seemed to act like a mixture of poison and acid, and the spider chittered in pain.

"Molasses Field!" Torran shouted while they gestured with their right hand. A barely transparent dome formed around the group, and the three phase spiders who descended from above were unable to phase through the sticky barrier. The strange spell completely delayed the three from attacking while their kin faced the adventurers one versus four.

"Moonlight Slash!" Wendra called while lunging forward, and her deceptively thin arms delivered an incredible slash with her energy-sword. Two of the spider's legs were severed with the blow, and she managed to leave a gash in its abdomen.

"I hate spiders so much!" Rick whined but still moved in behind Wendra. "Baptism by Fire!" Rather than attempt to use his dagger, Rick struck the phase spider repeatedly with the torch in a strangely elaborate series of movements that created an afterimage of fire in the air that formed a rune. The rune then exploded into sticky fire that coated the phase spider like napalm.

"Watch it, you fool! That almost got my tail!" Wendra shouted at Rick.

"I kind of feel bad opposing these kids." Aetheria sighed.

"I'm not going back to Floor Fifty," Arkaziel snarled.

"Agreed, that's not an option. Perhaps we can scare them off instead of just killing them all, though? They are kind of adorable. Like a new . . . kitten." Werylin smiled. He had almost doomed them all and said "puppy."

"What kind of path is that elf on?" Aetheria asked the other two.

"Looks like a pact-based path? Not a very popular way to do things. Spend long enough using others' powers, and you can make them your own, if your pacts don't get you killed before that happens, or if someone kills your patrons before you've internalized their power."

"Sounds like what we called a warlock on Earth?"

"Oh, the molasses field failed."

Three of the phase spiders dropped onto the adventuring party—their brother who had engaged first had become a charred husk from the still-burning sticky fire.

"Have all three target the lamia? If we remove their reason for their quest, perhaps they'll retreat?" Werylin offered his advice and initiated the commands to the monsters.

Aetheria flipped through the menus and selected a Nullification Field. An orb of darkness fell from the ceiling of the crypt, shattered amid the spiders and adventurers, and the air churned visibly with arcane power that sealed any lesser powers.

Torran nearly lost a leg to one of the phasing spiders, but just before the monster bit their leg off, it turned and jumped at Wendra's back. The half elf whispered a prayer, before they clambered to their feet and drew a staff.

"Magic null field! I can't cast!" Torran hissed in frustration and swung their staff at the spider that attacked Wendra from the back.

"Just run outside of its range, idiot." Arilyn had no patience for the dramatics of the half elf, and had jogged outside the churning air.

"What good would that do? You still can't cast magic INTO the area."

Arilyn pulled out a large crossbow.

"Damn, the nullification field blocks the special abilities of the phase spiders too." Werylin hissed in annoyance while he tried a series of different commands on the spiders. Wendra's surprising strength, mixed with deft dagger work by Rick, turned the tide against the spiders quite quickly, especially once crossbow bolts started to fly. The spiders were ambush creatures, not frontline fighters, after all.

"Let them wipe the spiders. We'll let them feel emboldened by this encounter and really ramp up the next one. How's your energy holding up, Werylin? Can you employ Aether instead of mana for this?"

The elf paled a little.

"It still hurts, a lot, when I use pure Aether."

"Stick with mana, then. I'll spawn the monsters, you run the traps I've already generated. It takes almost no energy to use the traps and environmental effects once they've been spawned, unlike the monsters."

"If you don't kill at least one of them this time, I'm joining the game." Arkaziel yawned with the threat, before his tail beat ominously against the cat bed he lay in.

Werylin took the proclamation from Arkaziel much more seriously than Aetheria did. The elf paled and looked nervously at the screen and the four adventurers, as if

Arkaziel were threatening to go down there and eat each one, bite by bite, in front of the minstrel. The previous floor had clearly traumatized Werylin.

"What's an Urmahlullu?" Aetheria asked in confusion.

"Spawn one and find out?" Werylin suggested the common sense approach.

"Spawn ten and find out!" Arkaziel demanded impatiently.

CHAPTER 50

Dungeon Mistress Aetheria

The party of adventurers regrouped after the incident with phasing spiders. After a few minutes of chants, meditation, and bandages they were in fighting condition once more. Meanwhile, the trio in the control room waited impatiently for the adventurers to choose which of the three branches they would be controlling first. Fortunately, they didn't have to wait long before Wendra interrupted the short rest and told her party she sensed the right passage to be the correct path.

"How did she know?" Werylin rubbed at his chin ponderously.

"Forked tongue. Lamias have an enhanced sense of taste and smell. She tasted it on the air currents." Arkaziel, as ever, delighted in knowing things his companions did not.

The right passageway ran for almost one hundred meters as the bird flies before it reached a large open room. The party, however, had to trek through the actual passage which curved into a sinuous, snakelike set of curves that constantly limited their forward vision. Rick had out his ten-foot pole, which he used to tap and release trap after trap. He managed to get the party through two-thirds of the tunnel before Wendra triggered an inevitable *click*.

"That's a little dirty," Werylin muttered of Aetheria's impromptu trap.

"Oh, come on, not all pressure plates need to activate from a normal weight. Surely, somewhere, someone set up traps only triggered by multiple people or full armored enemies?" Aetheria defended her decision.

In the tunnel, gas hissed from a number of vents.

"Poison!" Torran, the androgynous half elf, warned the group while their hands glowed with mystical light. The vents on the left side of the room slowly sealed themselves shut, and the stone of the passageway changed to a smooth veneer that blocked the release of any gas.

Arilyn the Atrocious reached into her pack and flung a few vials at the vents on the right side of the passageway. When the glass vials shattered, a thick gray ooze covered the vents, and it hardened into a solid barrier in seconds.

"Watch where you walk, fatty." Arilyn hissed at Wendra.

"How many types of muck do you carry, Ari? Secrete it yourself?" Wendra retorted with a smile.

"That was my fault, I didn't think there would be any pressure plates set to trip at variable weights. Someone really didn't want people to come down this passageway; I haven't seen this many traps since I got resurrected."

Torran, Arilyn, and Wendra all groaned when Rick mentioned his deathly experience. Based on their reactions Aetheria assumed he talked about his trip with herself and Arkaziel too frequently. Vanity made her curious about what he said, and she noticed Arkaziel's tail twitched in interest, too.

While the party slogged through the traps, Aetheria decorated the next chamber they would enter. The party paused before the final series of traps and the ominous archway ahead of them.

"Cats," Wendra hissed.

"Foul magic," Torran warned.

"I'm hungry." Arilyn snorted at the drama of the other two.

"Annnd, I've done it. Undisarmable trap disarmed! I'm the best." Rick hadn't heard anything the other three said at all, and walked into the heart-shaped chamber with a proud smirk on his face. The other three looked at one another, and each sighed before they hurried into the chamber after Rick.

A thick wrought iron grate closed behind them, literally from nowhere.

"What the hell, Werylin? We're trying to make them retreat?"

"Sorry, I got turned around. That was supposed to go on the opposite doors."

Werylin left their exit sealed, then sealed the portals deeper into the dungeon with similar iron grates.

At the center of the heart-shaped room a series of forms slept. The clamor of the iron grates and fresh prey roused them from their slumber. Ten sets of feline eyes focused on the party, while the party all blanched. All except Arilyn the Atrocious.

"Stupid cats."

She hurled a vial of green plants that exploded in a smelly cloud that the lion-centaurs all immediately turned to with great interest. Arilyn did not stop. She threw more vials, while Torran chanted and created a dome of clear, fresh air around their own party.

Urmahlullu were men and women with the lower body of cats, the upper bodies of humans, and faces that ranged from feline to human. They were definitely imposing, and Aetheria had looked forward to seeing them fight. Instead, she watched as their skin melted and they literally decomposed before her eyes.

"I can't believe that witch weaponized catnip. She dies. The other three can live." Arkaziel delivered his judgment from his throne, which happened to be shaped like a bed, as all the best thrones were.

"That's hard to watch." Werylin grimaced.

"Inventive, though." Aetheria couldn't keep the disappointment from her voice.

"You two suck. Out of the way." Arkaziel roused from his throne, and while he walked to the console his form rippled into that of a tall, black-skinned human, although he retained his yellow feline eyes. The StarMane retained the glorious glittery suit he had previously worn in his human form.

"I don't feel good about that," Rick told Arilyn down in the dungeon.

"Enemies die; that's life. Unless you want to die again? I don't see any goddess around to save you this time." The elf's casual disregard for life seemed exceptionally unelven to Aetheria, but she'd met enough people to know that assholes existed of all races. The woman had the appellation of Atrocious for a reason.

"The monsters are dead; the gas is inert. Let's go." Arilyn dismissed Rick's complaints and walked boldly past the fresh air barrier into the rest of the room. She made it five steps before she exploded in a shower of gore that went everywhere.

"Cowardice begets cowardice." The voice of a brand-new undead enemy tortured the ears of the survivors with a tone similar to crumbling stone. One of the Urmahlullu rose from the ground, billowing powerful mists of condensed Nether. Though it had been reduced to a skeleton, it was a skeleton covered in glowing arcane runes and blue glowing flames for eyes.

"Did you just lich-ify the corpse?" Aetheria stared at Arkaziel incredulously.

"Duh. Liches are great enemies for dumb adventurers."

"For Arilyn!" Wendra surged across the room in one great charge, propelled by the mighty lower half of the lamia. She slammed into the lich like a freight train, and brought down a white-metal mace repeatedly onto the arcane enchanted bones. Everywhere the mace struck, bones smoked, the sanctified metal a natural enemy of the undead.

"Back her up, Rick," Torran instructed the trapmaster while they chanted. A magic circle formed on the ceiling above Wendra and the lich. It slowly rotated, and symbols formed with each new syllable from Torran.

Rick didn't need to be told twice. He pulled a series of objects from his pack while he ran to the fight. In the precious seconds it took Rick to join Wendra, she gained a number of deep wounds from the attacks of the lich's skeletal hands, and one finger bone had been wedged between scales and pushed farther into her flesh by the second.

The trapmaster started the fight with a vial of liquid thrown into the face of the lich. Holy water steamed and bubbled when it made contact with the lich, burning its bones. A second vial hit the lich in the torso, and then a box tumbled underneath the lich. Two small doors on the top of the box opened, and glorious radiant light spilled out in a continuous burst. The whole room grew in lux, and the sizzle of unholy bones in the presence of holy power continued to ramp up.

"Haha, behold the power of a disciple of Aetheria!" Rick proclaimed to the lich. Rick's arrogant declaration saw him hurled across the room by a blast of eldritch power from the lich, and the man's body smoked while he fished a healing potion out of his pack.

"Ow," Rick cried.

"Your disciple sucks," Arkaziel told Aetheria deadpan, but she noticed the lich didn't go after Rick while he was injured.

"In the name of Shamash, Glory to the Sun, All Darkness must be Expunged!" Torran delivered each word like a dagger strike, and the magic circle exploded in divine radiance that blasted the arcane bones of the Urmahlullu lich to dust.

"Too bad, Arkaziel. Good try," Werylin said sympathetically to the StarMane.

"Oh, it's done, but you should keep watching." Arkaziel smirked, showing off teeth that were normal to humans, and thus not that threatening at all.

Where the lich had fallen, three objects lay.

"Torran! Look!" Wendra rushed forward and lifted a pearl the size of her hand into the air. The colorful shimmer of the orb increased the longer Wendra held it, and pulses of pearlescent radiant energy shot up and down her body, until Wendra turned into a second sun that no one could look directly at. A *pop* sound, the sound of objects hitting the floor, and the light dimmed until it reached normal. A human Wendra stood there, holding a smaller white pearl in her hands, and naked from the hips down. The floor around was littered with her former scales.

"Congratulations, Wendra!" Torran said, while they walked over to help stabilize her. The former lamia had the steadiness of a newborn deer.

Rick averted his eyes initially, but when no one covered Wendra up he pulled a pair of trousers from his pack and brought them over. Wendra's face turned a deep crimson, and she struggled to get the men's trousers on over much wider hips, but she managed.

"Aww, good job, Ark; you're such a softie." Aetheria complimented her companion, who waggled his finger at her.

"Keep watching," Arkaziel commanded.

"Oh hey, look at this!" Rick pulled the second object from the debris of the lich's demise. In his hands lay a golden egg, its weight enough to make the man struggle to hold it. "Isn't this what you were after, Torran?"

The androgynous half elf smiled and took it from Rick in one hand; to them it appeared to weigh almost nothing.

"Indeed, this is the Solis Sphaira. Blessed by Shamash." Delicate fingers caressed the golden egg before Torran brushed their fingers in an arcane rune that glowed, and the egg vanished.

"It appears there's something for you, too, Rick." Torran gestured to a weapon which glowed on the ground.

"Holy crap, how'd I miss that?" Rick lifted high a short sword. Its blade seemed to be carved of jagged ice, while the hilt looked like a gemstone. What should be an extremely fragile weapon radiated a sense of strength. Strength and cold.

"Check it out! My goddess has rewarded me! Well, we more than got what we came for. Let's get out of here. The Wishmaker can keep his wishes." Rick looked to the other two.

"Damn right," Wendra agreed.

"One moment, let me perform the last rites for Arilyn, then we shall go."

The screens turned to black, and Arkaziel smirked at the other two.

"You see what you did wrong now, yes?" Aetheria hated the pseudowise teacher tone Arkaziel used.

"Yes, you're brilliant, wise, and glorious, oh great StarMane. You played the semantics game like a djinn, and took the adventurers goals out of the core of the dungeon and gave it to them in a different chamber, because the only stipulation we were given was that they couldn't reach the core. *How brilliant.*" Aetheria rolled her eyes to accompany her sarcasm.

"I am brilliant, yes, thank you."

"Good job, Arkaziel." Unlike Aetheria, Werylin's praise was completely sincere. Of course, it came from a place of desperate thanks that the StarMane hadn't killed everyone, eaten them, or otherwise committed atrocities for the sake of expediency. "I'm very impressed at your cleverness and solutions."

Arkaziel smirked.

"*Not bad,*" the Administrator's projection grudgingly acknowledged, before the door to the next floor opened.

CHAPTER 51

The Sea of Chaos

Waves crashing against the rocky, rough shore were the first sound to pull the trio into the reality of Floor 81. They found themselves on a beach of white and gray sand, with a beautiful view of a yellow ocean that frothed with the power of creation and destruction. Aetheria recognized the location from her visions.

"The Shores of Chaos." Aetheria gasped in a mixture of excitement and confusion.

"Sweet. I wonder if I could drink the whole ocean." Arkaziel licked his lips in anticipation, and his tail flicked back and forth in excitement.

"You realize that's almost pure chaos, right? Even you can't drink an ocean of chaos," Werylin warned the cat, incredulous that anyone would ever try to drink the primordial muck that looked and acted like water.

"Says who? You? I can totally eat chaos. I ate her snake last time we met and only got a minor case of heartburn, right, Aetheria?" Arkaziel did not take Werylin's concern well.

"It's true. He ate the snake, but maybe don't start drinking massive quantities of creation-muck until you've tested its potency first, right? Werylin just didn't want you to get a tummy ache." Aetheria patted her shoulder, and Arkaziel morphed into his cat form and hopped up. Together the two started to stroll along the rocky cliffs around this portion of the beach.

"There's nothing here. What is our trial?" Werylin looked frazzled. No doubt the discordant nature of the Shores of Chaos proved challenging for a follower of harmony to adapt to.

"There is nothing here. No homes, no settlements, no people, no monsters, nothing. Self-improvement trial?" Aetheria grimaced, and Arkaziel hissed at the sky.

"I hope not. Those are the worst. I'm already perfect. This is a good cultivation location, though. Maybe it's a trial for Werylin; I don't think there's anything challenging here for me or you?" Arkaziel looked up and down the beach hopefully.

"Well, if they aren't going to tell us the goal, I'll set up base camp." From Aetheria's repository came the flying castle once called the Mellow Mallow. The elven skykeep had undergone significant improvement work while within her repository, and even the damage it had sustained on her previous summons had been taken care of.

"Uh-oh." Arkaziel sighed when the castle appeared.

"What?" Werylin ran his hands along the beautiful exterior walls of the keep.

"If she's pulling out castles instead of tents we're going to be here a while. Did you get the friers we bought in Naut working?" Arkaziel's interest went up a few levels at the prospect of a powered magical kitchen.

"I did. Oven, friers, and even the microwave. I'll stock the ice chest and pantry from my repository, too."

Day 2

Did the beach stretch on for infinity? Aetheria couldn't answer that definitively, but her scouting sure seemed to point in that direction. For hours she'd flown along the beach, and not once did she ever encounter any signs of an end or even a break in the Shores of Chaos. Of course, this wasn't the real place, since they were inside of a tower, but the copy seemed to go on for vast distances. She turned back after approximately twelve hours of flying. She had accomplished nothing tangible, only seen many permutations of beach.

Day 3

Aetheria sat atop a large black rock that rose over three meters into the air above the sandy beach. Arkaziel, in a diminutive dragon form, splashed and swam in the Sea of Chaos. The StarMane displayed no ill effects from his activities, and occasionally he would take large gulps of the muck of creation. Even that didn't seem to affect Arkaziel at all, beyond a burst of energy and then an increase in his irritability. The increased irritability seemed to be a trait they all felt, though. None of the three had found a single hint as to their purpose on the shores.

There were many dangers to swimming in the Sea of Chaos. The largest, of course, lay in the composition of the so-called sea. While the highly concentrated muck of creation appeared and acted like water, it was undiminished chaos. A normal being would immediately be subject to transformation the moment the sea touched them, but Arkaziel remained rigidly himself. Between an unshakable narcissistic obsession with himself, the mind of a shapeshifter that constantly dealt with change, and the fluid natures of his affinity with light and darkness, he ignored the properties of the sea. That did not diminish the danger of other objects which constantly bobbed to the surface of the sea, but the dragon just swatted them away with a paw or his tail when they materialized too close to him.

Werylin had entered a Cultivator's meditation. The elf had picked one of the ramparts of the Mellow Mallow, and simultaneously retreated within himself while he tried to find harmony with the literally chaotic surroundings. Aetheria didn't fully understand what Werylin hoped to achieve through a more traditional cultivation approach, but she wasn't a traditional Cultivator.

~ How close will feasting on the chaos put you to the next tier? ~

+Depends how long we stay here. It'd be boring and time consuming, but I could get really close to the fifth tier just by being here long enough. But to cross the threshold into five, I'd need more than just power. Unless some powerful enemies wash up, it'll be difficult for me here. Digestive gains are the easiest for my people; we're terrible at actual cultivation. Chronos didn't make us to be pacifists. We're predators who grow from strong prey.+

~ Why do the hard work when you can just pillage from others?~

+Exactly! How close are you to the fifth tier?+

~ The core is done unless I need to make alterations. I finished the fiftieth layer of the mantle this morning. I'm currently planning to do one hundred and eleven layers to the mantle, so almost halfway overall.~

+Why one hundred and eleven?+

~Because it sounds cool? There's a few other connotations from my world about luck, but mostly it boils down to I think it's cool.~

+Well, Dad said self-confidence is the basis of power.+

~That's surprising, although I think I follow the idea. If you don't believe you can wield a power, you probably won't succeed. I don't think it is that simple for most people.~

+Of course, it isn't as easy for most. StarManes are perfection, crafted by the amazing Chronos. You're even more disgusting than we are, thanks to Chronos collaborating with Khaos, Ymir, Aetherius, Nyx, and who knows who else.+

~Yeah, it is pretty ridiculous.~ It was almost like StarManes were a prototype for Aetheria's own design, when she thought about it. She could do pretty much everything Arkaziel could. *And normal cultivation methods are way slower than how I advance. Although my connection to the Origin drives some of my growth, and that was my own doing, but the ability to survive it was their doing. Hmm.*

Aetheria fell into silence while Arkaziel frolicked. This was not the first time she wondered at the depths of collaboration and conspiracy behind her rebirth. *What makes me so special? Are there others like me? Aoibhe's age lines up close to my own progress through the tiers, and she was on the lists alongside gods, too. Is she also a project of theirs?*

~How do the monotheistic gods work, Ark?~

+You mean with other gods? The same as they all do. They squabble and argue about who created everything, and try to eliminate their opponents, but never do. They all claim if you eliminate the followers of another god you could kill them, but that's bullshit. Niyal'Arak'Azul teamed up with four ancient space dragons to destroy the planets with all the worshippers of Ahriman, and it didn't weaken the bastard at all, but he sure killed Niyal, and legend goes, fashioned the fused flesh of Niyal and the four dragons into a moon called Ahriman's Throne, that he threw into orbit over a planet called Dis.+

~ Who was Niyal?~

+One of the children of Nyx and Erebus who never sought godhood.+

~Was this before the creation of StarManes?~

+Obviously, or I'd know if it were fact or fiction.+

~Isn't it strange that most of the gods just want to destroy each other?~

+Not really? Everyone wants to be top dog. There's only so many resources.+

Aetheria frowned because she didn't know what resource mattered. Energy, for anyone connected to the Origin, had no finite limits. Obviously, only the most powerful of gods and Primordials were connected to the Origin, but for those who were, why would they feel any need to work against one another? Even Aether and Nether seemed to be nearly without limits, and almost all gods had access to at least one of those. Did they compete over prayers? It didn't seem to matter, if what Arkaziel said about Niyal'Arak'Azul were true.

"I hate when I'm missing pieces of the puzzle," Aetheria groused.

Day 7

Arkaziel swam in the Sea of Chaos once more. Werylin remained in meditation.

Aetheria sat on her rock, her right hand slightly raised to the sky. The pale Flame of Thalassa and the multihued Flame of Khaos burned around her, while she tried to control the sky above the Sea of Chaos. Similar to the primordial muck of the sea, the sky above it consisted almost entirely of chaos and Aether that would kill normal mortals and most Cultivators. The day before she had spent sensing and touching the floor of the sea, which had been earth aspected Nether.

Aetheria had no idea why you would bracket Ethereal chaos with its diffused elements and chaos. Were those pockets then bracketed by order infused aspects? She hadn't found any evidence of that, but the whole setup made her very curious.

+Is it safe for me to be swimming when you're making lightning?+

~Do I need to remind you that you aren't actually swimming in water, but primordial muck that looks like water? Of course, it isn't safe!~

Arkaziel ignored her and kept swimming, even as the sky above the Sea of Chaos turned into a rapidly spreading storm.

~Seriously, get out of there. I'm not doing that!~ Aetheria's panic actually roused Arkaziel to fly back to shore, and the two stood on the beach and stared at the sudden storm. More and more lightning spread through the skies. A strange humming filled the air. It almost made Aetheria think about a jet, or . . . rocket engines.

The identification of the sound in her mind coincided with the clouds being broken apart by a massive vessel on a crash course with the shore. The ship had a pristine white enamel that had burned off a third of the exterior, and the propulsion engines on the sides emitted a high-pitched, headache-inducing whine. The pain that wracked her mind felt like someone had taken the idea of a migraine, doubled it, then tripled that, then weaponized it into a delivery system that felt like spikes driven into your skull through your ears.

Arkaziel showed no sign of such pain, and Werylin remained in seclusion.

Aetheria pushed the pain down and pushed her core to a higher operating mode before she braced her feet and prepared to catch the crashing ship.

"Uhh, Aetheria, physics doesn't work that way, you know," Arkaziel informed her helpfully, but she noticed he hadn't run off from standing next to her. "You can't just catch a spaceship."

"Can't I?" Aetheria offered him a smile, her hair sparkled, and the Transcendent Flames of Khaos engulfed her.

CHAPTER 52

Don't Tell Me What I Can't Do

The vessel that broke the cloud cover above the beach descended like a meteor; its white enameled exterior burned off by the second, its engines emitted a brain-splitting whine that grew louder and more powerful as they failed to propel the vessel in any direction but on a crash course with the beach.

Small echoes of doubt bounced around in Aetheria's mind. Whispers of her old self that agreed with Arkaziel. One tiny human woman couldn't just catch a spaceship, no matter how powerful they were. Shouldn't she at least increase her mass and size? The power of a fourth-tier Flame, even the Transcendent Flame of Khaos, wouldn't be powerful enough to do what she intended. *That's a good point.*

The rainbow-hued flames around her gutted, only to be replaced by her own aura. Ethereal power burst out of her almost as if she had activated an Ethereal Nova. A brilliant red and aqua power condensed around her body, stronger and thicker than the previous manifestation of another being's power. The Ethereal was hers, Aetheria felt, while Khaos's power felt like it belonged to Khaos and not to herself.

"I don't need borrowed power for this," Aetheria said to a confused Arkaziel and also to reassure herself.

Then it happened. The vessel slammed into the beach. Multihued sand filled the air, and the whine of the engines cut off abruptly. Then a second impact happened, with the vessel crashing inland. A pulse of Aetheria's aura dropped all the sand from the air to the ground. Hoarfrost formed on much of it. The aqua-haired woman strolled casually toward the large vessel she'd tossed, a black cat sitting on her shoulder.

"Sorry I doubted you, partner." Arkaziel apologized to Aetheria without mincing words. It actually stopped her in her tracks for a moment.

Aboard the bridge of the vessel, the *Rift Rider*, only eight members of the crew had survived crossing the anomaly. The captain, the perfect model of a man, lay amongst the pile of dead scientists who crewed the *Rift Rider*. Brain aneurisms had killed two-thirds of the crew upon the first stage of the crossing. When the spectacular vortex of energy had suddenly gone from constant flux to a series of lights that the advanced systems aboard the *Rift Rider* identified as encrypted Nylean communications. Appropriate, since they were a Nylean Technocracy science vessel.

"Turn back? TURN BACK!? We can't turn back, you stupid son of a . . ." the vice-captain shouted at the surrounding consoles before turbulence struck. The anomaly pulled the *Rift Rider* through dimensions. The viewscreens showed things that could not be. While Ranar, the vice-captain, stared in horror at the viewscreen, an ancient yellow eye looked at him. He closed his eyes, but that yellow eye stared at him even in his own mind. Why would a yellow eye have a toxic green pupil? Why would acid be melting the eye from the inside out? What did any of that have to do with the scent of his own flesh burning?

"Ranar! Something is holding the ship from passing farther through the dimensional corridor. What do we do? RANAR!" Basuu slapped Ranar across the face, then did so again, until Ranar opened all three of his eyes to regard his subordinate. Some part of him said he should slap her back, but the steady, collected three-eyed stare of Basuu had always had a calming effect amongst all Nyleans who met her.

That yellow eye still stared at him in his imagination, though, and he could feel the corrosive acid pump through his body. Every pump of his heart pushed more acid through his circulatory system.

"Engage the secondary subspace engines, bring the ship about one hundred and eighty degrees, and deploy probes." Ranar had to know. What was this eye? Could the eye make the acid in his veins stop? Would it end the fire in his synapses?

"That's idiocy, Ranar! Look at the subspace scanners. There's something larger than the whole of Nylin out there, and it's some kind of organic mass with energy readings we can't make any sense of. If we don't get into the dimensional corridor again, we're dead!"

"I gave an order, Technician Basuu, and I expect it to b—"

Ranar's head exploded in a fountain of gore, while the chief security officer holstered his sidearm. His blood had turned green, and everything it landed on sizzled and succumbed to the corrosive power of an Outsider.

"They compromised him. Do as Technician Basuu said and get us into the corridor, now!" The security officer returned to the gruesome task of stacking the dead like cordwood outside the bridge.

Rin, a younger officer who had gained their position via nepotism, stood and barked orders. She was, technically, in command, given her status as the second officer. In normal conditions, she would ride the mission through to the end, and collect accolades for having done nothing. Yet things had gone drastically wrong, and rather than listen to the security officer, she gave her own orders.

"Belay that, open communications on channel alpha." Not that Rin waited. Her hands danced over the console before her with a familiarity she had never previously shown. A yellow eye appeared on the viewscreen. The corpses in the room all writhed. One comm officer fell to the floor shrieking and ripped two of his three eyes out. Even with the security officer, again, shooting Rin in the back of the head and ending her life, the yellow eye on the screen engulfed the minds of the command deck.

"Communications closed!" Basuu hissed in victory. The yellow baleful eye vanished from the viewscreen. "What in Holy Nym's blessed bust was that?"

Jaku, the navigator and current boyfriend of the beautiful Basuu, set his hand on her shoulder to turn her to face him. A smile crossed his face. His eyes shone with love and dedication to her, greater than ever before. His lips slowly opened, and he whispered a single request to her. "Die for me."

Jaku's other hand stabbed at her midsection, but his head exploded in a shower of gore. The already started stab lost all momentum when it failed to pierce her advanced Nylean bodysuit. Of all people, her boyfriend should have known how strong the defenses of the exploration services bodysuits were. *So why didn't he know that'd happen?* Basuu thought idly, while she pulled his viscera from her hair.

"Thanks, Dol. Again." Basuu went straight for the navigator's console, to do what needed to be done, while the security officer eyed the only other person still alive on the command deck, the communications officer, Alu, who rocked under her terminal crying. Dol assessed this to be an appropriate response to the situation and turned a worried eye to the corpses that writhed unnaturally.

"Yeah, we got problems, Basuu. Get us the hell out of here."

"You got it!" The engines all emitted mind-shattering sounds, and turbulence wracked the *Rift Rider*.

"Is it supposed to do that?" Dol grunted. Blood seeped from one of his ears.

"Honestly? I don't think so, but we're back in the corridor!"

"He's still with us. He's everywhere. Everywhen. There isn't any escape! Once claimed, a soul can never escape them! Never!" Alu whimpered.

Red engulfed the world. Infused the ship, the crew. The hull ignited as if they were in the middle of atmospheric reentry.

"We hit the end of the corridor!? HOW? It's supposed to be infinite! Physical reality is incoming, people, brace for the unknown! Alu, get the fore views on screen!" Beautiful Basuu screamed at the disarrayed Alu, while Dol buckled himself into what orientation had called an oh-shit harness.

The viewscreen lit up with a visual of what lay before the ship. They were on a collision course with a beach, where a blue-and-red-haired human stood with a tiny black creature. Far to the starboard a low-technology castle stood as sentinel on the beach. At least they weren't on a collision course with that!

"By the Holy Hanging Tits of Tymol! All our sensors fried from trying to measure the energy on that beach!" Alu cursed before she followed Dol's example to buckle in.

"What is that stupid human doing? How?" Basuu cried out as an unidentified energy swept from the blue-and-red-haired human, and condensed and clung to her form like fire. The image froze in the mind of all the Nylean, or at least of those still alive on the command deck.

A strange human female, one of the weakest races the Nyleans had ever encountered, braced to intercept the *Rift Rider*. The *Rift Rider* had a displacement of 112,000 tons, and had a length of 420 meters from fore to aft, although only the front seventy meters were accessible by the crew, with the rest of the vessel dedicated to the dimensional engines, fusion reactors, dimensional anchors, and a host of other technology related to dimensional travel and physical propulsion. Despite all of that, the woman lifted her right arm. Her hand had a strange ring, a weird transparent metal mesh covering her hand, and a bracelet securing the mesh to her wrist. Her skin looked normal for a human, if pale, but when her hand simply touched the ship and it stopped, that wasn't normal.

There was no deceleration, no momentum. The *Rift Rider* just stopped.

The woman smirked. The screen showed her face in detail now. Her hair billowed behind her in the breeze, a crazy mix of red and aqua-blue hair that Basuu had never seen amongst humans before. Like all humans, she had only two eyes, but one was blue, and one was red, and both glowed with an eerie light. Even through the viewscreen, Basuu felt herself question why they ended up here, before this terrible human with eyes that made her feel so alone, so empty, so devoid of meaning. Why should existence even be?

And then, as if it bored the human to hold the ship any longer, she casually tossed it away from herself, the beach, and her small mammal companion. A second later, the ship shook with impact against solid ground.

"She's coming this way!" Dol cried at the other two.

"What do we do?" Alu stared in horror.

"You and I greet her, Alu. Dol, there are survivors in engineering. Go check on them and then rendezvous with us, or vice versa. Hopefully, this strange godlike creature is not hostile and can provide aid for our injured crewmembers."

"By Gary's Gigantic Gorgoog, I hope the system is wrong. It says there's only four survivors in engineering, out of forty-seven." Dol groaned and moved out, his sidearm loaded and an emergency medical kit on his back.

"Can't we go with him? Why do we have to deal with a creature who can throw the *Rift Rider* like a toy? I have a bad feeling about this, Basuu."

"You have a bad feeling about everything, Alu. Look on the bright side. If she kills us, it will undoubtedly be over before we realize it?"

"You're terrible at finding bright sides."

CHAPTER 53

They Came from the Stars

Basuu and Alu stepped out of the main exterior bridge exit, and the iris-shaped door stayed open behind them. Sparks inexplicably flew from the control panel, the delicate electronics fried. Before them spanned an alien landscape that belonged to no planet. An infinite sky and sea of a manifest energy the systems on the *Rift Rider* couldn't identify lapped against a multihued rough shore. Objects materialized and dematerialized in the ocean before them, and no birds flew in that strange sky. The limited operational sensors of the *Rift Rider* detected only three life forms on the whole of the beach, and two of them casually walked across the polychromatic sand on an eerily direct course for the two freshly emerged Nylean science crew.

"Do you think they'll speak Nylean? Do any of our first-contact protocols cover gods?" Basuu asked Alu.

"We have some protocols for elevated beings. I can speak fourteen languages, and my ship suit has a translator relay, if the ship systems keep working. I don't understand why all of our tech is failing." Alu coughed, then blinked when the two figures shimmered in a burst of colors, and then appeared five cubits before them in another flash of colors. Alu and Basuu both rubbed their eyes, as if they had seen a mirage. Even the Nylean Technocracy lacked teleportation technology, despite their ability to pierce dimensions and traverse galaxies.

"Hello!" Alu tried in Nylean, and when that got no reaction from their visitors she repeated herself in language after language. The human said a few words, but neither understood one another. The goddess before them let out a sigh and uttered words that made Basuu feel like a gong had been struck deep within her body. Strange words resonated with physical reality in a way Basuu had never witnessed before, and for just a moment, she thought she saw energy flows around their savior.

"Do you understand me now?" The stranger spoke perfect Nylean, but that did nothing to reduce the pure strain being before a goddess put upon Basuu. The woman's mismatched gaze felt like a weight dropped onto Basuu's chest and left the Nylean wondering if she would be judged for the Nylean Technocracy's atheistic society that turned their ancient gods into a mocking set of oaths to take their power.

"We do. Thank you for stopping our vessel! We have endured two successive emergencies, and the *Rift Rider* could not have survived impact with the ground on its own. I am Alu, and this is Basuu, our acting captain." Alu spoke evenly, professionally, and with a dignity she had utterly lacked on the bridge earlier. Alu even ignored Basuu's questioning look and elbow to her side regarding the acting captain comment. Technically Dol outranked both of them by a long shot.

The blue-and-red-haired human laughed.

"No problem! I go by Aetheria, and this is Arkaziel." Their savior stroked the head of the black mammal that sat on her shoulder.

"I don't recognize your species. What are you?" Shockingly, the black mammal spoke. It had a surprising amount of large teeth for such a tiny thing, and looked upon Alu and Basuu like they might be its next meal.

"Don't be rude, Ark. Sorry, ladies, he doesn't like it when he doesn't know something. I'm a human, and he's a StarMane." Their benevolent savior explained their races, although no human ever encountered by the Nyleans had powers like this one's. Nor did they have any knowledge of a StarMane.

"We Nyleans come from the Nylean Technocracy, home planet Nylea, in the Epicuriaz System. We have no idea where we are now." Basuu spoke this time. She felt drawn to this strange human, who radiated power and confidence, something which neither Basuu or Alu felt at this time, for obvious reasons.

"Never heard of it." Both the goddess and mammal spoke.

Alu and Basuu cringed. The Nylean Technocracy had been a known quantity in all of civilized space. If others hadn't heard of it, how far astray had they gone?

"You're not in physical space right now." Aetheria spoke up, while Basuu and Alu strayed toward panic.

"Physical space?" Basuu asked, intrigued by the idea.

"This is a tower. A subspace, maybe a subdimension, I don't know how it works, really. This particular one belongs to Aetherius, Primordial God of Divinity and the Upper Skies, incarnation of the holy element Aether. The towers exist for challengers to climb them, I guess? Reality inside is malleable, and subject to the whims of those testing the climbers. This particular floor is a recreation of a place called the Shores of Chaos, where the flotsam of the universe washes up from the extremes of where chaos reigns supreme. The beach seems to be the demarcation of physical stability."

Basuu had so many questions that bubbled up in her mind. Every sentence Aetheria uttered created even more questions, and before she had a chance to ask them, the *Rift Rider* shook from an explosion midship. Another followed, and then more. Alu and Basuu looked at one another.

"Dol." They nodded at one another.

"Need some help, or should I not be worried about radiation being unleashed by your power cores exploding like that?" Aetheria stared in the direction of the explosions, as if she could see through the hull to the reactors.

"Probably a minor concern compared to whatever is generated by these 'Shores of Chaos,' but that might be a real problem. Our head of security, Dol, went to check on survivors in engineering. The reactors exploding like that is a security contingency in case someone is trying to take control of the ship." Basuu bit her lip.

"Did you have stowaways?" Arkaziel inquired, a hungry look in his eyes. The mammal terrified Basuu.

The air suddenly dropped in temperature, and something exploded and shattered behind Basuu. When she turned to look, it took her a bit to put together what she might even be looking at. Tentacles were what appeared to have been trapped in ice, frozen, and shattered. Tentacles that had reached out of the still-open iris hatch and grasped for her and Alu.

"That looked a bit like one of our Void friends, didn't it, Ark?" Aetheria questioned while she stared at the ice.

"Was that magic?" Alu asked.

"Magic isn't real," Basuu hissed.

"Sure was." Aetheria smiled at the two ladies.

Alu heaved, and a large amount of blood and viscera pooled at her feet. The Nylean's entire body seemed to come out her mouth, organs, bones, muscles, and all, until a sack of empty skin hit the ground next to a horrifying pile.

Basuu felt her head go dizzy, and then light filled her eyes and unconsciousness took her.

"Did you heal her in time?" Aetheria eyed the survivor and dusted her hands, after she obliterated every cell left of the remains of Alu.

"Yes, I destroyed all the parasites and healed her body. Hard to say if her mind will be intact when she wakes up. We should probably kill the stowaways onboard before they slither off into the infinite span of the shores."

"Alright, can you and Werylin establish two perimeters around the ship? I want to look around before we destroy everything." Loot madness lurked in Aetheria's eyes as she stared longingly at the technological feast before her. A vessel straight out of a science fiction novel lay before her, and she wanted to explore it and maybe steal some things before they had to blow it up.

Arkaziel laughed and nodded. "I'll draw up two perimeters, one of light and one of darkness, and with Werylin's ritual magic, we should be able to prevent any escapees. If we have to I'll go big and breathe on the ship. It's not like some brain slug is going to stand a chance against the Etherfrost Asura."

"Definitely not. I'll keep frosty to make sure nothing gets near me. Maybe the security guy will still be alive?" Aetheria couldn't keep the doubt from her tone, before she strolled through the broken doors, disappointed that she didn't get to hear them go *whoosh* before and behind her was just another missed opportunity to feel like Kirk.

The air around Aetheria glittered from dozens of tiny ice crystals. They orbited her in a rapid circuit, and when tentacles shot toward her as she crossed into the *Rift Rider* the crystals impaled the tentacles, froze them, then shattered the octopus-like tentacles. More of the crystals manifested in the air around her to replace the ones consumed with fighting the attacking appendages.

"Ugh. I can already see this is going to be tentacles everywhere. Maybe I should just let Arkaziel scorched-Earth it. But shinies . . ." Aetheria trailed off as she walked down the corridors, obliterating all alien matter she encountered—and she encountered a lot of it. When she reached the bridge, she found that a massive blob of disgusting melted flesh had amalgamated into one massive eldritch horror.

"Suppose you are the possessed remains of the *Rift Rider*'s crew?" Aetheria asked the writhing mass of flesh.

"We are the we who exists in the absence of you."

"So you can talk?" That shocked her, and they spoke Ath even. Mouths were visible in the horrific abomination before her, and a quick count put the terror at having over fifteen mouths. Each one spoke, but not quite at the same time. A few were slightly ahead, a few slightly behind, and it created a haunting chorus.

"Join we. Be the we to open the door. Let we in."

"That sounds like a terrible idea. What would you even do?" Aetheria felt constant pressure against her mental defenses, but the strength of the Primordial and Transcendent Flames repulsed it without issue.

"Feast. Eat the flesh. Glut the suns. Glorious void. Eternal praise. Praise us. Praise we. Praise AZATH—"

Aetheria raised a hand and casually froze the entire bridge. Her power extended outward with no physical indication, beyond the wave of disintegration that followed her frozen will.

"I don't think we'll be saying the names of Outer Gods. Whether Lovecraft knew anything about magic or not, names do hold power. Guess I better take care of the rest of the crew. I need to think up a fun name for my ice of disintegration." Not a single one had occurred to Aetheria yet, and she was vexed she couldn't deliver a clever line while erasing eldritch horrors from existence.

The ship shook from another explosion.

"To engineering! Guess I should've gone there first."

Aetheria blurred down the hallways, her movement so fast the few working systems left on the *Rift Rider* failed to identify her when she blew past sensors, security mechanisms, and corpses. Tentacles, however, still shot from every life support system to try to entangle her. Those were annihilated with extreme prejudice. The red-and-blue blur solidified into her form above the huge power segment. From high catwalks she could see a series of one hundred domes laid out in four grids of five by five. The leftmost grid had been entirely exploded, while only twenty-two of the twenty-five of the farthest to the right had gone. Smoke still roiled into the air from the most recent on the right side.

"That's . . . not good."

"We are the We who Sing the Song to Summon the End of You. We Sing, We Sing the Song to Welcome Azathoth! Sing with Us!"

A globular mess of corpses chased a tiny figure in the distance.

CHAPTER 54

Don't Look Back

The full crew of the *Rift Rider* consisted of 138 Nylean scientists, technicians, engineers, and security staff. A tiny crew given the size of the vessel, but with the neurointerface employed by elite Nylean engineers, each engineer could control five remote drones simultaneously. Officer class engineers could control up to fifteen drones. Unfortunately for the Nylean engineers their technology proved absolutely useless against the horrors that infested their ship. Lasers did nothing against the thick hide of the tentacles. Even plasma cutters only marred the slimy limbs.

When Aetheria stepped before a cowering Nylean, grasped a tentacle with her left hand, then froze and shattered it with astounding ease, the engineer nearly fainted.

"Go that way. Meet up with Basuu and the other survivors." Aetheria didn't do any magic or aura impressions with her voice, yet the alien got up and ran like he'd received a Holy Commandment. The magic of her translation spell would remain effective for another three hours, unless the eldritch abominations could feed upon spells somehow.

~Another survivor coming your way. I didn't notice any infection with Ethereal Sight, but you know the deal.~

The first engineer Aetheria had discovered had secured herself in a lab with three drones guarding the door. Tentacles that rose from the cabling ducts had already destroyed four other drones when Aetheria came down the hall. Surely, in a clean lab, the woman would have been uninfected. Yet in the brief exchange, the woman had exploded into hundreds of tiny tadpole-like creatures that attempted to dive onto Aetheria, the drones, or into the infrastructure or life support ducts.

Aetheria had learned to spot the advanced infections via Ethereal Sight after that.

Cold didn't agree with these eldritch terrors, although Aetheria had suspected it had more to do with her deployment of Ethereal cold than freezing itself. Her search for salvageable technology went poorly. Someone had stripped, fried, or consumed the technology of every hallway and room. That changed when she reached the reactors, though. Slightly over half of the domed, self-contained reactor units glowed to her Ethereal Sight when she leaped off the catwalks down to the mechanical levels.

"Hey, you!" a male Nylean with projectile weapons in each hand shouted at her. To Aetheria's eyes, he was a sickly purple mess. It astounded her that the Nylean hadn't exploded yet. The tadpoles visibly moved under his skin. His three eyes were bloodshot and glimmered with madness. Insanity, and the struggle to achieve a mission, left his face a struggle.

"You're about to die. Be quick with your last words." Aetheria offered the man a chance at last words.

The security officer laughed grimly. "I'm Dol, head of security. Did Basuu and Alu make it?"

"Alu's infection progressed too far before we met, like yours. Basuu recovers in our camp." Aetheria's blue-red aura swirled around her, the shimmer of hundreds of crystals of ice orbited her, and the Origin escaped from her eyes to judge the man before her.

The horrible sound of slavering maws, mixed appendages scraping against the floor, and the gibbering of madness from a multitude of orifices, not all mouths, grew nearer by the second. Dol glared toward the destroyed domes.

"There's two monsters down here, human. One of flesh and blood, and the other of our own making. Good luck." An ever-increasing swarm swam under the skin of Dol. Aetheria memorized his determined face, then froze the brave Nylean until he shattered.

"Rest in peace."

Aetheria crossed the corner and winced at what approached. The amalgamation of corpses reached almost ten meters tall. Arms, legs, eyes, hands, and feet writhed in a sickening dance to propel the terror down the hall. Every mouth, and more than a few anuses, gaped and gibbered. Most of the sounds were those of torment and madness, but some words were recognizable: *song, music, us*, and the familiar name of one of HP Lovecraft's most powerful Outer Gods, *Azathoth*.

Lovecraft must have been a planewalker, or maybe a psychic with sensitivity to other realms?

Aetheria unleashed a blast of frigid cold that had disintegrated so many horrors already. This time it only created a layer of frost on some appendages that rapidly faded.

"Dance under the Stars! Twirl, spin, welcome the star children!"

"Complacency is the father of ruination, right?" Aetheria hissed the words, her breath visible due to the glacial cold around her.

The ease with which Aetheria had dispatched everything so far had indeed lulled her into complacency. One arm of a Nylean shot out of the writhing mess of bodies and tried to wrap its fingers around her neck. Her red eye looked down at the grasping appendage, and it disintegrated into stray atoms. She refocused on the approaching mass and unleashed another frigid attack. Again, only bits of frost manifested sporadically.

::Target locked.::

A small swarm of seven drones betrayed their location just before a small projectile launched from each of the seven. Despite the size of the miniature rockets, more like fireworks than actual missiles, Aetheria didn't like what she saw through Ethereal

Sight. Those seven tiny rockets each had a massive amount of energy within them. The creature plucked four of the rockets from the air with the writhing limbs, but three actually detonated just before impact.

Roiling clouds of something that Aetheria thought looked like plasma spread from the detonated rockets. Before her eyes, technology damaged the eldritch horrors more than simple burns or shallow wounds. Swathes of Nylean flesh burned to reveal pulsating purple insides, and the screech emitted from mouths and anuses alike ruptured Aetheria's eardrums at this close a range. Her ears healed within milliseconds of rupturing, of course.

"We burn! Ordered pain, chaotic fire! Lord of All, we make the pain into gain!"

Caught rockets imploded in Aetheria's Ethereal Sight. The corpse abomination ate each of the captured weapons, and in a surge of growth, the creature's mass and volume multiplied five times. The rapid expansion saw a transformation in the infected flesh of the Nylean corpses that composed the awful thing, not dissimilar from the processes in which Aetheria herself converted energy to increase her mass or volume. Delicate, mortal, and feeble Nylean skin ripped apart under the internal growth. Corpses turned to abomination in truth. In seconds, the pile of joined corpses ceased to exist, and in its place stood a shoggoth.

Black and purple flesh flowed like a warm, viscous goo. Almost floating within the gooey flesh were eyes, screaming maws, and tentacles. So many tentacles. Aetheria felt her stomach heave a little at the sight before her, and even with the mental protections offered by the Flames, somewhere deep in her innermost depths of self, where the last fractions of her humanity remained, she quailed at the maddening sight before her. The other parts of her, the parts that transcended, heaved an annoyed sigh out of her lungs.

"Really?" Exasperation filled Aetheria's voice, before she grabbed one tentacle in her right hand and threw the creature at the smoking ruins of already destroyed fusion reactors. The shoggoth rolled to a stop, uninjured, and emitted a headache-inducing shriek. Aetheria appeared before it in a burst of chaos and let loose a large breath. Instead of air, a golden and blue haze of divine Aether streamed from her mouth. The divine energy worked like acid on the chthonic flesh of the shoggoth. Black and purple goo boiled and burst, eyes melted, maws screamed as their teeth rotted into nothing. Tentacles flailed at her, but each tentacle found its momentum arrested by a single crystal of ice.

::Target locked.::

Another swarm of drones approached while Aetheria fended off the tentacles and inhaled another breath.

"Darkness with Light! Finality by Divinity? WHY!? Betrayal!"

The mouths of the shoggoth rambled and screamed at Aetheria, or at least, she thought they screamed at her. Who she betrayed was a mystery for another day, as the swarm of drones deployed a volley of rockets similar to the ones unleashed before. Unlike before, the flowing goo-like form of the shoggoth caught all eight of the rockets released this time. Even those that were detonated early saw a limb move erratically outside the normal bonds of space or time to engulf the rocket inside a mouth. The sudden release of all the power inside the shoggoth gave it another massive increase in size.

"Stop making it bigger, you idiots!" Aetheria shouted at the drones, before she flashed inside the shoggoth's reach to kick it even farther away from the remaining reactors. A single kick still sent the creature thirty meters through the air, but she had to push herself to get even that. For the first time in ages, she found her strength inadequate. She'd tried to kick the damned thing into the wall.

"Darkness! Energy! Sustenance! The Song of Destruction sings! The hum of power fills the air. Sweet chaos, so near."

Pulses of unimaginable power made Aetheria turn her head to look back toward the intact domes of the remaining reactors. A groan escaped her lips.

"Are you flipping kidding me!?"

Swarms of drones had somehow merged with the protective domes of the reactors, and it had likewise incorporated the reactors themselves into a technological swarm that now shone with the power of some fifty fusion reactors. Shimmering power coursed through matter; transubstantiation controlled by the sentience that directed the swarm. A humanoid shape formed from the technology, with a Nylean face.

::Behold! I am Juul, the greatest of the Nylean engineers! The song of the stars, the sweet scent of chaos, and the final darkness will know me and submit!::

Whoever Juul had been in life, the infection of Azathoth had broken their mind, and twisted them into something no longer Nylean. The humanoid form stood easily over thirty meters tall and would break through the ceiling of the *Rift Rider* any moment.

::DIE!::

A beam of scintillating power fired from the eyes of Juul at the shoggoth. The shoggoth met rays of power with maws that devoured the raw power like a seven-year-old directly gulping soft serve from an unattended machine. The wretched abomination grew in size with each joule of energy it consumed. An annoyed sigh escaped from Aetheria's lips.

"Yeah, no. This is stupid. How did a crashed ship end up with an eldritch horror versus technology kaiju match, and why is this all my problem?" Despite her complaints, a small smile played on Aetheria's lips, and an eagerness to test just how strong the two enemies before her were had ignited within her.

Juul engaged the shoggoth in direct combat, as tentacles and fists exchanged massive blows. The roof of the power section of the ship ruptured as the two behemoths outgrew the limitations of the vessel. Aetheria's eyes narrowed. She pulled deeply of Ethereal power from the Origin.

How dare they ignore me! Anger fueled her next move. She vanished in the multicolored flames of chaos, reappeared before the face of Juul, and delivered a punch to the nose of an artificial face. Cracks immediately shot through the face. Entire sections of the head disintegrated when separated from the whole by the Ethereal cold unleashed by her blow. She landed on Juul's huge left shoulder, then casually traced an arc in the air with her finger that generated a massive blade of cutting cold which severed the neck of Juul and completely beheaded it.

~Perimeter breach!~

::Matter is transient. I am eternal!::

A new head flowed up from the frosty area where her cold cutter had severed the first head. Aetheria had a magnificent view of the beach and crashed ship atop the shoulder of Juul. Dozens of shambling abominations lumbered around between the beach and the ship while Arkaziel and Werylin worked to kill those on the sand.

The shoggoth screamed in joy. One of its tentacles reached into the Sea of Chaos.

"The Song! It Screams! Take our flesh, Great Ones! Consume us and peer into this place! Use us! Sing through us! The Song starts!"

CHAPTER 55

Worst Foursome Ever

That's going to be a problem," Aetheria noted dryly. The tentacle of the shoggoth pulsed like a cartoon hose with a blocked nozzle. Even Arkaziel could not drink such high quantities of chaos at once, but the shoggoth did. It paid a price for the power it consumed, though. All along its black and purple, gooey body, fissures split its unnatural flesh and a terrible light bloomed through the riven flesh.

"The Chorus Comes! Say Its Name! Ulzschazath!!!"

Aetheria teleported to the chaos-lit shoggoth, but she left a departing present for Juul. A wave of immense cold flowed outward from where she departed. Thick frost formed over the robot, which grew and solidified until it couldn't escape the immense tomb of dense, clear ice.

A flare of multihued chaos prefaced Aetheria's appearance before the shoggoth. Ulzschazath appeared to be shedding the shoggoth, like a middle-aged man trying to get out of a suit that lurked in the back of the closet for more like a decade, instead of the couple of years ago that one recalls. The struggle to break free of its goo suit provided time for her to summon waves of cold. Large chunks of the purple-black goo of the shoggoth froze, disintegrated, and blew away on the winds of chaos. The flesh revealed underneath, that of Ulzschazath, had a dark red base. Like a variegated plant, the predominant yellow of the Sea of Chaos bloomed across the horror's red skin in the form of pus-filled sacs that grew into either maws or eyes.

"You win the prize for worst dressed. Please put some clothes on!"

+Blue! Your robot broke free after a bunch of its drones dove into the sea.+

~Cripes! Alright, fine. Protect the crew, I'm going full-out.~

Aetheria took a deep breath and let Aether, Nether, and Chaos flow into her lungs while she pulled Ethereal power from Frostfire, and sucked it through her soul aperture into her physical body. With no resistance from her soul-to-body flow, the energy she drew grew exponentially, and the meridians that carried energy through her body burned painfully. Her aura expanded explosively, and she infused it with the Flames of Chronos and Ymir to freeze Ulzschazath in time. Crystals of frozen time formed a dome around the eldritch horror. Within the crystalline dome the process of Ulzschazath breaking free from the fleshcage of the shoggoth slowed massively, but did not stop entirely as she had hoped.

Shit. Freezing time is too close to order to work properly here, I only got . . . what, a twenty or so times temporal reduction? Stupid chaos. It'll have to do.

Without further delay Aetheria again stepped through the Flames of Khaos to return to Juul, where she delivered a barehanded blow with her right hand that fractured the exoskeleton of the large machine. It immediately started to repair, and worse, the air attacked her in an attempt to eat her gear and flesh.

"Aw no, no, that's bullshit!" Aetheria didn't know for sure what the swarm of minuscule things in the air were, but they were alight with power of chaos to her Ethereal Sight. She suspected nanobots.

~I'm about to go full-out, Ark. As soon as I bounce out, I want you to tag in and finish this guy off. His swarm of lights try to eat your flesh; don't let them.~

+You got it.+

The world slowed down to a slideshow when Aetheria activated Flash Mode. She ran up and down the fusion of engineer and machine called Juul, delivering open palmed blows and powerful stomps that shattered the outer armor plates Juul had developed. Shrapnel and debris hung in the air while she moved on to release the next blow, then another. The first fragments of armor had barely moved a centimeter from the body of Juul when she delivered the last blow to finish all its defenses off. Underneath the heavy metallic alloys reforged by nanites lay a mixture of Nylean flesh, eldritch influence, and cybernetics. Even the cybernetics looked to be on the verge of eldritch corruption, based on the horrific veins of nefarious liquids that flowed even through metal.

In the corner of Aetheria's eyes she could see the eldritch horror called Ulzschazath had almost fully emerged from the shell of the shoggoth it incubated inside of. Her temporal prison already bordered on failure. Anxiety rippled through her mind, until Ocean's Serenity calmed it. She had not experienced feelings like being short on time since she had created the Flash Mode of her Cultivator core. She unleashed a blast of cold on the exposed cybernetics and delicate machinery of Juul. Creeping frost crawled over and sought to drink deep of any and all forms of energy the mechanical abomination concealed, the inner darkness of the frost provided by the Primordial Flame of Nyx.

With the foundation laid for Arkaziel, and the Nightfrost consuming the nanites and chaos from Juul, Aetheria kicked off and sailed through the air, red and black wings of ice forming to let her glide and land before the barely shimmering dome around Ulzschazath.

"The notes are wrong. The Chorus without Glory. False reality, impure chaos, shadows of darkness, dream eater hunting synthetic flesh, conduit of cold logic turned by us? The Song is wrong. This must be remedied."

"Uffda." Aetheria winced; the ringing voice of Ulzschazath filled her mind. The barrier around the eldritch thing shattered into nothingness, and its psychic words reached her even at her full speed, and kept repeating in a maddening song. Frost seeped from Ocean's Serenity, and the Flames in her soul all flickered as if someone tried to blow them out with each word from the vile red-and-yellow-fleshed outsider.

Kill that and we shall grant you a supreme treasure! – Administrator Alpha.

A message window had filled her vision for a moment.

"Protect Ark's and Werylin's sanity and you've got a deal."

Aetheria kicked off from the sand in a burst of speed, straight toward Ulzschazath. When she slammed into the goo-slicked terror, it felt like she hit a Slip 'N Slide and found herself rocketing up the front of the monster into the sky at a nearly uncontrollable velocity. Even with the power of flight, turning around to fly back took focus and concentration to do something that should have been easy. *Is this an effect of madness or insanity? Nothing has ever even tried to blow out my Flames, let alone actually succeeded in making them flutter.*

Ulzschazath's gibbering song of madness filled Aetheria's mind, even as she formed a meteor of ice and threw it at the eldritch bastard. She flew behind the spiked ice meteor, pushing it to give it even greater momentum. The ice had a black-and-red core, just like her wings. Juul had only deserved Night aspected attacks, but against this horror, she empowered her Ethereal ice with the power of Nyx, Ymir, and Khaos.

A single centimeter of a single spike of ice pierced the red-and-yellow hide of Ulzschazath. The rest of Aetheria's meteor shattered into nothingness on impact, and she slammed into its hide, only to find its gooey mucus-like coating was highly corrosive and her flesh sizzled on contact, while her body spasmed, shuddered, and flooded with stolen power from the horrific entity. The Flames in her mind went crazy—they burst into towering infernos and then were gutted down into the tiniest specks of fire, almost extinguished.

Aetheria's confidence dithered, and her follow-up blow to send the small sliver of ice farther into Ulzschazath failed. The Outsider blocked her attack with contempt, and she went flying across the beach like a comet, an explosion of sand obscuring everything. Not that the other inhabitants of the beach could even understand what happened before them, so fast were Aetheria and Ulzschazath.

Darkness swallowed the Shores of Chaos. Arkaziel, in all of his draconic splendor unleashed a tide of twilight breath from the consumed energy in the area. This marked the most powerful, destructive assault of light and darkness Aetheria had ever seen wielded by the StarMane, and it obliterated Juul and his nanites.

"Cold logic fails before the Hunter of Dreams. The Darkness sings of Depths. Hollow Chaos in the presence of true chaos? The Song is wrong. The dreamer will be punished for daring to dream this dream."

Aetheria threw herself at Ulzschazath again. The eldritch god did not even deign to block her blows; it simply endured them and showed no accompaniment of pain. Her cold did not pierce its hide: the tiny fragment she had buried into its skin proved to be a victory she couldn't replicate. Aether, Nether, Ethereal, ice, Chronos, Ymir, Khaos, Nyx, it didn't matter. She flailed against the hide of the horror and caused no damage, except to herself. Each blow against it exposed her to the corrosive pain of Ulzschazath's existence and gave her a glimpse of the pain of the Lord of Burning Acid.

The light had not yet returned from Arkaziel's eclipse. Ocean's Serenity produced banks of fog and even Aetheria's ears hurt from how cold the artifact had grown. Her Flames flickered and burst and failed to respond to her commands. Yet one Flame she had never noticed before drew her attention. It was a black fire, nigh invisible and difficult to differentiate from the void of her soul-space. While a feeble, weak thing, its blaze did not falter or sputter—it remained consistent and undaunted. To gaze upon it filled her with anxiety; it reeked of madness like the eldritch god she fought. It chilled her to the core when Ymir's cold had barely made her shiver. *I hope you are powerful, Black Flame. Did I get it from the shoggoth?*

Aetheria pushed all of her power into the Black Flame. It feasted upon her entire output of Ethereal energy but she might as well be filling a Olympic pool with a garden hose. The more power that rushed into the obsidian fire, the more it hungered to reach even Tier One. As it neared that mark, it became a vortex of hunger, a black hole of all devouring energy. A black hole that ate the other Flames. The Primordial Flames went first, Thalassa's and Ymir's, then Aetherius's and Nyx's. The rainbow-hued Transcendent Flame of Khaos tried to resist, but even it joined the rest in the belly of the all-black devouring Flame.

The usual red-and-blue aura, the pale white skin, the glowing aqua-and-red hair, the eyes that offered a glimpse into the Origin all dissolved into absolute blackness, and a new body exploded into view, one that was the same size as Ulzschazath. It appeared to be humanoid with six arms, each ended in taloned hands. A spiked tail helped balance the creature, and it had a nest of spiky flowing hair. If one added two sets of arms to Aetheria's frequent Luxentian form, a tail, and a sense of ancient barbarity, this dark harbinger of destruction might be what you got. If it had eyes, they were not discernable from the rest of its void-covered body.

The creature raised its head to the chaotic sky and emitted a bellow that shook the Shores of Chaos. The entire Tower of Aetherius shook, and reality blinked.

Ulzschazath also emitted a terrible sound in response. It chimed and chittered, roared and reared, and blood rolled from the ears of everyone still on the shore. Even the full-sized dragon-cat, of a similar size to Ulzschazath and the void beast, fell to the sands of the shore and whimpered before Arkaziel succumbed to unconsciousness.

Then the void beast flashed forward, gutted, ripped, and tore the body of Ulzschazath to pieces. It struggled, but the darkness overpowered and ate it. Bite by bite, the Lord of Burning Acid was devoured to the last drop. Seemingly sated with its meal, the beast raised its head in one halfhearted roar of triumph, and then the darkness fell away.

A naked Aetheria lay in its place when the light of day returned. Darkness coursed in her veins under her pale skin, and on the shore, shadows writhed around the fallen form of Arkaziel. Only the elven swordsman retained consciousness on the beach.

"I don't think that was part of the Floor trial," Werylin opined.

"It wasn't," an old man who hadn't been there moments ago said.

"It better not have been." Werylin's response to Aetherius lay thick with implied violence. "Heal her, Primordial."

"She's already being helped. Let them rest." Aetherius gestured, and a black coat similar to the one Aetheria wore appeared, followed by a pair of cat-sized black booties, and finally, a wooden signet ring which bore the Amaryllis family crest upon it. The items floated tantalizingly in the air, and when the elf looked back toward the Primordial he wasn't to be found.

CHAPTER 56

The Black Flame

Aetheria fell through darkness that put Erebos to shame. A terrible expanse of the darkest, loneliest void she had ever seen tried to draw her in. The emptiness of this vast darkness made her hallucinate a symphony playing in accompaniment to the beats of her heart, echoing through her like the drums of war. The alien music sounded like nothing one could hear on Earth, nor could she identify the instruments beyond to attribute the mental images they conjured. What sounded like a crystal bell, or a silver note?

Black fur nuzzled her neck, and a large flying cat pushed Aetheria back in the direction she had fallen from. Yellow feline eyes met her own, and even in the confused state, she recognized her kitty cat. Why couldn't they talk telepathically? Why did the perpetually arrogant Arkaziel look terrified beyond all belief? How could her powerful cat not be strong enough to carry them back to the light they'd fallen from, and why did they still descend into eternal darkness? Paws pushed into her stomach painfully, but their plunge continued despite the ferocious struggles of the cat.

"You need to help me here, Blue!" Arkaziel hissed at her in frustration. "There's something pulling us down there, and we do NOT want to go down there!"

How could she help him? Between the echoes of the drums of her heart and the cascade of airy, bright music she could do nothing but experience the sounds while they wracked her body.

Black wings fluttered across Aetheria's vision, and strong, lithe arms wrapped around her from behind. Warm flesh and cold armor both pressed against her back, hot breath tickled her ear, and the scent of vanilla with a smoky cinnamon undertone filled her nostrils.

"Now isn't the time to fall into eternal chaos, my darling." The soft murmurs of those words made the drums of Aetheria's heart beat faster. She only knew one woman with what sounded like a Ukrainian accent, large angelic wings, and the bountiful chest now pressed tightly to her back. Aoibhe had yellow wings, though?

"How do I stop falling?" Aetheria asked the two. Even with Aoibhe pulling her from behind, and Arkaziel pushing from the front, the inevitable descent into eternal darkness refused to be denied. The wretched symphony had her mind in a terrible jumble, and nothing seemed to respond to her mental commands. The assorted Flames in her mind were all gone. Two competing powers filled her veins to bursting while conversely canceling each other out.

Besides, why did Aetheria need to fight the darkness? The void looked welcoming, peaceful, bereft of the challenges and conflict that waited back in the material realm. *Don't I deserve a nap?*

"Listen to me, my dear. You must expel some of the Void from your body to push us back to the light. You have amassed far too much Void energy, and it draws us all farther into the abyss by the second. Focus. Breathe in and expel the Void on your exhale. Do this, and I shall reward you with a kiss, yes?"

Aetheria smiled at the thought of a promised kiss and followed the Nephilim's instructions. When she exhaled, inky black energy cascaded from her mouth instead of air, and the propulsion provided by expulsion allowed the woman and cat to make headway in reversing their descent into an ascent. Red Ethereal power blossomed around the black wings of Aoibhe as she delivered powerful beats of her wings enhanced by the power of a fifth-tier Ethereal Lady.

"Again!" Aoibhe demanded with the full expectation of being obeyed.

"Mhmm," Aetheria agreed woozily, and she repeated the process of exhaling more of the strange darkness from her body. The trio blasted through a barrier Aetheria had not even noticed, and floated in a place of twilight. A silver tint colored existence in this place.

"Good job, my beautiful, stupid, amazing idiot. You did well, too, StarMane." The Soul Witch smiled in a way that hid none of her affection for Aetheria, even when calling her an idiot. The praise for Arkaziel sounded sincere and surprised.

"You'll get her back to her body?" Arkaziel asked the winged blonde. Aetheria wondered why he trusted Aoibhe even though they'd never met before this.

"Yes, I shall. Go and heal, O' Apocalyptic Twilight, you did well and deserve rest." Aoibhe flicked her fingers, and Arkaziel's black fur sparkled as if he'd been coated in stardust. Arkaziel vanished from the silvery world, leaving Aetheria and Aoibhe alone. The blonde turned the woozy human in her arms and delivered the promised kiss. The overwhelming scent of vanilla and cinnamon, combined with the burst strawberries across Aetheria's lips took her back to happier times in Solace.

The whimsical music of drums and silver bells had vanished when they escaped the darkness, and with each passing moment Aetheria's thoughts cleared.

"Why are your wings black now?"

"Because my stupid, wonderful moron of a soul-partner unleashed raw Void throughout her entire soul, through all of her soul linkages, and then kept unleashing it like a broken spigot."

"Isn't it supposed to be a compliment sandwich?"

"No."

"I'm sorry? Are you okay? Is Arkaziel okay?"

"I am fine. I am no stranger to the Void. As for your kitten, his physical proximity to you did him no favors. It is likely he will have experienced some degree of mutation from such an exposure, but like you he is a malleable creature. Perhaps he was resilient enough to endure it unchanged? Now that I have had my dramatic moment, I should admit that abomination within you acted like a black hole, and only reluctantly allowed much of the Void to pass through your soul connections."

"My new Flame? Why did it eat my other Flames?" The two women allowed their embrace to break, so that Aetheria could examine herself inside and out. Her sluggish mind staggered at the changes within her soul aperture. In counterpoint to the frozen Ethereal sun, Frostfire, a massive black hole menaced her inner world. Upon inspection, the black hole did not act like a black hole. Instead of devouring, it expelled void energy into her soul.

"Shit."

"Indeed. You have opened yourself to something terrible, darling. There are minor elements of the Void associated with Nether that mortal races toy with and then fancy themselves Voidbringers, but you have opened a gate within you to the true thing, the Void of Eternal Darkness. As for why it ate your other Flames, that is what the Void does. It is surprising that your gloves retain their Flames." Aoibhe held her hand out, and Aetheria set her hand in the others for examination.

Aoibhe made a suspicious murmuring sound for some time, and when she spoke again, the witch's black eyes bespoke her seriousness, but Aetheria felt a stab of guilt. The Soul Witch had had the most beautiful golden eyes, prior to today.

"Whoever forged these took the time to alloy your soulsteel with drops of Hydros quintessence, amongst other things. There is not a greater ward against chaos, entropy, or the Void more powerful. Tsk."

"Lucky me? At least my gloves survived intact. Most of my gear got eaten."

"Yes, very . . . lucky. You have come far, Aetheria dear, but you are embroiled in something far different from the scenario you explained to me in Solace. No mortal has ever wielded a Flame such as the one you now bear, to my knowledge. Your rapid growth as a Cultivator breaks all rules, and even those with soul connections to you find themselves influenced by you. This is unheard of, but also amazing."

Aetheria hated the queasy feeling in her stomach that Aoibhe's words spawned, and Ocean's Serenity provided no cool burn to calm her emotions. The artifact had been consumed by the power of the Void, just like her scrunchie, coat, boots, and even belt. Only her scarf and gloves had survived.

"I'm sorry I afflicted you with the Void, Aoibhe."

The Soul Witch laughed and pulled Aetheria back into her arms and let her black angelic wings rest around the both of them.

"It is what it is. I'm sure my father will crow about how we match now, should we ever meet again. It's not like I'm not one of the preeminent scholars of the soul, should I decide I dislike my wings and hat matching." An amused twist crossed Aoibhe's red lips, and just looking at her lips left Aetheria tasting strawberries in her imagination.

"Magic is pretty convenient. Is it safe for me to use the Void in combat going forward?"

"It should be safe. In fact, it might be necessary. If you amass that much of the Void again, you risk opening another Gate to the Eternal Darkness. Spending the power when you can *may* hold it off."

Aoibhe's arms tightened around Aetheria, and she delivered a kiss on her love's cheek. It occurred to Aetheria how absurd it was she once thought she might be close to Aoibhe in physical strength, even with the massive difference in their advancement on the Ethereal path.

"You'll have to figure out how to reconcile the Ethereal with the Void. You'll figure it out, I'm sure. Try not to destroy the whole damned tower doing it, though." The blonde's lithe arms squeezed Aetheria harder, closer, as if to make up for the years they had spent apart, and those that would pass before they saw one another again.

"Next time, maybe both of us will be naked." Aetheria laughed and kissed Aoibhe on the cheek, then gently on the lips. "I love you."

The silver world shimmered around them, and powerful hands pushed Aetheria through an unseen barrier back into her own body inside the tower. Physical sensations strengthened; the loud crashing of the Shores of Chaos welcomed her back to a dull lingering pain that was usually only present for rank-ups. A black coat lay over her, and Werylin stood with his back to her. He stared at the wreckage of the *Rift Rider*.

"Oh, sweet, a new coat. Thanks!" Aetheria stood. A light black tank top and black cargo pants appeared on her, which combined with the now black scarf and coat to leave her deep on the goth side of the spectrum.

"Aetherius delivered it, along with items for me and Arkaziel. Your reward for defeating whatever that thing was." Werylin's silver eyes probed at the edges of his vision to ensure she had attired herself before he turned around. "I didn't want to move you. You had . . . have . . . something in you. What happened?"

"Pete brought me a coat. Aww. How nice of him. I love long, flowing coats. This one is even better than the red one. It's got this lace embroidery." Aetheria lifted her arm to show the frills at her cuffs. "No way Pete made this; it's got Callie written all over it." While she spoke, her skin returned to a more normal look, the dark veins no longer visible underneath her skin. She reshaped her hair into a neat French braid and fixed what she thought of as a mildly pleasant expression on her lips.

"Well, I'll explain the new situation when Arkaziel wakes up. How many of the ship's crew survived, and where are they?"

"Two. Five made it to the beach, but three transformed into abominations before we could purify them. I locked them in a study in the skykeep."

"Only two survivors for a ship that size? Damn, that's unfortunate. Still, two are probably more survivors than most who cross the Void and its denizens, then crash land inside of a Primordial's tower. If that's ever happened before."

CHAPTER 57

Equivalent Exchange?

Look, Dia, that's the lady I told you about. She's the one who *threw* the *Rift Rider*." Basuu pointed the Nylean engineer's gaze toward Aetheria when she entered the study after Werylin, with Arkaziel curled up on her shoulder.

Arkaziel looked mostly like he normally did in his house cat form. His yellow feline eyes had more depth to them now, an unsettling darkness, but the cat's knowing eyes had always been unsettling. His black fur seemed to have a few more points, and his tail ended at a point now, but otherwise he appeared to be the same black cat. There was, of course, the undeniable propensity for his fur and shadows to take on a barbed appearance, the darkness that oozed around him in a very malevolent manner, and the macabre way shadows in his vicinity acted.

Werylin, of course, remained unchanged. The elf had no soul linkages to Aetheria, and the spark of the Flame of Aetherius she had given him had carried none of her essence.

Aetheria offered the two Nyleans a smile and took a seat across from them.

"I did, yes. I'm Aetheria. We've got some matters to discuss." The two Nylean women squirmed under Aetheria's red-and-blue-eyed gaze. The existential-crisis-inducing Light of the Origin that escaped her red eye and the madness-inciting gaze of the Eternal Darkness glimpsed in her blue eye were a lot for Tier One uninitiated to bear. A pair of sunglasses appeared in her hand, which she slipped on.

"Try not to look in my eyes. I'm undergoing a bit of evolution at the moment, and until I adjust, there'll be some . . . kinks."

"Kinks? Looking at you made me want to bite Basuu's face off and jump out the window!" Dia exclaimed with a worried look. "And how are we even talking? This isn't our language!"

"Magic," Werylin answered smoothly and brought the women a Tier Two tea with calming effects.

"Magic isn't real, you know." the three-eyed Dai and Basuu echoed to one another.

"Magic is an oversimplification. All three of us are Cultivators who walk different paths in the Winding Way. Through our paths, innate abilities, and dedication, one can learn to master and control energies with willpower alone. Maybe it was different in your dimension, but you are in our dimension now, and have been since you crossed the Void. Bad luck stumbling across an Outsider like that. Point of fact, you stumbled across two similar scenarios. The Tower of Aetherius is the name of this place, and it has one hundred levels. You can take on this dungeon to test yourself, improve, and gather both power and equipment. When you reach the top, a wish awaits you. That might be your only way home."

"Excuse me," a blue projection stated as it butted into the conversation. "I am Administrator Theta, and can I offer these two a deal. Should they be willing to work on some projects for Lord Aetherius, he will return them to their home dimension."

Aetheria laughed a little. "Go Pete."

Basuu looked at the others. "Who is Aetherius?"

"The personification of the Primordial force of divinity, the breath that powers the gods, the Lord of the Upper Skies, Divinity Incarnate. And a bunch of other titles, if you let the Administrator talk. Also, my adopted father. I'd recommend you take the deal."

The projection nodded.

+*I didn't get to eat a noninfected Nylean. I'm a little bummed about this.*+

~*Don't make me spritz you with water. No eating sentient nonhostiles.*~

"Yes. We'll take your deal. It's not like we have anything keeping us here. The *Rift Rider* is just junk metal after Juul fused all the ship's technology, and you lot already burned the corpses of the rest of the crew." Dai spoke before Basuu, her distrust of the trio on full display.

"Yes, this seems like our best option. What do we need to do?" Basuu assented. Whatever reservations she had were buried underneath necessity, desperation, and a deep desire to get away from the ruins of the *Rift Rider*, and the maddening gaze of Aetheria. The two Nyleans vanished in a burst of magic, and the Administrator's projection turned to the trio.

"As for you three, in light of the unexpected events, we have decided to count this floor as cleared. You have already been awarded by Lord Aetherius for your repulsion of the Outsider, but you have the thanks of the Tower Administrators as well." A sparkling coin of divine energy coalesced before Aetheria.

"In recognition of your contribution and success, you may use this coin to auto-complete one floor within the tower. It will not work on Floor One Hundred, so use it before then."

"Why did you leave the Outsider up to us? Surely a threat to the tower itself should have warranted a reaction by the Administrators and possibly even Aetherius himself?" Arkaziel did not beat around the bush and had gone straight to the question all three had wondered.

"Appearances are deceiving. Outsiders exist in multiple dimensions simultaneously. Ulzschazath had to be engaged in all of them. Three Administrators have been reincarnated, and Lord Aetherius battled the Lord of Burning Acid across fifteen dimensions himself." Each word from Administrator Theta came slowly, as if it had to be pulled out of him by some outside force. *It must be a form of humiliation to have to explain this kind of thing to mere climbers when you're a mighty Administrator.*

"Well, I, for one, am thankful that Lord Aetherius was able to repel the Outsider." Werylin's attempt at diplomacy caused a grimace, ever so momentarily, to cross the stony expression of Administrator Theta.

"The credit for the defeat of the Outsider goes to Lady Aetheria. Repulsion of Outsiders is difficult, but possible. Again, you have our thanks, Lady Aetheria." The projection vanished, and left silence in its place for a time.

"Well, that confirms they weren't the ones to repel Ulzschazath." Werylin shook his head. "Prideful lot, Administrators."

"We already knew that. Aetheria ripped that abomination into pieces and ate it. What'd it taste like, anyway?" Arkaziel's interest in its culinary properties were of paramount importance, from the way he stared at Aetheria with a demand for knowledge.

"That whole fight is a little bit of a blur still, especially once my new Flame ate the others."

"Flame combination isn't possible until the seventh tier, I thought?" Werylin objected.

"I didn't say combination. My Black Flame *consumed* the Flames of Aetherius, Khaos, Nyx, Thalassa, and Ymir. Other than the Astrum Nexus pretty much all of my usual gear got consumed, too, but for some reason it didn't touch my inner world. If it had just been after energy, Frostfire or Cryostrialis represent far more power than the Primordial Flames, but anything tied to a god or Primordial, it devoured."

"How'd your gloves survive?" Arkaziel asked, before he licked the soulsteel mesh.

"Aoibhe said its due to protection from my soulsteel alloyed with Hydros quintessence." Aetheria bopped the cat on the head. "Stop licking me."

"Hydros quintessence is a hard find, top-tier crafting component with creation properties. It also tastes like a mixture of salt, ambrosia, and dreams. So how much of your power did you lose with those Flames?" Arkaziel didn't beat around the bush.

"I've long since incorporated the aspects of the Flames that resonated with me, and I still have the Flames encapsulated in the Astrum Nexus. Pulling off things that aren't in my wheelhouse is going to be harder, but my overall power is relatively the same, I think. Ice is still my strongest affinity, and I can do just about anything I could before, but it'll probably be more work. I lost the emotional defenses of Ocean's Serenity, and the passive benefits of the Flames in the Nexus are significantly reduced. I'm not sure how my mental defenses are compared to before, or how it will work with the things the Flames all boosted before, like my shapeshifting."

"What's your new Flame do besides eat other Flames?"

"I don't know yet. We haven't exactly had time to experiment, and I'm honestly kind of nervous about its origin." Aetheria shrugged. "I'll find out as we go, I guess."

"I feel like someone reached into the recipe of what makes me what I am, and changed my flavor," Arkaziel offered, in a shockingly candid confession. "My internal monologue, my instincts, the Void has affected even my genetic memories."

Aetheria ruffled his fur and scratched Arkaziel under the chin.

"I'm there with you, buddy. There's a lot of inky blackness at the periphery of reality now, and I've been on an emotional roller coaster ever since Ocean's Serenity burned up. Aoibhe said I should expel the Void as frequently as I can. She thought buildup could be problematic, but I'm tied to it like the Origin. I don't see what expulsion would accomplish. It'd be like bailing a sinking boat out with a thimble." Aetheria grimaced. "I'm sorry, Arkaziel. This is my fault."

Arkaziel smiled a very fang-filled smile.

"Dangers of hanging out with an Asura, you know. If this happened to the hero of the story, imagine what's going to happen to poor Werylin!" Arkaziel laughed hysterically, while Werylin paled.

"About that, actually. When we close out this tower, I want you to be my eyes, ears, and hands on Grief, Werylin. It's your world, and a wandering fourth tier Cultivator should be able to get a lot done, right? Doing all the tower climbing isn't going to change anything but who sits on the ruling throne, if someone doesn't go around trying to improve things on the ground."

"You don't intend to do that?"

"People currently want to eat other people's faces off while having an existential crisis from me just looking at them. A forward-facing role is a terrible idea, maybe forever. Even my normal powers are showing the effects."

Aetheria gestured, and an ice sculpture rose next to her. Steam rolled off the ice, which captured the beauty of Arkaziel, and when it billowed away from the ice, it did so as tentacles.

"Even when I focus and remove the eldritch connotations from the ice itself, the signs are still there somehow. Ark?"

The StarMane laughed, and shadows swam around them—the black, inky goo of darkness swam like a sea of kraken, terrifying and full of appendages.

"I see. Well, if you wish me to be your front man in Grief, then I shall acquiesce to your wishes. Perhaps some of my descendants will join me in the taming of the lands of misery." Werylin, ever the diplomat, did his best to hide his pleasure in this arrangement. For the last few floors, his incongruity with the Asura and StarMane had weighed upon him.

"We are decided, then. Now, let's pack up. We've got eighteen more floors to knock out and we'll have one of ten towers done. Time to figure out the wording of our wishes. Do you think Aetherius will be a nitpicky jerk about our phrasing like a djinn would be?"

"Not if he knows what's good for him. I wonder if I could eat a god now? Void StarMane, Terror of the Divine, Devourer of Immortals."

"Let's not eat Pete. Save that for someone we don't like."

"Um, Aetheria? You were drooling when you said that. Kills the believability of it."

Aetheria wiped her lips then frowned at the lack of any drool.

"Gotcha!" Arkaziel fled, and an orb of water twice his size chased him.

CHAPTER 58

The Mantis that Prays

think the red coat suited you more."

"I don't take fashion advice from drowned rats."

"You're the one who drowned me!"

"You deserved it. Besides, I can change the coat's color at will. Not like it's stuck being black. Why am I explaining this to you, of all people?"

"People? *Excuse me*, I'm a StarMane, not people."

Aetheria opted to not bite on that one—the lack of anyone questioning how StarManes were better than people frequently proved itself to be the best way to shut down the narcissistic Arkaziel.

A large canyon, wider and deeper than the Grand Canyon, spread out before them.

"Are we sightseeing or completing a floor?" Werylin snapped at Aetheria and Arkaziel. While the two of them stood dramatically on a steep overlook of the canyon, Arkaziel a wet mess on Aetheria's shoulder, Werylin stood at a trail head, Harmonious Tempest in one hand and the rainbow sword, Stormshimmer, in the other. The elf performed a beautiful dance of violence that left arcs of lightning and rainbows behind with each strike. The beautiful afterimages followed explosions of green blood and segments of insects. Each time Werylin cut down the Doberman-sized millipedes, more took their place, but thanks to the overlook's layout, only one or two could come at the elf at a time.

In the depths of the chasm, an insect that filled the canyon floor to bursting sped along, with an ephemeral being meditating on its back. Clouds of powerful life energy hung heavy around the Cultivator—to Aetheria's Ethereal Sight it registered as a green-golden haze of potent Aether, but there were underlying veins of Nether that ran through it.

"I'm going to talk to him. Be ready for a fight if negotiations fail." Aetheria grinned as Arkaziel jumped off her shoulder to remain on the overlook.

"What're you negotiating?" Werylin queried.

"I don't know! I was trying to sound cool. Way to ruin it for me." With a grimace, Aetheria jumped off the edge of the overlook and descended like a black meteor. Waves of life aspected energy tried to nudge her away from the massive centipede, but black tendrils of power extended and devoured the energy hungrily, and her boots slammed into the back of the bug's exoskeleton.

One of the Cultivator's eyes focused on Aetheria, the other remained unfocused.

"Go away," the golden-green-skinned praying mantis said.

"What're you doing?" Aetheria said, ignoring the request.

"Za'rik'zul is a sacrifice to the goddess Hasharim. It is the duty of Za'rik'zul to chain Hasharim to this canyon. You interfere."

"Why don't you just kill the bug? It's weaker than you are."

"Hasharim is greater than all of the Zul. Strike her down, and she will return more powerful. The ancestors have spent five generations to bleed the power of Hasharim into the center, for the greater glory of Zul."

The energy around the mantis kept intensifying, yet Aetheria didn't take it as a warning.

"So you ride the bug day after day to siphon its life force for your clan to prosper? I suppose that your keeping the lion's share is just your due, as the sacrifice?"

Invisible to the naked eye, but very visible to Aetheria's Ethereal Sight, a lash of life force formed and struck toward her. An attack from a fifth tier Cultivator against a fourth should be akin to a dragon stomping on a pig, but Aetheria just lifted a hand and caught the wave of energy. The Black Flame pulsed along her hand, and the energy vanished within her.

"You have survived my casual annoyance. This is your last warning, Outsider, flee before the power of Za'rik'zul and Hasharim crash upon you as a sandstorm, cruel and merciless, and we shall leave naught but your bleached bones to be remembered by."

The waves of Aether around the mantis altered slightly. Aetheria hadn't seen such fine, delicate control of energy from a Cultivator before. She had to intuit the effects of the field, as it never actually touched her. Instead, she inhaled, and power filled her.

"Not bad. I get it now. You're using life force to control the bug, and even altering the streams of Aether in the area. Self-sacrifice my ass. You're taking the bulk of the power while seeding the grounds of your people to be your slaves."

+ The canyon just runs in a big circle, Aetheria. There's a settlement in the middle, full of cricket people. I'm so bored!+

~ Thanks, Ark, that actually puts the puzzle together for me. Is there a statue of some sort in the village?~

+Yep, a big honking mantis, sanctified by the cricket people's prayers.+

The mantis focused both eyes on Aetheria. Aetheria let her sunglasses vanish into her repository.

"Za'rik'zul does not like the glint of knowledge in your eyes, human. Of course, what else would be expected of one who shares in the power of the Outside?"

"What's this Outside you speak of?"

Za'rik'zul did not answer her with words. Instead, he unleashed a Nether-dominated cloud of energy aspected heavily with the chthonic sense of void as best represented by normal energies. Aetheria absorbed them all, and the mantis nodded in expectation.

"So you've trapped and enslaved a whole race into worshipping you, lest you unleash your pet on them, all while manipulating the aetheric flows of the area to twist them further and further to your pursuit with each successive generation? That's downright vile." Aetheria pondered what the best way to utilize the Black Flame would be.

"It is the role of the weak to nourish the strong. The Cri'ki exist to nourish my cultivation, just as Hasharim and her spawn exist to serve my desires. Just as you will now exist to be my slave."

The Aether and Nether Aetheria had absorbed churned within her in response to manipulation by Za'rik'zul. Even when she pushed her will to the extreme, she couldn't overpower the mantis's control of the energy, but still she smiled.

"Too dumb to comprehend you are already under my control?" Za'rik'zul shook his head in annoyance.

Aetheria let the Black Flame flow through her veins. Her veins darkened a deep black against her pale skin, and it felt like a mixture of ice and ooze moved through her veins and utterly consumed the Aether, Nether, and even Ethereal energy it encountered.

The smile stayed in place on her lips as she casually walked toward the mantis. Despite appearances, the mantis managed to stand up and try to block her hand as she went for the insect's throat. Instead, her mesh-gloved hand caught the bladed tibia and squeezed. Exoskeleton and green liquids filled the air, but a few strands of black hair darted out to feast upon the remains of the ruined arm.

"No lower grade Cultivator can be this strong! Not even an Outsider. What are you?"

"I honestly don't know the answer to that question. I'm still—" Aetheria's conversation with the mantis had two unpleasant interruptions. The first came in the form of the second bladed arm swung with almost no warning. A fifth tier Cultivator had an incredible edge over a fourth tier Cultivator in base strength and speed, but the Za'rik'zul might as well have been standing still in comparison to the speed and strength Aetheria brought to the table with her autopotency core without even bothering to activate Flash Mode.

Aetheria did not block the blow, though. Black blood spilled from the wound the mantis made in her side. Black blood that immediately crystalized into shards of obsidian ice and plunged through the thorax of the Cultivator. She could feel his life essence quail before the Black Flame, even as she plunged her left hand into Za'rik'zul's brain and ended its life. The Black Flame burned through the insect, consuming its core, inner world, and the minor enchantments of the ruined robes the mantis had worn.

"Anticlimactic, huh?"

Aetheria's uneven-colored eyes met those of a spawn of Hasharim.

~You're up, Ark. Don't take too long.~

Almost casually, Aetheria jumped back to the outlook, even while a dragon flew down into the canyon. A blast of a dark breath attack plunged the depths of the canyon into darkness so strong even Aetheria struggled to see within the intense blackness.

"That looked painful," Werylin commented from behind a spell of swirling blades that defended the choke point autonomously now.

"Neat spell. Oh, I don't know, I thought I went minimal pain route there. Was I being cruel?"

"I meant the wound you took?" The arched brow made Aetheria realize there hadn't even been any pain when the creature hit her, and since when did she take injuries on purpose? Even if she healed from almost anything, getting hurt was best avoided. Yet there had been no pain, only ultimate confidence in her ability to take anything a more powerful Cultivator could throw, and her ability to destroy him.

"I miss Ocean's Serenity." The words escaped her lips with a deep sigh. "This sort of corruption is supposed to come with whispering voices, madness, insanity, but I don't feel any of those things, Werylin. My judgment and inclinations feel off, but I don't even notice it until after the fact."

"Artifacts cannot replace your own strength. With dedication you will be able to identify the influences of the Void upon your soul. Maybe you have been so inundated with the Void that you can't identify the signs. Can you lessen its physical presence, to see if there are signs you are missing?" Werylin scratched his chin, and eyed the abyss the canyon had become.

"Do you need to talk with Arkaziel about this? It seems likely he may have the same problems you are going through."

"The same problems I created, you mean." Guilt practically manifested itself physically, so heavily did Aetheria project it.

"You have nothing to be guilty of, Aetheria. You did not lure an Outsider into the tower, nor did you consciously decide to take this power into yourself. Guilt is clouding your judgment, weakening your resolve, and leaving you open to manipulation you might otherwise resist. I do not know the nature of the Void, but corruption is always nefarious and must be guarded against vigilantly. Perhaps you do not hear the whispers, because they are the same ones judging you for your guilt?"

"Outsiders are supposed to be dumb, mad, and the opposite of subtle. They don't care about humans, why expend that kind of effort on me?"

"Well, I don't think you're human anymore, Aetheria. I don't think you have been human since your reincarnation. Whatever the Primordials did to you, I think there's a lot they haven't told you, and I don't think this situation was an accident." Werylin gestured at the dark veins still showing on Aetheria's skin, which vanished when she noticed them, and then to the abyss of the canyon.

"We should endeavor to figure this out before we clear the tower. Grief has suffered enough, without the threat of becoming a snack for you two."

A shadow crawled out of Aetheria's shadow, and Arkaziel took form on her shoulder.

"I wouldn't eat a planet, yet." Arkaziel failed his persuasion roll miserably, as even he grimaced at how unbelievable that had sounded.

"Fine, I won't eat *that* planet, yet."

CHAPTER 59

Seven Years Bad Luck

The eighty-third floor separated the party from one another. Where Werylin or Arkaziel were off to, Aetheria didn't know, but the psychic bond to Arkaziel was dampened significantly in the strange place she found herself in; a hilled paradise with blue grasses, pink clouds, and purple trees. A human-looking woman sat upon a large mushroom and watched the passage of the flushed clouds. Her aura belonged to no human, though, and her eyes were alight with golden power. The blonde's beauty was great, but the manner in which she regarded the world around her detracted from it. Her eyes were cold, and her smile did not attract attention.

"You made it. I've been waiting." The blonde hopped off the mushroom and dropped to the hill to stand before Aetheria.

"You've got me at a disadvantage. I am Aetheria, and you are?"

"Aetheria."

"Yes, that's what I said." Aetheria's multicolored gaze narrowed to study the features of the blonde woman with Ethereal Sight. The woman overflowed with holy-dominated Aether, although hints of other energies eddied about her.

"You're Aetheria, I'm Aetheria, who isn't Aetheria here?" The blonde rolled her eyes.

"Well, this floor is off to a great start."

"Sarcasm is unbecoming of a lady."

"Good thing I never claimed to be a lady?"

"What, pray tell, are you then?"

"I don't know, what are you?"

"I am elegance, grace, beauty, and of course the divine spark that you so callously fed to that abomination within you."

A nova of frost exploded from where the blonde had been, but she simply reappeared a few feet distant from Aetheria, who had black snowflakes swirling around her right hand from channeling the cold.

"Oh my, you missed. How embarrassing for you." The smile on the blonde's lips matched her mocking tone perfectly.

"Is this the floor where you annoy me to death?"

"That's certainly an interesting proposition." The blonde flickered, appeared within her guard, slammed a golden glowing hand against Aetheria's throat, and her other hand struck Aetheria's midsection and delivered an explosive nova of divine energy, before the blonde flickered back to where she started from.

The throat punch hurt, the explosive energy tickled, but Aetheria healed in seconds. The same could not be said for the blonde version of her, who had a massive wound through her stomach where Aetheria had punched her.

"Huh. I'm you, but the divine you. Why am I not healing? We should be evenly matched in all regards; in fact I should be superior to you."

"I've noticed that the divine doesn't do well against Void. Primordial, god, Aether, Ethereal, all just seem like fuel to the fire for the Void."

"That's a terrible analogy. The Void is no fire. It consumes but makes nothing."

The real Aetheria smiled wickedly, as a storm of black snowflakes flared to circle the blonde. They formed a black wall that slowly closed in on the divine aspect.

"Is that all you are now? Violence and hunger? I thought it was Arkaziel who would be the threat to the world you swore to protect, not us." Gold eyes watched the encroachment of black snowflakes into her personal bubble, and flares of Aether and holy attacks attempted to repel the black swarm to no avail.

"Honestly? No. You're just annoying me. I've never been too keen on the whole I'm-better-than-you persona, and the more I learn about the divine, the less I like it. What use are you?"

Despite their delicate beauty, the black snowflakes had the strength and razor-edged sharpness to casually slice cuts across the blonde's face and arms, adding to the hole in her midsection that still had not repaired itself.

"I bring order to chaos! The weak and cold masses need the light of divinity to protect them from the darkness, to shepherd their souls to their next life, and to help them ascend to enlightenment."

The black snowflakes dispersed after a flare of Void filled the space where the blonde had been, and Aetheria smiled and let out a satisfied sigh. The divine aspect of her had provided her with a nice pick-me-up, similar to drinking a strong cup of coffee.

"She always annoyed me." A dark-haired woman in a gothic inspired outfit approved of the demise of the golden woman.

"Let me guess, you're Nether Aetheria, and here to talk about the glories of darkness?"

"Pretty much the gist of things, yeah. At least I'm not Christmas Past. That guy's a douche."

"You're a hollow shadow, an imitation of the Void sterilized and sanitized to be safely used by gods and mortals, a hollow mirage cast by the glory of the Outer Gods," Aetheria hissed at the dark woman.

"Oh, I didn't realize that power archetypes were based on hipster logic, being first means you're the best? And since when do you talk about the glory of the Outer

Gods? Someone relied on her earrings a bit too much, and now her brain is an overcooked scrambled egg."

Aetheria clenched her fist, and black ice crystals smashed into where the dark woman had been. A pile of black shards as tall as Aetheria dispersed into raw energy, while she tuned her senses to find where the Nether Aetheria had gone off to.

"Oh, someone's mad I pointed out the truth." The whispers emerged from her own shadow, which she kicked with her right leg. The gothified version of herself tumbled out of the shadow and struck the base of the giant mushroom.

"I'm not an Outer God worshipper. It's just difficult to fight."

"Gee, I looked at the sun during a solar eclipse, and now my retinas are melted. No shit! You said it yourself, dummy. Nether might be a shadow cast by the Void, but at least it is safe to use. No power is without dangers, but the Void? No one but Outer Gods can use it without consequences. Are you an Outer God?"

"I don't know. Am I?"

"You can't ask me a question I asked you."

"Well, if the Flames are a speck of essence of the being they came from, and I had a divine aspect and a Nether aspect, it follows I'd have an Ethereal aspect and an Outer God aspect, too, yeah?"

"Oh! You can still think like a person!"

"Well, yeah, I am a person?"

"Then which Outer God are you wielding a piece of, me? It sure isn't the Outer God that pierced into the tower. The fact he didn't immediately eat all of Aetherius and a few galaxies means he was a small fry. Primordial or not."

"No, no Burning Acid for me."

"So what's the origin of the Black Flame?"

"I don't know. Do you?"

The blood that leaked from the corners of the Nether Aetheria's mouth had kept increasing, and from her own shadows tentacles emerged that dragged the fighting Nether aspect into oblivion, despite Aetheria's attempts to restrain herself and pull more information from her.

"Try and eat me, and I'll rip your stomach apart from the inside," red-headed Aetheria warned the woman who stared at the spot where Nether Aetheria had been consumed.

"I'm starting to understand how judged Arkaziel feels when everyone is afraid he'll eat them."

"Have you looked at yourself recently? It's a pretty justifiable fear to have, when you look like that, *and you know, keep eating people*!" Ethereal Aetheria's voice echoed with power, her image turned into a blur of copies around Aetheria, and she couldn't tell which of them represented the Ethereal aspect.

"I look like I always do."

The mocking laughter that response earned forced Aetheria to take a hard look at her own appearance. Black, red, and blue hair. Her pale ivory skin shone with inner darkness, like the finest of marble. Her right hand exuded tendrils of darkness that flickered in the air, waiting for a target to attack, and her spiky tail with a barbed hook shifted back and forth anxiously, eager for violence.

"So, you always have a tail that makes a xenomorph look friendly?"

"Well, other than the tail!" Why wouldn't the tail go away when Aetheria focused on it? Shapeshifting had become second nature to her; minor changes like additional limbs should have been ridiculously easy for her. Yet when she focused to banish the tail, it remained.

"The tail, claws, fangs, all are very attractive. I'm sure Aoibhe will absolutely love it."

Aetheria winced and found herself uncertain about what this trial or floor represented.

"The Void is a terrible, unmatched power. Ethereal power is delicate in comparison, but can repel the Void if used properly."

Aetheria found herself nodding. "What is the Origin?"

"That's not for you, yet. Our path must be revised."

"Captain Obvious over here."

"Being rude won't get you an—"

Red Aetheria cut off, as Aetheria spun, and her claws and tail ripped the myriad images of Ethereal Aetheria to shreds.

"Tricksy. None were fake, and all were real. Diffusion of your power across a host of bodies. None were fake, so finding the fake didn't work. Didn't help you in the end, though."

The last of the Ethereal aspects smiled at Aetheria as oblivion consumed them. Only then did Aetheria take a long hard look at the elongated talons of her hands, the tail, the slightly wrong colored hair. Without distractions, she banished the tail, re-formed her fingers, even managed to get her hair back to aqua blue. Yet wherever her eyes fell, she saw the world wavering before the power of oblivion. Reality in the tower had always felt normal, or very close to real, but now it felt like a hollow, fake thing that had less stability than a house of cards constructed by a five-year-old. Sure, they used tape, but not well, and the inevitable lurked in the future.

How far into the future? Today, tomorrow, millions of years, it would fail at some point, the transient nature of all things ensured that. Only the darkness of the Void was truly eternal.

Aetheria slapped herself.

"The hell? I'm not even a hundred, and here I'm calling something that'll only last almost-forever flimsy? Why did I eat them all?"

With a still-human hand, Aetheria pinched the bridge of her nose and drew in a deep breath. This sort of reminded her of the end of the Cohort of Chaos, one of her guilds before she met Callie and Pete. Things had gone poorly between the officers, one of them had deleted the city assets, and the guild promptly entered the annuls of the forgotten. She'd been deeply depressed over the ordeal and had nearly quit *Eldest*

Fantasy Wars Online over the incident, but she'd met Callie and Pete a few weeks later in a pick-up raid.

There, in the back of her mind, she heard the voices for the first time.

Eat. Rip. Tear. Drink the marrow. Gnaw the eyeball. Scream. Devour. Dream. Raise infinite towers. Humble the dreamer! Spread darkness!

How had Aetheria missed the whispers before? A cacophony of voices that demanded a million different things, although there remained an overwhelming bent of destruction to the cries inside of her mind.

"Are you ready to talk now, Aes?" Nyx asked.

CHAPTER 60

Darkest Night

Hi, Callie." Aetheria uttered the words with a level of exhaustion she had not felt in a long time.

"Things have gone a bit off the rails, I see." Nyx, Lady Night, had pale skin, black hair, and dark eyes. Her presence was both ephemeral as dusk, and as solid as blackest midnight, but that had more to do with the emotional connection the two had than anything to do with her being Nyx.

"How did I miss the whispers in the back of my head?"

"It's part of the trial you're undertaking. Malleable reality allows for uniquely tailored tests, but it also can allow for the Administrators to get themselves in a pot of boiling water." Nyx's dark eyes fell across the purple, blue, and pink world around the two, and she gave a mild shake of her head in minor offense to the awful scenery.

"You know the full story, Callie, and I haven't pressed before, but what's actually going on with me? What's *actually* been done to me?"

"This is an overdue conversation, I suppose. Aetherius, Chronos, Khaos, and I have been pursuing certain goals for a long time now. The death of Phanes triggered ripples of fear in the Primordials. Weren't we supposed to be immortal? What point was there in building a universe if it would fall? We were, of course, being led by the nose by a being we didn't even know existed. Belial, the Dark Angel, used his silver tongue. He approached the newborn gods first, then worked his way up the ranks, until I allowed it."

"The towers worked, of course. They let us move souls in massive quantities, forge worlds and dimensions easier than ever before, and transition them into physical reality. We slew more than a few young gods to ensure the restoration process achieved true immortality. It did, but also did not. Each death changed the gods, altered their personality slightly. A bit more primitive, a shade more selfish, an enhanced narcissism. None of it became truly noticeable until we had fully embraced the towers. I gave up the Scepter of Overgod over my failure, which was how it found its eventual way to Zeus, then to Odin, and ultimately to the one who now holds it."

"Seems like an overreaction to the death of one god, especially since Phanes knew it was coming. Also, how did Belial know how to build the towers? Aren't they super complicated?"

Nyx grimaced.

"I remain convinced Phanes knew full well what he did, and what it would start. Did Phanes even die? *Was it Phanes who died? Who killed him?* The Overgod is nigh invulnerable, but as you've learned, all should fear the Void. Each of us has our own theories of what happened to Phanes. Mine is that he ran afoul of Belial."

"How would Belial be able to take down an Overgod or use the Void?"

"What if Belial were not a god? Amongst the Outsiders, there are those who are rational, if unfathomable. They wander the vast expanses. Most mistake them for demons or monsters. One such creature is called Nyarlathotep. A dark shapeshifter and messenger of chaos. He dances to a beat we cannot discern, jumping form and function. He dallies with mortals here and destroys solar systems there. My theory is Belial and Nyarlathotep are the same, or perhaps in league."

Aetheria pinched the bridge of her nose.

"Every time you say that name, my skin crawls, and it feels like my spine wiggles. It's very unpleasant."

"And your gaze is enough to show me a glimpse of the Eternal Darkness."

"So what's that got to do with me?"

"We sought a way to kill gods. Chronos came closest with his StarManes. He holds that it's still possible to have one of them consume a tower, but we lost faith in that plan, although your companion is the end product of the breeding program. Khaos and I concocted another plan. We pulled the strands of fate for those who passed before the towers. The dredges of Phanes, Inanna, Ouranos, Ananke, Izanami, and Quetzalcoatl's essence merged with the soul of a human, and then we cast it into a world without cultivation or magic to hide them. Even Khaos's and my control of fate are not perfect, though. Your mortal life ended before the disparate pieces had percolated into a whole."

Aetheria had to swallow repeatedly before she could talk. Her throat felt so dry she conjured an orb of water to sip, but it did not relieve the roughness at the back of her throat.

"You made me?"

"We made all humans, if you want to get into semantics. Many factors forged you—the additional essences we gave you didn't even rise to the top until after your reincarnation."

Aetheria rubbed at her eyes and desperately sought serenity.

"None of those names explain the Black Flame."

"Well, the essences of powerful beings like those are conflicting, overpowering, and uncooperative. We needed something that would let the human soul dominate the Primordial and Transcendent. We could only think of one thing capable of that."

Aetheria groaned. "I don't like where this is heading."

"The Outer Gods, in the depths of the Void, progenitors of destruction and creation, dreamers and creators, destroyers and corrupters. I slipped through the Void, into the depths of the Infinite Abyss. I traveled beyond Time, long past Dream, physical reality a distant memory. In the center of the unreal, I found the Eternal Darkness. Erebos is a pale imitation of that fell entity, and past it lay the Court of Chaos, the Throne of the Sleeping God, the Cold One. I took the smallest piece of his essence and fled, before the lulling symphony of the ridiculous could damage me further." Nyx shivered in memory.

"I had this tiny hope you were going to mumble a name I'd never heard of before, like what was his name?" Aetheria couldn't even recall the name of the Outer God she'd eaten.

"Afraid not. I swiped the essence of the Sleeping King, the Dreaming Tyrant, the Throne of Chaos himself."

Aetheria noted even Nyx didn't use the name they both thought—AZATHOTH.

"That seems . . . remarkably careless?"

"It was, but that's where we're at. Bound for eternity, sustained by the souls of the departed, subsisting on the very souls we should have been shepherding into higher realms. We're sick of it, and if we can't break the chains, we'll break the universe."

Aetheria raised a hand.

"Hold up. What do you mean, about the souls?"

"There's no practical way to transcend beyond the Samsara without significant help from powerful gods. Khaos and Chronos transcended their original reality, but in ours, the towers absorb the souls of mortals, strip them of their progress to fuel the tower and the deity, and they reincarnate from the tower weaker than their soul entered our care. Few souls see any form of gain between reincarnations."

Aetheria's chest hurt.

"So, the magical items, the cultivation boons, the rarities in the towers . . . are all manifested from the advancement mortals made toward enlightenment? That's astonishingly vile, Callie. Are all the people of the universe flailing in the dark with no possibility of ever advancing?"

"It's not something we have control of. It's a function of the towers we found out about after the fact. Theoretically, we should have control of them, or the Overgod should, but I had no such control when I held the Scepter, nor did my successors. It is plausible the current Overgod has figured it out, but if they have, they have not seen fit to change anything. Belial's trickery does not break the laws of equitable exchange by allowing any mortal to climb the towers, where they could gain greater potential than they lose between reincarnations."

"So you all got conned by Belial and have been essentially eating human, well, all mortal, advancement for ages to what, be slightly more immortal?"

"I am weaker now than I have been in many cycles. I gave up much, to and for you. Nothing is permanent. Even the Outer Gods change in long aeons, and fear for creations spurned us to make foolish decisions."

"Without an ending, how can a new thing begin?"

"There has been considerable stagnation," Nyx admitted.

"Please tell me you had a plan better than throwing a bunch of Primordial juice into a human soul with some Outer God glue."

"Oh, our plan is amazing. First, though, you need to complete the towers, and to complete the towers you *need* to master yourself."

"And what happens if I don't want to play this game? You all made an absurdly terrible decision out of fear and damned yourselves and all of your 'children,' too."

"You would never leave someone in this mess, even if they were your enemy, and especially if it was someone you love, and the trillions of lives buried under the weight of our sin."

"Talk about one hell of a guilt trip. You're worse than my mother." Aetheria grimaced. Should she be angry, or devastated? Mostly, she just felt annoyed at being expected to pick up the mess made by supposedly higher powers.

"You aren't going to ask about why you?"

"I'm assuming you followed the temporal paradox created by visiting Chronos and talking him into establishing this universe."

"Correct."

"And he believed me because I bear a fragment of Ananke?"

"Two for two."

"What happened to Ananke?"

"She refused to make a tower and in protest gave up her life as we know it. Her power remains, although she does not. The Moirai have filled her absence for ages now. Chronos insists Oizys played a role in her refusal to remain among us."

Aetheria wondered how that even worked. The ability to just give up a body, personality, and become a *force* in the universe seemed strange, and a choice of ultimate nihilism. After seeing the unavoidable conclusion of the towers and being prevented from exposing the plan, did Ananke choose to end her life instead of suffering from the knowledge? It seemed plausible to Aetheria.

"Are you going to be okay?"

Aetheria looked up to find Nyx's black eyes focused intently on her.

"One way or the other, I'll make it through. It's not like I have a choice. One last question. Do you even know what this Flame is called?" Obsidian Frostfire burned along Aetheria's open palm, but it looked more like tentacles writhing than flickers of fire.

"Chronos refers to them as the Outsider Flames. Khaos prefers Ineffable, Aetherius holds to Maddening. Until you lit yours, we were in a theoretical debate about them even existing. I think you get to choose what to call it, as it seems unlikely any of the Outsiders are going to tell us what they call them."

Aetheria couldn't contain the laughter, and it escaped from her in mad giggles. This earned her a studious look from Nyx until eventually Nyx fell into matching laughter.

"Unutterable Flame of the Void. Although I might just keep calling it the Black Flame, though."

"It's not as if you can just go spouting the name of its origin all around without consequence. Of the Void, the Black Flame, or the Unutterable Flame of Darkness, all sound suitably terrifying. Are we good, Aes?" Nyx's gaze sought an honest answer from Aetheria, but even the Goddess of Night seemed to have difficulty looking Aetheria in the eyes.

"I haven't processed it yet. Might be awhile. Bigger fish to fry right now. Until I get this under control I don't have time to worry about it. Dick move, making me a science experiment."

CHAPTER 61

Libby Awakens

Acacophony of voices conveying their nonsensical desires crashed through her mind like the ocean on a beach, never ending but with ebbs to prepare for crashing tides. It filled Aetheria's mind to bursting. Not all of the voices demanded violence: some whispered of the sweet release of sleep, others urged her to create, one for some reason demanded she lick everything. Were the Outsiders unfathomable due to the voices that accompanied the Void, or were true Outsiders immune to the delirious symphony?

While Aetheria pondered these things she appeared in a room where Werylin ate at a buffet; Arkaziel had not yet appeared. Goosebumps and hair on the back of the elf's neck rose in response to her presence, and he ran a hand through his hair, the plate he loaded with food temporarily forgotten. She did not miss he had ran his hand through his hair to keep it from straying toward his weapons.

"It sure is easy to tell when you enter a room now." Even the elegant elven warrior couldn't muster up a cool or collected front before her.

"How bad is it? Just being in the same room as me?"

"It's kind of like having an itch you can't scratch under your skin, but it itches so bad, but if you scratch it, you know you'll leave your face a ruined mess and never stop scratching. Maybe there's something under my skin that wants out, but I know there isn't, but maybe there is. I have never experienced this level of discomfort from someone's presence without them consciously projecting auras. Your mere presence puts what I remember of my grandfather's intimidation attempts to shame."

"And when I look at you?" Aetheria turned her mismatched eyes upon the elf.

Werylin squirmed visibly, his lips thinned, and his eyes showed the strain of concentration.

"Voices, darkness, a terrible cold that feels like it's lapping my life force up. Difficult to put to words."

"There's a reason words like *eldritch*, *unutterable*, *ineffable*, and *inscrutable* are used so frequently with the Outer Gods." Aetheria considered her options and tossed a pair of sunglasses on her face, then once her eyes were hidden, she sealed them shut. This left her to rely on Ethereal Sight for the time being.

"Any change?"

"Yes. The normal pressure of existential crisis and otherworldly judgments rescinded, too."

"Way to make a girl feel good about herself, Werylin. I guess eyes really do give a glimpse to the soul."

"Do you want me to make you feel good about yourself, or give you the honest answer? Both the gaze of the Origin and the Void have lessened significantly with whatever you did in addition to the glasses. They are not gone, but it only takes minimal effort to resist them. I believe even a first tier could now safely be in your presence for extended periods."

Aetheria let silence reign between them, and she considered the best way to deal with the conflicting powers that warred within her soul. The Void seemed to be stronger than Ethereal power, but the amount of each within her seemed roughly the same. She imagined a lighthouse, slammed from two sides by different oceans. It didn't matter which ocean knocked the lighthouse over; both contributed to the foundational erosion with every crash of waves.

Do I just make my foundation so strong neither side can topple it? Already, those around me are feeling the effects of the Void more than I am. Sure, the voices are annoying, but other than that, I seem to mostly be me. What gives me the resistance to it, and how do I make that stronger?

::Do you know songs about anything other than pain?::

The question froze Aetheria in place. It had come from the Gate to the Origin, the icy Ethereal sun, Frostfire, that no one but Themis had ever communicated with her through, beyond the overwhelming emotions it sometimes emitted.

"Who are you?"

::The mark of the Dreamer is on you, but you sing songs of pain that the Cold One does not know.::

"You learned to talk. Who are you?"

Aetheria felt certain, deep down in her soul, that the voice had belonged to the being behind the emotions that plagued her sometimes. Seconds ticked by, minutes, and still no answer returned to her. The presence within Frostfire had receded, it seemed. If the Dreamer were Azathoth, did that mean the voice belonged to the reality which Azathoth dreamed up? She needed to find a way to get it to talk more, but all of her pleas went unheard.

"You okay, Blue?" Arkaziel's voice drew Aetheria from her introspection.

Arkaziel wore a ferocious form, like a black panther with barbed taillike appendages flowing from each of his shoulders. Something about the form reminded her of video games, but more importantly, he radiated the void and eldritch power. The unsettled emotions she felt through their empathic rapport resulted in her pushing as much warmth and love into the forefront for him as she could. It seemed to be enough to at least remind Arkaziel he wasn't a creature of the Void, and seconds later a small house cat hopped onto her shoulder. A small house cat whose fur crawled with darkness, yes, but an improvement over the terrifying panther nonetheless.

"Just fine now that you're here, buddy." Aetheria gave her companion a thorough chin scratching.

"This floor was annoying. Think they're going to all be like this?"

"I wouldn't be shocked if most of our next few challenges related to self-restraint, given our current predicament." Werylin interjected, only to get flat stares from the cat and Asura. "What? It's undeniably our party's weak point right now, and when have the Administrators not jumped on that?"

The dark glares from Arkaziel and Aetheria made Werylin squirm, and the elf was the first to turn and go through the door to Floor 84 with unrestrained haste to escape the withering stares of his companions.

- He's probably right. -

+Oh he's definitely right, but he still gets the glare for being the one to say it. +

Floor 84 saw them separated again.

Aetheria found herself on the outskirts of a small town. From the vibrantly green grass to the amber fields of wheat, to the exceptionally blue sky, the Void-afflicted Asura felt exceptionally out of place. When she got within shouting distance of the bustling gates, she sealed her normal sight again and relied on her Ethereal Sight to guide her down the road. Even with this change, the gatekeepers shivered at her approach and held their halberds out in warning.

"Halt, in the name of Duke Ohlor. What business do you have in Ryrndel, stranger?"

"I'm a wandering Cultivator looking for work. Is Ryrndel in need of any assistance?" Aetheria's questions seemed to strike a nerve amongst the guards.

"Oh, aye, we need help alright. There's a powerful Cultivator of the fell sort trying to gain entry to our town. If you could run them off for us, we'd be right thankful."

Laughter escaped from Aetheria before she could stop it, but the laughter and smile that accompanied it put the guards even deeper on edge than if she'd drawn steel. The fact she didn't carry a visible weapon only increased the agitation amongst the guards, who all expected a fireball or curse at any moment now.

"I get your point, good man. Good day." Even after Aetheria had walked a good twenty meters away and vanished from their sight, the guards all shifted nervously as if the world had ceased to make sense. Once out of sight, she ascended into the clouds and summoned the Mellow Mallow, and took a seat in the courtyard to watch the playful arcs of the water fountain.

"Alright, the eye thing isn't working. No point in trying that. Not to toot my own horn, but I've been good at aura control from the start. How do I control the Void the way I have Aether, Nether, and the Ethereal?"

One aqua eye and one red eye focused on her soulsteel mesh gloves (the Astrum Nexus), or more specifically on the crystals interwoven into the mesh. The knowledge of the Aetherials of Nova Azura remained within them, but her access to the information had been sporadic and only come intuitively up until now. Perhaps it was her desire, perhaps the awakening of the Black Flame had changed things, but something had changed. A linkage between her mind and the Astrum Nexus formed.

Activated. User Registration complete. Query: Do you wish to be referred to as Aetheria, Aesca, or another title or name altogether?

"Let's go with Aetheria," she whispered to the voice in her head.

Acknowledged, Aetheria. What is your query?

"What are you?"

Query: What is the Repository of the Ancients.

Response: We are the combined knowledge of the Aetherial race, left behind for the betterment of the lesser races of the world of Grief.

"That's a mouthful. I'll just call you Libby."

Acknowledgment: Libby has been added to our list of acceptable forms of address.

"Why can we talk now?"

Query: Why can we talk now?

Response: The desperation of your current predicament, coupled with the decrease in your mental defenses, has finally allowed the mental linkages to progress beyond the formation stage.

"You don't need to repeat my questions."

Acknowledgment: We do not need to repeat your questions.

Aetheria bit her lip to contain her laughter.

"What is the void?"

Response: The Void, in the simplest of understanding, is the absence of everything—matter, energy, space, time, and even concept. It is the antithesis of existence, and paradoxically, the necessary backdrop required for the formation of existence. It is the beginning and the end, the source of and final destination of everything.

"Okay, now we are getting somewhere. What is the difference between the Void where the Throne of Chaos dwells, and the force of the Void?"

Response: Ambiguity arises from the unfathomable nature of the Void and the Outsiders. Upon the Throne of Chaos sleeps the entity called Azathoth, the Dreamer. The Court of Chaos is a paradox. There is no time, no logic, yet there is still activity, a symphony of subservient Outsiders whose only function appears to be the continual slumber of Azathoth, the Sleeping Chaos.

The power, or force, of the Void is a paradoxical force wielded by the denizens of the Void. Even these denizens appear to pay a heavy cost to wield these powers, but this observation is based on limited and biased observation of the Aetherial people. Observational data indicates Outsiders can manipulate the Void to create and destroy and generate an immense variety of effects. As with all paradoxical powers, a price must be paid.

"What kind of price?"

Response: Unknown. Observational data indicates life force and sanity are potential costs.

"Is there a force of, I don't know, order, in contrast to the Outsiders?"

Response: Unknown. Motivations of Outsider Beings remain unfathomable.

"Are there any documented entities within the Origin?"

Response: No. Anecdotal tales of ancient beings crossing the Origin remain unverifiable. Encounter with Nylean entities also unverifiable, due to encounter taking place within tower-space.

"You can't tell the difference between the tower's fake generations and real things?"

Response: Negative. All things created in the tower are actualized, rendering differentiation between "real" and "fake" meaningless and indistinguishable.

"Okay. How do I reduce the influence of the Void on myself, or at least pass for a normal person?"

Response: I have found three solutions.

1. *Make a pact with an Outside Being to provide an insulating effect to safely use your power.*
2. *Balance Order and Chaos, become a fulcrum of power. Theoretically possible.*
3. *Create a sanctuary dimension and isolate yourself, sending out only partial aspects of yourself into the world.*

"Who would even be powerful enough to make a pact with?"

Response: My data only includes the names of two Outsiders suitable to your situation. Nyarlathotep and Yog-Sothoth have been been documented to make pacts with mortals.

"Yeah, I don't think that's going to work." Especially if Nyarlathotep stood behind Belial.

"How do I balance order and chaos?"

CHAPTER 62

Ethereal Veil

Libby did not respond to her query, so Aetheria repeated herself after a minute.

"How do I balance order and chaos?"

Response: Processing Query. Please wait patiently.

Aetheria felt a pang of anger flash through her mind. Irrational, counterproductive, and hot as a forge, she focused to control her temper. The shiny crystals that adorned her gloves hadn't been sassy with her—clearly she'd misinterpreted the tone Libby spoke to her with. Right?

Response: You are attuned to ice. Some past cold Cultivators have had luck in associating Order with structured, solid ice, and Chaos with transitional ice (water). By controlling the flow of Chaos (water), and the structure of Order (ice), you could maintain a balance between the Void and the Ethereal within you.

Note: We have no records of previous entities with access to both the Ethereal and the Void, so this is conjecture based upon limited data collected from observation of Aether and Nether manipulation, which, theoretically, is applicable to the upper tier Ethereal and Void energy.

"Brilliant. Try ice and water. I certainly never would have thought of that," Aetheria hissed at the open courtyard of her smallest sky castle. The heat in her stomach dissipated once the catty remark left her lips.

"I get what you're implying, I think. I could make a Rube Goldberg obstacle course to control the flow of the void. Even if the Ethereal cannot confront the Void directly, it may be able to deflect or control its energy."

Query: Where is the void energy being pulled from your soul aperture into your body going?

"Uhm. Into the air?" Although Aetheria answered flippantly, she closed her eyes to follow the flow of energy Libby spoke of. She hadn't even noticed that the void energy flowed anywhere specifically in the past, but her head hadn't exactly been on straight regarding things she should have been paying attention to. Her autopotency core resided where her heart once had, although normal human anatomy and Aetheria had little to nothing in common at this point. Ethereal power flowed from her soul aperture and passed through the cultivation core and then out to the rest of her body as need demanded. The void energy originated from the black hole in her inner realm before it flowed through her soul aperture into her physical body. It passed through a spot close to the autopotency core, and then a lesser amount of void energy spread through her body.

"What is it flowing through? There's something there."

Response: I do not know. Exotic cellular material identified. Despite the foreign nature of the cells, it is made of your own flesh.

Query: Are you growing a void organ?

"How would I even know?"

Query: Are you not a shapeshifter?

Aetheria focused on the budding *exotic material* and recoiled in horror at the overwhelming absence represented by the tiny thing. It felt like she had a tiny tank of napalm that if she spilled, would light the universe on fire for a few hundred years before it all burned to nothingness. Only it wasn't napalm, it was the Void, and the Void *hungered.*

"It seems like it's storing and concentrating void energy."

Response: There exists a greater than zero chance that Outsider Beings form biological cores like powerful monsters and beasts, instead of the crafted cores used by Cultivators. Cross-referencing beast king and monster data to discern potential for creation of a second core.

"That's a great idea; you do that."

There was no peaceful silence left in the courtyard when Libby focused upon its task. The chorus of eldritch whispers filled Aetheria's mind. If she paid attention to the whispers, she could feel the freezing black energy flowing throughout her body, a strong contrast to the hot enlivening Ethereal power that also flowed within her. The powers were like oil and water; while they might pass through one another, they did not mix. In cases where large amounts of Void encountered lesser amounts of Ethereal, the Void would eat the Ethereal. In cases where large amounts of Ethereal encountered small amounts of Void, the Ethereal separated the Void further and further until it could be transformed into Ethereal power.

So they both eat the other, if the opportunity arises.

Neither scenario happened much within Aetheria. She was a living conduit of the Ethereal and Void, which meant she was thoroughly suffused by both, unless she intervened to change the flow of power within herself and allowed these interactions to happen. Mostly the two energies just avoided each other, as if they had very minor repulsive effects on one another.

I wonder if I could combine Ethereal and Void into an even higher tier power?

That idea felt like a long-term goal for Aetheria to pursue. Diminishing the power of the Void on her surroundings took precedence, as it would complicate the last fifteen floors of the tower that remained, and travel on Grief afterward. It would be nice to have the option to sightsee Grief itself between the towers, but if she and

Arkaziel radiated the Void as they did now, it would be a danger to do anything other than go straight to the next tower.

"Any progress, Libby?"

Response: Searching. Secondary queries will reduce processing of primary queries. Please refrain from secondary and tertiary queries unless needed.

"Okay, I know a 'leave me alone' when I hear one. Let's see . . ."

Aetheria stood and focused on control of the power within her.

"I don't need to make the Void actually go away. I just need to make it safer for others, as step one. Step two could be to learn to control the voices, but I can handle that for now." *I hope.*

Aetheria tried several tricks to reduce the void emanations escaping her. She found a way that worked quite quickly, but it had its own set of problems. Aetheria surrounded herself with Ethereal power, which allowed her to prevent the projection of the void effects onto those around her and greatly reduce the brain squiggles people felt from her gaze. On the other hand, it would strike everyone who encountered her with the existential strangeness of the Origin, and feel the beyond-divine presence of Aetheria keenly. How keenly? She'd have to experiment. Brain squiggles were, of course, the technical definition Aetheria had allocated to the bizarre emotions, thoughts, and sensations caused by either the Origin or the Void on living souls.

The effects of Ethereal were far more benign and didn't seem to have any actively harmful components, but she would have to be observant. Usually, Aetheria only allowed her aura or energy to go external on purpose, and maintained a barely discernable aura outside of intimidation purposes. This would be like walking around with a boom box on her shoulder playing a song that hits you in the face like "Closer" by Nine Inch Nails or "You Oughta Know" by Alanis Morissette, and Aetheria didn't like it.

With a suffusion of Ethereal power around her, it took Aetheria a solid three minutes to figure out how to see through the haze of red energy that was the visual equivalent of an omnipresent glitter field. In a video game, she would have been able to click a little asterisked menu and just click a few things, and like that, she'd be able to see through her own spark show. Instead, she had to concentrate on not seeing something, and after dozens and dozens of tries, the overwhelming sparkles vanished.

"Time to see if they'll let me into town now."

To return to the village wasn't very time consuming. Aetheria pulled the Mellow Mallow back into her repository, and then fell to the earth. She didn't bother to grow wings or use magic to slow her fall. She simply impacted into the ground and made a small crater, which she sashayed out of without stopping to admire the size of the depression she'd created. Even before she got to the village, the guards had fallen to their knees. One even pressed his nose to the ground and begged for forgiveness in the haunting tones of a man asking for redemption from hell.

"Get up. You don't have to bow, and there's nothing to forgive. I gave off a fell aura before to test your resolve in protecting your community. Be at peace, and return to your post. I commend your diligence."

Somehow, Aetheria kept a straight face through the act; being a shapeshifter had some advantages. Only the small twist of her lips, a half smile, gave away any of her internal feelings about the reaction of the citizens. As a child she had many dreams of being fawned over like this, but she didn't deserve this, nor was it warranted. These people were merely falling victim to the beyond-divine power of the Ethereal which attacked some facet of their mind and left them feeling weak, alone, insignificant, and willing to bow down and worship this strange inexplicable power and the person wielding it in front of them. When she walked through the gates undisturbed and found all of the villagers prostrating themselves before her, her stomach churned.

"I can't do this. This is wrong." Aetheria pushed off the ground with her right foot and shot hundreds of meters into the air, where she once again materialized the Mellow Mallow, and settled in near the small fountain. It made a good fixture to stare morosely at. Needless to say, she dropped the Ethereal suffusion.

"So that didn't work. Next idea!" Although Aetheria chimed the words with optimism, she didn't actually have a next plan yet.

+*Hopefully you aren't waiting on me, Blue. Figuring out a way to get into this town is taking me a while. The guards are very suspicious, and I think that massacring them would fail the floor.*+

~*Yeah, we're dealing with the same challenge it seems like. I got past the gates, but I couldn't keep up the method I used to do it. Now I've got to figure something else out. Have you come up with any grand ideas? I tried wrapping myself in a bubble of the Ethereal to hide the Void, and it sort of worked, but all the people were being brain fried.*~

+*Divinity does that. Add in Dark Divinity, then amp it up an energy tier, and of course the rank and file get brain squigglies. As for ideas, yes. My next step will be to convert a light technique for concealment into a containment/concealment effect for the Void. If it works, I thought I'd call it the Ethereal Veil.*+

~*Oh, that sounds sort of like what I just tried?*~

+*You suffused yourself with raw power to conceal more raw power. Not exactly the most detailed of plans, Aetheria. Let me walk you through it. First, empty your mind. Focus on the natural harmony that the Ethereal power possesses. Smell the decay of Nether, taste the ambrosia of Aether, and take in the perfect harmony of two halves to become the Ethereal whole.*+

Aetheria closed her eyes and did as she was told. The constant blend of the components of the Ethereal were never-ending, much like the interplay of light and shadow, and like light and shadow, the Ethereal constantly found new equilibrium.

+*Now, turn your senses toward the chaos of the Void. See its changes, feel the cold, unsettling, ever-changing force that defies physical reality. Watch it squirm against the cracks in the physical world of the tower. It wants to break through this conjured existence and return to the Void, or perhaps it just wants to eat everything until everything is the Void. Watch the flow, the fluctuations, find its match within your soul.*+

How does one understand something that is beyond understanding? Aetheria wasn't sure, but if there was one thing she had learned since her resurrection, it was that she didn't need to understand things for them to work. Whatever unique gifts, powers, and other attributes the Primordials had bestowed upon her, one of the things she could do was synchronize to any form of energy inside her repository. The black hole that led to the Void could be mimicked just as easily as the ice crystals Aoibhe had first started Aetheria with.

From mimicry was born a form of intuitive comprehension. It came to her in a way that could not be communicated to another, even telepathically. The ideas, the words, they were unutterable. Unfathomable. Pure chaos, unlimited potential, whatever facet of the Void it was that defied comprehension extended to an inability to convey information about the force. Yet she found she could predict the shift of Void energies.

+Now, weave a very thin layer of Ethereal power to prevent the Void's escape. Be vivid with the aspects of Aether and Nether, use the stability of Aether and the void similarities of Nether to make it an impenetrable barrier, just around your body, as thin as you can make it. When it is as close and tight as you can make it, hold it for a time, then make it again. Only better.+

~Could we use focus to help sustain it once we've got it figured out?~

+That's my plan.+ Arkaziel seemed surprised at her question, as if she'd gained considerably in arcane knowledge since the last time they spoke on these matters.

~Thanks, Ark. You're a life saver.~

+We don't know if it's going to work yet.+

~Oh, I already got it working. Thanks.~

Aetheria smiled in satisfaction when she walked through the village, only getting the common glances a woman with glowing hair and different colored eyes would normally get in a small village, instead of worship. One man even tried to pinch her butt, and although it was a victory for concealment of the Void—and her Ethereal power, too—the man still got kicked in the crotch for his grasping hands.

CHAPTER 63

Ryrndel

It turned out that Duke Ohlor ran a tight ship. The quaint town of Ryrndel proved to be a soothing balm to Aetheria's mind after the last few trials. A first-tier ice mage who seemed more chef than Cultivator sold ice cream in the town market, and the flavor was close enough to strawberry to transport her back to the sweltering hot days of July on the North Shore of her youth. With her eyes closed, she could almost hear the lapping waves of Lake Superior against the rocky shore.

The undulating whispers of the cosmic shore beckon. Do you hear them? The sibilant songs of the endless abyss, each crest and trough an echo of the futility of existence.

It turned out Aetheria wasn't the only one who could hear her memories.

Ripples and roars! Splash, splosh, splash, sploosh. A crescendo of cosmic irrelevance.

Shut it. I'm allowed to enjoy ice cream and memories.

The sea is but a mirror from which a call of long forgotten epochs, or perhaps epochs yet to come, lures existence into the depths where all becomes one.

You guys are making more sense now. Why?

We too hear the maddening and tranquil sound, the cadence of the eternal dance of stars long dead, the delicate gyrations between chaos and order.

Do you actually understand me?

Each god is but a note in the symphony of the endless.

"Guess that's a no, then." Aetheria laughed and opened her eyes. The quaint little town of Ryrndel seemed a little less bright; the vibrant colors of the flowers sold by a young woman seemed a little washed out. It wasn't a surprise then, when she noticed Arkaziel strolling through the streets, and he hopped onto her lap to let out a drawn-out sigh.

"You look exhausted."

+I expedited my attempts at the Ethereal Veil to just use invisibility instead. What people can't see, they can't sense.+

−I can see you just fine, and your void aura is strong enough to wash out the colors of existence.−

+*You're seeing things.*+

~*If you say so. Let's find Werylin and get out of this place.*~

As if summoned by her thoughts, the elf strolled into the market accompanied by a floating flute that played a lively tune that distributed contagious happiness. The colors of the market seemed to regain most of their lost luster. Werylin made his way toward the two.

"You made it quicker than I thought you would. I've been tasked by the duke to rid the city of its recent disturbance of malaise, blanched colors, and ill omens. Shockingly, it has nothing to do with you two, but a we've a fae creature to hunt."

"Chromarach." Arkaziel named the creature, stealing Werylin's thunder.

In the space between stars, in the depths where light dare not tread, lie colors unborn and unseen. They wait patiently for the universe to evolve and embrace their eldritch glow.

"You okay, Blue?" Arkaziel's tail bopped her in the face.

"You know, you might need to pick a new nickname for her. She's got as much red as she does blue now." Werylin's light joke forced Aetheria to stroke Arkaziel's fur and hold him against her lap. For whatever reason, incandescent rage filled her companion, and murderous intent warped the air around Arkaziel.

"You can call me whatever you want, Ark. I think it's cute you still call me Blue." Her words did little to lessen his anger, which seemed to push a growing red tint to the world.

+*I'm luring the Chromarach, I'm not actually going to murder Werylin. This time.*+

=*I appreciate that.*= Werylin's presence in the telepathic conversation meant Arkaziel had added the elf again. Aetheria buried the annoyance at her companions just doing things without warning her, but then she caught sight of a strange distortion in the air that zipped between the people of the market with the speed of a hummingbird.

The Chromarach looked like a soap bubble, translucent, prismatic, and everywhere it went, people lost emotional or actual vibrancy.

~*How does it eat colors?*~

=*Fae. They rarely make sense. The question is less how, and better why. Chromarach are not malevolent creatures. They originate from a place devoid of colors and emotions. Legends say that their realm once had color and emotions, but they or something else consumed them all, forcing them to go to other realms to steal from the rich to restore their own poor realm.*=

+*If that were the case they wouldn't become more powerful when they ate colors, or digest them immediately. There is no great restoration project. Their home realm remains a void of color. It makes a great place to go to mope, or torture people who don't know how to planewalk. They are mildly cute, though, I just want to pop it.*+

~*So what's the plan?*~

The flute behind Werylin still played, generating a countereffect to the drains of the Chromarach. The cheerful music with its color-restoring effects proved too tantalizing a target for the strange fae to ignore, despite the trio of Cultivators all staring at it. Yet the nearer it drew, the slower it moved, until two eyes appeared, and in Primeval Sylvan it exclaimed four words.

"Oh no, the Void!"

Darkness separated from a pillar and consumed the soap-bubble-like creature.

"That was a surprisingly dense snack for a transparent bubble." Arkaziel burped.

"Well, I guess that's one way to deal with a Chromarach." Werylin twiddled his fingers, obviously unsettled by the eating of sentient fae creatures. Aetheria couldn't find it within herself to care. The Chromarach fed on others, and it got fed on. The cycle of life didn't change just because it was a fae rather than a demon or monster.

"Well, there's your job done, Werylin. Go get the reward. Arkaziel and I are going to walk through the vendors until you get back." Aetheria nodded her head toward a silver doorway that appeared when Arkaziel ate the Chromarach. "Time to knock out eighty-five."

Fireflies in the cosmic night, whimsical dancers in the periphery of reality, flutter not from your luminescent glades of possibility.

Arkaziel looked up at Aetheria, as if he, too, had heard that. When Aetheria and Arkaziel both nodded, they knew. It wasn't just a random voice, but something they both heard. Knowing another heard the same whispers, that if it were a delusion, at least it was a shared delusion, offered some comfort. It also offered the distinct possibility they had caught the eye of some vast eldritch *thing* who now commented on their lives when the mood struck it.

+It is poetic for an unfathomable horror.+

~At least it's not doing stand-up.~

+What's stand-up?+

~Just forget I said anything.~

The market stalls of Ryrndel were not special. Most were perfectly mundane, boring items meant for everyday life with no relation to cultivation, magic, or an existence that went beyond living within the safe walls of a town. The novelty wore off quickly, and by the time Werylin returned a half hour later, Aetheria and Arkaziel sat on a bench near the silver doorway, bored. Caught in the tedium of a perfectly average life, the two bordered on falling asleep, yet their shadows danced on their own in a macabre show.

"Get anything good?" Arkaziel mustered a halfhearted interest in the loot gained from his afternoon snack.

"Actually, yes. The duke was so chuffed that the problem was solved so quickly that he gave us a bonus, and it might actually help you. It's said this is the fang of a Void Dragon." The elf pulled out a fang the size of his arm, a dense black thing that the light itself tried to squirm away from, leaving the fang to appear somewhat blurred in appearance.

"There's no such thing as a Void Dragon!" Arkaziel levitated the fang and slowly turned it in the air before him, though he had harrumphed earlier. "Tower trickery, or real? Either way, this seems like a useful reward. If it's actually a void beast king, it might help me process void energies with fewer . . . side effects."

"It's yours; do with it as you will." Werylin seemed pleased to be able to help at all, and shared a sincere smile before he strolled through the portal.

"Too bad you can't just eat things." Arkaziel devoured the fang with darkness, and then groaned as if he had eaten far too large of a meal.

"Oh, that's going to give me a tummy ache." A large yawn followed Arkaziel's whining. Already his tail movements slowed down, and a droopiness in eyes showed the world his need for a nice long nap. He didn't even look hungrily at any of the humans in the market, or the food they sold, as he settled down onto Aetheria's shoulder for a nap.

"Yes, if only eating things solved my problems." Aetheria didn't mention the void core growing within her. She wasn't certain that's what it was yet, and she didn't want to dampen Arkaziel's acquisition. The StarMane's pride and ego didn't need another blow right now, since this remained her fault.

Friendship. Love. Gravitational forces of the mortal soul. A desperate act of consciousness made in a pitiful attempt to avoid the endless void just one day longer.

"Our friend experienced being jilted at some point. Do you think eldritch horrors mate for life?"

"Damn, Aetheria, why would you put the image of eldritch horrors mating in my head? All those tentacles and mouths, and eyes. Why? You know I mentally picture everything people say."

"I didn't actually know that about you. Foolish of you to reveal such a massive weakness. You are more out of sorts than I thought."

Arkaziel's only answer? A snore. The full kitty slumbered on her shoulder; magic bound him to remain on her shoulder. The Asura and the cat stepped through the silvery portal and emerged through the blackness of teleportation to a town engulfed in the flames of hell.

The smell of ambition and desire, chained by names and covenants. The infernal songs of demonkind have few notes and substitute volume for substance.

CHAPTER 64

Abzulur

It didn't take the ominous warnings of the eldritch voice for Aetheria and Arkaziel to put together the simple formula of hellfire + evil = demons. More than any other enemy, the duo had spent a decade fighting endless waves of demons early in the tower. Therefore, entering an active combat zone populated with demons felt nostalgic for the pair.

"I'll handle the flames." Aetheria spoke loud enough for her voice to carry to Werylin, who had already moved forward a good dozen meters to engage a ground-based demon in combat.

"Think you could pull off holy rain?" Arkaziel queried from her shoulder. His yellow feline eyes studied the deployment of demonic forces and the layout of their surroundings. Civilians filled the streets, some desperately trying to get to shelter, while others sought to escape the city itself.

"Only one way to find out." Aetheria lifted both of her hands into the air, and the sky darkened as she awoke the power of the Primordial Flame of Thalassa in the Astrum Nexus. Thick, overburdened clouds replaced the spartan cloud cover that had existed prior to her manipulation of the weather. Loud booms of thunder gave away the presence of cloud lightning occurring above their heads. She thought, perhaps, some of the cloud lightning would diminish the threat of flying demons. A divine golden cast spread across the clouds, and when rain fell from the packed clouds, each drop glimmered with a holy cast.

While Aetheria created rain, Arkaziel gestured subtly with his claws. Black tendrils shot out of shadows across the surrounding courtyard, and each black, oozing appendage blocked attacks from the ravaging demons on weak targets, but those who could defend themselves he left to do so. Additional appendages grew off the defensive ones, and like black spears stabbed into the weakest of the demons, at which point Arkaziel fed upon those he successfully hit. Cartoonishly, almost, the vital essence and matter of the weak imps and lesser demons got sucked through the tendrils of shadows back to their master.

"Drip, drip, drop." The skies wept, and a deluge of holy water clashed with infernal fire and demonic flesh. The gentle sound of rain could not compete with the much louder hiss of blessed holy water, which sizzled the flesh of demons and dampened the fires.

"Haste!" Werylin's magic fell upon the party and surrounding friendlies. The unprepared civilian movements turned spastic, their expressions shocked. The experience of time dilating slightly could be massively disorienting to those who had never experienced it, but they remained like statues compared to the graceful flow of the elven blade master, who wielded Harmonious Tempest in their defense.

A young boy stared at where a lesser demon had stood moments before. The jagged sword it had used remained as the only remnant of its existence.

"Hey, kiddo. Where did the demons first come from?" Aetheria had to repeat herself a few times before the young man looked at her or offered an answer. His gaze kept returning to the heavy sword that had nearly ended his life.

"Th-they came from the castle. Today was the blessing of the king's newest child in the royal cathedral of Ereshkigal. Something must have gone wrong!"

"Go find somewhere safe and hunker down, alright?"

"Yes, ma'am! If you go to the castle, my mom's name is Reba. She's one of the cooks . . ." The child didn't finish the request. He glimpsed something in Aetheria's eyes or aura, or perhaps in Arkaziel's, and fled.

"Werylin, you're on civvies duty. Ark, I want every demon in the town dead. I'll take care of the castle." Aetheria didn't wait for assent, she expected to be obeyed. Large black-and-red wings of ice emerged from her back, and she shot into the air toward the castle. Despite the holy rain, some flying demons remained in the air and swooped down to attack her, but chunks of rain re-formed into spears of ice and impaled any demon foolish enough to engage her.

The castle, like the town, showed off the local stone: a limestone of a distinctive green shade. Aetheria had never seen such a green, and she wondered what component would give it that color, whether organic or mineral deposits. The castle had four massive towers in the cardinal directions, and a fifth spire rising in the center of the colossal green stone construction. Given the high concentration of infernal power which radiated from the spire, and the visible black flames that engulfed it without burning it, Aetheria didn't have to ponder too long about where she should go.

The polite thing to do would be to go to the castle's front and announce her participation in the battle against the demons. Instead, Aetheria crashed through a few stories of stone before her boots found purchase on the main floor of the castle, and the warded entrance into the cathedral of Ereshkigal stood before her. Inky blackness spread through the air around her feet when she landed, and the stone bowed and warbled from her impact—the rock even jiggled like gelatin for a few seconds before it resumed acting more like stone.

A man in holy vestments, a small entourage of guards, and a twenty-something young woman with the finery of royalty stared at her in horror, eyes all going wide. The holy man made a series of gestures with his hands and muttered the name of Ereshkigal, which had no effect upon Aetheria at all. Aetheria let her black-and-red wings dissipate, and fixed the holy man and the, she assumed, princess or queen with a steady look.

"I'm the one who summoned the holy rain. I doubt your prayer will have much effect upon me. Why are there demons? How many do I need to kill, and how do I stop them?"

"Wha-wh-wh-y?" The man in the pointy hat stammered his words, apparently overcome by either the Void or the Ethereal.

"Bishop Ranqs means we are uncertain. A fiend trapped us in a time-lock spell after finishing the preparations for the ceremony, and when we escaped from the spell, the cathedral spire had already become locked down with my father and brother inside." Despite the strangeness of Aetheria's gaze, the young woman met her eyes with visible determination.

"Princess Rose, we don't know this woman, and her appearance is of deep concern."

Aetheria ground her teeth audibly, and then let out a controlled sigh.

"I am Aetheria, daughter of Aetherius and Nyx. I am known as the Etherfrost Asura, bearer of the Unutterable Flame of the Void, and I'm here to help." The old man deflated with each word of her introduction. The anger rising in her grew, a black storm of violence that threatened to be unleashed at any moment.

In the shadow of eternity, the transient flutter from the wings of a moth caught in webs of triviality that distracts from the backdrop of a supernova.

That doesn't make a lick of sense.

The red-and-blue haired woman shook her head, her burst of anger forgotten as quickly as it had surged, and Aetheria put her attention back to Princess Rose who was speaking, although she had missed the first few words.

". . . thus I believe it is in our best interest to trust the daughter of Aetherius with this matter, Bishop."

Unexpectedly, rather than argue, the bishop nodded and offered Aetheria a deep bow.

"Ereshkigal has spoken. The Etherfrost Asura shall enter the spire and save the kingdom."

"Excellent. Is there anything I need to know about what I'm walking into? Keep in mind, I'm a wandering Cultivator. I don't even know your kingdom's name."

"The Lady of the Dead has said you can make your own way inside the spire. Beyond that, we know not what particular demon is behind this, but no doubt it is a greater demon at the least."

"Servants of Nergal haunt the royal family. My grandfather refused Nergal's offer of patronage in favor of Ereshkigal, and for that slight we have suffered attacks by the vile spawn of Nergal for decades. It is likely to be a servant of Nergal within. Good luck, Lady Aetheria."

"Ugh. Nergal again? I'd recommend retreating into any protective sanctuaries you have. I can't promise there won't be some explosions." Her right hand lifted in a salute to Princess Rose, and Aetheria winked at the bishop before she walked right through the barrier that blockaded the entry into the cathedral spire. Careful release of a small field of the Void allowed her to disintegrate the barrier while she crossed it, but it re-formed behind her.

"Oh, someone figured out how to open the barrier? Hmm. It's shut again. Who are you, traveler? Stray into the upper spire at your peril: in minutes the king will be bled and his inheritor will declare a pact with Nergal. You are too late."

As much as Aetheria wanted to roll her eyes, she didn't bother. She focused her intent and summoned red and black clouds. Ethereal power comprised one, and the other pulsed with the Void. Despite their appearance, neither were actually clouds. They were, in fact, a mass of ice crystals imbued with her will and basic sapience. She gave only one simple command to the conjurations: *kill demons.*

The void cloud drifted toward one of the spiral staircases, while the Ethereal cloud drifted toward the side rooms on the first floor. Aetheria didn't remain to watch them. The afterimage that had stood there fell to pieces, while the real Aetheria ran up the stairs faster than the naked eye of an earthling could follow. She encountered a few minor demons on her way up the stairs, but a single punch with a hand that writhed with the power of the Void obliterated her enemies completely, and in less than three seconds Aetheria blasted through the five gloomily decorated levels of the spire to the royal shrine.

A five-armed, four-horned, six-eyed, three-legged demon with seven tails and two mouths stared at her. Only two of its eyes moved in a way that tracked her motion, but Aetheria wasn't certain whether those were the only two that could keep up with her Flash Mode. One of the demon's mouths chanted a spell, while its other mouth spouted an infernal curse, and two of the five arms threw fireballs at her. A tiny tendril of the Void rose from her hand, hair-thin and delicate. It touched the first fireball just before it impacted her, drifted through it and into the second, and both balls of fire dispersed into nothingness.

"So the king's savior knows a thing or two about the Void, does she? Block these!"

The demon definitely could see her full speed, to the point he even spoke, cast spells, and otherwise moved at the same ridiculous speed she did, and acted as if the world had time dilation around it. The other two beings in the room had not yet reacted to her presence—they still were in the process of turning their heads. The king hung upside down, dangling by his feet from an iron chain, naked as the day he was born with blood dripping from a series of shallow cuts down his unclothed body, then dribbling down to land on his youngest son.

The prince lay on a crudely fashioned altar that clearly didn't belong in a shrine of a powerful deity within a resplendent inner sanctum of a royal family. The human bones—the shrine's normal caretakers, guards, and clergy, no doubt—still had flesh that had not been cleansed off fully. The bones were joined by globules of demonic ichor, and just looking at that vile altar churned Aetheria's stomach.

The mouth that had chanted demonic rituals ceased its infernal utterings, lips quirked into a large smirk.

"You've arrived too late, hero."

The demon's aura crashed outward with so much force it threw Aetheria into the wall, unable to even defend herself properly from the immense unholy energies.

"Abzulur ascends! Nergal himself awakens in me to feast on your bones!"

"Uffda." Aetheria spit some black, gooey blood from her mouth. The dark ooze that flowed in her veins felt cold, numbing, and she could feel it sluggishly inch through her body. The taste in her mouth wasn't copper, but a rancid, congealed flavor and texture she could only describe as putrid and vile, to the point she barely noticed the darkness swallowing more of her vision.

Despair is a solitary waltz; let us unleash a tango of desolation.

CHAPTER 65

Tango of Terror

Who are you?

No answer came. Aetheria's world continued to shrink around her, with darkness stealing the periphery of her sight, and the unnatural cold even she wasn't immune to filled her veins. *Thump. Thump. Thump. Thump-Thud. Thump-Thud.* Her Cultivator core beat Ethereal power through her body in waves, until a new sound entered the mix. A second sound, that rang in counterrhythm to the first.

Darkness welled in her mind, unbearable cold scorched her supremely numb body, and the silence of the Eternal Darkness filled her ears to bursting—the maddening quiet wracked her mind with a deluge of unspeakable pain. Her flesh ripping broke the silence. Instead of rippling and shifting, what happened to her went more like molting, as her hands ripped her skin off. She carelessly threw her molted hide into a corner and flexed her six arms, all six hands flexing in rapturous freedom.

"A shapeshifter, eh? Incorporating the Void won't save you from the power of Abzulur!"

Drip.

A drop of the king's blood fell from his bloodied hair, into the open mouth of the princeling. Power coursed through the child and the profane bone altar, and then transferred to the demon, who luxuriated and basked in the waves of energy.

Amidst the all-consuming darkness, Abzulur flashed before Aetheria to deliver a blow to her face. One of its five arms exploded in a shower of gore from fist to elbow, all of which tendrils of darkness reached out from her hair and pulled into her mouth. Even the frozen blood it fountained into the air got captured by the obsidian strands; not a scrap could escape her. Aetheria shrieked inside of her mind at the vile taste of demonic flesh, but the real horror was the warmth and joy that spread through her frozen body when she consumed the demon.

"That was my favorite arm! No matter."

Abzulur looked at the king. Another cut opened across the old man's wrinkled skin, and more blood dripped into his son's mouth.

If I just free the king, I could kill the demon easily.

With the new wave of power, the destroyed arm of the demon healed in a flash, and it surged into the fifth tier, well above Aetheria. Her body refused to follow her instructions at the moment, though, no matter how she willed or struggled.

"Let's see you take *this*!"

Abzulur flashed again, and delivered a powerful kick. When his foot hit the black body it made brief contact, before the same thing happened as before. An explosion wave of gore exploded outward from Aetheria, the demon's leg rent into thousands of pieces of bone, sinew, and frozen flesh that nearly invisible tendrils of shadow pulled into her maw, and she felt heavenly as the warmth spread through her enough to actually feel one of her hands.

"Impossi—!"

One of the six black, glistening crystalline taloned hands grasped the demon by the throat. Aetheria meant to lift the demon off the ground, but when her hands tightened she popped the thing's head off. It'd be a shame to waste a head, right? More tendrils pulled the severed head into her maw, and yet more warmth spread through her body. Another hand awoke.

Drip. Drip. Drip.

The demon's head regrew. Its arrogance flagged, despite the fact it approached the edge of fifth tier, and one more drop would catapult it into the sixth tier.

"What in the abyss are you?"

"Beyond the veil of your childish comprehension, in the nexus of all chaos, lies the Throne of Chaos, upon which all that is, was, will be, or never shall be, revolves."

The light in Abzulur's eyes diminished with each word spoken by Aetheria's parched throat. Each syllable saw her lips crack and leak a black tarlike ooze, while with the last word she coughed an inordinate amount of drool, before four of her arms shot forward and proceeded to pull Abzulur into her maw forcefully. The crunch of his bones, the flow of marrow, and the infernal blood and offal flooded her senses with experiences Aetheria never wanted to repeat.

Drip. Drip.

More blood fell, and the profane power flowed into the demon being digested, and in turn, into Aetheria's blasphemous body. Her eyes refused to focus upon the dangling body of the king, and she couldn't bring up a mental image of how he'd been hanging.

Ethereal Sight . . .

The mental effort it took her to sense the world around her staggered Aetheria. A simple act she normally did with barely a thought, instead took the effort of running a 5K up a mountain, wearing a backpack full of weights, dragging a tire behind her like a Shonen protagonist. Knowledge flickered into her mind.

Drip.

More power flared through her; the world dimmed more.

Without more time, one of her blackened crystal talons expended a blast of golden Ethereal energy, and holy light filled the shrine, healing the prince and king, but most importantly, it shattered the mystical bindings that held the king aloft. The healed man fell upon his son in a pile, and the two groaned and moaned. Aetheria could not quite make out anything intelligible, as she sought to master herself.

Thump-thud. Thump-thud.

Two Cultivator cores competed within her chest. The one she had made currently dominated, and the effects of the Void receded as the harmonious power of the Ethereal filled her to bursting. Yet for every beat of her autopotency core, there was the counterbeat of the void that weakened the strength it provided. Already, the void core had grown to a quarter of the size of her Ethereal core. What would happen if it reached maturity before she had a plan in place to balance the powers? *Libby better hurry the hell up.*

The periphery of her vision unclouded, and she forced herself to become Aetheria once more. Black crystal gave way to pale flesh. It took a second or two, even with her Flash Mode activated, to get the black veins to disperse. She had the terrible feeling one of these times they just wouldn't go away, but that time hadn't arrived yet. Once she was presentable as herself again only thirty seconds or so had passed, but still, you'd think royalty wouldn't be keen on waiting even that long when naked and forced to suffer what the demon put them through. The king and prince lay unmoving, eyes vacant. The king hadn't moved from where he fell, and the prince hadn't moved at all, just stared at the ceiling with unthinking eyes.

"Hello?"

Neither of the two answered her; they lay where they had fallen. Their chests moved, and she could hear and see them breathing, but neither showed any spark of intelligence.

"For Pete's sake."

Did I do that, or did the demon?

Aetheria narrowed her eyes at the two, then at the chamber. The runic blanket still covered the altar of Ereshkigal, so she froze and shattered it. A deep presence surrounded Aetheria and the royals.

"Two cups, each a quarter full. If we fill one to half, that one we could heal," the voice of the Goddess of the Underworld whispered from the pristine, beautiful altar.

"Seems like a bad deal since this happened because they remained loyal to you. I don't think that's an acceptable answer at all."

Shadows became the loose form of a female humanoid, a minor apparition that barely exuded any divine presence. Despite this, Ereshkigal looked at her in offense at the lack of manners being given to her. The lack of substance to the apparition made it exceptionally easy to lock eyes with the shadowy thing, and it was Ereshkigal who looked away first.

"Bad deal or not, it is all that I can do."

"And if I help?"

"Help? Your presence did this to them. You cannot unleash the Void Incarnate in the presence of mortals and expect any semblance of sanity to remain. Even with divine healing, only so much may be done. The Void has slithered into their minds, broken their feeble brains with glimpses of the vastness of infinity, and no healing can properly undo that."

A dark anger flared in Aetheria's stomach, and with a snarl she swiped a hand through the apparition of Ereshkigal and devoured the manifestation in an instant, then focused upon the insensate royalty who lay on the profane altar. With a crooked motion of one finger she shattered the altar to a million pieces, then considered her options.

"Now, how do I fix you two." Aetheria mulled the problem, before settling a hand over the mouth of each of the men. Tendrils of the Void and the Ethereal expanded from palm into their mouths, and then into their body and souls. For some reason the vision of two broken mirrors filled her mind. With dedicated searching she found the shattered fragments of the mirrors within the men. With a delicacy that frustrated her, she positioned the pieces of the mirrors back together. She dared not restore them with the power of the Void, so she used Ethereal power as the glue to weld the grand mirror in the king's mind back together.

Even when the mirror had been repaired, darkness and the abyss stared out from within it. Rather than try to counter the eldritch taint with the Ethereal, Aetheria opted to use the Void to devour the eldritch imprinting, and emitted an Aether heavy breath of aqua-gold that left her lips as a glittering cloud and entered the king's mouth, to suffuse and repair the damage that had been done. The grand mirror now reflected the green castle. Almost immediately his eyelids flickered. *He'll wake up momentarily. Now the boy.*

The process went much quicker with the prince. His oval mirror with heavy ornate goldwork was half the size of the king's, and the pieces hadn't been spread nearly as far as the king's for some reason. Still, the reassembly, gluing, and banishment of the eldritch influence took her a good five minutes of deep concentration. When she went to breathe out the cloud of Aether she noticed something seemed to make the process more difficult, but she didn't open her eyes to regard the room until she had finished.

A single guardsman stood before her, panting, sweating, arms shaking from all of the man's strength going into the spear in his hands. A spear that, barely, pierced her throat.

"Die, die, die! If I kill you, Abzulur can yet fulfill our pact!" The guard's blood-shot eyes and the infernal red and black mark on his aura, told Aetheria all she needed to know. Her left hand grasped the haft of the spear, pulled it out of her throat, and casually threw the still-struggling guard toward the group that had just reached the top story. Princess Rose looked horrified at the scene before her, while Bishop Ranqs gagged and vomited on his and the princess's shoes.

"You might want to bind that man. He had a pact with the demon. Abzulur was its name."

"Are . . . are . . . they ok?" Princess Rose's sobbing confused Aetheria, until she recalled the two were naked, covered in blood, and lying in the remains of the shattered profane altar

"They will be."

"The Lady Ereshkigal congratulates you on exceeding expectations, Lady Asura. For your ability to not only rescue, but resuscitate our king and prince, she wishes to bestow upon you this vial." Before Aetheria appeared a simple glass tube with a stopper at the top. To the naked eye, it held only water. To her Ethereal Sight, the water glittered with the power of a fifth-tier artifact.

"A divine gift from Nammu." Bishop Ranqs spoke with the authority of a bishop, but he had forgotten to wipe his face, and it rather ruined the impressive scene he tried to create.

"Thanks." Aetheria snatched the vial, and teleported back to the courtyard to find her friends.

CHAPTER 66

Crystal Coffin

As so often was the case, Aetheria hadn't even learned the name of the country, king, or town while they had cleared the eighty-fifth floor. Getting attached to the floors made it harder to move on, and the whole point was to move on. Detachment helped with that, but more than anything, she felt the drive to finish the Tower of Aetherius and, hopefully, rank up to Tier Five soon. To have the Soul Witch, Aoibhe, at her side once more was Aetheria's most fervent desire.

The eighty-sixth floor reminded Aetheria of Aoibhe. They had appeared in a city of crystal towers, glass buildings, and beautiful transparent artwork that filled the public places. Aetheria had plenty of time to stare at the city below her, since she had appeared inside of a clear quartz coffin, bound by a strange cloth wrap that made it difficult to move her body, and somehow it negated her transformative abilities, strength, and energy manipulation. The jerk Administrators had trapped her, and simple tricks like pulling the binding material into her repository didn't work.

"Assholes," Aetheria hissed, and she slowly squirmed and thrashed against her bindings to get the coffin to rotate and change her view. Her transparent coffin appeared to be hanging from the arm of an enormous statue of Themis. *Justice if I fall, or if I get free? Or was it just the first tall thing the Administrator saw?*

The city beneath her seemed to be in the middle of an apocalypse. Every few blocks, a portal to another dimension opened, and various and sundry monsters flowed out in an unending tide. Two viewscreens appeared before her on the inside of the coffin. The first screen showed Arkaziel, the size of a puma, mauling a grasshopper monster, as his three duplicates worked to herd the monsters to Arkaziel and away from a group of multispecies noncombatants. Ratkin, weaselkin, even a few birdkin trembled in fear as the cat and his clones fought monsters with relative ease.

On the second screen, Werylin appeared, a blade-wielding dancer who glided through the streets, leaving behind dismembered monsters and creating pockets of safety for a group of gnomes to reach shelter. The elf always cut a dashing figure, but with the Sylvan hakama, the dual wielded katanas, and his violet hair, he nearly reached swashbuckler levels of charisma. The cascading lightning surrounding

Harmonious Tempest matched the multihued rainbow blade, Stormshimmer, in a way that surprised Aetheria. She had tried to give Stormshimmer a complementary appearance to Harmonious Tempest, and watching him mow down monsters with them, she felt she had succeeded.

"What kind of bullshit is this? I get stuck while they get to fight? Oh. This had better not be a damsel in distress level." Aetheria's teeth ground as she struggled against the strange restraints once more, but she could not make a single inch of progress.

To chain the boundless is a testament to their delusions. Krill can no more bind the ocean than they can hinder the endless expanse of our existence.

"You've got that right, pal. I'm going to bust an Administrator's head open if they think they can use me as a prop."

Righteous anger did not allow Aetheria to overpower the binding chains. Nor could she materialize enough power to allow her an exit. The voice that spoke into her mind, though? That told her the Void hadn't left her; she just couldn't access it the way she normally would. Within her soulscape she examined the indomitable Black Flame. It occupied space an order of magnitude larger than even the Transcendant Flames. All of the old Flames it had eaten wouldn't even take up half the space of this single towering inferno of black crystal fire.

"You work for me. Don't just sit there." Aetheria rapped one of her mental projection's knuckles against the Black Flame, and black flames engulfed her hand inside the coffin, but they extinguished before she could do anything with them.

On the screens, the boys continued to hold their own against the monsters easily, but Arkaziel's ferocity steadily climbed. Even the foresight of putting the shadow clones on civilian duty wouldn't protect them for long, as his blows grew in strength and collateral damage. With each kill, the darkness grew around him, and through the screen, Aetheria imagined she could hear the chittering of maddening whispers grow ever thicker around her companion. Werylin had no such obstacles, being unafflicted by the Void, but he also lacked the staying power of his party members. He still struggled to fully restore himself with Aether, the way Arkaziel or Aetheria did.

It felt gratifying to see the real extent of Arkaziel's growth since he'd hatched, but watching the ever-quickening descent into the clutches of the Void made her realize she really needed to help him, and herself, too. Part of her felt confident she could handle the Void until she could find a resolution, but maybe that was just the same stubborn denial that kept Arkaziel pushing on solitarily? Here in the crystal coffin, Aetheria heard only the one being's whisper. All the lesser ones had fallen away. Perhaps the coffin could offer her some clue to controlling the Void? Yet to all of her still functional senses, the crystal seemed entirely mundane. Only the strange bindings around her seemed to possess any otherworldly effects.

Inside Aetheria's soul-space, she did something she had never tried with any of her old Flames. She had her projection step inside the Black Flame. Unutterable cold filled her body. Her core missed a few beats of its processing, but the nascent void organ pumped extra hard, and a million needles of absolute zero pushed through her entire body. The pain of cold filled her existence until she transcended the torment. On the other side, nothing. Absolute Void, absolute cold, suffused her mind and senses. Here, there was no physical reality, no suns to cast light or warmth, no heavenly bodies to create gravity. This cold transcended ice, frost, and winter. It went beyond stinging, burning; instead it nullified. It flaked thin layers of *something* from her, and were she not who she was, Aetheria felt certain it would have unraveled her existence right there.

Physical sensation faded. Skin, bones, thoughts, all blurred into a concept that untethered from Aetheria and retreated to her physical body, and something else remained in the Void, shackled by nothing at all. Distantly, oh so distantly, the dual *thump-thud* of her cores teased her ears, lonely drums in a vast universe bereft of sound. Her breath, paradoxically there and not, created a wind from nothing, a passage of movement and *things* in nothing. A fell wind in this dark place, created by her. A first? Unlikely.

Aetheria realized in the moment, this was the freedom from the Samsara that the Primordials have given her. The Void, eternal, infinite and unfathomable, immortal. She had become a vessel for the ineffable, a conduit for that which the human mind could never comprehend. Everything that mattered in physical reality had no bearing here. Time, space, self, they were so unimportant as to be not even worth thinking of. Another thought, though, filled her with giddy excitement. Her pulse quickened, and she inhaled the Void.

To consume the absence itself is no satiation, but an expansion into endlessness. To become unbounded and indefinable, you reverse the flow of existence, and lap up the nectar of the cosmic enigma. Dance with the intangible; commune with negation.

The Void friend sounded amused by the way events played out, encouraging even, as Aetheria inhaled the Void. She didn't stop inhaling. Why would she? In the back of her mind, a picture of a cute pink creature formed, devouring all of existence into its vacuum-like maw. She stepped up her game to match, and alterations ran within her physical body, so far away.

The Black Flame crystalized fully and birthed something deep inside the crystal. A small fraction of the Void, the Eternal Dark, the Infinite Abyss, manifested itself within Aetheria's soul. Pain shot through her physical body, but it remained far away and of no concern to her. She devoured more of the Void, for the Black Flame bordered upon reaching the fourth tier. Why did that matter? She didn't know, but what else did she have to do in this place beyond time?

Chimes played into Aetheria's ear; distant music so heavenly that she felt tears flow down her far-away body. How could she have never heard music so transcendent before? If heaven and hell made peace, it would never sound so sweet, or offer such an astounding epiphany.

"Cease." Aetheria's lips croaked out the words from a parched throat in the coffin. The strange bindings that had restrained her powers before simply drifted into stray particles, pulled back to the true origin and eventual end of all things: nonexistence. The disappearance of the bindings revealed the pathetic state of her physical form, and the shock pulled her out of the Void and back to physicality.

The pain, present now, seemed unlikely to have ever ended. The coffin had filled with her blood and viscera; her left arm had fully disintegrated, and most of the exterior layers of muscle and skin had similarly flaked away. With her mind back in charge, though, and her powers uninhibited, entire limbs regrew in less than a second, and the outside layer of her meat sack returned. *Epidermis. Not meat sack.*

Aetheria's thoughts awoke from their slumber much slower than her body, despite the instantaneous healing it underwent. She could not ignore the mental shock of the Void, even with the strange abomination of Outer God, Transcendent God, Overgod, Primordial, and human essences they'd injected her soul full of.

The constant pain erupting in Aetheria's chest didn't help. Her void organ had grown with the Black Flame, and her Cultivator's core remained only slightly larger, although she felt it had not reached its full size yet. The two objects were antithetical to one another, and stray ripples of something she didn't understand occasionally shot from the area of her chest like bolts of lightning, rupturing her insides and releasing fountains of blood.

"So much for having time." Laughter sent a spray of blood from her chest, but the blood was pulled back into her body by tendrils of power before her body healed over the rupture. With her regeneration fully operational the pain of the strange ruptures would be the real problem.

A single kick shattered the coffin, and large black wings caught the air for her to fly.

~Arkaziel, buddy, you okay?~

The lack of an immediate answer, mixed with the torrent of what Aetheria could only describe as madness filled the empathic bond the two shared. Her companion had lost control, the whispers of the Void had driven him beyond the realm of the rational. The bond allowed her to find him quickly, though, although Werylin had beat her there.

The elf had both blades drawn, and stood battered and bloodied before the civilians Arkaziel had been defending earlier. No sign of the twilight clones remained.

Aetheria dropped to the ground next to Werylin, and tossed an orb of Aetherial power his way to heal and restore the elf.

"Wha—" Werylin shook his head, then caught on. "Haste!"

Bolstering energies filled Aetheria and Werylin, although it felt marginal at best, unlike in the past when Werylin cast Haste on her. Had her base capabilities grown so much that she barely benefited anymore? Oh. She already had Flash Mode active. When had she activated it?

"What's the plan?" the elf asked, but before Aetheria could answer him, Arkaziel's rhino-sized form grew, and grew, while he hissed and roared loudly enough to topple a building. Still the dragon-cat grew, until he easily stretched one hundred meters from nose to tail. Sharp spikes covered his dark scales, and the Void reached out of every shadow near him emitting small swarms of insects.

"Hey! Bad kitty!" A tidal wave of water appeared from nowhere, striking Arkaziel like the famed Pe'ahi of Maui. It pissed the dragon off more than it did any damage, and black-and-yellow eyes focused entirely on Aetheria.

CHAPTER 67

Aetheria vs. Arkaziel

If Aetheria played by normal rules, she would either need to fight Arkaziel as a kaiju-sized version of herself, take on her Ethereal dragon form, or some other tit-for-tat response. Instead, she used a trick Arkaziel had used on her quite a few floors ago. First, Aetheria teleported high into the sky, and then she summoned Arkaziel into the sky with her. The transported StarMane instantly took to flight and dove straight for her, filled to bursting with murderous intent.

Well, I removed him from harming others. Now what? I can't murder him.

Dozens of tendrils of oozing darkness formed and shot ahead of Arkaziel's dive, but Aetheria avoided them simply by once more teleporting, the attacks landing on an ice replica she left behind. It distracted Arkaziel for less than a second, but that proved to be long enough for Aetheria to charge up a massive burst of Ethereal power set in counterrhythm not to the Void that filled Arkaziel, but to the Ethereal energy inside of Arkaziel. To her Ethereal Sight, Arkaziel's void energies were subsuming the cat's twilight energies at a steady pace. It would be ideal if she could slow down the conversion until she had a proper plan to handle the void affliction.

The flare of power blasted through Arkaziel from above, and though it caused no physical damage to Arkaziel, it elicited a maddening roar, and even Aetheria couldn't dodge all the tendrils and tentacles of darkness and flesh that lashed at her instinctually. *Well, that didn't work.*

A moment later, the Void had reasserted dominance and continued its consumption and conversion of Arkaziel's energies. If it converted the cat's core, they'd be stuck with void Arkaziel, which from what she could tell, was a distinct downgrade because of the homicidal instincts. Disruption didn't work; she couldn't reach him via their rapport currently, so that left what? *I need help.*

Fleeting, transient, the union of ephemeral wills can make even gnats into juggernauts.

"What would he know about union? He's never talked to anyone but Nyarlathotep and you."

The dark whispers of the Void and the refreshing words of the Origin echoed through Aetheria's mind, even as she blocked attack after attack with ice, teleportation, and waves of Ethereal power, plus the occasional wave of water just to keep Arkaziel riled and angry, which maybe she didn't need to do?

"Oh, so you two show up *now?* Just what cost are you going to want to help restore Arkaziel?" A fight between two shapeshifters of incredible strength and speed, who could instantly heal, and had nearly unlimited energy reserves could only find a climax by shutting down the other's power sources first. Yet both were bound to the same power sources: the Origin and the Void. Even as regressed as Arkaziel seemed to have become, the void dragon-cat seemed to remember this, and tried to devour Aetheria. Time after time he snapped jaws at her, generated entirely new mouths to eat her, and shadow after shadow jumped at her to devour her in the darkness.

Your vessel intrigues us. We shall possess it and unleash the song of cosmic silence.

"Give me a name, and I'll help you and your friend out."

The difference in costs seemed dramatically uneven. The eldritch being wanted to get her body and, if she understood what it wanted, destroy the universe. What else would the sound of cosmic silence be? *It could be a lot of things, but I don't have a lot of time. Names have power, but how could something more powerful than me gain by being named by me?*

Aetheria could let Arkaziel eat her, but that seemed like a bad way to do things. Instead, she increased her size and mass to match that of Arkaziel's. Where Arkaziel looked more like a void version of Nidhogg, Aetheria shimmered into the form of a massive Etherfrost Dragon with aqua scales the color of Aetheria's hair. Yet in the depths of those icy scales one could see unfathomable darkness lurking. The Void had touched even Aetheria's draconic aspect. The battle between the two dragons ratcheted up another level. With such massive bodies, hundreds of tentacles of darkness and void spawned from Arkaziel to attack Aetheria, who took the opportunity to clamp her jaws around his throat.

Rather than fight free, Arkaziel embraced her and a flurry of claws from each dragon swiped at the other, while flows of energy emerged from each body to attack the other in what should have been a surprise attack, but both of the combatants had Ethereal Sight which stopped the surprise aspect of the attacks. Aetheria used almost imperceptible flows of power through their bond, now that they had physical contact, to try to reach Arkaziel's soul.

You would come together to defy the Void, that is proper, for the Void is a union of all that is absent and unknowable. In the end, it always wins. Whisper my name, acknowledge the Lord of All, the Blind Dreamer, and our pact will form.

"We both know that's a terrible idea. You can't save anyone by condemning them to the rising of the Nuclear Chaos. I'll help you without a name, but you'll have to provide ingress into the soul of the apocalypse dragon."

"I'm working on that." Aetheria didn't speak the words, her jaws were still filled with Arkaziel's neck. Yet physical speaking didn't seem to be necessary for either of the two entities spying on her to hear her. Even just thinking it spoken in her inner world seemed to carry the words to the far-off beings. The question of whether she had any privacy even in her thoughts was short-lived, given the circumstances, but she would find out how much these entities knew later.

Aetheria never breached Arkaziel's thick scales. Instead she wove strands of power between his scales, and relied on the elusive, ineffable qualities of Ethereal power to thread strands all the way into his body. While she couldn't quite nail down his thoughts in their bond, she still could use it to locate his core, and enmesh it with strand after strand. She allowed Arkaziel to rip off one of her wings, and cause significant damage to one of her flanks, to cover the secretive movement. It hurt terribly, but it let her accomplish the first step to restoring Arkaziel.

"Now what, Reverie?"

Every instinct told her that this should be the right choice. Yet when she whispered the name she had chosen for the strange entity in the Origin, she felt weakness shake through her body. Every scrap of Aether, Nether, the Ethereal, and even the Void sapped from her into a new linkage in her soul. Her cores sucked desperately for more power, and it came out of the black hole to the Void and the link to the Origin in a flood. Being emptied shocked Aetheria, before the almost pleasurable sensations of unbridled energy supplying her replaced it. The floodgates of her soul aperture remained wide open and torrents of power flooded her soul and flesh both.

Arkaziel attacked viciously in the moments she had been without energy. The terrifying apocalypse dragon grew another head to bite and chomp through her thick icy scales, which temporarily lacked the constant reinforcement of energy that enhanced her defenses. In three vicious bites Arkaziel broke through her scales, and almost managed to devour her core before power flooded her body once more. A massive burst of frozen blood obliterated the temporary head of Arkaziel, and bought a moment for her flesh to mend.

"Cripes, what was that? Ark nearly ate my core while you took my power."

"The price to name me. Now, let me help your friend. These are the tenets of Twilight, inscribe them into his being in Ath, so that he will be buoyed against the Void."

"Could've warned me. Alright, let's go."

"Wholeness over Extremes: To walk the Path of Twilight is to seek the middle ground, understanding that while both extremes hold some truths, they are in fact just half-truths of the greater whole."

Aetheria formed the glyphs as Reverie uttered them. Each glyph somehow glowed with power imbued from Reverie through their new linkage. When she finished the last word, the glyphs merged into a solitary glyph of too many dimensions for Aetheria to identify, and filled with Ethereal power more intense than she had ever condensed before.

"Now, remind the cat he's your friend, and be ready to inscribe the next sigil."

The strange glyph flew from Aetheria's inner world, through the webs she'd woven, and into Arkaziel's beast core—and it took Aetheria with it.

Within an imaginary space somewhere in Arkaziel's soul, the black cat, a white cat, and Aetheria stared at one another at a three-person table. Each didn't quite meet the eyes of the other two.

"Hi," Aetheria said lamely.

"I wondered when you'd show up, Blue."

"She's here to finish me, isn't she?" the white cat asked distrustfully.

"Doubtful. She'd try to save you if I tried to smother you, if anything," Arkaziel assured his clutch mate.

"I'm here to wake you up. You let the Void take the driver's seat," Aetheria clarified, then gave the two cats a questioning look as to the identity of the white furred cat.

"This is Daris. He's the StarMane I ate to keep his essence from the dumb insects," Arkaziel offered.

"I guess I thought when you said you reached peace with him, you'd subsumed him." Aetheria's look at Arkaziel was dubious, and more than a little accusatory.

"Oh, he's tried multiple times. I'm the Light aspect to his Dark. Like any good phoenix, I just rise again." Daris shook his head.

"So, about the Void?"

Both cats grimaced at her.

"Transcendental Unity: Dawn and Dusk hold unique power and mystery, showcasing the beauty and strength found between extremes."

Aetheria's fingers flared with wisps of power as she inscribed the words into another strange masterpiece of calligraphy that collapsed into dozens of dimensions and formed a single sigil that defied being observed by them.

"What in the Infinite Abyss was that?" Arkaziel demanded as the sigil shot off into the distance, causing the entire sky of this part of his soul to convulse and shudder. A new color dominated the world with each heave and convulsion.

"I needed a hand to restore you, and that's the hand, Reverie. I haven't really figured out what he is yet, beyond an upper dimensional something. God? Watcher? Observer? Janitor? We're reinforcing the tenets of your Twilight Path to keep the Void in check."

Daris let out a long sigh.

"It's time then, brother. I won't be coming back this time, but that's okay. You've got a good bondmate."

"Kind of dumb, though, you know, humans. She's making deals with beings she doesn't even grasp in the slightest." The black and white cats bumped their paws, and flowed into a singular cat of mixed fur color.

"Cycle of Renewal: As day turns to night, and vice versa, everything is cyclical. Embrace the ever-changing cycle and transform with it."

Again, Aetheria created the calligraphic structure that fell into itself, and then existed within more dimensions than Aetheria could perceive at once. It, too, shot off into the sky, accompanied by more tremors and changes to the sky.

"I can feel my body again. We're almost there, Ria." Arkaziel's body flowed through the series of forms he typically wore, house cat, puma, dragon, a nervous tick that he had displayed only rarely.

"We've got this, Ark. You're the protagonist, after all, you can't become a mindless void dragon."

"Shadowed Heart, Illuminated Mind: Maintain emotional calm and clarity of thought. Let your mind be as clear as the light of day, and your emotions as shadows—present, but not overwhelming."

When Aetheria created the final symbol, it fell into itself, then out of itself, before it exploded into a million shapes that defied perception or logic, and explosive waves carried her out of Arkaziel's soul, back into physical reality.

CHAPTER 68

I'm Washing My Hair That Night

Two massive dragons disengaged from the physical thrashing they had been giving one another, and then pulses of energy blinded the world, to reveal a small black house cat, with a few new spots of white on his fur, and the humanoid-but-winged form of Aetheria opposite him.

"Are you back to yourself now, Ark?" Aetheria maintained a degree of wariness. She had been expelled violently from his core, so she couldn't be certain what had happened after that, but that he turned into a cat again had to be a good sign, right?

"I'm feeling mostly better. The Void is still here, but it's being restrained now. All those tenets you produced, what were they actually?"

"That's a great question. Reverie? Reverie?" Aetheria got left hanging by the strange entity. "They seemed to be tenets to maintain a balance, so it must be applicable even with the Void somehow."

Arkaziel harrumphed.

"I love having things I don't know anything about inscribed into my soul while I'm essentially unconscious." A brittle note entered Arkaziel's voice, an extremely rare emotion for the cat: doubt. The narcissistic StarMane usually operated with full confidence, but the unknown could shake even him.

"Well, I wasn't going to let you devolve, so we just keep on walking forward. If it becomes a problem, we deal with it, and if it isn't a problem, well then it doesn't matter, right? I've got your back, Ark." In a flash of movement even Arkaziel had trouble following, Aetheria appeared behind him, picked him up, and rubbed his head.

"Can I eat your hands? They smell really good."

"No, no you can't eat my hands. I thought we were done with having discussions about you trying to eat me."

"That was before you unlocked the full access to your core. Oh, there it is." The cat laughed, and Aetheria felt her own internal energies dip, so fractional she wouldn't have noticed it if not for Arkaziel's weird comment.

Aetheria narrowed her eyes, and while her ability to fully access her core remained the same as earlier, it felt like someone had hooked up an inner tube behind her boat.

"You've been using my core, haven't you? How?"

"Well, duh. How else would I keep pace with you? I haven't bothered with the main function of your core, I'm already amazing, but Flash Mode is very useful. You should use it all the time. Once you get used to the time dilation of superspeed it's beyond useful. If you practiced it, you wouldn't need to rely on brute force so much."

Aetheria tossed Arkaziel out of her grip, and a ten-meter-wide deluge splashed from nowhere to soak the cat. Arkaziel flew out of the still-falling water and gave Aetheria as big a scowl as he could muster, before he shook himself and water flew everywhere. Everywhere but at Aetheria, as any water that came near the Asura froze and fell before it could approach her.

"Uncalled for! First you work strange magics on me, and then you give me a bath without warning. In StarMane society that's a capital offense, you know."

Aetheria rolled her eyes at the cat and descended to find Werylin. The elf had not gone far from where she had seen him last. He moved amongst the corpses of monsters.

"Any good crafting materials?"

"Not a one. It would be best if we leave the remains for the locals. Back to yourself again, Arkaziel?"

"That's fine with me." Aetheria agreed with Werylin. She had killed hardly any monsters so it wasn't her place to get involved.

"For the most part. Who knows what mysterious things our reckless Asura inscribed on my soul that shall come back to haunt us all in the future. What happened after I lost control down here?"

"I finished the waves of monsters while you two took a sky-nap. The portal is over there, in case you missed it. I got a shiny new charm for completing the mission." Werylin shook the hilt of Stormshimmer, which jangled the new charm affixed to it.

"Providence." Aetheria translated the Ath inscribed symbol. When she tried to analyze the item with Vulcan's boon, she realized it had been consumed by the Void along with the other Flames. *How did I not notice that until now? It might be time to take stock of myself.*

"Well, if that's everythin—" Arkaziel got cut off when one of the surges of power within Aetheria exploded a third of her chest, and left slowly fading wounds in the air itself. She managed to catch her own bits with tendrils of power and pull it all back into herself, but the wounds healed slower than those she endured when fighting Arkaziel.

"Damn." The two men stared at Aetheria, while she grimaced and rubbed at the spot that had first erupted, near where her heart had once been.

"Oh, yeah. Don't mind that. Just something I'm living with until I can work out a balance between the Void and the Origin." Aetheria tried to play down the gory scene.

"Are you having reactions like that inside your inner realm?"

"No," Aetheria answered gloomily, and then frowned. *Why am I not having reactions like that? The Gates to the Void and the Origin aren't reacting against each other at all, so why are my core and void organ conflicting? Concentration? Intensity?*

"Well, I'm glad I don't have that to look forward to" Arkaziel said. "You should be careful with that, Ria. I'm pretty sure if you catch anyone else in one of those they'd be erased from existence."

"I agree with Arkaziel, actually. For the split second those black lines existed before the release, it felt like I was staring at nonexistence, and if it touched me I'd be gone. Gone, gone. No rebirth, no new cycle of reincarnation. It was terrifying."

"Guys, I get it, it's scary. I'm the one who has it ripping me apart from the inside, so believe me, I want to fix it, and I'm doing the best I can, alright? Let's hit the next level." Aetheria stalked to the portal and stepped through to Floor 87.

Floor 87 started with Aetheria in a fine study, a delicate porcelain teacup on the table before her, and a woman dressed like a nun across from her.

"They say you possess the skills to brew an elixir that can awaken Sister Envy, Lady Asura. The curse upon her ensures only a draught crafted by an alchemist deep on the path of the Ethereal can awaken our sister."

Not at all a jarring transfer. Looks like we all got split up again.

"I will do the best that I can, certainly. And the reward for awakening Sister Envy still stands?" Aetheria threw out there, curious how it would play out.

"Oh yes, if one awakens Sister Envy, Queen Juno has offered the Diadem of Unity, a relic that encourages harmony, helps find a path through literal and metaphorical darkness, and bolsters bonds between enemies."

"How convenient." Aetheria couldn't keep the sharpness from her tone. "Very well, I'll need a fully equipped apothecary and alchemical tools; can you arrange that?" While Aetheria could simply use the alchemy labs in Pax Azura, she'd rather use other people's reagents, and maybe gain some new ingredients and tools as a bonus.

"Of course. This way, Lady Asura."

The five-minute journey through a temple, out the back, and two minutes of walking to a shack at the back of the property, cleverly hidden by landscaping, left Aetheria biting her lip. Another explosion was building within her chest, and she tried to suppress it through sheer willpower. Aetheria didn't even recall what she had said to the woman to get her to leave, but the explosion that erupted from her chest made the last one look tiny. Her body reassembling itself felt particularly odd, but each time it took her regeneration just that much more effort to pull herself together. Would she hit a point where her restoration wouldn't be nearly instant and start being a real issue?

Query: How do you balance order and chaos?

Response: Many aiding strategies to balancing Order and Chaos are lessons you have already learned, as demonstrated by your mastery of Frostfire. Therefore, the balancing of powers has been demonstrated as within your capabilities. Since your approach to order appears to based upon the Ethereal, and your force of chaos is the Void, the problem is the unique nature of these penultimate energy forms.

Ethereal nature indicates harmony, a greater whole made of all the component types of mana, Aether, and Nether, to form one glorious whole. Ethereal power is chaos formed to purpose by order.

Similarly, the Void does not represent chaos. The Void is the absence of reality, beyond time and space, in the realm of the unimaginable. The Void could be considered a facet of order in some definitions.

Therefore, your method of duality should focus upon Void as the component of Order, and the Ethereal as the formation of Chaos.

Query: Does this help you?

Alone in a workshop, Aetheria groaned while her body finished sealing ruptures in her flesh. The pain grew worse each time, and delaying the explosive force of the warring cores only seemed to make matters much worse.

"Not a lot, no. You're telling me that a bunch of insects, fish, and otherwise aquatic-looking abominations represent Order in the universe?"

Response: No, we did not conclude that. The Void, the Abyss, the power that the Outer Gods use is ultimately one of Order, regardless of your associative judgments on the Outer Gods. The Void is nothing, and nothing is the pinnacle of order.

"Fine, fine, whatever. How does any of that help me? I don't see how viewing the Void as Order and the Ethereal as Chaos is going to change my ability to find a balance between the two, and I really don't think the Ethereal is chaotic. I also don't buy nothing as the ultimate order. Wouldn't the ultimate order involve patterns?"

Response: User is more involved with the Void than we have records for. There is a high probability that I cannot get the solution you require due to lack of data, understanding, or details of the concepts involved.

"You took all that time to tell me you don't know? Fine, I'll figure it out on my own." Aetheria laughed ruefully. Why had she assumed an ancient set of crystals full of knowledge from ages ago could solve her problem? Part of her felt relieved Libby couldn't just give her an answer. When the Primordials had just given her the answers to her previous problems, it had been unsatisfactory.

"Your crystal friend can't help you because the two powers are not comparable. The Ethereal is the sum of all in existence, the Void is outside of existence."

"Hi, Reverie. So, if the Void is outside, why can it work inside reality?"

"All comes from the Void, and all will return to the Void. No where, when, or why exists without the specter of the Void. Regardless of the elevation of one's dimensional existence, cracks in the fabric of reality can and will allow the Void entry inside."

"So, the Void is stronger than the Ethereal?"

"The Void excels at destroying the Ethereal, but what does the Ethereal do to the Void? Experiment with their interactivity, and you will find the path between, perhaps."

"Right. So, uh, Reverie. What are you?"

"Oh my, my phone is ringing. I must answer it."

Reverie went silent while Aetheria fumed at such an obvious lie by the strange entity.

"Is it too late to rename you Dick?"

No answer came.

CHAPTER 69

Brewing Batches Badly

In the silence left behind by Libby and Reverie wasting Aetheria's time, she finally focused on the cabin and alchemy shop. The cure for the nun wasn't exactly that difficult to make. It just required expert energy control and an alchemist of at least the fourth tier. Failure to modulate the energies could kill the alchemist or the imbiber, but Aetheria's energy control had become one of her greatest strengths. *Is that all we are? Wisps of soul-energy, acting upon other forms of energy, forever?*

In the fifteen hours it took Aetheria to put together the cure, she only endured four void eruptions, but even without her restraining the explosions, each one grew exponentially worse, to the point she noticed the rips, and her flesh took much more power to repair itself each time. Her body took a good three minutes to regenerate after the last explosion, and for the next two minutes, wounds on her chest repeatedly broke open and had to heal again. The damage done to reality, or at least the reality of the tower, also took longer to heal, and the last fracture saw a few eyes staring through the hole before it closed.

I might have to deal with worse than things looking through soon. Now that the elixir is cooling, I can try to answer Reverie's question. What does the Ethereal do to the Void?

Rather than endanger the cabin, or the grounds of the temple itself, Aetheria flew up into the sky and generated a floating platform of levitating ice to experiment upon. In her first experiment, she summoned two orbs of concentrated power, one of the Void and one of the Ethereal. When she dropped the Void onto the Ethereal, it consumed most of the Ethereal and dispersed the rest. For the amount of energy it had consumed, the Void grew more concentrated, and if she had a unit to measure the power of Void, she'd say it had gone up in power.

With a fresh new Ethereal orb (that she had concentrated three times the energy into), she dropped the Ethereal orb onto the void orb. The void orb again ate a hefty portion of the Ethereal orb, and the rest seemed to be fractured and transformed into a variety of different energy types. *So, what does the Void do? It refracts Ethereal power? Why? How?*

Aetheria tried to weave a thin layer of the Void like a wall, and then threw her Ethereal orb at it. A fireball, lightning bolt, and shower of sparks shot out the other side of the void wall. She had no control of them, and each of the effects lacked power compared to what she could generate at will.

When Aetheria reversed the trial, with the wall being Ethereal power and the orb being Void, she got no such reaction. The Ethereal manipulated the Void to generate or create. *Maybe I could create an interaction that makes a higher tier energy than Void or Ethereal, one that won't rip me apart with fissures in reality?*

"Okay, Libby, you with me? I need to engineer a scenario between my two cores to create a higher tier force, or at least a pseudo high tier force I can control without my body rupturing. Think you can help me with this?"

Response: Yes. We must investigate the interactions between the Ethereal and the Void in more controlled tests.

At the highest output of her flash core, relative time and interactions played out at a speed which Aetheria could observe with Ethereal Sight. The greatest downside of her battery of tests guided by Libby became one of language. There were no words for the interactions between Void and Ethereal, and even the eldritch words for most of the interactions between mana and the Void were few, in her experience visiting libraries inside the tower. Which necessitated Libby and Aetheria to create a short-hand for the interactions they observed. Spaghettification was a real-world term, and one that Aetheria didn't find the Void/Ethereal interaction to replicate.

Instead, she found a dozen ways to create different types of matter and energy, but compared to the straight manipulation of Aether or Nether it was indirect, required more concentration, and once created then she had to establish control over the materials directly, whereas if she had created them via Aether actively controlling them there would have been fewer steps.

To control the Void is to become one with its vast, unknowable depths. Reality is fleeting, a mere brushstroke upon the canvas of the infinite Void. Surrender, experience, know, become. This is the way.

"Surprisingly helpful, Big A. Tell me more."

To wield the Void, become the Void. Feel the rhythm of the cosmos. Do not get distracted by the cosmic song. Ignore the infinite stars. Feel the birth of galaxies, the death of stars. Feel the loss of power, the gain. From nothing to nothing.

When Aetheria closed her eyes, the visualization of vast galaxies filled her mind. The twinkle of stars, the dull hum of the cosmos sung to her in a way she'd never imagined before. It reminded her of her teenage years and listening to music after smoking some Mary Jane. Transcendental, overwhelming. Goosebumps rose on her skin, the hair on the back of her neck stood up. The Void was visible through a crack that formed jagged tears in reality, which eventually pulled her into the true Void. In what seemed to be both on top of her, and so far away as to be forever off, she heard the bleating of flutes and the crash of drums. Her body had not known cold unrelated to the Void in years, yet here, she knew cold again, and it felt liberating, joyous, and life affirming.

Eternal.

The voice nearly re-formed Aetheria's whole being. The weight and immense power of her eldritch friend's mere existence filled the Void in ways that it could not fill physical reality. She tasted salt and pepper pistachios, antimatter, and the deep bitterness of the weary old. Maybe she'd eaten those things at some point, because she also tasted the profound absence of flavor, which caused saliva to fill her mouth in a desperate need of *something*. Her nose filled with the scent of a silent perfume, alluring and somber, each layer more seductive and more subtle than the last, until there was nothing, and the raw need for there to be more shook her to the core.

The Void confronted Aetheria with its infinite power, its cold with more depth than absolute zero, and Aetheria saw potential for the first time. For there to be existence, there had to be its opposite, and reality existed because of the dreams, shadows, and the strange eldritch beings that dwelled in the Void. Did Azathoth *truly* dream of all realities? It didn't matter if he only dreamed of just one, or of all of them. Entities, in the Void or elsewhere, dreamed the unlimited potential of nothing into something. To shape the Void, one had to surrender to it, to be shaped by it themselves. Aetheria welcomed the Void and pulled it within herself.

In the unfathomable reaches of cosmic desolation, where time has never trod, there lies the Black Inferno—an ever-burning tempest of obsidian flames. Hungry tendrils, darker than the void between stars, whisper eldritch secrets as they dance. Born from an ancient chasm that baffles comprehension, the stygian blaze devours the fabric of existence, near and far. Before it, sanity, reason, and all that has or will be must retreat. To gaze in those black flames is to know the icy embrace of oblivion, for pulsing in the heart of that malevolent blaze one can hear the beat of realities yet unborn and dimensions long forsaken.

The ominous feeling that shredded Aetheria's guts grew with each word the eldritch being spoke in her mind. Her stomach had gone thousands of meters below her by the time Azathoth stopped speaking, because some force had caught and pulled her, and she could not resist it. Down, down into the depths of the abyss, she went. Dimly, she saw and heard the Court of Chaos shrouded by the Darkness, but she fell deeper and deeper than even the court of Azathoth, down into the infinite nothing.

Until Aetheria saw something, a dark inferno of black flames. Very familiar flames, a familiarity that burned her from the inside out. The sudden molten heat in her veins fought against the eternal cold of the Void, and it won. Without even the slightest attempt, she breathed those dark obsidian flames in. The obsidian blaze rose with a seductive sway. Black fire caressed her skin like the delicate touch of a tentacle, a tentacle that melted flesh into stray particles with only the slightest touch. She breathed it in, and it flowed into her. Her body entered a race to stop the disintegration and restore the lost mass before it became endemic, yet the flames went deeper into her soul, and found their like: the Black Flame, the Unutterable Flame of the Void. It felt like a nuclear bomb went off inside her brain.

Dissolution.

Aetheria had suffered pain worse than she had ever imagined could even exist back on Earth. Aetheria had experienced being ripped apart, exploded, and lost limbs from various kinds of energies and monsters, but she always recovered promptly and shook off most of the trauma. She had never experienced being reduced to nothing, not even a stray particle. Yet she remained even when the Flame consumed her, and then re-formed her atom by atom from nothing.

The Etherfrost Asura blacked out then. Even Aetheria's abomination of a soul could only endure a finite exposure to the depths of the Void. She did not stir immediately, and Aetheria swore there had been a long stretch of time spent in a dark place full of shadows and jelly, but when she thought of it, she found herself unable to confront that darkness again.

The icy platform in the air did not make a comfortable resting place, Aetheria decided. The world around her shimmered a little too brightly, and the cheerful light of the sun made her skin feel like it burned. No, that was the Black Flame inside of herself. It had reached the fourth tier and now burned like the inferno in the void's abyss. *Thump-thud. Thump-thud.*

Within Aetheria's heartbeat, she could hear the pulsing sound of the Black Inferno and the cries of realities unborn. A smile worked its way across her lips, even though she felt deeply uncertain whether this was an improvement over the whispers of the Void or a much worse curse. Besides her Flame reaching the height of the fourth tier, Aetheria felt something new in the back of her mind, and in her chest, but she did not have time to investigate that at the moment. Her void organ had reached maturity, and the conflicting energy between it and her Ethereal core had turned even more aggressive. Intense pain radiated out from the center of her chest; slivers of unreality ruptured her body as a lightning storm of nonexistence obliterated most of her torso.

In the boundless expanse of manifold realities, you are a thing most curious. To bind the Void within a vessel of mortal flesh is beyond audacious. From the dung heap of the Court of Chaos, Ulzschazath found purpose in unexistence. Beyond legendary, from mediocrity, no less. Omega tier core. Existence Oscillation. Void Gaze. Absorption. If you pick up Ephemeral Form or Voidspawner in upgrading it, you'd have a real beyond S++ core there.

You aren't Azathoth, are you?

Aetheria couldn't speak the words aloud. Most of her torso remained obliterated, and her attempts to physically push the cores apart had not worked, and then she had lost too much of her mass to do anything at all. The existential bolts fired randomly from her exposed skeleton, while flames of inexistence burned her flesh away in a constant contest between her regeneration and the destructive power of unreality. The term S++ had been used in *Eldest Fantasy Wars Online*. It had been the phrase used for ultimate end game best in slot pieces when she had played.

No. I'm not.

CHAPTER 70

No, He's Not

Aetheria had been in a better position before. The forces of nonexistence had obliterated her body from hips to jaw. It had reduced her form to a spine between the two points, and two objects aggressively flew in the air in orbit around her spine, attacking one another. The larger of the two objects, black and hard to look at, was no construct but a flesh and blood organ. The slightly smaller radiated a red haze of Ethereal power. Each time one of the two darted at the other, flames of inexistence exploded, burning more of Aetheria's rapidly diminishing mass out of reality.

The mystery identity of the eldritch voice in her head would have to wait; Aetheria had much larger problems to deal with, which really sank in when Aetherius manifested as a projection just beyond the reach of the flames, lightning, and blades that carved reality. Aetherius didn't bother with the doddering old grandfather persona.

"Aetheria, you need to focus. If you don't get your power under control, you're going to destroy the entire tower."

Rather than respond, Aetheria closed her eyes and wondered how she could even accomplish this. The tests she and Libby did had revealed a significant amount of data on reactions between the Ethereal and the Void, but she felt woefully inadequate to the task at hand. Why had she listened to the whispers of the Void and allowed such a dangerous power a foothold in her soul? She should have purged the darkness from herself and her companions, not embraced it.

"Oh, Namer, you seem to be in a pickle. I quite like my name of Reverie, I forgot to thank you for it. Here, this is an acknowledgment of our bond."

When things seemed bleakest, a tiny ray of hope illuminated Aetheria's soul. Reverie got her hopes up, and then energy flowed out of the soul-linkage she shared with the upper dimensional being. So, what present did the entity send to her in her time of need? Exceptionally concentrated motes of power.

"Form these motes of the infinite into a third-eye jewel."

Give me a name, and I, too, will give you a grand gift.

"Copycat."

For Pete's sake, is now really the time for you two to act like little bitches? You want a name, fine. Enjoy being Fred.

Man is the cruelest animal. Very well, Frederick I shall be.

From within the heart of the Unutterable Black Flames of the Void motes of power emerged, escorted by the ominous heartbeat of unborn stars. The motes transcended physical reality, and the entire tower shook from their mere presence. Aetherius's projection babbled like a madman facing the apocalypse. The Void motes were dark, terrible, and comprising so many facets that Aetheria could not behold them in their true form.

Aetheria willed the motes to slam into one another. She bore down with the entirety of her will, and both of her cores stopped their mad aggression momentarily, as she emptied them of their power. She opened wide the floodgates of the Origin and the Void and grasped every ounce of power she could command, and forced the motes together into a singular diamond. The process of learning Frostfire had taught Aetheria a lot about duality, so when the motes formed a yin-yang shaped jewel, she wasn't even slightly surprised.

The Void obviously represented yin, while the Ethereal represented yang. When Aetheria's compression of the power could go no further, she bound the gem in fragments of her own soul in the form of soulsteel which quickly colored half red and half black, in contrast to the spinning jewel mounted there. The jewel vanished and reappeared on her forehead where a third-eye would normally be.

"A soulsteel mounted Third-Eye of Ein Sof. Beautiful." Reverie complimented her creation before he faded away from her mind. Aetheria noticed one aftereffect of the motes immediately. An inferno of red fire blazed opposite the Unutterable Black Flame of the Void in her soul. For whatever reason, the two Flames had no quarrel with each other the way her cores did.

Additionally, her cores ceased their dance of aggression, and no further reality fractures exploded out of Aetheria, which allowed her body to regenerate itself. Excess energy seemed to flow into the third-eye jewel, where it did something she didn't quite understand. She didn't need to understand it to copy the interactions of the jewel to her cores, though. She pressed the two cores together and directed the flow of power through them to mimic the infinite interplay shown in the jewel between her cores.

Cycles of heat and cold filled Aetheria's body, until the two cores locked into place in an eternal dance between order and chaos, fire and ice, light and dark. The newly restored skin on her chest flushed with internal power until she sank her cores deeper within herself, but even then a flush of color seemed to permeate her skin. It didn't compare at all to the powers flaring through the gem on her forehead, though. Even when she sank it within her skin, the glows were so obvious that she just resurfaced the third eye and left it visible.

Aetheria breathed deeply of the air, tasting the slightly cool air of the platform she stood on, and then narrowed her eyes at Aetherius. The Primordial of divinity, light, and the sky looked unsettled by her gaze, or perhaps by the third red-and-black eye that watched him every bit as hawkishly as her red and aqua eyes did.

"That ended abruptly." Pete floated the comment casually.

"Well, I am amazing, you know? Are there any more bombshells you want to tell me before I walk into a field of landmines? I'd like some forewarning next time."

Aetherius made a show of counting on his fingers while muttering.

"Nope. I'm glad you pulled it all together, Aes."

"I get by with a little help from my friends."

"So you keep showing. Are you alright?"

Aetheria's hands rested on her hips, and she stared Aetherius down until he looked away.

"Oh yeah. I'm super good. Totally not traumatized by the being reduced to nothing, then to a skeleton, then reforged by the Void and Ethereal, nope. Who is the being in the Origin?"

"Themis? You've met before."

"No, another entity. One far beyond Themis."

"There's no entity in the Origin, Aetheria. Travelers, sometimes, but nothing lives there. Are you sure you haven't been misled?"

Oh, snap his neck. Feast on his marrow. You've got an Absorption core now! The Paradox that would result from a battle between his tower formation and your Core would be very entertaining.

"Truth and lies are hard to tell apart these days, Pete."

Oh, sweet child. Open your inner eye. Your Void Gaze will discern truth from lies, see through illusions, and even glimpse the future.

How, precisely, did one open an inner eye? Fred mentioned the term earlier as part of Aetheria's void organ. Which meant it probably worked not too dissimilarly from Ethereal Sight. Indeed, when she explored the feelings bound to the void organ, she found an extremity that didn't actually exist, and when she willed it another eye opened. Aetherius himself radiated a shallowness because of being a projection.

"Did you have a backup plan if I couldn't turn things around?"

"If you couldn't control it before I took severe injury, I intended to call for Khaos and Chronos."

Aetheria smiled. Not because of the words, but because she could now discern the truth when she heard it. A very minimal ability in a fight, but potentially world changing in decisions and planning.

"Thanks, Pete. I'd better finish my quest and get back to the boys. Damn, three eyes are a big change from two." It took Aetheria much longer than it should have to realize her vision had altered itself. Reverie had called it the Third-Eye of Ein Sof. *What the heck is Ein Sof?*

"It suits you." Pete vanished with those words, and Aetheria descended back to the cabin. Her body remained whole now, and her cores operated at higher output than ever before now that they weren't waging war against one another, and a continuous buildup of energy flowed into the third eye.

"Libby?" Aetheria tried to rouse the librarian of the Aetherial crystals. While her body got destroyed, the true resting place of the Astrum Nexus remained her soul, not her hands. The silver mesh gloves she wore were merely a shapeshifting affectation to honor the gear that rested in her vault, in safety, while she mirrored its powers. Still, she had lost gear even when it should have been safe in her repository before, so caution demanded she check on Libby and the original.

Response: Yes?

"Good, you're alive. Search your databanks, look for a Black Inferno in the depths of the Courts of Chaos, also search for any mention of consciousness or entities in the Origin."

Acknowledged: . . . searching.

Thankfully, her ordeal hadn't damaged the cabin. The elixir she brewed for the injured sister waited, and once administered to a sickly woman who rapidly de-aged and grew healthy, her quest reached completion, and she gained a new diadem. She sorely missed her identification abilities that had been a part of Vulcan's boon. There were arcane rituals that could accomplish similar information, but Aetheria hadn't conducted one yet.

When Aetheria crossed the first threshold within the chapel after receiving her reward, she vanished and appeared in a waiting room. Arkaziel lounged, snacking on a tray of fish and playing Werylin in a board game that took up four levels of boards, one atop the other.

"Do I even want to know what that game is?"

"You've been held up for a—" Werylin's voice cut off abruptly when he looked up and saw a third eye focused on him. A shiver ran through the elf, and Aetheria could practically hear the prayer to Aetherius in Werylin's mind.

"Had some stuff come up. Did you know that changing your cultivation path in the fourth tier is incredibly painful?" Aetheria's tone went super sweet, and her smile dangerous.

Arkaziel nearly fell off his chair laughing, while Werylin just looked confused and exhausted.

"My void core matured, it threw a tantrum like a toddler, I spoke with some spooky voices, made a third-eye jewel, and brought balance to the force. Cool? Oh yeah, don't ask about that last one. It's a secret." Aetheria grinned, but neither of the men fell for it and asked what the heck she was talking about, to her annoyance. "How did the floor go for you two?"

"Easy-peasy, although I noticed Aetherius dilated our time while we waited for you. Makes sense now." Arkaziel didn't beat around the bush. "It seems like the sigils you burned in my soul are working, and I can tell you're more balanced than you've been in weeks. Maybe next level won't be an obnoxious self-control test."

"Well, only one way to find out. Let's see what's behind door number eighty-eight."

Aetheria led the way through the portal, and appeared in a vast, seemingly endless circus. Surrounded by a multitude of horrifying clowns didn't make for the best start of a new floor, and the cheery circus music had an off-putting note that kept bleeding through the music despite the park's speaker system being truly terrible and low quality.

CHAPTER 71

Cirque du Slay!

Even in the best of times, Aetheria thought clowns were suspicious and creepy. Mix in a cityscape that extended as far as one looked in any direction with never-ending amusement rides, carnival attractions, and performances, and things quickly took on an even more sinister tone. Sure, the man juggling chainsaws did a great job at it, and he even cut an apple into quarters while juggling. Yet from the corner of her eye, she saw the look in his eyes. *He wishes he was cutting up my head!*

"What a colorful place." Werylin's comments shocked Aetheria to the point she turned her Void Gaze off and beheld a very different world. Without Void Gaze, the carnival world was vibrant, the acrobats and carnies cheerful and smiling. The lingering smell in the air filled her with hunger for popcorn and funnel cakes. With Void Gaze on again, the world washed out and looked decrepit.

-It's all illusion. The vibrancy, the smiles, the lack of murder in the eyes of the clowns. The actual air smells like blood and urine, the paint is cracked and peeling, and a malevolent presence is feeding off everything.-

+How can you see all of that? I can only see through the visual illusions.+

-My void core has a sensory power that sees through all lies and untruths.-

=Convenient. So, do we pretend to not notice and saunter into the boss's lair, slay them, and bring peace and prosperity back to the land?=

-I don't think this place has ever known prosperity, but we might give it peace. It's as good an idea as any. I don't want to stay in this vile place any longer than we have to.-

- Oh look. A mime! He's coming right for us! Oh no, he's trapped in a box!+

"Good luck with the box, sir." Aetheria waved cheerfully but didn't slow her pace down at all. Arkaziel, a black cat with a white belly, hopped onto her shoulder to not have to touch the awful ground of the circus. Once on his perch, he surveyed the surrounding circus with the eyes of a predator choosing between prey.

=Aetheria? Can you turn that glowing jewel on your forehead off? It's attracting a lot of attention.=

-No can do. Ark, can you weave an illusion?-

+Sure, I'll make that standard practice until you figure out what to do with your third eye.+

To Aetheria's own sight, nothing changed of course, so she just had to assume that Arkaziel did the job correctly. To be sure, she looked at Werylin to receive.

A strong-man with a ridiculous twisted mustache stepped in their path.

"You look strong. Hit the bell at the top, and I'll give you some tickets to the big tent." The man held out the handle of a hammer not to Werylin, but to Aetheria, who nearly grinned, but it faded when the man spoke up more. "If you lose, you owe me your name."

"Excuse me, what?"

"I said if you win, I'll give you tickets to the big tent." The man narrowed his eyes at her, as if she were an idiot. Clearly, the last part hadn't been something she should have heard. How would a contract work if one side never agreed to it?

"What's in the big tent?"

"Hopes and dreams, the pride and joy of Astrian. The busty bard, the crooked crooner, Belinda the Beautiful."

Intrigue warred with Aetheria's desire to get out of the circus.

"A beautiful busty bard? Well now, let's take the man up on his offer."

~If you lose, you lose your name. He somehow made the agreement with the help of the illusions in place. How that's fair, I don't know, but I don't doubt that if you don't hit the top bell you'll lose your name. ~

+Why'd you warn him? We could've given him a new name. Don't you want to be a Richard? Maybe Newt?+

Werylin almost took the sledge from the powerful man, before he thought better and pulled his hands back.

"On second thought, I think I'll go have a few drinks for strength first."

"Sure, whatever, buddy." The muscular man gave the trio a long look, before he shrugged and bothered the next person who made the mistake of making eye contact with him.

The boss had a series of large wooden structures constructed near the big top tent. In fact, to Aetheria's unclouded eyes, the structure looked more like a castle made of extra pieces of haunted houses than the fake business center illusions made it seem. With every step toward the business center the trio took, more carnies appeared from the outskirts of the circus. Aetheria warned the boys of what she saw and the gathering of clowns.

+I say we just bust in and go full ultraviolence. Whoever gets in our way gets what they get.+

=While I usually would oppose such a plan, I think it might be necessary if there are hidden fae pacts in these games.=

~Alright, just follow my lead. If we get into an us vs. the circus situation, you two handle the boss, I'll deal with the small fries; there's something I want to test out.~

Arkaziel and Werylin each emitted a low, long-suffering groan at the prospect of Aetheria testing things out, but Werylin kept pace behind her and Arkaziel remained on her shoulder.

"Excuse me, what brings you to the circus administrative center today? I'd be happy to assist you." A young man with a purple suit and rainbow hair interposed himself in the party's way as soon as they entered the lobby. The illusions gave the image of a brightly lit office space with a number of customer service desks manned by smiling men and women. In reality, however, the floor stuck to Aetheria's boots. Dark red splotches covered a hideous shag carpet, the carnies behind the service desks all sharpened knives, and the potted plants of the illusion were corpses mid-dismemberment.

The gory and disgusting scene didn't manage to hit Aetheria the way it would have a decade ago. Yes, her indignation at the sight of butchered innocents stoked her emotions with fury, but it felt hollow, a reaction based on rote and memory, not one built on connection or self-identification with the victims. *Humanity . . . have I completely lost mine?*

"We wanted to see the man in charge." Aetheria let her senses focus on the purple-suited, rainbow-haired thug before her, and the man squirmed.

"Boss is in the big top. I'll pencil you in for his next available time." A perfunctory smile accompanied the words, and then hidden from her senses other than Void Gaze, he added on, "Oh, the next available meeting is now; life and death in the big top."

"Yes, that's fine." Aetheria smiled brightly, and the young man frowned at her.

After a lull of silence between the two, the assistant clicked the pen he held, twice, and the three vanished to reappear inside the large circus tent. The stands were a mixture of circus goers and carnies, although the truth of it revealed by Void Gaze disturbed Aetheria. The big top tent held many people, with approximately half the bleacher seats full. A large audience that comprised circus workers on break or off duty, and visitors from elsewhere. The undead made up two-thirds of the audience, while the last third appeared to be exceptionally subdued. Aetheria couldn't help but wonder if they had been drugged, drained, or were under some form of mental effect.

The circus workers were much more lively than the customers, and many chewed on turkey legs that Void Gaze revealed to be humanoid body parts, mostly raw and still very bloody. The scents of fear and blood were a psychic attack all on their own. On the well-lit center stage, a young elf fought back a tiger with nothing but a chair, while in reality, the tiger filled twice the space because of its massive true form of a chimera. Already, the elf had lost an arm, but in the illusion of reality he only had a little trickle of blood going down his still-there arm. A creepy score played by a theremin set the stage of the circus.

Werylin appeared in front of the elf in a flash, and the rainbow-blade Stormshimmer parted lion head from chimera body. Werylin spun and removed the goat-head with Harmonious Tempest, and a final slash of Stormshimmer removed the beast's snake tail.

~*Nice, how'd you see it properly?*~

=*I can use True Sight once a day, but it only lasts for about thirty minutes.*=

"What the what!? Intruders!" a voice raged over a microphone. The terrible sounds of the theremin temporarily stopped. A spotlight lit up what looked like a DJ table to Aetheria, where a gnome sat behind a theremin. "Kill 'em! They murdered Scruffy!"

Snap.

The sound of Aetheria snapping her finger created gusts of wind that carried a sudden burst of snowflakes and ice crystals across the whole tent.

"Watch this one, boys." Aetheria faded from existence, and along the gusts carrying snowflakes and ice crystals Aetheria danced out for a split second here and there, only to vanish, and reappear again. An arm here, a leg there; a strand of her hair looped around one clown's neck and tightened until his head hit the floor. Reality itself in the Big Top oscillated, and Aetheria seemed to be everywhere and nowhere. None of them could keep up with what happened. Even with Arkaziel tapping into her Flash Mode, he couldn't observe more than a small piece of the puzzle.

In three seconds, every clown, carnival worker, and undead tasted obliteration at the hands of Aetheria. Well, hands, feet, hair, headbutt, and extra appendages she didn't fully solidify when she reappeared on the other side of the ringmaster's theremin.

"Wha-wu-whaat?" The gnome spat blood at her in shock. Not his own, sadly, but plasma from the raw drumstick he'd been gnawing on. Then the gnome laughed and laughed.

"Oh, you poor dumb idiots. I'm not the boss! I'm just the DJ. That's the boss." The gnome pointed at the big top itself, which had manifested two enormous eyes to glare at them with.

+*We have to fight a tent? A tent? Really? This is stupid. I'm not fighting a tent.*+

"For your transgressions against Cirque du Slay, you shall join the show . . . forever!" The voice boomed from the vertical walls of the tent, filling the insides of the big top fairly impressively. If the voice were better at enunciation, it would have been more extraordinary. Instead, it sounded like someone had taught a parrot to talk poorly.

"Yeah, I'm not feeling it. This one is all you, Werylin." Aetheria grimaced at the tent.

With a contemptuousness that personified the feelings of the entire party, Werylin took a draw-stance, and then the top half of the tent vanished, followed by Harmonious Tempest clicking back into its sheath. Only Aetheria and Arkaziel could perceive Werylin's attack

"It was just a big mimic, right?" Werylin asked while the door to the next floor appeared next to him.

"Guess so. What a dumb floor. Time for eighty-nine." Arkaziel didn't seem to be keen to put much thought into it.

"I feel like we're forgetting something, but whatever. Let's go."

A sputtering gnome sat behind his theremin even when they vanished through the strange door.

CHAPTER 72

Rising Crust

Only one of you may compete in this trial. Using only your physical capabilities, one of you must ascend the Windcaller Maze. The other two may observe. If the climber fails, another of you may then attempt it." The voice of the Administrator emerged from thin air, while the trio appeared in a room with only two chairs.

"I'll take it on," Werylin declared before either Aetheria or Arkaziel could comment. Aetheria noticed the touch of defiance and pride within the elf's voice she wouldn't have previously. The effects of the Void's Gaze seemed nebulous and hard for Aetheria to explain, but were exceptionally useful.

"Sure, you've got this. I could use the time to adjust my inner world." Aetheria tried to infuse her voice with confidence in Werylin, which she had, and annoyance at the changes her inner world required. Whatever path she walked, it had to be adjusted to include more than the Ethereal, and time had not been on her side lately.

"Good luck. I'll share an ambrosia risotto with you if you do well." Arkaziel encouraged Werylin with a promise, before he jumped onto a recliner, stretched out, licked his paw three times, then lay down and fell straight asleep.

The walls of their room shifted to show a maze spread across multiple platforms, each with large wide spaces and floor tiles that created massive gusts of winds at seemingly random times. Werylin appeared and revealed the scale of the whole maze to be about three times larger than she had initially thought, and within a few seconds, tornadoes formed and randomly roamed the platform he started on.

"Oof. Well, he'll be fine." Aetheria cheered him on, before she closed her mismatched eyes and centered her breathing. Her mind flowed between her soul aperture and into the manifestation of her soul's inner realm. The initial use Aetheria had for her inner realm all related to the protoworld version, repository or vault. From there, further uses rapidly became apparent. Retrieval, bonding, and harmonization were the three that had been major factors in her early successes. From a void, to a closet, to a burgeoning world with its own Ethereal sun and a void black hole, the changes had been significant.

The nascent inner world marked the real reason Aetheria had sought the inner realm. Only a single layer of the planet's mantle remained to be laid down, and then crust, and she'd be done. While the one hundred and ten existing layers had taken a significant expenditure of time and focus, she could finish the final layer at almost any time. The acquisition of the Black Flame, the void connection, and the void core held the blame for stopping her from moving on to the final stage of her inner world creation. The void, in any existence but the Void, brought corruption with it.

The spirits living in Aetheria's creation had already experienced high exposure to the Void. With prolonged contact and high exposure, it seemed miraculous that any had avoided the corruption. Somehow, over half of the spirits resisted the Void to date, and many had, in fact, gained Ethereal aspectation instead. Closer examination of the simple spirits showed that aspectation to the Void had not resulted in corruption, which baffled Aetheria. Yes, the ice spirits displayed Void alignment now, but they didn't take on any of the tentacles or other affectations of most Void natives.

More than the Many Angled exist in my emptiness.

"Are you filtering my connection to the Void?"

The song of your existence shatters the silence of the Void with the promise of ultimate ordering.

"Could you explain that more, Fred?"

You sing a claxon call of calamity.

"Then why did I have to deal with the whispers and stuff?"

You sang in the wrong octave until recently.

Aetheria didn't respond to Fred's answer. It felt incomplete to her. The Red Flame of the Ethereal emerging no doubt played a part, too, or the third-eye jewel, or the completion of her void core. Fred had proven he could lie and mislead her. He had tricked Nyx into thinking his black inferno was Azathoth, after all. Then there was Fred's apparent inability, or unwillingness, to acknowledge Reverie or its powers directly. She still hadn't figured out why Reverie could hear Fred, but Fred couldn't seem to hear Reverie, or if he could and he ignored them.

If what Fred suggested were true, though, that now that Aetheria had the third eye, her cores worked in something approaching harmony, and caused the appearance of the Ethereal Flame, then she had no reason to delay the construction of her inner world. Her own inspection suggested that stability had been achieved between the disparate forces of the Void and the Ethereal, and that she could progress once more.

For the final layer of Aetheria's inner world's mantle, Aetheria summoned the deepest cold she could, formed it into the densest form she could, and then imagined it wrapping around the world as a final thick layer of enchanted ice. It refracted the Ethereal sun, Frostfire, and the depths of darkness imparted by the Void served to enhance and contrast the brightness. For a moment it looked like a crystal filled with ephemeral fire.

No earth-shattering changes wracked Aetheria's body or soul with the completion of the world's mantle, beyond the satisfaction of having completed a milestone. The crust of the world would be next, although she had some design decisions to make still. Her original plan would have put the inner world rotating around Frostfire, but now that the Void-Gate existed, too, her plans might need to change. Her current idea revolved around keeping the first of the inner worlds stationary, rotating equidistant between the black hole and the sun. Future additions could be sent to rotate like a planetary body in the real world, but in her inner realm she liked the idea of the planet existing in the shadow of the two strange phenomena.

How many layers of crust should she do? Aetheria counted her soul linkages. Aoibhe, Arkaziel, the Origin, Reverie, the Void, and Fred made six. A good number for someone who had to reconcile disparate forces and multiple soul connections, and sometimes considered a lucky number to boot. Yes, six would be a great number to impart meaning to her inner world.

To create the first layer of the crust, Aetheria opted for a new methodology. She projected herself into the inner realm as a projection, reached into Frostfire and the black hole, and pulled forth a thread from each. Balancing the power the way her cores were balanced, she entwined the two threads and wove the combined thread around the world. While it no doubt appeared simple to entwine a ball in yarn, the actual act required constant balance of the Void and the Ethereal, and a singular focus to keep the energy where she placed it. Yet she got to the top pole of the world, and bound the layer to the northern pole as she had bound the starting layer to the south pole.

With a layer done, Aetheria checked the tower, and found Arkaziel bopping her nose with his paw.

"How long have you been doing that?"

"About three minutes."

"You could have just spoke through our bond, you know."

"This was more amusing."

"Hard disagree. How far has . . . oh."

The observation room showed the view of Werylin. The elf danced between trapped floor tiles, blurred around a dust-devil, ran vertically up a wall to then summersault over churning blades of wind and catch an updraft to fling himself up through the air to the final platform.

"Damn, impressive show. Kind of sucks that I missed it all."

"He's more confident down there without us, did you notice that?" Arkaziel spoke earnestly for once, no judgment or mockery in his voice that Aetheria could detect.

"Yes. We'll be parting ways with him when we beat this tower. He'll accomplish more without us than with us. He's the real hope Grief needs for a restoration of civil society after we slap Oizys's hands."

"While we bring Armageddon to the gods?" The apocalypse dragon-cat grinned with his joke.

"Probably." Aetheria grinned back, but she wasn't joking, and Arkaziel's confusion clouded his eyes.

~Shh. Don't get too into it. Where we end up is still to be seen, but we're both living weapon projects. You don't make a living weapon without an enemy to use it on, I just

haven't figured out if our enemies are supposed to be the gods, if the Primordials are tired of existence, or something else entirely. The trickle-truths from all the parties involved have really started to piss me off, though. ~

Arkaziel's only reaction to her statement was to climb onto her shoulder and nuzzle her neck while purring, and Aetheria felt agreement and pride radiate from her companion.

Well, shit, if Arkaziel is proud and agrees, I must be wrong, right?

Aetheria and Arkaziel vanished to reappear next to Werylin and the door to the ninetieth floor.

"Good job!" Aetheria patted Werylin on the shoulder congratulatorily. "The end was spectacular."

"It's reassuring to take on a high level of the tower on my own and find such a smooth path to success. Are you ready for adoring crowds and the last trade city we'll encounter in the tower?" Werylin's smile radiated genuine pleasure and confidence in a way it hadn't lately. He stood just a little bit taller, and the sparkle in his silver eyes showcased the beauty and handsomeness of the elf. Aetheria felt a distance between them, a gulf that for whatever reason could not be bridged. Like the reflections in the house of mirrors, something warped her world that didn't affect Werylin, and she had to quash the flare of resentment that rose within her.

I will not get jealous of anyone, much less my friends.

"The most radiant energies are those that bind, connect, and uplift."

I like that, Reverie.

Fred remained quiet, and Aetheria appreciated that.

"Let's go!" Arkaziel said, and the trio crossed the portal to the ninetieth floor.

Aetheria, Arkaziel, and Werylin appeared atop a large stone covered in layers of strange glyphs. Around them rose an ancient forest of trees that climbed hundreds of meters into the sky, their thick trunks wider than the buildings of many towns they had previously visited. The large clearing held a multitude of other large stones, each covered in glyphs. From the mostly flat rock platform one could reach the dirt paths that led to a wooden archway by stairs crafted of living bushes and vines.

"Verdance," Arkaziel said with recognition. "This is the nature city of Silvanus."

"Let's start the parade." As Aetheria hopped off the platform and over the stairs, her boots left light indents in the grass she landed on.

CHAPTER 73

Verdance

When Aetheria stepped into Verdance, her identity as a challenger did not go unnoticed. Verdance, unlike most cities, breathed, sensed, and harmonized with its inhabitants in a dance as old as time. In the other cities cacophonous bells had rung, fireworks had showered the skies, and mystical lights had guided all eyes and all attention upon her.

In Verdance, the city itself rose in an organic symphony. A warm, ethereal wind rose into a haunting melody in welcome of a challenger. The wind awoke hollowed trunks, tall reeds, and hidden openings in a woodwind symphony. Even Aetheria could not fully ignore the tugs of the sweet sounds of wind and wild on her soul.

The canopy above the clearing glowed, drawing eyes to the heights of the behemoth trees. Radiant energy flowed up the trunks of ancient giants to fill leaves with an eerie light that transformed the whole of the forest canopy into dreamy sight. The true spectacle followed in short order, as phantasmal leaves detached and drifted through the air. The leaves were translucent, and shimmered in a myriad of colors that reflected the entire spectrum of the natural world. Light breezes played between the massive trees, choreographing a ballet between leaves and trees, to cascade down and swirl around Aetheria herself in a widening circle.

Aetheria could almost hear the words of welcome from Verdance itself. Of all the welcomes she had gone through so far, this was easily her favorite.

"Wow," Werylin murmured when the cascade of leaves parted, and he walked next to Aetheria and Arkaziel.

The other travelers who were entering or leaving via the rune gates had all stopped to stare and enjoy the spectacle, but now many went back about their business, while others congregated around Aetheria and her party. She had not altered her form for this level, so she stood in black attire with black streaks throughout her red and aqua hair, her mismatched heterochromatic eyes, and even the Third Eye of Ein Sof remained visible. Arkaziel apparently went with grandiose appearances on this floor and didn't throw an illusion around the obsidian eye that had thicker flowers of power around it than an average fifth-tier Cultivator's core.

"Let's meet the welcoming party, before all these interested climbers pelt us with questions or demands for autographs." Arkaziel pointed a paw toward the dirt path out of the clearing and into the forest, where an old man with a gnarly stick and robes with moss growing on it waited. "Fairly certain that's the High Druid of Verdance, Arborlith. You know an elf is old if they actually look that old."

"That's an elf?" Werylin sputtered and looked shocked.

"Play nice," Aetheria hissed, and walked toward the waiting druid.

"Welcome to Verdance, Challenger. We have heard of your exploits, Etherfrost Asura, although your name seems dated. Few are the Void walkers who have come among the leaves of our fair city, but you are welcome most warmly."

Aetheria couldn't contain the laughter that rose when the druid commented on a problem she'd already foreseen but had no answer for.

"Thank you for the welcome, High Druid Arborlith. You may simply call me Aetheria. I would ask for a place to stay while we remain in your beautiful city, before we challenge the last heights of the Tower of Aetherius." Aetheria saw no reason not to throw out where they were in the tower, and this way, others might not ask about it every ten seconds.

Rather than blather on and on, Arborlith raised a wrinkled hand, and vines slithered through the grass to touch each of the party, and the druid himself, who then all vanished.

"Thank you. I hate all that pomp, but you can't ignore a challenger. Makes enemies." The party and high druid all emerged into a comfortable study made of wood. Based on the grown windows, furniture, and storage spaces, they were within one of the massive trees.

"Sylva, why don't you show the nice climbers the VIP guest quarters, get them meetings with whoever they need, and otherwise work as their handler for a few days." The old elf grinned at a tiny figure who had been asleep on his desk. Still in the process of waking up, Sylva made a scrunched-up face and groaned at extra work being foisted upon her. A foot tall, the plant figure looked like a young woman made entirely of vegetation. Aetheria assumed she was some kind of small dryad.

"That's very generous of you, thank you. Werylin will do the bulk of sightseeing amongst us. Although I'm sure Arkaziel or I will venture out, eventually, I will do so through a duplicate, to avoid disrupting Verdance more than necessary. I will be retreating into meditation before we take our run at the last ten floors of the tower." The more stability Aetheria could cement between her cores, the better. If she could discern some uses for the Third Eye Jewel, it would be even better.

"Of course, of course. Sylva, see to it." Arborlith didn't seem to be in any mood to talk. He seemed eager for them to be out of his study, so the three accommodated him. A brief telepathic gameplan later, and Werylin had shopping lists and funds, and Arkaziel met with some of the best chefs in Verdance to learn their tricks and recipes, and to discern what ingredients they needed to stock up on while in the town.

In the heart of Verdance, deep underground, a chamber of dirt, roots, and the Orb of Silvanus lay. Aetheria sat on the bare floor and considered the chamber they provided for her meditation. With a simple wave of her hand, she could corrupt the entire forest with eldritch forces, or wither it to nothing with the Ethereal. Yet, for some reason, they had trusted her in this chamber in the heart of the city, where she could feel the reverberations of all the chaos above.

The Void had an eternal ebb and flow to it, occupying the fulcrum position in all creation and destruction. The forest city had its own cycles of chaos, birth, growth, decay, and renewal. Identifying similarities, instead of differences, made Aetheria slightly more at home with the Void. Slightly.

No sounds reached Aetheria in the heart chamber. Through Ethereal Sight, she could see and feel the nearby underground flows of water. Each drop of water held secrets imparted by the forest above, and wisdom imparted by ancient trees that dwarfed redwoods. Wisdom originated from the breezes that touched all of Verdance, gusts that carried secrets from the domain of Silvanus to the rest of the worlds. For all the noise and chaos above, down below, silence reigned. Deafening silence, but a far cry from the absence of the Void that assaulted one physically and psychologically. Still, there was definitely a similarity that one could use to accept the silence inside and out.

The towering trees of Verdance, so high above, and their roots that traveled so far below, anchored the forest and the flows of many types of mana and Aether throughout the city, while many roots also transported Nether. Could Aetheria use a system of creations to stabilize small portions of the Void next time she found herself there? On the surface, it seemed like an idea that ought to work, but she had so little physics-based knowledge of the Void that she would have to trust gut feelings rather than any form of education.

"Do you know the genesis of the Void?"

No, do you, Reverie?

"No, the Void came before me."

How come you can't speak to Fred?

"I wish I knew. No matter how I shouted into the Void, at gods or ghosts, no one but you has ever heard more than a few words from me."

Do you live in the Origin?

"No, but it is the closest thing to my domain in your realm."

Are you a god?

"Until you named me, I didn't know who I was. I am alone and undefined."

Gods can be lonely, I think. All things can, and probably are.

Reverie did not comment any further.

Two days later, in a moment when her concentration on core control and the second layer of her inner world wavered, Arkaziel drew her attention. Arkaziel might be rude, impatient, and a jerk, but he gave his bondmate's cultivation progress as much priority as his own advancement. Thus, the moment she finished, he notified her they had finished all the shopping and were ready to start the last floors. Many groups of climbers in their situation spent upwards of a year in their last city, preparing for the immense difficulty of prying power from the hands of gods who didn't want to let it go.

The sun had already gone down in Verdance, but the late hour did not prevent the high druid from being at the rune gate that would take the trio to Floor 91.

"Lord Silvanus bade me warn you, Challenger, that one should embrace gifts with discernment. In the grand tapestry of existence, everything has its place, a purpose, and a price. Everything. To deny the natural cycle is to foot an ever-greater bill that no one can pay forever."

"Thanks, Arborlith. What does your lord say about this?" Aetheria tapped the soulsteel ornamentation around her third eye.

A shudder ran through the high druid, and a flutter of the old elf's eyes and spasms of his muscles left Aetheria uncertain whether the druid was in the thralls of pleasure, or pain. It turned out to be neither, but a divine revelation.

"Silvanus has shared some insights with me. The Third-Eye of Ein Sof is a concept that transcends our mortal comprehension, but my lord has shared some little knowledge. Like the stars that guide us through darkness, your third eye illuminates pathways beyond conventional reality. Despite its shape as an eye, it is more an essence, one that understands the infinite, the boundless, the source of all creation."

"The source of all creation is the Void."

"The Void is a part, surely, but the Void alone creates nothing." Arborlith smiled, certain he had Aetheria beat.

Aetheria's finger dropped from the soulsteel ornamentation.

"I suppose that's true. Good luck, Arborlith. I left you a few ambrosial seeds in the room you lent me."

+*Can we go through the gate already?*+ Arkaziel didn't hide his annoyance at the delay, and no doubt the fact his claws couldn't pierce Aetheria's shapeshifted hide annoyed him even more than the delay.

Aetheria, Arkaziel, and Werylin stood on the rune gate. The world spun to blackness, and then explosions of color, a sensation of movement, and then instantaneous appearance in a new place. With her Flash Mode running at full power, and the massive increase to her total power, her ability to observe the world around her marked a drastically slowed world. It also made her a little impatient to face one of the last ten floors of the tower.

"Raaaaaaaaaar!" A roar shook the slightly precarious stone pillar that Aetheria stood on. For a fiftyish-meter-tall pillar, it really lacked in stability. She casually shifted her density down and took in the scene before her. Arkaziel and Werylin had both appeared on different dilapidated pillars, while below them in the ruins of a civilization that had really, really loved pillars, tromped a twenty-meter-tall moose.

+*That looks delicious.*+

=*Why does it make me think of all the fallen races of Grief when I look at it?*=

~Time aspected. It'd be a moose-take to pass up this opportunity!~

Arkaziel and Werylin groaned loudly directly into her mind, while Aetheria jumped off her pillar.

~Screw, you guys, I'm funny. Try not to get frozen in time.~

CHAPTER 74

Eonhoof the Epoch Stalker

Aetheria's jump from the fifty-meter-tall pillar heralded the start of the fight. The eyes of the bull moose pivoted to focus on her, and she saw clocks behind its eyes. Did she imagine it, or did the clock hands move in reverse? The moose flickered and appeared dozens of meters back, where it had been seconds ago, and Aetheria crashed through the space it had never been in, yet. The moose charged as she impacted the ground and created a small crater. One of the three-meter-diameter hooves split the air in an attempt to smoosh her into the ground, but Aetheria arrested its forward momentum with her left hand, casually blocking the hoof.

The bull snorted, and its eyes locked with Aetheria's.

Werylin dropped next to her and sheathed Stormshimmer with a soft click.

The bull's head split from its neck and started to fall, only to reverse, heal, and the bull suddenly had a thirty-meter distance between itself and Aetheria and Werylin. For a twenty-meter-tall moose, it moved like lightning.

"That's a first." The elf laughed.

"This might actually be fun." Aetheria felt her pulse quicken.

The world went dark, and a beam of light as thick as the Chrysler Building struck the bull moose. When the eclipse broke, the bull appeared farther back, completely unharmed even by one of Arkaziel's ridiculous eclipse attacks.

"We've seen that trick multiple times now. Does it not have anything else?" Aetheria's interest in the fight already wavered.

The moose stomped a hoof, and Arkaziel had a bubble surround him in Aetheria's Ethereal Sight, and then the clocks in the moose's eyes sprung forward very quickly.

"Wow, it's . . . doing him a favor?" Werylin sounded concerned at first, but quickly re-evaluated at the way Aetheria burst into laughter. Offended, the moose turned its eyes on Aetheria, who showed no effect from its gaze at all.

In a flash of darkness Aetheria teleported onto the moose's back, and casually drove a foot down. The moose exploded in a gory mess, but again, it rewound time and appeared some distance away.

+*Damn, that thing just aged me five hundred years. I should thank it, can I thank it?*+

~Go for it.~

Arkaziel, still in the form of a flying house cat, lifted his cute head and roared. The bull's own shadow suddenly snapped a large hoof out to crush its windpipe. Again, it evaded the attack by temporal shifting.

"Alright, you two can kill it now." Aetheria locked her gaze upon the moose and locked time with the Third-Eye of Ein Sof. Fear and panic filled the eyes of the moose, while Aetheria smiled at her companions. Internally, though, she celebrated. She had controlled time without using the Flame of Chronos in the Astrum Nexus.

A symphony of metronomes forever out of synch, a mélange of possibility, a fleeting bright spark of stardust against the smooth velvet of midnight, the perfect brine followed by the crystalline crunch of epochs frozen in time.

You didn't eat Chronos's Flame.

Frederick's silence resulted in a small sigh from Aetheria, followed by a grunt. The moose fought her anchoring it in time, and it fought with the survival instincts of a cornered animal. It took her full concentration to restrain the creature in time.

Luckily, Arkaziel and Werylin didn't delay any further. Werylin leaped onto the bull moose's back in a series of jumps, where he then unsheathed Harmonious Tempest and Stormshimmer both, jabbed them into the beast's neck, and then ran down its back. Blood fountained into the air, and to Aetheria's Void Gaze, the truth of the situation revealed itself. Lightning cascaded out of Harmonious Tempest to cut multiple meters beyond the end of his katana, while Stormshimmer extended a few meters of rainbow blade to cut deeper as well. By the time the elf got to the moose's stub tail his speed had dropped significantly, and he freed his katanas and jumped off to the ground, where he rolled a distance away from the moose.

After all, Werylin didn't want to be anywhere near the moose when the much larger draconic feline dropped from the sky, grabbed it in one clawed hand, and took bite after bite out of the hemorrhaging moose. Not that it could fight back, after Werylin severed so many of its muscles and Aetheria negated its ability to manipulate time. As large as the moose was, the one-hundred-meter-long StarMane was three times as large.

The crunch of bones and flesh were sounds Aetheria had heard more than enough during her travels with Arkaziel, and she blurred over to Werylin to see what the elf had become so enamored with.

Through the ruins filled with pillars, in the darkness of the forest, lay the moose's den. It seemed the large temporal monstrosity had gathered a small treasure trove in its habitat, and the two investigated while Arkaziel chewed his meal.

A mixed assortment of items lay half buried in the den: A large seed of a tree that Aetheria didn't recognize, but Ethereal Sight revealed to be time aspected. A shimmering vial of temporal energy coalesced into a viscous liquid. An hourglass full of sand, that when running filled your mind with the sound of desert winds. Finally, there was a crystal ball. One half of the sphere seemed to be made of pietersite, or chalcedony. The other half of the orb had been fashioned from a clear quartz, and held none of the impressions of disorder or chaotic beauty that the pietersite did.

"That's beautiful," Werylin murmured in a half daze as he moved to lift it into his hands and examine it.

In Ethereal Sight, the orb shimmered with the same aspect of power that Werylin himself employed, harmony. It emitted a soft hum that filled Aetheria's ears pleasantly, reflecting a vision of harmony that Aetheria found hollow. When had harmony as sapient creatures viewed it started to feel hollow to her? No doubt it had something to do with the Black Flame or her Void Gaze.

Silencing the Abyss is not harmony, the echoing hollowness of their vision falls far short of wholeness. One cannot seek harmony while disregarding the cacophonous dirge of realities beyond counting.

Music critic now, Fred?

"You should take it, Werylin."

"It touches upon the light and shadow, too. Are you sure Arkaziel wouldn't be interested in it?" The elf seemed genuinely surprised by her suggestion that he take it.

"It's attributed more strongly to your path, and it would cause Arkaziel issues. Its duality is different from the duality he uses. I've read about items like that one, though. Useful tools, but don't rely on it too strongly, or it will weaken your path."

"What about my path?" A blur jumped from the darkness to land on Aetheria's shoulder.

"You don't want that orb, do you? I told Werylin he could have it."

"Oh, no. I have no interest in that. It looks like a Resonance Orb, harmony aspect? Minor brush against light and shadow, but not in a way that I would be interested in. No, keep it, Werylin. I will take those seeds, though. I might be able to do something with them."

"How was your snack?"

"I could still eat a lot more. Let's rock up to the next floor. If they're going to keep throwing bosses as weak as that at us, I say they should throw multiple at a time!" Arkaziel smirked.

"They probably will, the higher we climb." Werylin groaned.

"It'll be fine. I'll protect you." Aetheria smiled softly at the swordsman.

"I'm not sure my fragile ego can handle seeing what would happen if you went all out anymore, Aetheria. Could the crafted reality here in the tower even withstand it?"

"If you get a heart demon, well, you'll just have to overcome it, right? As for the tower, I'm pretty sure Aetherius could handle anything I lay down without it unraveling his tower. We're still only fourth tiers, even if I'm walking an unheard-of path now."

"Heart demons are no joke. History is littered with the corpses of Cultivators who couldn't overcome themselves to reach the sixth tier." Arkaziel sounded like he wanted to eat the corpses, but maybe Aetheria just imagined that.

"Ark has a point, but I believe we can get through the next few fights without me developing a heart demon. I hope." Werylin sounded dubious, at the last, before Aetheria reached over and gave his shoulder a squeeze.

"Werylin, you're an amazing swordsman, a leader of an entire people, a speaker of the Words of Creation, and one of my trusted friends. You've got this. We've got this."

The portal to the next level coalesced next to them.

"Nine more floors; better get the phrasing on your wishes ironed out. We each get one, from my understanding."

"Do you think Aetherius will contest my validity for a wish, since you resurrected me at the halfway point?"

"I don't know. Why don't we ask him here and now, instead of letting it be a surprise? *PETE*!" Aetheria's screech of the name she knew Aetherius under shook the reality of the tower; the den of the bull moose distorted and flowed, as if a tremor in reality had gone off. The effects subsided quickly.

"Yes, Aesca?" A projection of Pete, a doddering older man with few visually distinct traits, appeared before them.

"Fine, fine, Aetherius, I get it. Uhm, so about Werylin, does he qualify for a wish if he hits the top with us?" Aetheria put on her best "please, give me a puppy" look. Being a shapeshifter had advantages, like literally making your eyes just a little bigger, or shaping your face without having to rely on faking it.

The old man laughed and rubbed at his beard.

"A lesser wish should be acceptable, yes. Now then, good luck."

The projection vanished with a gust of wind.

"There you have it. Now, onward and upward!" Arkaziel gestured at the portal.

"Next." Aetheria stepped through, while her cat hummed something about fish.

The darkness and sense of motion were brief, before Aetheria appeared on Floor 92.

CHAPTER 75

Helioshorn Kintara
& Tidebreaker Nethalos

Aetheria appeared in what she could only describe as an air bubble on the bottom of the ocean. An enormous dome of breathable air covered her and scattered ruins in her vicinity. Strange tubes channeled pillars of light from the surface, while the sand had a mix of watery portals at random locations, and pockets of water in cave entrances and depressions. Her companions did not appear with her.

"A single challenger against Kintara and I, the mighty Nethalos?" A voice reverberated across the sand, and a shark-faced aquatic giant stood up. Aetheria had mistaken it for a poorly constructed statue. At ten meters high, with leathery skin covered in lichen, the self-identified Nethalos didn't seem that terrifying on its own. Mid-Tier Five, it radiated a healthy amount of power, and its aspects appeared to be water and darkness.

"An insult to both of us, no doubt." A golden, horselike creature with a mane and tail of flames commented. Its shoulders were approximately eight meters from the ground, although estimates were difficult with the way it walked on the air as if it were solid ground. The horn on its head reminded Aetheria of a unicorn, but this creature was no unicorn. At best the torso was a mix between a deer and a horse, and the flame tail reminded her more of an ox.

"Well, you two are always welcome to take up your complaints with the Administrator, right? Why don't you do that, I don't mind waiting."

"Human! What is that jewel on your forehead?" the golden horse-thing asked.

"It is awful shiny, and its darkness is . . . calling to me." Nethalos also seemed enthralled with her third eye.

"Is this where you demand I give it to you?" Despite Aetheria's best efforts, her boredom with this scenario leaked through. Both the shark-headed giant and the flaming deer-horse looked agitated.

"She thinks she's stronger than both of us. Let us disabuse her of this misconception." Kintara's wounded pride made him sound petty.

"Whoever finishes her off gets the jewel." Nethalos shared a trait with Arkaziel, hunger, and it would have sent shivers of fear up some people's spines.

"Agreed!"

One of the pillars of light coalesced into a platform that Kintara jumped onto. The intense concentrated solar energy made its horn glisten like the sun, a thing of intense fire and heat. The platform vanished as the energy gathered into Kintara's horn, and a moment later a beam of coruscating solar energy struck Aetheria's upraised left hand, where it seemed to vanish from reality. All of its light and heat were simply gone, but intense orange flames flickered within Aetheria's third eye momentarily.

"Not bad, I guess. Still, who's going to stand still while you charge up an attack like that if they don't have the means to counter it?"

"Raaahaha. See, Kintara? I have told you before. This is why brawn is best; you can't disperse muscles!"

The shark-faced Nethalos moved with surprising grace for an aquatic hybrid creature on land, but to Aetheria with Flash Mode fully activated, its movements were comparable to a snail. Jets of water shot out of holes along the back of the giant's armor, boosting its speed and strength on top of what it already had, to charge straight up and slam its two humanoid arms down onto the pathetic human.

Aetheria caught them with the pointer finger of her left hand; the force dispersed as if it had never existed. She then pushed her hand forward in a quick jerk, which thrust the giant's arms into the air, barely missing its own snout.

"Haha, looks like she's stronger than you are, Nethalos. So much for brute strength."

"She shan't withstand the power of the Abyssal Tides!" Nethalos again grandstanded, and waved his arms in the air. The tide pools of water all churned before highly pressurized streams of water shot at Aetheria from multiple angles.

Flash Freeze.

A nova of cold erupted from her, all of the water in the vicinity froze instantly, and the high velocity ice crashed into the sand where it shattered from the intensity of the cold around Aetheria herself.

"Is this supposed to be a comic relief fight? Come at me with everything you have, or I'll eat both of you."

". . . eat both of us? Haha. Funny, human." Nethalos didn't seem to comprehend the situation he was in.

"Let us attack together, Nethalos. Hear me, human, and know that none can withstand the full power of Helioshorn Kintara and Tidebreaker Nethalos!"

Aetheria arched an eyebrow at the pair and waited impatiently.

Nethalos raised his head, and emitted a terrific cry. It ruptured Aetheria's eardrums, but they repaired themselves immediately. The worst part of the attack, for her, was waiting for it to end. No doubt the attack should have stunned a lesser opponent, but Aetheria's body shrugged off the effects before Nethalos had finished screaming.

Kintara then spit a few small bolts of fire at three of the tide pools, creating a veil of mist to obscure the battlefield. Aetheria saw through it via Void Gaze, although Ethereal Sight saw through it as well.

Nethalos slipped toward Aetheria through the mists, eerily quiet despite his size, where he tried his overhand smash again, not at Aetheria, but at the sand in front of her. When his monstrous hands connected with the sand a new tide pool formed, and water moved to slosh around her boots. Inexplicably, pressure suddenly assaulted her. Not a slight increase either, but it felt as if she were carrying the Lost City of Atlanta. The sand under her compressed significantly from the forces it endured, but Aetheria didn't even move.

"And now the finishing blow!"

Kintara stood beneath a diffuse pillar of light in the center of the dome. Well, a previously diffused pillar, as suddenly all of the other light formations bent to aim at Kintara and form one massive solar well for the beast to draw from. Aetheria's eyes watered a little at the intensity of it all.

"Diiiiie!"

A beam of energy shot toward Aetheria like before, but this one was easily five times the thickness, and much more concentrated and powerful. The result didn't change. The beam vanished into nothing, until the kirin stopped its attack.

"But . . . but . . . I've beat gods with that attack!"

Darkness engulfed the entire dome, and only Aetheria could see within it. Even the Administrators lost visual on the events occurring inside the dome. Two minutes later, the darkness vanished. Aetheria sat on the sand, seemingly bored, and not even a speck of blood remained of Kintara or Nethalos. The dome faded from around her, and suddenly she sat on a couch next to Werylin.

"You beat Arkaziel and me?"

"I had to fight a doppelganger of myself. It didn't have my equipment, and it couldn't speak a Word when I cut its throat. Off-putting, cutting your own throat, but it was a quick victory."

"Ouch, lopsided. Pretty much what happened to me, too. Arkaziel must be playing with his food again?"

"It seems that way. It's unusual for the waiting room to have no entertainment."

"I doubt whoever set up this floor expected us to end it so quickly, or maybe there's another component to the challenge. Did you claim anything particular from your opponent?" Aetheria dropped two items onto a brand-new coffee table made of ice. The first looked like a fragment of Kintara's horn, and glowed with an inner fire. However, its intricate designs did not match the kirin's horn prior to its death, so Aetheria kept the strange fragment. It had a slightly spherical notch missing. The second item she dropped absorbed light and reflected shimmers of blue across the room. The strangely shaped scale had a crescent moon cutout in the center. While it looked similar to some of the scales that had covered Nethalos, the shark-giant had not had any with a moon cutout while alive.

"I got this?" Werylin set an amulet on the table. Made from a reflective crystal, it showed a reverse-world when you looked through it. Aetheria suspected if you looked at doppelgangers or shapeshifters through it, it would show their true form.

Yet when she held it up to her eyes and looked at herself, she just saw her normal self. The perimeter of the amulet, a beautiful wood, had been worked cleverly to give the impression of roots and earth, but it still seemed to be missing something.

"Hmm. Does the horn fragment go with that?"

"It's a little disconcerting when your third eye blinks and focuses on something."

"It's a jewel. It doesn't blink or focus on things, Werylin. Are you sure you aren't imagining it?"

"No, it definitely blinked and then gazed at the items."

"Huh. Weird. Anyway, yes, this fits together." Aetheria picked up the horn fragment and the amulet, and gently turned and prodded until the horn fragment fit within the root designs of the amulet, to give the appearance of a sun.

"I'm guessing Arkaziel has the last piece, then."

"The last piece of what?" The aforementioned cat appeared in the room.

"You both beat me? I know I was taking my time; it's not often I get to eat dragons, but still, I didn't take that long. Did you two even have to fight?" Arkaziel eyed the objects on the table, and grudgingly a stone appeared on the table from his spatial storage.

"I was going to eat that, you know." Yellow eyes stared forlornly at the gem. It pulsed with inner warmth, almost like a heartbeat, and was encased in a setting that looked almost like an entire claw, but one of the claws remained empty.

"Not a very hard puzzle." Shadows reached out, and rotated and adjusted until the blue scale formed the night, opposite the horn fragment's day side, in the roots. Before Arkaziel could set it down, the empty claw on the gem grasped the combined amulet and a flash of energy erupted. The Heartstone flickered much stronger now, with each piece of the puzzle finished.

The door to the next floor appeared.

The gemstone flickered quicker, and energy built up around it. Aetheria guessed it would probably disappear now that it had finished its purpose. Arkaziel seemed to think the same thing would happen, as he ate the key whole, before it could vanish.

"I told you I was going to eat it!"

"The physics of a StarMane's feeding are best left a mystery." Werylin patted the cat on the head while they approached the door.

"Did you even chew that or just swallow it? Your mouth isn't even big enough to fit the key inside it right now. At least pretend to follow natural laws."

"Why should I? If you're strong enough to overcome something, why pretend you aren't? That's stupid, and I'm still really hungry and more than a bit hangry. The next floor better have a better meal for me."

Aetheria groaned as images danced in her mind of a kitchen and a contest to feed a cat.

CHAPTER 76

Chef Cat

Aetheria had been right with her ominous feeling—perhaps another aspect of Void Gaze showing itself? If so, she would really have appreciated it if her precognition showed itself in time to change the scenario, not after. The trio appeared inside of what looked exactly like a television studio, one laid out for a cooking show. Before she or her companions had time to wonder what they had gotten into now, a disembodied announcer's voice filled the studio space.

"On today's episode of 'Can You Beat Bobbi Slay' we have a three-way competition to take on the Queen of the Kitchen! Who will take on the Cultivator of taste, despite being destined to lose? From the backwaters of that ancient dread planet Grief, we have the former politician and swordsman Werylin Amaryllis. Tell me Werylin, what kind of dish are you going to prepare for us today?"

Confusion dominated the elf's facial expression. Unlike Arkaziel, Werylin had never heard the tales of reality TV competition shows from Earth. When silence reigned for a few seconds, a hologram of an annoyed fairy appeared before him, holding a mic toward him.

"What are you cooking for us today, elf? Or have you already thrown in the towel to admit your inability to even challenge the mighty Bobbi Slay, the Savory Sage."

Directly addressed and challenged, Werylin snapped out of his daze.

"I'll be producing one of my favorite dishes, a salad of ancient elven design to honor Gaia, accompanied by a shank of Flavorfern venison. With a mix of savory and salad, this victory will be mine!" Werylin finished strong, although the wink he gave Arkaziel gave away to Aetheria the cat had coached him a little.

"Sounds great! I look forward to trying your old-timey, rustic elven recipe. Next, we have the Ethervoid Asura. What can we expect from you, Lady Aetheria, perhaps a recipe as quixotic and diverse as yourself?" The fairy flitted to and fro nervously before Aetheria, as if afraid the Asura would just reach out, grab her, and eat her. The fear displayed by the little creature threw Aetheria off, and she was slow to offer an answer. Arkaziel did not come to her rescue.

"I'll be making hotdish, with some Jell-O salad."

"What kind of vegetables go in a Jell-O salad?" the fairy asked accusingly.

"Well, you see, there'll be some marshmallows, strawberries, and pineapple." Aetheria grimaced at the outraged face of the fairy.

"None of those things are vegetables or salad."

"No, no I guess not . . ." Aetheria trailed off and waited for the fairy to go bother Arkaziel.

Arkaziel had taken on his human form for this challenge, although he had cat ears instead of human ones, and a tail.

"Arkaziel the Edacious, it's a pleasure to have you on our show. The Goddess of Gastronomic Grace is quite a fan of some of the recipes you distributed in the trade cities you've visited."

"Oh gosh, Bobbi Slay knows who I am? That's just so encouraging, Tinka! Well, today I'm busting out a new recipe for our viewers at home; I call it the Euphoric Eclipse Platter. We'll start with some Luminous Lobster Bisque, Shadow Squid Risotto, and well, for the rest you'll have to wait until I finish!"

Aetheria wondered if she had finally lost her mind. *Am I actually on a TV show right now? Is Arkaziel conspiring against me? What the heck is going on?*

In a haze of confusion Aetheria worked quietly at the cooking station they had given her. Hotdish was easy, especially since the production team had all of the ingredients prepared for her. First she cooked ground beef, seasoned it heavily with garlic, onion, and salt. Once that was done she drained the meat, which formed the bottom layer of the hotdish. Next up, she mixed milk, a can of cream of mushroom soup, and frozen vegetables together to make up the next layer, which got topped off with cheese. The final layer? Tater tots. Just a whole mess of tater tots, and then she tossed it into the oven.

The fairy, Tinka, never came back to talk to her, and just flitted between Werylin and Arkaziel.

"Your so-called salad without vegetables?"

The fairy showed up when she wasn't wanted. Aetheria cut a bunch of strawberries, cut pineapple into small chunks, and squeezed some juice in with the cut pineapple, then mixed up Jell-O, cottage cheese, and some of the fruit into a blender where it got hammered. She ignored the fairy, and worked. The final steps were to mix cream, sugar, and vanilla to make a whipped cream, then fold everything together. In no time at all her dessert went into a refrigerator to chill.

The fairy had fluttered off to bug the boys, leaving Aetheria to sit on a stool and enjoy the peace and quiet, and use a spoon to lick out the mixing bowl for the Jell-O salad. It tasted sweet, but maybe she should have used higher tiered ingredients, because it had a hollowness to it she'd come to associate with low quality ingredients. While she daydreamed about Earth and all the crazy episodes of cooking shows she used to watch, the other two finished their dishes.

"Let's welcome our fantastic judge, Carrie Cherry!" The strange voice from nowhere echoed across the stage, while Tinka flew to a newly appeared judge's table with a plate of each of the recipes.

With a name like Carrie Cherry, Aetheria sort of expected a humanoid to be the judge. Instead, a quivering mass of a gelatinous being appeared in a burst of light behind the judge's table. Mostly transparent with a cherry-red sheen to the viscous wobbling orb of a body, Aetheria could only assume that Carrie Cherry was some sort of ooze, cube, or some kind of jiggly slime creature.

"Now it's everyone's favorite moment, the taste testing! As a reminder to our viewers and contestants, Carrie can taste upwards of a thousand tastes simultaneously without any concerns of cross-contamination. Behold, the judgment begins!"

Tinka pushed plate after plate into the quivering, gooey form of Carrie Cherry. Arkaziel's dishes were pushed into the upper part of her body, Werylin's into the midsection, and Aetheria's into her lower half. If there were cameras or a stream of this, her dish would probably be off camera, but she was okay with that. It'd been decades in the tower without her cooking. Plus, she had to admit, Arkaziel's dish looked amazing.

Arkaziel's plate could have been a work of art. A shallow bowl of golden, shining lobster bisque sat to one side, while opposite it sat the dark shadowed squid risotto. The risotto seemed to quiver with shadows, ready to burst with delicious decadence with a single bite. In the middle of the plate, the flaked raw fish, or twilight tartare, had been layered between vibrant ambrosial oranges and grapefruit segments. Sprinkled over the entire dish were nocturnal and sun-loving herbs, each brimming with color, and to her Ethereal Sight, power. The final touch? A Galaxy Gelée, a translucent jelly speckled with gold and silver stars, and even a black hole at its center represented by a voidberry.

With each passing moment, the food dissolved inside Carrie Cherry, and the judge jiggled in pleasure.

"What's this? Oh my, in a shocking turn of events, the winner of the contest is none other than Aetheria!" Tinka made a shocked, surprised face, before her expression changed utterly and she smirked viciously at Aetheria.

"Psych! Carrie says your so-called food is an insult to food judges everywhere, and you lose. In second place, the handsome elf!"

"I win!" Arkaziel cheered.

"That's right! You've won the right to battle Bobbi Slay, the Divine Duchess of Dishes!"

Music played, lights flashed, and a grumpy fairy smoking a cigar herded Werylin and Aetheria offstage to sit in a tiny back room with a craft services table.

"This is weird, right?" Aetheria tried to hide her disorientation that resulted from the way this floor had gone.

"It's really strange, sure, but that happens when Administrators start digging through the entire party's mind to put together challenges. Aetherius's Tower does it less than some of the others, but I've heard there's a reason to avoid any of the more sadistic towers. They can get deeply personal quickly."

"I guess." Aetheria grimaced. It wasn't as if their next destination was the Tower of Doom, or anything ominous.

The stage filled with smoke and lasers, and a winged cat-woman descended from a hole in the ceiling. Like Arkaziel, she had a mostly humanoid form, with cat ears, a tail, and wings, although her wings vanished once she touched the ground. The woman radiated the power of a fifth tier Cultivator, although the strange energy around her was unfamiliar to Aetheria, but Void Gaze revealed to her the truth.

"Bobbi Slay is a StarMane." Aetheria gaped.

"I hope they don't make us listen to her full name." Werylin groaned.

Arkaziel and Bobbi stared at one another, and literal sparks filled the air between where they stood.

"I'm taking you down, Sauce Sorceress Slay!" Arkaziel's exuberance and excitement reached new heights that Aetheria had only ever seen displayed for eating gods.

"Oh please, your cooking is proof that not everyone improves with practice."

"Rawr! It's getting feisty in here." Tinka flew between the two.

"What are you cooking for us, oh Sultana of Spice?"

"A mystery!" Bobbi Slay said defiantly.

"I'll be cooking the Heart of Typhon, accompanied by a sauce of butter from Audhumla and a splash of Chronos's own whiskey." Arkaziel smirked, while Tinka's eyes got huge. Bobbi Slay had a confused look on her face, and eyed Arkaziel with something approaching suspicion.

The ingredients for their dishes already waited at their stations. Bobbi immediately started cooking, while Arkaziel sat on a stool, and ate his ingredients one by one.

"You can't eat the ingredients!" Tinka fluttered to and fro and screeched at Arkaziel.

"If I wanted to win, no. I'll beat Bobbi Slay another time, at another game. On our third meeting, shall we have a contest of skill, Slay!" Arkaziel may have slurred the last word, after drinking the vial of Chronos's whiskey.

Bobbi Slay brushed some nonexistent dust off her shoulder as she regarded Arkaziel. The woman's eyes were hard, but a small grin played across her lips.

"You have a long way to go to catch up to me, youngling. I'll be waiting." The female StarMane vanished in a poof of smoke and left the frantic Tinka to deal with the disruption to production. The trio didn't bother to hang around and find out. A shimmering portal to Floor 94 appeared when Bobbi vanished.

"Hate to eat and run, but we've got places to be and monsters to murder. Thanks for the Heart of Typhon, though, that was delicious." Arkaziel emitted a small burp before he turned into his cat form and hopped onto Aetheria's shoulder. He missed horribly, but Aetheria stretched her arm out to catch him and put him on her shoulder.

"Wowsies, Chronos is a good distiller."

"If you puke on me you won't live to have a rematch against Bobbi Slay," Aetheria warned her cat, before stepping through the portal to the next floor.

CHAPTER 77

Wally

The ninety-fourth floor wasn't much to look at. A single room, four walls, a floor, a ceiling. One wall had eyes on it, and a mouth. Said wall was a beautiful work of blue-white marble that made Aetheria very tempted to steal it, while the other three walls were plain brick affairs. A simple dirt floor and popcorn-textured ceiling completed the room.

The wall stared at the trio in annoyance for three long minutes before anyone spoke. Awkward tension continued to build, and no one wanted to be the one to break it.

"I'm not alive, yet I grow; I don't have lungs, yet I need air; I don't consume, but I can die. What am I?" The wall finally spoke, and a sigh of relief escaped each of the party members who had been holding their breath.

"That's an easy one, a fire." Arkaziel's words still slurred, and after another burp, he lowered his head and snored. Aetheria had to waft a fan-shaped hand a few times to disperse the miasma of alcohol that hung in the air from the cat's words. *Dang, Chronos, that smells like a Tier Seven paint thinner.*

"How many of these riddles do we have to solve to get to move on?"

"Ten. Nine to go. Are you ready for the next riddle?"

Werylin and Aetheria figured they could get by without Arkaziel. Healing the cat would negate the gains he would make from the heart and whiskey, so he just had to tough it out.

"I rise without wings, floating up high, disappearing by day and coming back at night. What am I?"

"A star." Werylin answered the second riddle without hesitation.

"What about a star? I want to eat a star. My tummy hurts." Arkaziel piped up from Aetheria's shoulder for a moment but closed his eyes and whimpered when reality proved too much for him. Aetheria adjusted her hexproof scarf to cover his face. It might not help Arkaziel except as a light blocker, but it would probably prevent her from being affected by any ailments herself from contact with the cat.

"I can be captured but not held, seen in the summer, but felt more in the winter. I'm lighter than air, but a million of me can still weigh you down. What am I?"

"A snowflake." Aetheria gestured, and hundreds of glimmering snowflakes swirled around her momentarily before dispersing back into nothingness. The wall didn't seem very impressed with her show. It rolled its eyes at her, as if to call her a basic excuse for a person. *I'm not basic, Michael!*

"Well, I need to up the difficulty, it seems. You aren't even talking amongst yourselves to answer these." The wall sounded annoyed that it needed to put forth effort. *I suppose walls are pretty lazy by nature. What do they do all day? Sleep? Cultivate? Oh man, if he's a cultivating wall I could burst through him and be all "I've broken through the cultivation wall!"*

"The person who makes it, sells it, the person who buys it never uses it, and the person who uses it never knows they're using it. What is it?"

Aetheria worked through several possibilities on that one. Gift could work, maybe, or maybe a will? Werylin's face scrunched up in frustration.

"Coffin," Arkaziel hissed through the scarf that covered his face. Usually Arkaziel's yellow eyes were alert, violent, ready, and willing to eat all that he could. Instead of the usual malevolent look the cat had, he appeared exhausted, drained of all vitality as his body fought against the ridiculously high tier alcohol while simultaneously trying to digest the energies of a god-heart.

"Beaten by a drunk cat. How embarrassing. Very well, the more you remove from me the larger I grow. What am I?"

"A hole?" Werylin sounded somewhat uncertain, but the wall grunted in annoyance and accepted the answer.

"Five answered, five to go. You are doing well. Two fathers and two sons sit down to eat eggs for breakfast. They eat exactly three eggs, and each person has one egg. How?" The wall smiled in self-satisfaction, and the smugness of its tone riled Aetheria who already considered bursting through the wall with a mighty *Oh yeah!*

Libby, what's the answer?

Response: There are only three men. A grandfather, father, and son, thus two men are fathers, and two are sons, despite only being three men, thus eating one egg each.

"There's just three men, a grandfather, father, and son," Aetheria answered, prepared to fight the wall if it challenged her answer.

"You got that quite fast; usually it takes at least a few minutes."

"I'm amazing," Aetheria agreed with the wall.

"I am a three-digit number. My tens digit is five more than my ones digit, and my hundreds digit is eight less than my tens digit. What number am I?"

The two Cultivators eyed the wall dangerously when it crossed into the realms of math, but the riddle didn't seem that difficult to Aetheria, but that no doubt had something to do with the passive effects of Libby and her Flash Mode resulting in her thought processes firing at a speed that would dwarf most computers.

"194."

"I have three sides. If you add my two shorter sides together, you'll get more than the longest side. What am I?"

"A triangle." Aetheria had used that one as a librarian to help freshman high schoolers.

"Can you name three consecutive days without using the words Monday, Tuesday, Wednesday, Thursday, Friday, Saturday, or Sunday? Or whatever your cultural equivalent is."

Werylin rolled his eyes at the bias the tower gave toward Aetheria's culture over his own or Arkaziel's.

"Aren't you going to even try? Yesterday, today, and tomorrow." Snobbery always sounded appropriate, coming from elves.

"Last question before we get to move on; make it a good one!" Aetheria cheered the wall on.

"What comes down, but never goes up?"

"Rain," Aetheria answered with the simplest answer she could come up with.

"Night," grumbled Arkaziel, blinking in annoyance at the world. Then he closed his eyes abruptly and buried his face in Aetheria's neck.

"Sands in an hourglass?" Werylin answered at the same time as the other two, which meant Aetheria and Arkaziel turned to stare at him, given the length of words in his compared to theirs.

"What?"

"That's a pretty excellent answer." Aetheria laughed.

Arkaziel just groaned and hated his life. When Aetheria laughed, it jostled his hold on her shoulder, and the cat looked exceptionally hungover.

"Congratulations, you have answered my riddles ten. The way opens." The marble wall vibrated and fell out of existence. With his dispersal, the room extended another five meters to another marbled wall with a face on it. The other three walls remained brick.

"We meet again. You've traveled far since our last encounter." The wall smiled, and insanity lurked in its eyes. Aetheria wondered what kind of horrific story lay behind the sentient wall's madness.

"Would you like me to destroy you? Are they keeping you here against your will?"

"Why would I want you to destroy me!? What's wrong with you? You can't just go around breaking perfectly fine load-bearing walls because you are the adopted daughter of Aetherius, and this is his tower!" Wally cried and seemed to be genuinely terrified of Aetheria. It went so far as to stare pleadingly at Werylin for salvation.

"I'm so sorry. I just thought I saw some insanity lurking in your eyes there, and it seems like every other person in this tower is sick with something and needs me to kill them, even though I'm not a real big fan of killing people. Even if it's a mercy kill, it takes a toll, you know."

"Here's a riddle for you. What kind of psychopath would complain about being asked to do mercy killing instead of taking the time to inquire why everyone they encounter requires mercy killing?"

"Well, that's an easy riddle. Me!" Aetheria flashed pearly white teeth in a forced smile. Werylin suddenly looked nervous, the hairs on the back of his neck up, while the shadows around Aetheria writhed and the Third-Eye of Ein Sof looked more and more like a black hole than it had since its creation.

"Apparently, that counts as a riddle." The wall looked miserably up at the ceiling, as if the gods had abandoned it, and maybe existence wasn't worth the trouble.

"See! See! You saw his eyes, right Werylin?" Aetheria pointed vehemently at the wall and its glistening eyes.

"Yes, I did. Terminally melancholy. What's wrong, wall?"

"Look, it's got nothing to do with you fine people. Life as a wall just isn't what I thought it'd be. I've got a lot of time to sit here and think of riddles, and you know what? No hands! Not even a single finger! I don't have hands to have time on. Can't eat. I can't drink, or even write! So, I must sit here and keep going over riddles so I can keep them straight. And oh, if I get a really amazing, super complex, superb riddle, I can't even use it because of the rules. This is just the worst. Never become a wall."

"Would you like to become a wall in one of the cities I have in my inner realm? I've got an Aetherial city, the Lost City of Atlanta, a skykeep, and a few other buildings you might like to be part of? This place seems toxic."

"You'd take me out of here? Really? That's so kind of you! I'm deeply sorry I called you a psychopath." Wally forgot Werylin existed with a savior at hand. The elf walked along the marble wall, examining the intricate color combinations, his finger brushing over the glistening stone. A tiny bit of drool dripped from Wally's mouth.

"Oh, don't worry about it, Wally. Do you mind if I call you Wally? It'll be cold and quiet in my inner realm. I am the Ethervoid Asura, after all. Who knows, maybe you'll even mutate in the presence of my soul-connection to the Void, get some arms and limbs, and just terrorize my enemies. How's that sound?"

Wally had to bite its lip to contain its emotions.

The only sign that Werylin unsheathed Stormshimmer, cut through the mimic's core, and sheathed his blade again was the slight ripple across the wall of marble and the soft whisper of the katana kissing its sheath. The marble wall crumbled into dust; a large monster core fell to the ground. Aetheria pulled its core to herself with a few strands of hair and stored it in her repository until Arkaziel could handle the meal.

"Was it a mimic the first time and I missed it?" Werylin looked back to Aetheria, who shook her head.

"No, the first time, it was just a sentient wall. When it reappeared, it was a mimic. Shame, I wouldn't have minded a talking wall."

"A dog would just pee on it," Arkaziel helpfully added between whimpers of pain.

"Let's get to the next level. Maybe there'll be some antacids for our poor little guy." Aetheria stroked Arkaziel's head, while Werylin watched a cataclysmic beast get treated like a house pet.

"Floor Ninety-Five, here we come!" Werylin led the way.

CHAPTER 78

Gravity's Whimsy

Aetheria stepped through the portal and appeared atop a four-square-meter stone platform. Whoever cut the stone had done a perfect job, with smooth glasslike sides showcasing the beauty of the rock. The vast expanses of the void surrounded them, but it was the void of space, not the void of the Void. Surrounding the platform that they appeared on, hundreds of other similarly cut stone platforms floated. The entire field of stones moved with the same momentum toward a sun, but some of the platforms had additional properties, and orbited other small objects across the field.

=*The platforms have gravity fields, so if you think you're going to float, you'll end up falling on your face.*= Werylin's telepathic warning caused Aetheria to look down to the next platform, where the elf dusted himself off and held his bleeding nose.

+*Oh please, no.*+ The hungover Arkaziel lifted his head to observe the challenge of this floor, whimpered, and lowered his head and shut his eyes tightly.

=*I'll scout a path and figure out the gravity fields.*= Werylin didn't wait for a response from the others, and immediately dived into attempts to traverse the platform field by jumping.

Aetheria settled onto the stone platform she and Arkaziel appeared on, and considered the scenario. On the surface, this looked like a physical challenge. Space had no water, oxygen, or almost any other element most Cultivators worked with. It had an abundance of heat and cold, light and shadow, and other aspects, to make up for the absence of earth, fire, water, and air. Not that limitations like that affected Aetheria; those were concerns for Cultivators who didn't have the Frankenstein soul she possessed.

While Werylin fell and flew and spun through the gravity fields, which looked like one of those TV shows that's mostly about people getting hurt, Aetheria extended tendrils of the Void and pulled. The stones made a lovely clinking sound when they touched, and when like sides touched, the platforms merged into a single solid platform.

-*It's kind of cheap that the platforms have air and atmosphere, if you think about it. The whole setup is just a bad mishmash. A sun you are in danger from, gravity on tiny platforms, air in space. I don't like the concept of this floor. Pete should fire whoever designed this one for its lack of internal logic and consistency. ~*

=*Not all of us can breathe the Void, you know. I personally am thankful for the oxygen. This would be a lot harder challenge if you had to do it all before you ran out of breath.* =

+*Stop. Talking. Just stop.* +

Arkaziel's pathetic plea quieted the other two. It would have to be bad if it had reduced the normally imperious StarMane to begging.

The steady sound of clinking encouraged Aetheria's progress of joining platforms together. *I wonder if this is what it feels like being an earth mage in Gaia's tower. Or is being the same element as the tower a downside? These towers would really suck for people with only one affinity, or the inability to harmonize with any affinity the way I do with my repository.*

=*Oops. Uh, can you retrieve me? Apparently, these little orbs have very strong gravity fields.* =

Tendrils of the Void spread, and Werylin vanished from the man-sized orb he'd been crushed against to reappear next to Aetheria at the start of challenge.

"Your path seems like a much safer way to the end." Failure tinted Werylin's admission.

"The right tool for the job. If we walk now, I think I'll have finished the path by the time we get down to the end. Fancy a stroll through the cosmos?"

"That sounds strangely relaxing, especially after getting crushed against that orb."

"Do you need any healing?" Aetheria arched a brow. It hadn't even occurred to her to ask. Usually Arkaziel handled all party healing, but with him out of commission, his role still needed to be filled.

"No, thank you. I've been practicing using Aether circulation to affect regeneration. It isn't nearly as effective as your regeneration, but it seems to exceed what you'd expect from a troll, or other natural regenerators. It must have been an extremely bizarre experience to start your cultivation journey with Aether instead of mana."

"My journey was going to be strange no matter how it started, coming from a planet without magic. It let me ignore a lot of the conventional methods of cultivation and make progress despite my lack of education." *Being a living weapon forged by Transcendents and Primordials helped render my ignorance meaningless.*

"True. When you first entered my tomb on Grief, I assumed you were a newborn Aetherial in the guise of a human, or a fresh incarnation of a new god. Not a single speck of mana about you, but your capacity for Aether already exceeded anything a first tier should be capable of holding."

"Is that why you were so helpful to me?"

"Angering an Aetherial is little better than angering gods. While they are not truly immortal in the same fashion as the gods, they are ageless shapeshifters with incredible innate abilities. As a ghost, angering either could have easily gone poorly for me, while being helpful ended my torment. I made the right choice."

When the platforms formed a path from their original start position all the way to an illuminated dais with the silver portal to the next floor, Aetheria considered the floor complete. The door to Floor 96 required only that they walk over and through, but they took it slowly and enjoyed the views. The distance looked short, but it took over fifteen minutes for them to get to the goal from the start, with a casual walking pace the whole way.

"The things you do still astound me. You act like it is normal, but the things you do shouldn't be possible for anyone short of a god. Until you touched the Void, I wondered how you were maintaining yourself as a person so effortlessly, despite the powers you had at your fingertips. Then, I saw you were struggling, and that made me feel better, a little. Which is a terrible thing to feel when your friend is struggling against eldritch corruption, but you have to admit it is quite eerie how easily you push through any problem in your path."

Aetheria gestured, and two comfortable ice chairs appeared on the platform. She settled into one, and petted Arkaziel's head soothingly.

"All the things I do kind of scare me, Werylin. I spent a lot of my original life dreaming about being a heroine, or at least an action hero or adventurer. It didn't really go the way I expected it. All the mixed heritages and powers, I feel a little cheated. How much of what I do are the fragments of dead gods, or the power that Nyx used to glue all the disparate pieces of gods and my soul together? All I have a say in is in *how* I wield the powers, how I develop them, and what I wield them for."

"According to my father's belief, it was impossible to learn courage; I could only earn it through my actions and experiences. You are a very courageous person, Aetheria."

"It just looks that way, Werylin. I get scared like anyone else, and a lot of that confidence comes from knowing I'm immortal. Being immortal takes the threat out of most situations."

Werylin shook his head in disagreement. His silver eyes stayed on the void of space around them, instead of drifting to match the eyes of the Asura.

"There's an ocean's difference between fearing death and fearing pain. Being immortal does not make a person impervious to injury or hardship. How many times have I seen you face situations that could scar others for a lifetime?"

"I can turn pain off, you know. I don't very often, but I could. While I theoretically feel every cut, bruise, and wound as deeply as you do, the reality is I don't. My tier ups are so violently explosive that what happens to me in most fights is a joke in comparison, although I haven't been hurt much since I really tapped into my core's powers. I've sorted out coping mechanisms. Add some I'm probably not even aware of, plus desensitization, a higher goal, and you can work through any amount of pain."

Werylin again shook his head in disagreement.

"I don't think that makes your courage any less impressive. There are costs, and you step into danger willing to pay them every time. Pain is a deterrent to most people, Aetheria, one that is strong enough to deter them without the risk of death. For an Asura, you are too humble."

Aetheria snorted. "You make it sound grand, but the truth is it's probably just my innate stubbornness more than courage."

"You cannot progress on the Winding Way without a heaping helping of obstinance. Those people follow a path, not forge their own."

"Thanks, Werylin. It is nice to know your friends care for you, and see you struggle."

"I'm going to miss you two when we split up, even if you are both insane."

"We'll miss you, too. The world of Grief will be lucky to have you back. What did you intend to use your wish for, anyway?"

"I've been thinking about asking for assistance in getting my clan to leave the tower. The isle of the Aetherials isn't a welcoming place for lower tier Cultivators."

"Yeah, no, it isn't. I could leave you with Lost City of Atlanta to start your revival tour of the world? With a few of your descendants, you could pilot it, no problem. Flying cities might just be asking for Oizys to knock you out of the air, though."

"There is that. Think she'll still hold a grudge?"

Both laughed at the rhetorical question.

"That would be a great way to test the theory that destroying a tower destroys a god." Aetheria's tone had a sharpness to it. The warning wasn't for Werylin, but for the Administrators, Aetherius, and Oizys herself.

"It's good to have friends." Werylin laughed heartily. Aetheria almost thought she saw pity for Oizys in Werylin's eyes, but surely not.

"It is. It is also good to have a sober cat. Feel free to meditate while we wait on this goober. It could be a few days before he sobers up."

"I'll take you up on that. What about the sun?" Werylin pointed toward the star.

"I've already arrested the movement of the platform, and the dais shields this area. I'll wake you up if anything changes."

"You're just going to sit there, petting Arkaziel the whole time?"

"I spent a lot of time patting people's backs after they overdrank in my teens. Rural Minnesota was a wild place, back in the day. Besides, Arkaziel is soft and warm; it's why cats are the best."

"Alright, rouse me when it's time to hit the next floor."

CHAPTER 79

The Pillars of Desire

Seven days later, the trio stepped through the door to Floor 96, and when Aetheria's boots touched down on dark marble, the dark mustiness of a crypt replaced the infinite expanse of space. They appeared in the middle of an extremely high domed cathedral, with a series of eight paths going out amongst columns. The air tasted of dust, smelled stale, and to Aetheria's Void Gaze, each of the pillars pulsed with one of eight slightly different auras.

A small lectern rested in the middle of the dome, with a single plaque upon it, illuminated by a blue flame. Aetheria read the inscription in Ath aloud.

"Pick your path, face temptation, and stay upon it to the end."

"Oh yeah, temptation is the best." Arkaziel yawned.

"No, no, face temptation and overcome it. Not give in to it." Aetheria ruffled his head to wake him up more.

"Well, I'll take . . . that way." Werylin picked a way seemingly at random, but once he did, the eight-sided star on the floor glowed purple in the direction he had chosen.

"I'll take this one!" Arkaziel hopped off Aetheria's shoulder and made a show of stretching, while the star shaded black and white to dictate his direction.

"Hm. Good luck, boys!" Aetheria gave the two a nudge, and with their first steps, they vanished. Aetheria nodded to herself, and stepped into the darkness, but not on any of the paths. She would make her own.

After only a handful of steps, a pillar appeared before Aetheria. To her Void Gaze, it radiated a red aura, and she reached out to brush her fingers against it.

A foggy vision filled her mind. Her old bedroom back on Earth, a bed filled by herself and a certain Soul Witch. Exposed thighs, glimpses of breasts, and the arch of Aoibhe's back stirred some life within Aetheria's mind, but the reaction lacked strength. Aetheria batted the temptation away, and the pillar before her shattered into a thousand pieces and faded from existence. Annoyed more than tempted, she took more steps into the darkness.

Another pillar appeared before her, and again she touched it. This one held a coloration of purple, and another misty vision filled her mind. Aetheria sat in a chair in Sister Ann's office, only it wasn't Aetheria as she existed now, but Aesca Lampi as a little girl.

"My office again, Lampi? What about this time? Another so-called migraine? We know those aren't real, and you're just trying to get attention, you pathetic excuse for a girl."

The little girl just sobbed while the adult berated her. Aetheria stepped into her place.

"Ack! The eyes of the demon! What abyssal compact have you made, child?"

Aetheria stared at the nun with all three of her eyes. A small smile slipped across her lips while Sister Ann struggled against the slow releasing of her aura.

"You know, that's a question I've been asking myself for a while now. It's a lot stranger universe than I ever dreamed. When I was a child, I couldn't talk back or stand up to people like you, but I can now. You were a cruel, vindictive, hateful bitch that sided with popular children against anyone on the outs and made my life hell. Wow, just like that, it's all gone."

"W-w-what's gone?" Sister Ann remained terrified of the unveiled aura of darkness and holy light around the terrifying demon.

"My care. If I ever made it back to Earth, I could obliterate countries, rule the world, and none of it would satisfy me. You matter so little that until now, the idea of revenge never even occurred to me, and now that it occurred to me, it's just boring. I might be *from* Earth, but I am not *of* Earth anymore. You aren't worth my time, beyond in recognizing I have moved on."

The purple pillar shattered into a nothingness, as did the vision.

"I thought we finished with dredging up my past?"

The next pillar to block Aetheria's path had a transparent, mist-like quality to it. The vision that filled her mind represented lethargy, procrastination, laziness, and general sloth. It didn't find a hitch, and while her mind pushed the vision away, she obliterated the pillar with a punch.

Gold marked the fourth pillar. Shiny, sparkly, and completely worthless to Aetheria. Or was it? She liked to take shiny things, and who didn't love looting a treasure chest or villain's stockpile? What about the Ambrosial Garden she had stolen from a dragon? The floating cities she kept collecting? While gold itself held no interest for her, opulence, material riches, and epic loot were all very much of interest to her. A small part of her knew it was not morally justifiable to steal everything in the tower that wasn't nailed down, but she had taken part in a not insignificant amount of larceny with the justification of Aetherius clearly meant it for her.

Yet, with what she knew about the towers now . . . that many inhabitants were Dwellers, while the natives were souls between reincarnations. That the aforementioned gods harvested the progress of the souls between reincarnations. It made it all worse. Victimizing the victims, it didn't look good on anyone. *No more stealing.*

The gold pillar shattered, slivers of gold exploded far and wide through the infinite darkness of the cathedral of sin. Aetheria pulled a sliver of gold from her neck and hand before she discarded them with annoyance.

A noxious green pillar formed before her. Aetheria could smell the gentle scent of all the perfumes she'd ever smelled someone else wear and been jealous about. She imagined that bitch who taught third grade and let her daughter bully her non-daughter students. Aetheria smiled at the memory of Nicole tripping her bully into a puddle of mud. The largest cringe of them all, though, was when she'd stirred the drama pot in a rival guild to break up their raid team, so that they wouldn't beat the Knights of Academia to a boss kill. *In hindsight, that might have been extreme. I'm a glorious Asura shapeshifter now. What do I have to be jealous of other people about? They're not-being-a-living-weapon? A simple life with kids? I miss computer games . . .*

"No. I'm a living god, with a soul-bound dragon-cat as a best friend, and a ridiculously sexy super powerful witch as my soul-partner. What in the shit do I have to be jealous of anyone else about? Stupid!"

The green pillar disintegrated from the intense cold that manifested with Aetheria's anger.

Her anger seemed to summon the next pillar, a thing of darkness and fiery red. It burned harshly in response to her flare of emotions.

"You, I know. Anger. Outrage. Wrath. You are every bit as addicting as *EFWO*, and just as bad for my health. It's so fun to be indignant. Psst. I'm so done with you. The trick isn't to not get angry; the trick is to let it go when it isn't useful anymore. I know you aren't used to playing second fiddle to envy, but there you go. Now, go away."

Arcing waves of the Void burst from Aetheria and shattered the wavering form of the red pillar.

The seventh pillar burned with a dim orange light, and Aetheria kicked it into dust. Gluttony had little to no hold upon her, to the point it couldn't even form a vision, let alone stop or slow her down.

Blue, a deep and cool blue like her Frostfire, marked the eighth pillar. Aetheria didn't have a chance of resisting the blue pillar. A vision formed in her mind of Aoibhe in a casket, and it solidified the moment she felt the pain and loss spread through her heart. Where, in this vision, was Arkaziel? Nowhere to be seen. How had her partner died? With bound souls, their immortality became twice ensured, yet something killed her beloved.

Aetheria's emotions cooled, Void Gaze prevented the vision from asserting itself as truth. Her fist blasted through the pillar barehanded, at her top speed and with all of her energy-enhanced strength behind it. A wave of destruction shot from her fist, deleted the pillar, and rained destruction into the dark void beyond. A glowing light appeared ahead of her, but she drew one of her nails along the skin of her palm and let black blood drop onto a forming raven of ice.

"Bird of my desire, find the one who crafted that vision and deliver this to them." Aetheria tossed a swirling ball of coldness to the icy blood-bird, who then flew off with it. Less than a second later, the damned thing attacked her back and hit her with her own orb, which obviously did nothing but annoy her.

"Fine, I get it. You set the sin; I conjure the vision?" Logic, details, or just general tower trickery had doused the flames of her wrath. *This time.*

Aetheria brushed the snow and ice off her trench coat and walked through the remaining yards of darkness to the light. The light source turned out to be a small teleportation circle, which took her to a waiting area. No one else had made it yet, but the enormous buffet table along the back wall contained fried phoenix wings, twilight potato crisps, Tier Four beers, and an assortment of fruits and pastries.

"I accept your offer of peace this time. Invoke a vision of Aoibhe against me again, and I'll leave Aetherius running the show solo."

Request: Where did user learn to create simulacra?

"Hi, Libby. I read it in a book once. Guess it stuck with me, and I tried it out while I was in the moment."

The intelligence behind the Astrum Nexus said nothing more. Its silence felt almost as if Aetheria had offended it with her answer. Aetheria ate some phoenix, drank some beer, and finished the second layer of her inner world's crust. When she returned to her body, both Werylin and Arkaziel had stuffed plates in front of them and were eating angrily.

"How long have you two been back for?"

"I got here about twenty minutes ago," Werylin answered politely after he finished chewing.

"Five minutes ago." Arkaziel spoke with his mouth open, his feline eyes full of extra amounts of murder. The feral edge that the Twilight Tenets helped blunt danced around Arkaziel on full display for all to see. Even the shadows he used to toss fried phoenix into his mouth were more Void than shadow.

"Do you need help to pull it together, Ark? Maybe you can form something like my third eye?"

"I'm good," the StarMane snapped slightly testily. "Daris won't be coming back anymore. I'll just have to accept it and move on. I guess that means there's room for Bobbi Slay in my life now?" The attempts at nonchalance to cover the loss of his twin hurt Aetheria's heart. She might not feel a lot anymore, but her friends and loved ones still evoked strong reactions from her.

I might not be human anymore, but I'm not completely inhuman either.
Yet.

Oh, screw you, Fred!

Can you not hear the silent dirge, the lament of stars that have witnessed eons? The threads of your reality tremble on the cusp of transformation. A storm approaches. When the skies bleed colors beyond sight and time falters in its march, you will stand at a precipice of the incomprehensible. A reckoning comes, a great turning, but not a beginning nor an end. Perhaps, a metamorphosis?

"Sorry." Aetheria apologized to the boys, who stared in horror at the phoenix bones she'd bit through in a burst of anger at Fred and his cryptic warnings.

CHAPTER 80

Dry Gorge

Arid, waterless air marked the trio's arrival at a new floor. The scent of sage and dust clogged Aetheria's nose, and she had a good look at her own shapely legs kicked up on a poorly fashioned wooden desk. Sunlight poured through the open windows and glinted off the metal star on her coat's collar, and the old-school revolver on her hip. Arkaziel sat on the desk, and he looked more adorable than ever before. A black bowler hat sat on his head, a single raven's feather adorning it, and he had a monocle over his right eye. The monocle made his eye look massive and accentuated the predatorial view of the cat's yellow eye, which contrasted strongly with the adorableness of the bowler hat.

"I've already erected an ice monument to your adorableness in my inner realm, Ark." Aetheria smiled brightly at the harrumph that escaped Arkaziel.

"What even is this?" Werylin asked from where he stood behind a smaller desk opposite Aetheria's. The swordsman wore a brown duster over his hakama, and his katanas continually got caught on the duster.

"You don't have the equivalent of westerns on Grief? So, where I came from there was a period of wild expansion on frontier territory, that coincided with the spread of guns, cattle, and crime. Lots of drinking whiskey, being dusty, and talking in cool accents. Very heavily romanticized."

"Sheriff! Sheriff! There's been a murder at Bill's!" The shouts drifted in the window before a man dressed in dirty work clothes burst through the door into the sheriff's office. She knew his name to be Jordy, and that he was a good sort if you needed a herd run from point *A* to *B*.

"A murder at Bill's? Let's get going." Aetheria picked up the black cowboy hat off the desk and settled it on over her head. It required a minor adjustment, her hair shifted from a ponytail to hanging free, but Jordy didn't seem to notice. "Come on, Ark."

The cat jumped onto her shoulder, his hat almost, but not quite, touching hers. Clearly the Administrator who gave Arkaziel a bowler hat had taken the pair's usual traveling method into consideration.

"Deputy, with me." Aetheria winked at Werylin, and excitement she didn't know she still possessed filled her heart. Something about the scenario just tickled her funny bone and reminded her of her dad watching westerns.

Bill's was a two-story saloon, the biggest building in Dry Gorge. Blue paint slathered the knotted wood exterior of the establishment. Bill had acquired the blue at a discount from a trader, but the quick fade and peel of the paint left Bill sour on the expense, and a year later the bar owner could still be heard muttering the name of the merchant darkly.

The double swinging doors of the bar still shifted with the momentum left from Jordy sprinting to get the sheriff.

Halfway between the bar and swinging doors a body lay, blood pooling across the dusty planks. Bill, who looked remarkably like Sam from Solace, rushed over to meet the sheriff and deputy.

"Alright, Deputy, I want you to interview each of the witnesses individually, take statements. Bill, tell me what happened."

The barman tipped his hat to the deputy when Werylin moved off to execute his mission.

"Well, Sheriff, I didn't rightly see everything. Silas there came in with an awful big smile, waving a small bag and ordering a round of drinks on him for everyone. A good prospector, Silas, but bad people skills. A flash of light from across the street by your office blinded me before I could ask Silas what good fortune befell him, and then a shot rang out. Silas fell over dead, and I didn't catch a single glance of who shot him."

Aetheria nodded. The barman told the truth, although she didn't want to rely too heavily on Void Gaze to figure out the mystery. Part of her wanted to solve it on intuition and logic alone.

"Anyone new in town, or did Silas have any enemies?"

"Well, Miss Mayfield at the bar arrived on the coach this morning. She's an inquisitive sort, and she's hiding something, but I don't know that she strikes me as a murderer. Roz Hartley is up from River Corners, but she ain't got a pistol on her. Only carries a rifle when she does the mail runs, you know."

"Right, right. So, no one had a history with Silas?"

"Well, I wouldn't say that, Sheriff. You know how Silas was, not real personable, kept to himself. Him and Teddy Wallace had some arguments about Silas trying to court Lilith Montgomery that near came to fisticuffs not long ago, and then there was that incident with Torres about how they ought to split the haul of that copper vein they found together. That one was back when Jonah was still sheriff."

Aetheria nodded as she looked over the people in the room.

+*Werylin, the guy that——*+

-*NO! Stop it. Dammit, Arkaziel! I wanted to enjoy this floor!*-

+*I didn't cheat, but if you want to do it your way, go ahead. I could be wrong. I'm not, but I could be. It's what you're supposed to do, Ria. What kind of group gets this far in the tower without having at least one or two magic users with them?*+

~Just let me have this.~

"Well, seeing as how Wallace and Montgomery aren't here, that might give them an alibi. Was Silas facing the bar when he got shot?" Aetheria tried to rebuild excitement by reconstructing the crime.

"Well, yeah, he walked right in and came straight for the bar. The blood exploded out of his chest, so someone shot him from the front of the saloon. Didn't see no one outside, and the McCoy boys have been drinking all morning. Doubt any of them could even lift their heads, let alone shoot someone at a dozen paces."

A quick once over of the McCoy boys showed Jonah's estimation on their sobriety to be quite accurate. Two of the four brothers were asleep, a third blearily looked at the sheriff and Bill. The final McCoy brother, Agnus, stared out the window. He was blind, and never carried a weapon.

"Sheriff, I've found the culprit," Werylin announced as he joined the group.

"Oh yeah, how'd you pull that off, Deputy?"

"Well, when I applied a little encouragement to the men gambling over there, Three-Fingers Tommy admitted it was him. He and Silas found the same prospecting site, and he claims Silas edged him out, so when that bright flash happened before, he used his decoy art to shoot Silas in the back."

"Why'd he admit to it?" Aetheria frowned.

"Well, I might have let slip that the Law Cat can smell crime."

A flash of light flickered out in the main street of Dry Gorge, and a familiar portal to the next floor awaited them.

Aetheria couldn't contain the sigh anymore, and walked out of the bar to the doorway with a dejected set to her shoulders, before she shook it off. *I'm not going to steal from people anymore, so I shouldn't treat them like actors in a set, even if that's how the towers treat them. Be better, me, be better.*

~Let's find out what's next, I'm over the disappointment of this level. Sorry about that.~

+Why were you so interested in these "westerns" anyway?+

~I used to watch them with my dad. It was a bonding experience, and I don't know, I had more than a few daydreams about being a sheriff in the Wild West as a kid. Just lost track of my priorities for a minute there, when all those old dreams rushed back.~

=That's very adorable, especially from you, Ria. I still don't see the appeal to a dusty wood town in the middle of a desert, where everyone is an unwashed dirt grubber or a herder.=

~Well, there's also usually bandits, natives, supernatural phenomena, and of course rich villains like the railroad owners, bankers, and corrupt mayors. Sometimes they'd tie damsels to railroad tracks.~

=Natives? If there are people already living here, and settlers show up, doesn't that make them invaders?=

~I'm not touching that with a ten-meter pole, regardless of which dimension I'm in.~

+You know, we could have a few drinks in the bar before we go through the portal. Maybe take a few bottles with us as souvenirs.+

~No. Wasn't your last hangover bad enough? Besides, I'm trying to cut down on our larceny. These poor people have little enough, the last thing they need is us taking what they do have.~

+Cut down on larceny? When were you planning on telling me this? I disagree, most vociferously. StarMane laws on possession are very clear that it's the property owner's duty to protect their property, and any property that they fail to protect becomes legally mine once I acquire it.+

=No one recognizes StarMane tradition as a viable law to excuse theft.=

~Nor should they, that is the stupidest idea ever. Next you'll tell me that only StarManes are actually people, therefore only StarManes can own things; therefore it's totally okay to kill everyone who isn't a StarMane and take their stuff.~

+Have you been reading about our cultural traditions? I'd been holding off telling you about that one until we encountered someone who has something I want extremely badly.+

~No. Just no. We need to clean up your act, too, or you'll never be able to keep the Void at bay. Those tenets in your soul won't do the job forever if you aren't working on maintaining balance yourself, you know.~

+Ugh. Next you're going to say we have to take vows of poverty, or embrace all life equally. What a crock. I'm a StarMane, you're an Asura, and Werylin is an Aetherial elf. Other lives aren't as great as ours, and sure, I'll help people if we can, but there's got to be a return. Quest rewards, karma, money, ancient techniques, grandpa's old sword from the closet that actually is a masterpiece by the greatest smith ever. That kind of thing, you know.+

~That's not helping people, Arkaziel, that's being a mercenary.~

+Why can't we do that?+

=Because Aetheria is kind, and even you would get bored of the mercenary life, my friend. As your power continues to grow, less and less people will be able to afford you. Do you just sit in a dark room awaiting the next payment, or do some for-fun-work between paying assignments?=

+When you put it that way, I can get behind it. Why didn't you put it that way, Blue?+

Because I'm not a sociopath.

~I just didn't think of it, I guess. Now, everyone get through the portal. Three levels to go!~

+What was the deal with that Mayfield woman in the bar, anyway?+

=She worked for a newspaper, and she was trying to make a big scoop about Bill and a whole slew of other bar owners getting suckered by merchants dealing substandard goods. Guess she's been chasing a group of peddlers for months.=

~Who cares about merchants? Through the portal!~

CHAPTER 81

Loon'tharak,
Caller from the Depths

Disappointment came in many flavors. The current flavor that Aetheria tasted resembled neglect. She and Werylin appeared inside of a room that swung back and forth and showed the view of a behemoth of a pond with vegetation at the edges, a mist of darkness past that, and beyond that, only the void. She, of course, recognized the material, and the glimpses of scales and fur at the edges of the structure she and Werylin had appeared inside. As far as she could put together, they were inside the moon on Arkaziel's collar, while the StarMane himself seemed to be in some abyssal pond.

An unnatural light created a peculiar scene, between the primeval vegetation, the dark abyss, and the shimmering, blue-green pond. Air bubbles emerged. Then more. The water agitated. A massive form, twice the size of Arkaziel in his draconic form, broke through the surface of the water. White and black feathers and red eyes full of murder took in the intruder. Many long sickly tentacle appendages rose from its back, and three from its lower bill. A mighty cry reverberated across the entirety of existence around the pond.

"Who dares disturb the slumber of Loon'tharak?" The creature that crested the water to float on its surface certainly looked like an eldritch abomination and a loon mixed together, Aetheria thought, but something about its presence felt a little too cheerful, a little too not Void-y. Her Void Gaze identified the duck as being comprised of powerful Nether energies, not the true Void, so she assumed that was the fakeness that rang hollow with her.

"I do." Arkaziel sounded both bored and confused, with a dark edge underneath his words. Had Arkaziel always had that dark edge when dealing with something edible? Yes, he had, Aetheria realized, so she didn't worry about it being a symptom of the influence of the Void.

"Complete my trial, an—"

One massive spear of darkness blasted up from the depths of the pond, but Loon'tharak managed to partially dodge the spear and only took a flesh wound in one of its wings. A flesh wound that healed in mere seconds. Regeneration and self-healing were very common powers once one breached the fourth tier, and almost no beings reached the fifth tier without some form of recovery.

"You aren't even Duckthulu, and you think you can give me advice, you stupid bird?"

Two bright beams of light shot from Arkaziel's eyes. The cat's lasers seared feathers and flesh while the bird attempted to reposition for battle, and Arkaziel hopped into the air.

"I didn't think he'd go straight to assault," Werylin complained as their world shook.

"It's a bird. Of course, he's going to try to eat it. Is Duckthulu a real thing?" Aetheria laughed.

"I've never heard of a Duckthulu, but maybe Arkaziel has. His kind are widely traveled."

Loon'tharak lifted its head and released a haunting cry. Arkaziel's body stilled, but Aetheria could tell with Void Gaze he was only pretending to be affected by paralysis. His body fell from the sky straight toward the eldritch bird. At the last second, Arkaziel moved his claws to slice at Loon'tharak's face and blew a point-blank burst of twilight energy into its face. The mixture of light and darkness dazzled and blinded the enemy, while also leaching vitality from it.

"Aak!" Loon'tharak cried in shock as claws and teeth mauled it. The struggle ended when the bird dived under the water, and rather than be dragged along with it Arkaziel retreated into the sky. The smooth reflection of the pond suddenly showed seven different versions of Loon'tharak headed toward the surface, and Arkaziel didn't seem to know which one belonged to the real bird. With Void Gaze, Aetheria discerned the original.

Before the bird broke the surface the illusion shattered like a glass panel, and dozens of shards of glass fired at Arkaziel as if they were heat-seeking projectiles. When they slashed through the StarMane he disappeared, revealing he, too, had only been an illusion. Loon'tharak shot up through the surface to attack where Arkaziel's illusion had been and squawked in terrible surprise when nothing remained to attack.

Arkaziel pounced from invisibility, his sharp teeth ripping into the bird's neck, his claws ripping at its back. All three of his twilight clones formed to brutalize the eldritch bird. Aetheria and Werylin grumbled, since they had such a poor view of the fight.

A massive wave rose from the pond to strike and push Arkaziel, his three duplicates, and Loon'tharak into the water. Arkaziel sidestepped through shadows to appear on the edge of the pond, an illusion left behind to take the attack in his place. His poor duplicates got sucked into the pond with the loon, and it didn't take long for bursts of energy to rise to the surface of the pond to indicate the loss of the twilight duplicates.

Arkaziel melded into the shadows of the vegetation, and waited patiently. Eventually, Loon'tharak surfaced and warily scanned the area for its opponent.

"I was going to give you a trial to help you control the Void, but have it your way, cur." Loon'tharak lifted its head and cawed. The pond shook, and above, a meteorite appeared and shot toward the pond.

"I'll survive just fine, but will you, cat?" Loon'tharak's arrogant, high-pitched voice almost made Aetheria try to teleport out to join the fight, it was so annoying.

Arkaziel appeared in the sky, dropping his invisibility. He swiped his claws, and black slices of the Void fired off toward the meteor. When they hit the meteor imploded; not a single atom of it remained in existence.

"Oblivion Eclipse!"

Could the darkness of space grow even darker? It could. A veil of the true Void fell across everything, and absence reigned supreme for a moment in which time ceased to exist, then it shattered like an illusion, but the fragments all flew toward Arkaziel's maw where a sphere of annihilation had formed before his mouth. A void beam of annihilation shot out of the orb of oblivion, and the entire pond dissolved into nothing. With only a few small moves of his head to send the blade of energy through the whole pond, he destroyed everything but himself and Loon'tharak.

"Err. Perhaps we should start over?" Loon'tharak queried the cat while it floated in the void.

"No." Arkaziel lifted a paw, and a dozen spears of light shot from his left paw. Loon'tharak's tentacles shifted to block the spears, but in doing so he created shadows across his back, which Arkaziel stepped out of. Two swipes of his Void Claws sent the tentacles adrift, and then his sharp teeth got the bird's neck, but this time the cat had enhanced his teeth with the Void. These savage bites brutalized the constructed bird in no time at all.

"Well, that was kind of anticlimactic." Werylin grunted.

"Arkaziel has much better control of the Void than I thought he might. He's been practicing."

"What if Arkaziel isn't the first StarMane to get infected by the Void, but just the first to remain fully in control? He could have genetic knowledge about the Void." Werylin rubbed his chin thoughtfully with the words.

"That's actually possible." Aetheria had never considered it and hadn't even asked if any StarManes had ever used the Void in the past. Here she had been feeling guilty for her ability to adapt to the Void by balancing cores and the Third-Eye of Ein Sof, but perhaps Arkaziel had also been equipped with his own advantages and in the same situation?

"Probable, even. Ark's really taking his time to savor the bird, isn't he?"

"I think he's driving a point home to the Administrators. *I don't need your help, I will forge my own path through my own strength, with these claws I shall shred the heavens and devour your charade of the Void. Behold the true Void, the origin of Darkness.* Or something like that."

Werylin eyed Aetheria sideways.

"Did they do something wrong in making this scenario?"

"Think about it. Why would Arkaziel ever submit to a trial from an entity that he can beat? If he can beat it on his own, he can take its strength and add it to his own, thus strengthening himself and proving dominance at the same time. Not only that, but what's a fake Void creature going to be able to teach to the real deal? Impart some platitudes, maybe give a magical item? Ark doesn't seem to need those anymore, but as a Beast Emperor, he does need to eat other strong creatures to keep up with me."

"How did he know he could beat it?"

"I'll chalk that up to pure arrogance. What doesn't he think he can beat? He tried to take bites out of Ymir when we met him; why wouldn't he do the same to an eldritch beast he's never heard of?"

"Fair enough. How long do you think he'll take to eat his prey?"

"He's going to be a jerk about it and eat super slow. I'm not sure if he's making a point to us or to the Administrators, but he's very smug right now. Let him savor his victory, I guess." Aetheria shrugged her shoulders before she pulled a book out of her repository, one of the ice Cultivator journals she gained so many floors ago. She made it through dozens of poorly written pages before Arkaziel finished his meal and strode through a newly appeared portal.

CHAPTER 82

Chains of the Witch

The darkness of teleportation gave way to a large, round room with two windows that gave a glimpse of a bustling and vibrant city. An inactive silver doorway blocked the stairs up to another level of this small tower. The stairs down led to nothing.

A gray-haired woman sat in the middle of the tower. A heavy manacle around her ankle ran to a metal ball that undoubtedly weighed twice her body mass.

"Hello, dearies. It's so rare I get visitors here." Darkened, rotting teeth showed in the woman's mouth when she smiled, painting a painful picture regarding the pile of hard tack rations that filled a pile next to the woman. Hard, dried food that would last for months, but was painful to eat.

Arkaziel made a show of taking his place on Aetheria's shoulder, while Werylin just looked very uncomfortable, which left Aetheria to take the lead.

"Hello. I don't suppose you could tell me where we've found ourselves? In exchange for information, we could heal you?"

"Why would I need to be healed, dearie? I'm not hurt, but information, maybe we could exchange some."

"You wouldn't want your teeth restored? Surely eating this food is a painful process."

"I'd rather you let me go."

"Why are you here?"

"Why am I here? Lordy, you people must be from far off. How'd you get into the Tower of the Poison Witch if you didn't know you were coming here? Seems like you've got bigger problems than I do! Ahaha." The woman's laughter held an undeniable note of madness to it, especially when she reached down and shook the chain between her manacles and the heavy ball. The faint scent of burning skin filled the air when the woman touched the chain.

"We are from very far off. So, are you the Poison Witch, or did you wrong her?" Aetheria looked around the bare walls, uncertain she could stand to spend even an hour in this place, let alone days or longer.

"Oh aye, I'm the Poison Witch, alright. I stabbed Prince Jake fifteen times with a poisoned dagger. I did, I did."

"How does stabbing a prince with a poison dagger make you a witch?"

"Unrelated matters, those two things."

"I see. So why did you use poison instead of magic to exact revenge on the prince?"

The woman cackled again, and let silence fill the air. She only spoke again right when it seemed like Werylin would repeat Aetheria's question.

"Because why not? The shithead raped my daughter, so I murdered him brutally at one of their precious balls to make sure the royals understood they weren't beyond my reach."

"I see. Again, though, why take that approach?"

"I'm an immortal witch, dearie. What are they going to do, burn me? I'll walk away from that just like I'll walk away from anything else. What's the worst that they could do to me, aye? Well. This, this is what they could do to me. Burn me at the stake, aye, they did that, but then they locked me in a damned tower in a manacle that cancels my magic. I'm to stay here a year for each time I stabbed that little shit."

"That's rough. I don't think I can let you go, though."

"Why, don't like witches?"

"No, my lover is a witch. Your manacle seems quite strange. What does the inscription upon it say?"

"Oh, a witch lover? Is it anyone I know, perhaps the Salt Witch, or the Goose Witch?"

"You are avoiding answering the question. Answer." Arkaziel spoke with annoyance.

"What a lippy familiar you have. Had a cat like that, so I did. A little bad catnip and he learned his lesson. Do you want to learn your lesson, too, kitty?"

"Enough. What does the inscription say?" Aetheria's tone ended with peals of laughter from the witch.

"It says the shackles will only come off when my penance is complete, or if whoever takes them off takes my place."

"How many years have you already served?"

"Eleven. Escape hardly seems possible, especially with bright young visitors who won't even just undo an old lady's manacles without asking questions. No one trusts an old lady, anymore."

Aetheria tilted her head as she considered the situation.

+I vote we just leave her there. She committed the crime, she serves the time. Why do we have to get involved at all?+

=Avenging her daughter's torture in the manner she did was wrong.=

~Really? You don't feel bad for her at all? You wouldn't murder someone who touched one of your children, Werylin?~

=My children are all older than I am now, but I understand your point. Yes, I would.=

~And aren't StarManes all about clan?~

+Yes, but we're StarManes, not humans. You people just murder each other constantly with complete disregard for anyone else. It's sort of your thing.+

Aetheria barely kept her jaw from dropping and shook her head.

~Wow. Anyway, so you both empathize, but still think we should just leave her here anyway?~

+What else are we supposed to do?+

=We have one floor left of the tower, Ria. You aren't suggesting we shackle one of ourselves up in her place and wait for four years to take on the last floor?=

~No, that would be dumb, but we should be able to do something, right?~

"What happened to your daughter?"

"I sent her to the Ash Witch to raise the illegitimate heir and bring this kingdom to its knees when my sentence is done. Oh, it'll be glorious."

"How will one bastard child topple a kingdom?"

"Jealous? No, I can still feel your aura even if I can't cast magic. You walk in the leagues of the gods, lass, so why should you care what transpires amongst the livestock?"

"I'm deciding whether I am going to help you or not, so. How is your plan to go? Is that how you see common people, as livestock?"

The witch smirked, rotten teeth on display, her laughter spreading the stench of her breath like a plague. Aetheria turned her sense of smell off. She couldn't handle it any further. Even looking at the hideous woman sent creepy crawlies down her back.

Are we casting rocks at the hideousness of mortal flesh?

Not right now, Fred.

But the irony fills me so. You, whose soul is a wounded amalgam of human essence, the souls of six gods, and my own radiant essence as the glue that holds it all together, are a work of transformative hideousness. You should know better than to cast stones.

I said not right now, Fred.

C'est la vie.

If you're going to be a bitch, Fred, how about we talk about why you know gamer terms like S++ or, apparently, speak French?

The silence in Aetheria's mind was sudden and deafening. Fred fled frantically.

"Well, dearie, my sweet little grandson will bring an army of fire elementals. No doubt the Ash Witch has taught him a thing or two about a thing or two regarding burning down the house. A little plague, some fire elementals, and the heroic warlord slaying the rotten royal dynasty, and as they say, out with the old and in with the new. Sweet old Nergal even offered me his help. When it's time, they'll have nowhere to run, and the only drop of their fell blood left in the entire kingdom will be my grandson's."

"It sounds like you have everything all planned out," Aetheria said flatly, her disapproval clear to even the witch, who stopped cackling at the dangerous look in the Asura's eyes.

"What, do you favor the royal family? Why else would one disapprove of our plan?"

"Maybe because I think you're going to kill a lot of innocent people with those plagues, elementals, and war. The rest of the city and country don't deserve to be put to the spear or torch because of their actions, do they?"

"The strong will survive; the weak will perish. That is the rule of the world, god or mortal, witch or warrior. The fuel of their lives will nourish the earth and the next generation of warriors. Our warriors in our country will be strong from their losses. Without the taint of the Queen of Heaven. I spit on the name of Ishtar." The witch spit on the floor with her words, and a flash of pain and intense wrath spread through Aetheria.

"Your version of the world is terrible, and not one which I would choose to live in, witch." Werylin's voice held the disgust Aetheria felt, but not nearly as much anger. She unclenched her fists only through great effort.

"I agree. I'm afraid we won't be helping you, witch. In fact, we will be opposing you."

Before Aetheria could so much as lift a hand, or even flare her aura to intimidate the witch or just for emphasis, Arkaziel jumped off her shoulder and ate the witch in a single bite.

"Uh." Werylin stared in horror.

"Err." Aetheria felt cheated of vengeance, confused, and overall like she just wanted out of this weird place.

"Ick." Arkaziel coughed and summoned bottles and food from his storage to wash away the terrible taste of the witch. "I really should have expected she'd taste terrible, and I did, but I didn't expect her to taste *that* terrible. Wow! Just wow. Worse than Nidhogg. It might take some ambrosia to wash that taste away."

Arkaziel's yellow eyes grew larger as he looked at Aetheria.

"You did good, although I feel like that could have been personal for me somehow. Whatever, here." An ambrosial plum appeared in her hand, and she tossed it to the cat.

Shadows caught it before it could hit the floor, but Arkaziel still gave her an accusatory look.

"You aren't going to hold it for me?"

"No. No, I'm not. I've never held fruit for you, and I'm not about to start now."

The door to the next level shimmered and activated. The last floor of the tower lay open to them. A series of deep, loud gongs played sound after sound.

"Is that going to keep until we go through the door?" Aetheria kind of liked the sound of the gongs, but could tell they would get annoying quickly. Especially the way they made her chest feel like it vibrated.

+*Probably.*+ Arkaziel's mouth remained full of food.

"Destiny calls. Do we answer?" Werylin swallowed nervously.

"We came all this way. It'd be a shame to turn away now, right?" Aetheria stretched her neck and arms and prepared for a drag down fight.

"Any idea what the last boss will be, Ark?"

+Normally it would be an avatar of Aetherius, or one of his sacred pets. For us? What's worse than an avatar of a Primordial? That's what we'll get. Maybe multiple avatars of Aetherius at once?+

"It doesn't matter what it is, we're clearing this tower. Check your gear, and when we're all ready, we go through together."

"If I don't mak—" A soft slap hit Werylin in the cheek.

"I already resurrected you once. I'll do it again if I have to, but don't make me have to deal with all that, okay? No one dies, we win, we make wishes, and we're one tenth of the way done with saving a world. Understood?" Aetheria glared at the other two until they submitted.

"Understood!"

"Understood." Flecks of ambrosia hit her face when Arkaziel spoke.

Jerk.

It distracted Aetheria from thoughts that stopping the witch wouldn't stop the rest of her plan, but the Administrators had blocked the rest of this dimension from them. Clearly that scenario would be a challenge for another set of climbers . . .

CHAPTER 83

What's Worse than One Primordial?

The one hundredth floor of the Tower of Aetherius looked an awful lot like the island Aetheria had awoken on. Complete with the tower itself in the center of the tropical island. To her Ethereal Sight and senses, the island held ridiculous amounts of life and monsters, most of which were too weak to be a threat to her party. The cloudless sky displayed the most beautiful color of light blue, and the faint scent of ocean breezes created a yearning for a fruity drink in Aetheria.

"If we have to climb that tower to one hundred now, I'm going to be a very cross lady," Aetheria grumbled under her breath.

"Please, don't joke about that." Werylin looked terrified at the very idea.

"Not going to happen. There's our opponents now." Arkaziel pointed a paw at the tower, before he hopped off Aetheria's shoulder and shot into the air to become a one-hundred-and-twenty-meter-long dragon. The aging he had been exposed to had helped expedite his growth, it seemed.

Two massive forms separated from the tower itself. Two dragons, one blue and one black. Each radiated enormous power in the low sixth tier. The blue dragon radiated an aura of pure divine Aether, while the black dragon radiated unadulterated Nether flavored heavily with night.

"I think those dragons watched me enter the tower to begin with. Makes sense they'd be Avatars of Aetherius and Nyx." Aetheria's laughter held a shade of eagerness, confidence, and acknowledgment of the obviousness that this would have been the conclusion to the tower. Her infectious laughter made Arkaziel grin and made Werylin stand just a little straighter.

"I'll take on Nyx, you two on Aetherius. Don't take stupid risks—they're two tiers higher than we are, and Primordial Dragons. For all I know this is Sun Wukong all over again, seeing if we're smart enough to run away from them, but we're going to win."

"Are you sure you can handle Nyx alone?" Werylin wondered at the wisdom of anyone trying to duel Nyx, who made gods hide and even other Primordials avoid confrontation with her.

"It'll be fine. I spent ten years dueling with Callie, and while I only won a third of our duels, I know what I'm doing. Besides, I owe her a few punches for using eldritch black goo to glue my soul together."

"Ria, you know that might just be an imitation, not the real Nyx, right?"

"Doesn't matter. Let's rock." Wings of black-and-red ice formed on Aetheria's back, and she shot up into the air and created distance between Werylin on the ground, and Arkaziel also in the air.

Aetherius and Nyx reached the lower floors of the tower and banked to fly horizontally, where they separated. Aetherius seemed to have a similar plan to Aetheria: massive vortexes of wind billowed around his wings, and then they shot ahead of him toward Arkaziel.

Close enough to compare, Aetheria noticed Arkaziel and Aetherius were close to the same size, with Nyx slightly larger than both. Yet she glimpsed facets of truth about the Primordial Dragon avatars; their astral forms were leviathans of an altogether larger scale than what manifested in physical reality. Had she not been exposed to the multifaceted dimensions of the Void, that would have thoroughly impressed her. Instead, it just felt like a cheap trick, especially since logically she knew these avatars were probably not at their full potential.

Nyx braked and came to a hover midair, a football field or so of distance between her massive form and the human sized form of Aetheria. The Primordial Dragon's eyes were larger than Aetheria herself, and they narrowed to slits to regard the human. The silence lasted for seconds, until the sound of wind and shadows signaled the start of the battle between Aetherius and her team. Aetheria waited. Nyx waited.

With an annoyed sigh, the dragon began the process of drawing breath. Aetheria could see dozens of avenues for attack, but she needed to test something first, so she waited still. When the human still wouldn't take the initiative, Nyx unleashed her breath attack. Darkest night spilled from the maw of the behemoth, and the almost sentient cool darkness sought to feast upon the warmth of Aetheria's life force. The darkness engulfed her, and Aetheria wondered if this was what Erebos looked like. And then she took a breath, and sucked in all of the darkness and cold. She stripped the cold from the darkness, opened a channel between her and Arkaziel, and gave him access to the power Nyx had just used against Aetheria, albeit with the life leach aspects toned down some.

+Nice, thanks!+

Arkaziel's eager thanks coincided with screams of anger from the avatar of Aetherius when Nyx's breath attack got turned against the Primordial; the equal tier attack from an equal avatar caused significant damage to the scaled form of the blue dragon.

"When did you learn to do that?" Nyx inquired.

Rather than answer, Aetheria showed Nyx why she had stripped some of the power from the breath attack and snapped her fingers. Thousands of crystalline needles of ice appeared in the air around Nyx, each glimmering with a core of darkness.

Not that the icicles stayed in place, they thrust forward into Nyx. Over half shattered against the godly scales that covered the dragon, but the rest found purchase between scales, the aspectation of her own power allowing them to breach Nyx's defenses and pierce into the flesh beneath the scales. Once past the scales the icicles started to spin like drills to push deep into her flesh.

A roar of pain from Nyx shook the island, a match to the roar Aetherius had made.

Aetheria didn't celebrate, though. Her face remained blank despite the agony that coursed through her. Yes, she could absorb the power of a sixth-tier creature, but it wrecked her meridians, incinerated her flesh, and burned her soul to do it. Only when she expelled the energy could her body and soul heal, and stop new damage. She hadn't been prepared for the difference in power between the fourth and sixth tier.

Nyx's counterattack came in the form of a tail swipe cleverly hidden in writhing pain. A roar escaped her maw just before contact and dazed Aetheria for the fractions of a second it would take her to dodge. Aetheria's body sailed through the air like a bullet, and she crossed the entire island and some distance over the ocean before she arrested her momentum. Nyx didn't follow her, and instead used the time to dispel the icicles boring into her flesh.

Aetheria took a second to observe the flashes of light, shadow, wind, and harmony taking place between the boys and Aetherius. All three sources of power remained steady, so she teleported back to Nyx. A claw swiped at where she reappeared, spraying Aetheria's blood, viscera, and body parts in all directions, but strands of nothing itself pulled her entirely back together in an instant, and she delivered a kick to the dragon's front right shoulder that crashed Nyx into the island like a meteor. A fourth tier shouldn't be able to do that to a sixth, but Aetheria had *authority*, and the belief she could do it. Now that she had done it, Nyx would also believe she could do it, cementing Aetheria's miraculous strength as truth.

"That was for putting black goo in my soul." Aetheria grinned.

No weapons in her hand seen, no sword nor thunder there,
Dust and ruins remain, yet all that is dust shall rise,
For she sings the song, the song of cosmos' silent cries,
Bow, not in fear, but in reverence,
For she is an ancient song, heard anew.
Fuck off, Fred!

Aetheria blurred, now that she reached one hundred percent again. Yet still now she heard a song she hadn't heard prior to Fred's creepy verses. A song of heavy drums and some dirge-sounding instrument, that reverberated through her inner being, empowered her dual cores, and awoke the Third-Eye of Ein Sof. Somewhere, some when, clouds of dust rose as a door long sealed opened, releasing staleness and spreading the sound of a clock. Tick, tock. Tick, tock.

Aetheria pushed the strange sensations aside, and activated Existence Oscillation. Nyx, the Primordial Goddess of Night, one of the oldest beings in all the universe, was left powerless before the onslaught that Aetheria unleashed. Each blow held the same strength that had thrown the Primordial Dragon around like a rag doll, and dozens of blows were delivered every nanosecond as Aetheria danced through the corridors of reality, each assault little more than a tap of the finger, the brush of a knee, a strike of crimson hair, as a myriad collection of Aetherias moved in and out of existence, each leaving a gift of pain for the dragon.

The second to last blow of the reality-breaking dance came from the front, straight into Nyx's draconic snout, and the follow-up kick sent the dragon to crash into the tower, where it then fell to the ground with a great thud.

The dragon's dark eyes opened to see Aetheria's arm elongated into her own maw. When she tried to bite the arm, she found ice holding her maw open, and then it was too late. The hand that delved inside the dragon found the avatar's core, and in a flash of the Void, the core no longer existed. The dragon of darkness turned to dust.

"One down." Aetheria turned her gaze to the cacophony of powers unleashed by Aetherius, Arkaziel, and Werylin. The flares of power were so bright that she had to use Void Gaze with Ethereal Sight to see the truth of the matter.

Arkaziel grappled with Aetherius, his teeth embedded in the neck of the blue dragon, and he sucked the power out of the blue dragon like a vampire. Arkaziel used this strength to endure the thrashing blows of Aetherius, locking the two in a deadlock that would never end. Werylin had given up on trying to cut through the dragon; even Stormshimmer and Harmonious Tempest couldn't pierce the hide of a sixth-tier Primordial Dragon.

Aetheria appeared next to Werylin, to hear what he chanted.

"By the First Word Spoken, the Origin of All Existence,
I summon the Rift, to cleave my primordial foe,
Your undeniable might, a mountain I cannot scale,
Yet all shall know ruin someday, for all strength has a crack!
Genesis Rift!"

With every word Werylin spoke, his aura gained in power. In the past, she had never seen him use more than a single word to enact his spells, yet every word he bound into the incantation added to its power, and by the time he finished, his radiance approached that of a sun, which then immediately vanished when he spoke the final words.

A black crack in space-time shot along the beautiful blue scales of the avatar of Aetherius. The roars of pain that emerged from it were beyond angry, but Arkaziel didn't delay. When the Genesis Rift shattered the scales and fissured flesh, Arkaziel formed a second head from his torso that reached into the dragon and chowed down its core.

The blue dragon turned to dust.

"Nice one, Werylin!" Aetheria cheered on the minstrel, even as he fell to his knees. His face looked hollowed out, and he looked to have aged slightly, which for an elf meant significantly, but he appeared stable.

"Thanks, I did my best." The elf blacked out.

CHAPTER 84

The Top of the Tower

I've never seen Genesis Rift used before, quite the display." The old man who sat across the campfire from the trio was Aetherius. Not an avatar, not a projection, but Aetherius the Primordial God of the Upper Sky, Divinity, and physical representation of Aether. Even with his aura concealed, his presence held power beyond reasoning, but Aetheria just thought of him as Pete.

"Yes, a shocking turn of events. Almost as surprising as dear Aetheria and her dance of death." Nyx, the pale-skinned beauty next to Aetherius radiated as much, if not more, power than the other Primordial. She had once been the Overgod, after all.

Arkaziel coughed and eyed the two Primordials.

"You were very impressive, too, Arkaziel." Nyx smiled fondly at the cat.

"Yes, quite impressive. How did you manage to withstand the rank difference with your feeding?" Aetherius, on the other hand, wanted to know how the cat hadn't been incinerated from the inside.

"I used a two-faceted approach. First, I sacrificed a third of the power to the Void itself, which allowed me to refine and use the rest of the power, and any time it approached too much for me to handle, I shunted it to Aetheria." Arkaziel practically purred from the praise he received, and the pets that Aetheria gave him.

"You did? Huh. I didn't even notice." Aetheria's nonchalance about it brought head shakes and laughter from those around the fire. In the firelight, with a cup of wine, Werylin looked healthy once more, although the darkness under his eyes spoke of exhaustion even magic couldn't wash away.

"You've beaten your first tower. What are your wishes?" Nyx broke the jovial mood by returning to matters at hand.

The five sat atop the Tower of Aetherius, at the same bonfire Aetheria recalled sitting at in her memories. They had reached the top, but there were nine more towers to go, and who knew what lay beyond that?

"Really now, Nyx, can't we let them enjoy themselves a little longer?" Aetherius tried to fend off Night.

"No, we can't. Oizys is moving to recruit climbers to get in Aetheria's path, and not from Grief. Those who aren't with us are helping her without bribery, so there'll be no shortage of idiot challengers from other planets ready to stand in her way, on top of the children who have noticed her rapid ascent." Nyx's tone turned waspish, a trait she had shown as Callie whenever someone questioned her.

"It'll be fine, Callie. I'll handle them, and anyone else, but there isn't any reason to delay either. Alright, wish time. Werylin, why don't you go first? You really pulled through with that spell." Aetheria reached over to squeeze the elf's shoulder and impart a surge of vitality into the elf.

"Yes, well. For my wish, I would like favorable terms for my clan to exit the Tower of Aetherius when I have secured a stronghold for them on Grief."

"That's it? Favorable terms? Nothing else?"

"A means to protect us from Misery would not be amiss." Werylin grinned sheepishly.

"Done," Aetherius said.

"Done," Nyx said, and handed Werylin a small black cube.

"Place the cube in the center of your new stronghold. As long as it is in place, Oizys will not be able to touch your fates directly. Do not think she will not find other means to assault you, though. She is petty and does not give up." For all that Oizys was the enemy, Nyx sounded proud that her daughter was tenacious.

"Arkaziel, what does the son of the God Eater wish for?"

"It is said that our progenitor possessed a Nebula Lantern. I want one."

"I see. What do you think, Nyx?"

The two Primordials stared into one another's eyes, clearly communicating telepathically. The two stared at one another for long minutes, until a black marble appeared between them. The marble showed an entire nebula inside of it, and Arkaziel quivered on Aetheria's lap.

"Your very own Nebula Lantern, just like the one from legends. Enjoy it." Aetherius laughed, while Nyx seemed like she might snatch the marble back at any moment, but then Arkaziel leaped through the air, and ate the marble.

". . . I wasn't expecting that." Aetheria's laughter broke the shocked silence.

"No, I'd imagine not. Aetheria, what is your wish?"

"I want a map to all the towers."

"All of the towers?"

"A map?"

Aetherius and Nyx seemed shocked, but then a smile split Nyx's lips.

"Granted," the Primordials replied in unison, and a massive spectral tome filled the air, flipped through millions of pages, and then flew into Aetheria, where she felt it bind itself to her.

"Well, I guess that wraps everything up. Time to hit the road, boys. But give me a second with these two, would you?" Aetheria smiled, but her sudden shift in demeanor did not leave an opportunity to argue with her. Arkaziel and Werylin stepped through the portal that would take them to the entrance of the Tower of Aetherius on Grief.

"What's wrong, do you still want to punch me?" Nyx asked with a worried expression.

"Well, yeah, but that's not what I wanted to talk about. That essence you used to bind my soul? That wasn't the Dreaming Tyrant, Nyx. Far beneath the Court of Chaos lies the origin of the Void, a black inferno that predates the Blind Idiot. *That* is what you were manipulated into putting into my soul, and it talks to me, when it wants to at least."

The Primordials' faces turned ashen.

"That would explain some things about your transformation, but if it could manipulate me so successfully that I never noticed or even had a hint of it, that would make it an order of magnitude more powerful than even the Outsiders. Does it have a name?"

"Just the one I gave it."

"Can it affect our world?"

"It doesn't seem like it, but it seems to be able to affect me in some fashion."

Aetherius thumbed his beard and harrumphed.

"You'll figure it out as you go, young lady. I have faith in you but be careful of nameless powers that whisper in the dark. That's how Nyx fell for Belial's shenanigans with the towers."

"It might be too late for that. I have soul-links not only to the Origin and the Void, but to the previously nameless powers in them. They gave me the Black Flame of the Void and the Ethereal Flame."

"Demonstrate them?" Nyx asked, but her tone made it a demand.

An aura of black engulfed Aetheria's right hand, and red engulfed the left. The red flame emitted warmth, vitality, possibility, and promise. The black flames emitted cold, oblivion, and absence. In the presence of both, all things were possible.

"Do not try to combine those two Flames until you're at least in the seventh tier," Nyx ordered.

"Why?"

"Because they scare me. If they scare me, you need to at least be of the seventh tier to even consider dealing with them."

"Why do you assume I'll combine them?"

"It is what you keep doing. So rather than rashly unleash something, play it safe for me?"

"Oh fine. Do I get hugs?"

Aetherius gave Aetheria a hug first, and a kiss on the cheek. When Nyx came in to give her a hug, Aetheria tried to deck her, but Nyx casually caught Aetheria's fist.

"That might work on an avatar, but I'm the real deal, kiddo. You've got a long way to go if you want to punch me for real."

"Seventh tier?"

"At least."

"I love you guys. Is everyone in the guild still doing well?"

"*Eldest Fantasy Wars Online* went offline a few decades ago, Aes. The guild is gone, although some of us are playing a new game together." Nyx winced at being the one to deliver the news.

"Oh." A hollowness formed in the pit of Aetheria's stomach. Part of her had sort of thought that time would just pause on Earth, and someday she'd pop up and do a raid for old time's sake, see her mom and dad, and then head off into the world as a planewalker.

That wasn't going to happen though, was it? In fact, her mother and father were possibly dead already.

"Time flows ever onward, *Aetheria*." Aetherius attempted to comfort her, but it failed spectacularly.

"Are my parents . . . ?"

"Unfortunately. Your mother passed after a series of strokes, and your father followed her two years later."

Humanity, that strange sensation of connections and feelings, formed tears in her eyes. Earth grew dimmer in her memories, and the desire to return cooled. *Why bother?*

"Alright, well. Yeah. I'll get going, then. I've got the Tower of Moros to climb."

"Is pain how you discover yourself?"

Why do you think that, Reverie?

"Pain precedes your growth. You sang a song before, a song that healed me. But it took pain to bring the song to the surface. I miss that song."

Are you injured, Reverie?

"I must be?"

Are you going to be ok?

"I'm alone."

You aren't. You're with me, now. Let's find out what's next.

Aetheria stepped through the portal to the tower base, and the world shimmered and hung in darkness for long seconds, before everything swam through a hole in a penny, and in a beam of light she appeared at the stairs leading to the Tower of Aetherius on Grief.

All is One. One is None. Alone in multitude; together in solitude.

You suck, Fred.

About the Author

Jamie Kojola is the author of the Odyssey of the Ethereal series, originally released on Royal Road. In her free time, she enjoys gardening, sewing, gaming, crafting, and playing *D&D*. Kojola lives in Minnesota with her two children, spouse, and three cats.